THE
HOUSE
OF
DREAMS

Also by Kate Lord Brown

The Perfume Garden

The HOUSE of DREAMS

Kate Lord Brown

THOMAS DUNNE BOOKS   ST. MARTIN'S PRESS

NEW YORK

This is a work of fiction. All of the characters, organizations, and events portrayed in this novel are either products of the author's imagination or are used fictitiously.

THOMAS DUNNE BOOKS.
An imprint of St. Martin's Press.

THE HOUSE OF DREAMS. Copyright © 2016 by Kate Lord Brown. All rights reserved. Printed in the United States of America. For information, address St. Martin's Press, 175 Fifth Avenue, New York, N.Y. 10010.

www.thomasdunnebooks.com
www.stmartins.com

Designed by Steven Seighman

Grateful acknowledgment is made for permission to reprint from the following:

"The Great Lover" by Rupert Brooke, 1914, is used with the kind permission of the Rupert Brooke Society.

The Library of Congress Cataloging-in-Publication Data is available upon request.

ISBN 978-1-250-08453-8 (hardcover)
ISBN 978-1-250-10982-8 (Canadian)
ISBN 978-1-250-08454-5 (e-book)

Our books may be purchased in bulk for promotional, educational, or business use. Please contact your local bookseller or the Macmillan Corporate and Premium Sales Department at 1-800-221-7945, extension 5442, or by e-mail at MacmillanSpecial Markets@macmillan.com.

First U.S. Edition: May 2016
First Canadian Edition: May 2016

10 9 8 7 6 5 4 3 2 1

For LAW

Love is a flame; we have beaconed the world's night.
—*Rupert Brooke*

THE
HOUSE
OF
DREAMS

From the Desk of Sophie Cass

New York
August 28, 2000

Dear Mr. Lambert,

   Here's the thing. You can ignore my letters if you wish, but my piece will run in The New York Times *whether you, or your lawyers, like it or not.* If it weren't for our family connection, I'd sue you in a heartbeat. I don't like threats. I am a professional investigative journalist, Mr. Lambert, and I'm just doing my job. This is not some personal vendetta as you claim, nor have I used underhand tactics. As an artist, I'm sure you appreciate the key is to look, to listen clearly, and see the things that other people miss. I looked, and I saw the truth—plain and simple.

   My sources are rock solid, and more importantly I have new evidence for my claims. You see, I have discovered photographs, Mr. Lambert, taken by Alistair Quimby in 1940, the summer before you met Varian Fry in Marseille. Not only are there stunning photos of my great-aunt Vita, there are photos of you at work in the studio at the Château d'Oc. Both of you. I assume I don't need to explain any more?

   Your lawyers have done their damnedest to warn me off, but now I am warning you—this piece celebrating your illustrious career and 95th birthday will run. I'm going to give you one last chance to put your side of the story before I file my copy. I will come and see you after Labor Day, at midday on Thursday, September 7. I imagine now you'll be ready to talk.

   Yours,
   Sophie Cass

ONE

Flying Point, Long Island

September 2000

Gabriel

There are few things emptier than the space where a Christmas tree used to be. At least, that's what Annie always says. If my lovely girl had her way, we'd have a tree all year long and the white lights strung out on the deck. When I was younger, I'd swim out at sunset and see Venus and the stars above and that rope of lights guiding me home, luminous as pearls on the dark throat of the bay. When we walked the dogs along the beach at night, she'd take my hand or loop her arm around my waist. *Gabe,* she'd say, *look, it's like our own galaxy on the shore.*

Plenty are surprised by this home of ours. They expect the great man to have something grander, but they don't see I have everything I ever dreamed of here. I have the clear light of the sea spilling in through the square open doors to the barn where I work, and I have Annie. One summer I paid a bunch of boys to come up from Pennsylvania to raise the barn for me—it's an old red colonial, with a hipped roof and doors that open wide to the north. I need space to work, to spread my canvases, but Annie never wanted a studio. When I offered to build her one, she said, "What do I want with that?" She just set up a little table off the kitchen, facing the wall. She says she likes to be in the middle of things, so the kids can come and go as she sews her beautiful clothes. Her work's in collections across the country, but you wouldn't know it to look at her with her head bent over her embroidery. There's always a dog sitting at her feet and a cat curled up in the warmth of the lamplight beside her as she sews. First it was our own kids, and now there's always one grandchild or another in the high chair beside her or playing with their bricks or dolls on the floor and the radio singing away in the background. Maybe that's why people love her art—each stitch pulses and shines with life. My paintings scare people, intimidate them. They are big and intense, just right for uncompromising white-box galleries and soaring corporate atriums. I know which I'd rather live with. Over time people confused me with my paintings. Here's something I've learned—if you do good work, make it to my age, and keep your trap shut, you become a reclusive genius. I like my reputation, play up to it: the enigmatic old man of abstraction. People are afraid to ask too many questions, which suits me just fine. Only the bravest bother me out here. I glance over at the girl's letter on the table. Only the boldest find me.

My cup of coffee's grown cold as I rock the child in my arms and look out to sea. I'm listening to Billie Holiday singing "It's a Sin to Tell a Lie" on my 1959 Magnavox Imperial, and Lady Day's voice is dancing up among the rafters with the angels, the Calder mobile swinging with the tune as it rises into the air like bubbles in pure water. This song is Annie's favorite, and she always has a mischievous glint in her eye, singing along softly as we dance, our bare feet shuffling on the sandy deck overlooking the sea. My wife knows me well. I've lied about plenty in my life, but I never lied about loving her.

I love this time of year, too, always have. There's nothing like an empty beach for me, with the dazzling white sand, the sea turning to winter swells, and the pure blue sky above you. I can breathe here. Every day I wake feeling like the first man on earth, with his Eve at his side. After Labor Day, once all the fancy cottages along the dunes close down for the season and their topiary is tied up in its dust sheets for the winter, Annie and I kick off our shoes, get our toes in the sand, and take a walk down to our beach. We build a bonfire, grill a fish or two, and toast another summer's passing with a glass of Chardonnay. Annie doesn't drink much, but those nights she curls up under an old plaid blanket, and her cheeks flush, and she talks freely about the past, our life, and the future like the girl I met used to when we walked in the woods at Air-Bel like children in a fairy tale.

I am a contented man. This is all I wish for my children. I gave them each enough to help them start out in life, but not so much that they didn't have to work at it. Too much ease can ruin you; that's what I've always thought when I look at some of the kids of wealthy folks I've known. You lose your edge. I didn't want the kids to struggle as Annie and I did, but the rest I quietly gave away. If some fool banker wants to pay my dealers a million bucks for one of my early abstracts, then let him. Hell, I am the Robin Hood of the art world. There are plenty more folks in the world need the money more than we do, and I have so much to be thankful for in this life that I've had, this good and simple life I don't deserve.

TWO

WILLIAMSBURG, BROOKLYN

Wednesday, September 6, 2000

SOPHIE

A flurry of white wings wakes her, whirling, silhouetted against the bright morning light spilling through the curtainless loft window. Sophie leaps from deep slumber, sits bolt upright on the living room sofa, shielding her face with her arm from the light, from the bird. She squints her eyes, makes out the dove's frantic search for the narrow margin of space it slipped in through, helpless wings battering the high panes of glass.

"How did you get in here?" Sophie throws wide the window. The noise of the waking city spills into the studio on the warm breeze: honking traffic below, the whirr of air conditioners on the roof above, a tinny radio somewhere, playing "Said I Loved You . . . But I Lied."

Jess's favorite, she thinks instantly. A Pavlovian cocktail of memories swirls in her mind. She remembers teasing him about his taste in music when they met, how his unlikely love of power ballads became a running joke: *Seriously? Beneath that Brooks Brothers suit you're all big hair and stonewashed denim?* Sophie thinks of the night they slow danced to the song on the deck at some party in East Hampton—his request. Everyone had laughed and groaned as the DJ played the tune, but that gave the moment, the way Jess had walked toward her and held out his hand, a perfect lightness. She remembers his certainty, his focus only on her, the sound of the surf, and the sweet taste of strawberries still on her lips as he kissed her. She flexes her hand at the memory of the ring sliding onto her finger, the glint of the stone in the moonlight. Sophie gathers up the white bedsheet. *Of all the songs. Our song* . . . She corrects herself. *His song.* The tune carries up, up into the morning sky, from an open doorway on Grand Street, taking her thoughts with it.

Sophie speaks softly to the bird, calming its frantic search for freedom. "There you go," she says, dropping the sheet over it the moment it lands in the corner of the studio. Gently, she enfolds the bird in her hands, feels the staccato beat of its heart against her fingers, the fine, cathedral arch of its breastbones.

At the window, she releases it, watches it soar up across Brooklyn into the hazy morning sky. The air is hot, edible, laced with the scent of the streets—gasoline, coffee, ripe melon skins in the Dumpsters behind the grocery store. The dove joins its dull-plumed friends roosting on the pediment of the building opposite, a pale punctuation mark among the Morse code line of birds cooing and shaking the night from their feathers.

Sophie sits on the windowsill in the sunshine, the brick already warm against her aching back through the thin cotton of her white camisole. She closes her eyes, raises her face to the morning sun, and cricks her neck from side to side, loosening the tense ligaments. Her gold-blond hair spills across her shoulders, a glossy halo she scoops up and secures in a loose bun with practiced ease. Beside the window, the sagging red velvet sofa and single pillow still bear the imprint of her restless sleep. The tune ends, and as the radio station jingle releases her from thoughts of Jess, the letter runs through her mind again, as it has on a permanent loop since she woke at four A.M. *Was I too hard?* she thinks. *What if Lambert won't see me?* She has read the letter so many times that she knows it by heart. *"Professional investigative journalist."* She cringes inwardly. *Wonder what effect "newly graduated arts writer with zero professional experience" would have had on his hotshot lawyers?*

At the sound of paws trotting across the bare concrete floor, Sophie turns and smiles. "Hey, Mutt." The dachshund yawns and stretches, front legs extended, tail wagging high. "C'mon," she says, swinging down from the window. She freshens up, picks out a clean white shirt, and shrugs it on. Sophie reaches for the lead spooled on her suitcase. She rubs her thumb across a curling airline sticker on the case, thinking of the last trip she took with Jess to Mexico. A knot forms in her throat as she remembers it all—the color, the light, the heat. *Coming home,* she thinks. She remembers dozing on Jess's shoulder in the taxi as they drove through the snowy streets of New York to their cozy apartment in Greenwich Village and wonders if she'll ever be that happy again. *It's all gone. I made my choice.* She glances across at the dog, who sits waiting for her, his head tilted. "I know, I know," she says, peeling the sticker off and screwing it up. She flicks the ball of paper into a wire basket beside Alisha's drawing board and stops to look at the wedding dress designs her friend is working on. Sophie reaches out and touches the cool bolt of duchess satin. "Could have been me," she says under her breath, and she pads across the studio, sunlight warming the open space in wide parallelograms now. "It's just you and me, now," she says as Mutt follows her, tail wagging in hope. She clicks on the coffee machine, takes out a fresh pack of Zabar's coffee from the mercy parcel of provisions her mother insisted she take, and rips open the seal, inhaling the rich, smoky scent as she tips it into the filter. She glances at the bag of groceries, spots her mother's familiar, looping hand on a note tucked beneath some bagels. Sophie smooths it out: *Hang in there. I love you, Mom x.* It is pinned to a copy of a Henry James essay, and Sophie sees she has underlined a section.

At the door, she pauses to slip her tanned feet into a pair of white Converse sneakers and loosely buttons the shirt, rolling the sleeves and knotting it at the waist of her wide-legged chinos. Mutt's paws skitter impatiently on the floor, and he nudges her leg with his head.

"Just a second," she says. Sophie tucks a pair of Ray-Bans into her hair and checks her reflection, rubbing away a smudge of mascara from beneath her sea-green eyes. She wipes a trace of toothpaste from the crease in her bottom lip with her thumb. *You can do this,* she tells herself, her mind racing ahead to her meeting with Lambert, her stomach taut with excitement and nerves. She has imagined what it will be like to meet him, finally, a thousand times. "Be generous, be delicate, and always pursue the prize," she says under her breath, quoting from the James essay. She tucks the papers into her battered leather satchel and grabs her keys and a few dollar bills, then slides back the dead bolts on the heavy metal door. "Let's go."

On the street, her tension eases as they walk around the block to Bedford Avenue, the pulse of a bass line drifting from a pimped-up Chevy on a side street beating in time with her heart as she pauses for Mutt to christen his favorite lamppost near the Kam Sing Restaurant. The metal cellar door is propped open, and the scent of last night's cooking oil and spices drifts up to her. Sophie reaches into her pocket for her phone and dials her mother's number, stepping aside for a group of early gray-faced commuters heading toward the L. She catches her reflection in the window, a white ceramic lucky cat waving at her from the counter. Sophie frowns at the busy signal and slips her phone away.

"Finished? Sure?" she says as the dog walks on. She ties him up outside the grocery store on a wall scrawled with graffiti, and he waits, his unwavering eyes on her as she buys fresh orange juice. Sophie takes a copy of *The New York Times* from the vending machine. She sees his name instantly, there, beneath the headline. It's as if the print loses focus, leaving two words in dazzling clarity: Jess Wallace. Mutt barks, impatient, and Sophie can't help smiling as she walks over and unties the lead. "Hey, I was only a minute." The dog's good mood is infectious; joyful wags contort his whole body—they are together again, simple as that. Sophie loops the lead and bag over her wrist and flicks on through the paper as they walk, deliberately not reading the front-page article but instead searching for her latest column on a new exhibition that has just opened. She finds it way back in the "Arts" section, tucked among the advertisements. It feels like an afterthought.

In the studio, she hears the shower running, Alisha singing loud and true along to Macy Gray on the radio. Sophie pours a cup of coffee and clears a space among the sketches and bolts of fabric on the dining table, spreads out the photographs and documents from her satchel as if she is dealing cards. Each is labeled with a Post-it note, written clearly in black ink: *Gabriel Lambert, 1970? Last known photo. Varian Fry, André Breton, 1940. JC: Gabriel and Annie Lambert, party, Long Island, 1960s.* This last photograph Sophie picks up, studies closely. The young woman wears her blond hair fashionably loose, a heavy blunt fringe over dark kohled eyes that gaze, full of love, at the lean, tanned man at her side. His black hair is graying at the temples, worn long enough to brush the collar of his faded denim shirt. His eyes are fierce, the color of the sky. The chemistry between them is palpable, even down the years, no air between their bodies, his arm protectively around her waist, her palm resting flat against his chest. *How do you do that?* she thinks. *How do you keep that passion for a lifetime?* Her stomach tightens with nerves at the thought of finally meeting them. Their legendary love affair fascinates her; the idea that sometimes there is a happily ever after is a beacon of hope in the darkness.

"Hey, honey, I didn't hear you come in last night," Alisha says. The red of her sarong flares as she walks through sunlight, beads of water glistening on her freshly oiled skin.

"Didn't want to wake you. How was your break?"

"You know, Labor Day, my family." Alisha purses her lips. "How's your mom?"

"She sends her love."

"D'you manage to store all your stuff in her barn?"

"Just about." Sophie raises an eyebrow as she looks down at Mutt. "Mom suggested we should just move in there. What do you think?" The dog cocks his head, listening.

"Where's she live again?"

"Montauk."

"Could be worse." Alisha shrugs, takes a bright green apple from the bowl on the counter. "If the *Times* don't take you on full-time, you could get yourself a job in one of those fancy-assed lobster restaurants."

"Thanks for the vote of confidence," Sophie says. "Everywhere's closing for the season, but I'm heading out to Long Island again tomorrow, so I'll see if anyone's hiring, just in case."

"Ha, ha." Alisha bites into the apple. "Man, you spend more time out there than in the city lately. This article you've been working on?"

"Yeah." Sophie rubs the bridge of her nose, rests her lips against her index finger as she stares at the photo of Gabriel and Annie. "I'll be glad when it's done."

"Sleeping any better?"

Sophie looks up from the photo. "So-so. I've just got all these questions running around in my mind."

"Tonight you take the bedroom for a change. You need some sleep if you're going to face off with the great Gabriel Lambert, baby girl." Alisha comes over to her. "Were you up all night working again?"

"It has to be perfect." *It's got to be,* she thinks. What was it her editor had said? *The correction rate on your pieces is too high, Sophie. Accuracy is everything at the* Times. *You're quick, you're willing, but you're making too many beginners' mistakes. If you want to make it, you've got to check and double-check every lead, every line. I know you've had a tough few months, but if you can't nail this Lambert story,*

I'm going to have to let you go. "Talking of perfect, see this?" She taps the front page of the paper.

"Jess? Is he back?"

"Who knows? There's some big summit at the UN, maybe he's in town for that." Her stomach turns over at the thought. "I haven't spoken to him in weeks."

"Good." Alisha glances at the clock. "It's the best way. A clean break. You'll be back on top in no time, trust me." She raises her chin. "Say, hadn't you better be going?"

"Is that the time?" Sophie scoops up her papers, swings the satchel across her body. "Thank you." She hugs her friend. "I promise you, this won't be for long."

"Take all the time you need to find somewhere. Me and the Mutt will be just fine, won't we?" she says to the dog. "He's a big hit with all my clients." The dog looks up at her, cocking his head.

Sophie checks her watch and wheels her bicycle toward the door. "Anyone coming in today?"

"Yeah." Alisha gestures toward a mannequin draped with muslin sheets in the corner of the studio, near her drawing board. The shape hints at the full skirts of a wedding dress, and a crystal tiara rests on top, sparkling. "Damn, I didn't—" She hesitates, glances at Sophie.

"It's okay," she says, her voice softening. "I was thinking the same thing. It would have been last weekend." Sophie opens the door. "Kind of ironic, isn't it, bunking down in a wedding dress design studio." She glances back, forces a smile. "Like I always say, the universe has a sense of humor."

Alisha holds open the door. "I sure wish it would share the joke."

In the hall, Sophie drags the elevator cage open and wheels her bike in. "Catch you later?"

"MoMA at five?" Alisha raises her hand as Sophie disappears.

On the street, Sophie pauses as her mobile vibrates in her pocket, the old-phone tone rising above the traffic. She wheels the bike along the pavement with one hand, crooks the phone beneath her jaw. "Mom?"

"Hi, darling, sorry, I was just doing my Pilates. I saw you'd tried to call. Are you okay?" Sophie can hear an old James Taylor track playing in the background.

"Fine. . . ." Sophie pauses. "No, I'm not fine," she says. "I feel like I'm going round and round in circles with this story—"

"But he is going to see you?" Sophie hears her mother click off the radio. "I spoke to Gabe's son, like you asked."

"I feel like such an idiot, asking my mom to call for me. But thank you."

"Hey, that's what I'm here for. And honey, trust me. If I know them, they wouldn't have let you within a mile of Gabe if you weren't family."

"I just want to do it justice. Do Vita justice. I care about this story. . . ." *Our story,* Sophie realizes. "I miss him."

"Your dad? So do I, darling. So do I. Every single day." She hears the emotion in her mother's voice. "He would be so proud of you. You've sacrificed a lot for this."

"You mean Paris, Jess?" Sophie pauses. *Happily ever after?* she thinks. "He didn't get it at all, did he? But then I never told him the real reason I want to write this story."

"Well, we all have our secrets, don't we, darling. . . ."

THREE

Manhattan

Wednesday, September 6, 2000

Sophie

Sophie runs up the stairwell of the *New York Times*' offices on West Forty-third Street, the exhilaration of her ride across the Williamsburg Bridge into Manhattan still with her, her cheeks flushed with pink. The stale scent of cigarette smoke hangs on the air in the hall as she pushes open the door. "Hey," she says to one of the interns on the way through the dingy, windowless newsroom. "Is the boss in yet?"

"Not yet, Soph." The boy flexes his wrist and winces.

"RSI playing up, still?"

"Yeah, and the culture editor wants me to be his hands today."

She roots around in her bag and tosses him a gold pot. "Tiger Balm helps. Weren't you on the TV guide? Those grids are a killer."

"They're kind of boring. . . ."

"Shh!" Sophie's eyes widen. "For God's sake don't let anyone hear you say that. You've got to suck it up, we've all been there."

Sophie glances around for any sign of her boss as she walks on through the office. "Thank God," she says under her breath as she reaches her desk safely. She slings her satchel onto the back of her chair and swivels around to the computer just as the phone rings. "Sophie Cass," she answers, crooking the receiver against her shoulder as she begins to type. She waves her hand, clearing the cloud of fruit flies hovering above the bowl of red apples by her computer.

"Cass," he says. The hum of the strip lights and tap of keyboards across the room seem to intensify.

"Wallace," she says finally, trying to sound amused, playful.

"Damn, your voice is sexy as ever." She can hear his breath on the phone line. "You're late."

She eases back in her chair. "I prefer to think of it as making an entrance." Sophie pauses. "How do you know?"

"I always liked you in chinos. Very Hepburn, very yar . . ."

"Are you comparing me to a *boat*?" She swivels around and stands. Jess is leaning against a desk at the end of the newsroom.

"Why not? Trim. Responsive. Lively handling . . ." He flicks his cell phone closed and walks toward her as she replaces the receiver with deliberate care.

"What a surprise. I didn't know you were in town." *You didn't warn me,* she thinks.

"How are you?" He leans down to kiss her cheek, and she smells a new cologne—something citrus and fresh. "You look great."

"Thanks. I've been at the beach with Mom." She can't immediately place what has changed about him. He's wearing the same deep blue suit she loved the best, his red-blond hair is immaculate, as ever. "Are you here for the summit?"

"Yeah, I had some leave, so I flew in from Paris last night. Biggest gathering of world leaders in history, never know what I might pick up."

"You never stop, do you?" Sophie indicates the phone. "I should—"

"Sure." He holds her gaze. "Can we have a drink later?"

"I don't know."

"Old times' sake?" He leans over her, searching for a pen. She imagines for a moment reaching out to him, lacing her fingers in his. How simply it could all begin, again. "Around six P.M.?" Jess scribbles down an address.

"Why not?"

"See you later, Cass." As he turns, he calls back, "Don't be late."

And then, as he walks away, Sophie realizes. It is not Jess who has changed, it is her.

"I'm sorry, I'm sorry..." Sophie waves, running along West Fifty-third Street, her heels clicking. "The meeting ran over."

"Well, look at you," Alisha says. She shoulders open the door to the museum, and they walk against the crowds leaving for the day. "You shouldn't have gotten all dressed up for me...."

"I didn't, I'm meeting—"

"Jess."

"How did you know?"

"He rang the studio just after you left for work this morning. I hope you know what you're doing."

"Of course I don't." Sophie smooths down her black dress. "Do I look okay?"

"You look beautiful. Hold on a second." Alisha reaches around to the nape of Sophie's neck and snaps off the tag. "Don't want him to think you're making a special effort or anything." She screws it up and tosses it into a bin without breaking her stride.

"Oh God, I didn't?" She touches her neck.

"You did."

"Anyway, it's not for Jess. I bought it for tomorrow. I just thought I might as well wear it now. At least he won't be able to complain I didn't make an effort."

Alisha takes a breath. "Where are you meeting him?"

"Some cigar bar up on First and Forty-eighth."

"Typical. Convenient for his parents' place?"

"Don't start."

"Listen, I have seen you put yourself back together again over the last few months and it has been hard for you. He comes breezing in from Paris and you—"

"It's just a drink. That's all. It's over. I just—I just want to make sure he's doing okay." They walk on through the museum, and Sophie checks her watch. "So what did you want to show me?"

"I want you to know what you're up against." Alisha points the way, the gold bracelets on her wrist jangling. "When I was in here the other day I saw they'd done a rehang. I guess your Mr. Lambert's due for a revival with his birthday coming up and all." She glances across as a young guard walks toward them.

"The museum is closing," he says.

"Okay, honey." Alisha tosses a glance over her shoulder like a silk scarf as she walks on. "Over here," she says to Sophie, stopping in front of a series of huge dark paintings, broad abstract strokes gouging into the canvas. "Gabriel Lambert." They stand side by side in silence. "I know this isn't your period—"

Sophie squints at the Perspex tag on the wall: *Mars*. "Give me a Matisse or Monet's water lilies any day," she says quietly, stepping backward to take in the full scale of the paintings.

"Lambert makes the rest of them—Pollock, Rothko, all those abstract expressionists of the fifties—well, he makes them look like pussycats." Alisha sweeps her arm around the gallery, and Sophie turns a full circle, returning to Lambert. She stands in silence for a time, dwarfed by the paintings. It feels as though they are pressing down on her.

"We should go," Alisha says, noticing they are the last ones in the gallery.

"The thing is," Sophie says, pointing out canvases as they walk on through the museum, "these guys—the Europeans like Breton and Ernst, all the people Varian Fry helped escape from France, when they arrived in America it was like art exploded. They were the catalyst for all of that." She points back to the room with the abstract expressionists. "But Lambert's work changed so much, I just don't get it."

"Well, if you ask him why, you're a braver woman than me. Your man's like the missing link, isn't he? Born in France and made in America."

"I came into the archives here a while back, and looked at the 'Flight' portfolio of prints Varian Fry curated to raise funds for the refugee organization he worked for back during the war. I don't understand why so few of the artists he helped contributed work."

"Did Lambert?"

"Nope."

"Doesn't surprise me. He's a tough old SOB." Alisha pauses on the pavement, and Sophie hears the museum doors locking behind them.

"Maybe after everything he went through during World War Two he didn't want to look back," Sophie says, thinking it through.

"Perhaps once you start running, it's hard to ever stay still." Alisha puts her hands on her hips. "Look, don't let this old guy run rings round you.

From what I've heard he's tricksy. Did I tell you he blanked me at an opening once?"

"No? When was that?"

"Way back, way, way back. I was still at Parsons. It was a friend's show—I saw this old guy in a denim shirt and worn-out jeans, and espadrilles with his toes poking out of a hole at the front, and I thought: I know you. I mean, his hair was white as white, but those eyes . . . like those snow dogs, you know? Ice blue." Alisha whistles softly. "Man, he must have been fine in his day."

"So what happened?"

"I went over—you know me, I'll talk to anyone, and I started in with: 'Excuse me, Mr. Lambert, I just wanted to let you know what your work has meant to me. . . .'"

"And?"

"He just stared me down. Those goddamn beautiful eyes, cold as fire."

"That doesn't make sense."

"It will when you meet him. Hot and icy, all at the same time. He just walked on by me midsentence, gushing like a damn fool about how much I loved his work." Alisha shakes her head. "Take my advice. You want your story, keep it professional. Don't show a chink of weakness—"

"I won't."

"Sophie, you're a romantic." Alisha cups her face between her hands. "I know you've fallen for the story of Gabe and Annie Lambert, their mythical lifelong love affair—" Sophie rolls her eyes. "Okay, okay." Alisha holds up her hands in surrender. "You sure you want to see Jess? I'm going to see *Love and Sex.* . . ."

"Again?" Sophie laughs. "You and your thing for Jon Favreau." She kisses Alisha's cheek and walks on. "You're obsessed."

"Takes one to know one," Alisha says under her breath as Sophie walks away.

Jess is reading a copy of *Wonder Boys*, a plume of blue smoke rising from the cigar in his right hand. Sophie walks toward him through the dimly lit bar, conversation humming around her like bees in dense grass. Jess throws aside the book and taps his Rolex as he unfolds himself from the dark leather wingback chair to greet her.

"Give me a break," Sophie says, kissing his cheek.

Jess gazes down at her. "I'd forgotten how beautiful you are."

"That didn't take long."

"You cut your hair? I always loved—" He stops, registering her frown.

She remembers how light and free she felt the night Alisha cut it for her a few weeks ago, the heavy hanks of waist-length hair drifting to the floor. "I like it." She touches the nape of her neck.

"Fresh start?"

"I had a broken heart, didn't you hear?"

"You and me both." His gaze travels down. "You should wear this tomorrow, you know. You look professional."

"I was aiming for irresistible."

Jess smiles, his blue eyes creasing. "That too."

"How do you know about tomorrow?"

"I was talking to your editor about this arts story you're writing." He settles back in his seat and beckons over the waiter.

Sophie tosses down her bag and takes the chair beside him. "I feel like a kid with a bad report card."

"Don't sound so defeated. Show them what you're capable of."

"Jess, I'm not like you." Sophie rests her head against the palm of her hand. "I've tried, I really have, but I just feel like a phony—"

"Sweetheart, I've always told you—fake it till you make it—"

"You didn't just 'sweetheart' me?" Sophie raises an eyebrow.

"Sorry, sorry!" Jess holds up his hands in defeat. "Damn, forgetting who I'm talking to." It's an old joke they share. The moment's tinged with loss.

"Maybe I should have stayed on at the university," Sophie says, breaking the tension.

"Ironic, isn't it. If you were still at the Sorbonne, we'd be together in Paris now."

"Really? I hadn't thought of that."

"I see your biting wit hasn't left you." Jess looks up at the waiter. "What'll you have?"

Sophie takes a sip of his drink and pulls a face. "Neat vodka?"

"Whiskey started giving me killer hangovers. I miss it, though—few things finer than late nights and Scotch."

"Hemingway wannabe."

"Pseudo-Sontag." He holds her gaze. "Chablis?"

"Sancerre, thanks." She smiles at the waiter. Jess takes a drag on his cigar and exhales, tilting his face to the ceiling.

"Bravo," he says.

"Sorry?"

"Your taste, it's refining."

"It suits you, this place."

"Sophisticated? Old school?"

"Expensive. Up its own ass."

"I see you've forgiven me."

"And old. Not old school." Sophie glances at him, smiles. "How was your fortieth?"

"Lonely."

"I don't believe that for a moment."

"I missed your birthday, too. What was it? Your twenty-fourth?" Sophie nods. "Well, Happy Birthday to us." He raises his glass to her as the waiter hands her the wine, and they chink a toast. Jess offers her the cigar.

"I gave up."

"Doesn't count."

Sophie takes a drag, exhales slowly. "Happy?"

"Not really. You know me." The intensity of his gaze makes her head spin. "How are you?"

"Just dandy, can't you tell?"

"And Mutt?"

"Doing fine; he's doing just fine." Sophie hands back the cigar. "You know you have visitation rights, anytime."

"Weekends and holidays?" Jess shakes his head, drains his vodka. "No thanks. It was hard enough saying good-bye the first time. Does he still hog the bed?"

"He prefers his basket to Alisha's sofa."

"May I get you a refill, sir?" The waiter clears Jess's glass.

"Yes." He frowns, waits for him to leave. "Soph, why haven't you found anywhere yet?" Jess leans toward her.

"I've been busy. And you know how expensive it is."

"Christ, I feel terrible. Where is it Alisha lives? Williamsburg?"

"It's hardly roughing it." Sophie laughs. "It's up-and-coming, you know."

"Yeah, if you're a meth dealer."

"You watch. It'll be wall-to-wall artisanal cheese shops before you know it." She shrugs. "It's not Greenwich Village, but . . ."

"I'm sorry about that, leaving you to sort the apartment out."

"It was fine," Sophie says. *Fine. It's all fine.* How many times has she said that over the last weeks, when it's been anything but? *It's been hell, Jess, that's what she wants to say. I missed you, and my heart's still mending.* Her throat tightens at the thought of their home, the cozy rooms she had spent months painting and furnishing, all the hopes and dreams that came to nothing.

"I want you to have some of the money, Soph." He glances at the waiter. "Thanks."

"No," she says.

"Everything you did to the place added thousands."

"Your parents bought it for you—"

"For us."

"And we broke off the wedding."

"Only because I insisted on taking the job in Paris." Jess waits for her to look at him. "I've missed you."

"Don't, Jess. We've been over this a thousand times. My life is here." Her stomach flips over at the memory of the arguments toward the end. "What did you expect? That I'd just sacrifice everything and follow you?"

"That's what people in love do."

"Would you do it for me?" She waits, part of her still hoping. "I didn't think so."

Jess swirls his drink. "Your dad would be proud of you."

"Don't, please."

"No, I admire you, I really do." Jess knocks back his vodka. "Hell of a man to live up to, that father of yours."

Sophie closes her eyes, exhales. "Not this again? Jess, you are the one who wanted to go and be a foreign correspondent—"

"You could have come with me." He leans forward. "Don't you remember how it was, when we met? Don't you remember Paris?"

"Of course I do." She can't look at him.

"Soph, I wanted to see you tonight because there's something I need to tell you—" She picks up on his tone immediately. *Tell me. Something to tell me, not ask me.*

"You've met someone new." It's a statement, not a question. She places her wine carefully on the table. "Is it serious?"

"Nothing's happened, yet." He takes her hand. "If you won't come with me—"

"Of course. I'm happy for you." *What did I expect?* She rubs her thumb against the side of his, and they rest fingertip to fingertip.

"Jeez, Cass. Aren't we worth more than some job? People do write in Paris, it has been known."

"Not like this, not like the *Times*—"

"Still going for that Pulitzer, are we? Daddy's little girl. . . ."

"Be happy, Jess." Sophie swallows down her disappointment as she stands to leave.

"I'm sorry. Don't go." He reaches over to stop her. "I'm flying back just as soon as the UN summit ends on Friday. Once you've seen this old guy tomorrow, and knocked out your story—"

"Jess, this isn't just some story." Sophie squares up to him. "I care about this, more than anything—"

"More than me?" His brow furrows. "Come with me."

"I can't—"

"Just think about it. You're due some leave, I know." Sophie tenses as he stands and hugs her. *Too damn right I am. It should have been our honeymoon.* "Come with me to Paris, not for good, not yet, but just to see if we still—"

"Love one another?" Sophie reaches up and kisses his cheek. *Did you ever really love me? Or were you just in love with the idea of me?*

"Stay with me tonight." He turns to her, his jawbone brushing her temple. "My folks are out of town."

"I can't—" Her voice breaks. "I just can't . . . do this anymore, Jess." She steps away and smiles, her eyes glistening. "Besides, Mutt's waiting up for me."

"He watches too much TV. Does he still like *Friends*?"

"He's into *Frasier* lately."

"Is he? I guess we all move on." Jess gazes down at her. "Stay. Please."

Sophie shakes her head. "I've got to be at Penn Station early."

"It'd be quicker if—"

"Good-bye, Jess."

"No." He raises her chin with his index finger.

"What do you mean, no?"

"I'm not saying good-bye to you, Cass. Not yet. You've got a couple of days to think about it. Montmartre, the galleries, strolling along the Seine . . . Wait till you see my apartment near Sacré-Cœur."

"You don't give in, do you?"

"Never, with you." Jess drapes her jacket over her shoulders. "One last chance, is that too much to ask?"

FOUR

Southampton, Long Island

Thursday, September 7, 2000

Sophie

A little after ten, Sophie's train pulls in to Southampton station, and she jumps down to the platform. She slips on her sunglasses as she walks out through the low redbrick building and glances around for a cab. On the flagpole opposite the station, the Stars and Stripes snap in the warm breeze. A man with jet-black hair leans against the side of a dusty blue pickup truck parked beneath the flag. Spotting Sophie, he strides out into the road and calls to her.

"Sophie Cass?"

"Yes," she says. *Those eyes.* "Who—"

"Harry Lambert." He reaches out and shakes her hand. Sophie's shocked by his directness, his resemblance to Gabriel. Reading her expression, he shrugs. "Yeah, I know. Everyone says it's uncanny." He turns his head from side to side, an amused look on his face. "I haven't seen any photos of Grandpa at my age—"

"I have. It's amazing how alike you are." She thinks of the photos Alistair Quimby took, tucked safely in her bag. "How old are you?"

"Man, you're direct." Harry laughs. "How about getting to know a guy first?"

"I just meant—"

"I'm twenty-six, thank you for your interest."

"Who says I'm interested?" Sophie takes off her sunglasses.

"Say, I know you."

"I don't think so."

"You were at that opening in SoHo a few months back. Red dress." His eyes crinkle. "I tried to get your attention, but you were deep in conversation with some stiff in a suit."

She remembers the night, the argument. Jess had left for Paris the next day. "I don't remember—I mean, I'm sure I'd have noticed you." It was on the tip of her tongue to say: *I'm sure I would have noticed someone who looks so like the man I've spent months researching.*

"Yeah, well, sometimes you don't see what's right under your nose." Harry smiles. "I looked kind of different then, too—I'd shaved my hair off."

"Bad breakup?"

"No." He runs his hand through his hair. "Though there was that, too. I did it for charity."

"Well, small world."

"Gabe got your letter," he says. "We figured you might be on this train if you were coming in from the city."

"And what? You wanted to stop me getting to see him?"

Harry shrugs. "Just wanted to check you out."

"So?"

Harry searches for the word. "Unexpected."

"Look, I can appreciate you're protective of him." She pauses. "Hey—how did you know it was me?"

"Magic." Harry strolls toward the truck. When Sophie doesn't follow him, he turns to her. "Okay, I did my research, too." A smile flickers over his lips. "On Yahoo. Wanted to see what we're up against."

Sophie walks after him this time, and he puts his arm out, protecting her from the traffic. He opens the passenger door of the truck and helps her in. Sophie glances at the child's car seat strapped to the bench and throws her bag down into the footwell. She's surprised at the jolt of disappointment she feels. "Thanks." The cabin smells of fresh-cut timber and oil. She notices he's wearing heavy work boots. His faded jeans are splashed with white paint, but his crumpled blue-and-white-checked shirt is clean—she catches the fresh scent of detergent as he winds down the window.

Harry starts the engine, and *Bear in the Big Blue House* blasts from the speakers. "Sorry." He flicks the stereo to the radio station. "There goes my street cred."

"Very smooth," Sophie says, laughing. Harry ejects the CD and flips it out. He reaches for the glove compartment as he watches the traffic, the back of his hand accidentally brushing her knee. Sophie shifts her leg and searches for the case, taking the disc from him.

"I sometimes forget to turn it off—"

"C'mon, admit it. You love *Bear*."

Harry glances over at her as he pulls out onto Hampton Road. "Who doesn't?" Sophie tucks the disc back in the glove compartment, dappled shadow from the tree-lined road dancing over her arm. "Pick whatever you want." Savage Garden is playing on the radio.

"No, this is fine." She slides her sunglasses down and settles back, her arm resting on the open window. *I knew I loved you* . . . Sophie can't help thinking of the photograph of Gabriel and Annie as she looks at Harry.

"How old's your kid?" she says.

"Kid?" Sophie gestures at the car seat. "No, she's my niece. I just help my sister out sometimes, dropping her at nursery."

"Oh." As they drive on past high hedges, white clapboard houses peeking above, she relaxes. Sophie reaches into her bag for some gum, and she spots the Henry James essay, the note. Her mother's voice comes to her: *good-looking, sense of humor, good with children* . . . She offers him a stick, and the scent of fresh mint fills the air. "Tell me what you meant by unexpected?"

"Thanks. You've just surprised me, that's all. From those hard-assed letters of yours we were expecting—"

"We?"

"The family." Harry spins the wheel. "My dad spoke with your mom the other day, Miss . . . ? Ms.?"

"Doctor."

"Doctor?"

"Art history." Sophie looks over at him as they stop at a junction. "Though I do know a little first aid."

"I'll bear that in mind if I need mouth-to-mouth."

Those eyes, Sophie thinks, easing the gum against the roof of her mouth with her tongue. She feels the heat rising in her blood, molten, warm.

"Dad's normally so protective of Gabe he won't let any journalists near him." Harry glances at Sophie. "But your mom was pretty persuasive."

"She has a way with words. You may have heard of her—Paige Cass?"

"Vaguely. Poetry's not really my thing."

"What is your 'thing,' Mr. Lambert?"

"Harry. I'm an artist."

"Like your grandfather?"

"And you are a writer, like your father." Sophie looks at him, surprised. "I told you I checked you out, Dr. Cass."

"Sophie."

Harry drives on. "Jack Cass, Pulitzer Prize–winning *New York Times* journalist and all-round hero. . . ."

"Bravo."

"So what is this? Trying to prove you're as good as Daddy? Going in for the big story?"

"Something like that." Sophie folds her arms.

"What happened with him? I saw he was killed—was he on assignment?"

"Now who's direct?" Sophie shakes her head, a tendril of hair loosening. "No. It was the wrong drugstore, wrong holdup, wrong time to be a hero." She turns to the window, gazing out as a succession of identical brick driveways with impenetrable electric gates sweeps past.

"Damn, I'm sorry." Harry reaches over and touches her arm, waits for her to look at him. "There's never a wrong time to be a hero."

Sophie acknowledges his kindness, a tilt of her head. "Maybe you're right." She felt it, at his touch, a quickening. Desire blooms in her like hunger. She looks up the road, hiding her surprise. "I took you for a contractor."

Harry settles back, one hand on the wheel, his other arm looped easily across the back of the bench seat. "Got to pay the bills somehow."

"I assumed—"

"What? That none of us have to work, because of Gabe?" Harry throws his head back and laughs. "You really haven't met him, have you?" He indicates to turn off the main road. "Listen, I've got to do a couple of chores on the way. Do you mind?"

"Sure, no problem. As long as we get to Gabriel on time."

After driving for a time, Harry pulls into the yard of an architectural salvage store and switches off the engine. Weathered stone garden statues and a pair of Doric columns line the entrance to the clapboard barn, a brass bedstead leans by the doorway, basking in the sun. "I won't be long."

In the rearview mirror, Sophie watches him walking away. He moves with a lean, agile strength. A blue glass lantern hanging in the tree by the barn door swings in the breeze, catches the light. *What am I doing? I haven't felt like this since . . .* Sophie flicks back through her memories. *When? Since the first time I saw Jess? No, this is different.* She quickly flips down the sun visor and slicks some Carmex across her lips, lets down her hair. *Meeting Jess was crazy, and wonderful, and Paris . . .* Her green eyes are dark in the shaded mirror. *But it wasn't like this.* By the time Harry returns, arms laden with tiles, she is leaning against the truck, idly scrolling through her phone.

"What do you think?" he says to her, dumping the tile boxes in the back. "First impression?"

"Bit wary, but charming in a rugged artist slash builder way. . . ."

"Less of your lip, missy—as Gabe would say." He puts his hands on his hips. "Not me, the tiles."

"Kitchen or bathroom?" She stands beside him, feels him watching her.

"Bathroom floor."

"Those." She runs her fingertips over the warm limestone slabs.

"Yeah, that's what I thought." He walks around and opens the door for her.

"Is this for a project?" she asks as Harry starts the car.

"Nope, I'm renovating a place up the coast."

"Really?" Sophie turns to him, her leg tucked beneath her. "I've always dreamed of doing that." Her imagination runs ahead of her. She pictures an empty house, white rooms full of light, two chairs on the porch, talking late into the night.

"It's not much at the moment," he says. "But it's a start, and I'm going to build a little gallery on the side as soon as I can." He glances at her. "In fact, I could do with a curator—someone who could write the catalogs and so on."

Sophie shrugs. "You never know. If you build it—"

"She will come?" Harry grins. "I loved that film when I was a kid."

"Yeah, so did I." Sophie leans her head against the palm of her hand as she looks at him. It's like looking at Gabriel, but with none of the hardness and anger etched into every photograph she has seen of him at that age.

"What?"

"Nothing," Sophie says. She had been wondering what it would be like to kiss him. "You're just . . . unexpected, too." She glances at her watch. "Listen, do you mind if we head over to the house now? I don't want to be late."

He hesitates. "Sure." He pulls out onto the main road again.

"Is it far?"

"No." She feels a distance between them, suddenly. "Do you know Flying Point?"

Sophie shakes her head. "Nope."

"City girl, huh?" Harry looks on ahead.

Sophie frowns, doesn't correct him. "Any advice? I mean, anything you can suggest that might make it easier?"

"With Gabe?" Harry puts his foot down, heading toward the coast. "Just be yourself. He doesn't like phonies."

"Okay. Anything else?"

"Take it easy on him, okay?" She sees the concern in his eyes as he turns to her. "Gabe's not . . . I mean, he's ninety-five."

"About that—"

"Look. You're talking to the wrong person. You have some great theory about Gabe, then have it out with him. I tend to trust people, you know? Treat them how they treat me. And Gabe . . ." Harry pauses. "He's the best." They fall silent as Harry drives on. Sophie glances at her watch again. Five to twelve. "Not much further." The sudden edge in his voice cuts through her. "Look, in fact, do you mind if I drop you here? It's not far."

"Sure." She hesitates, uncertain whether to ask him what has changed so suddenly. *What an idiot,* she thinks. *I've been out of the game so long, I completely misread him.* Disappointment settles quietly on her like mist on a lake. Harry pulls in to the side of the narrow road. "Thanks." Sophie hops down from the cab. "It was good to meet you." She reaches over and takes her bag from him.

"Sophie . . ."

"Yes?"

"Don't do this, please?" He touches her hand. "I know your mom said you've been working on this for months—"

Sophie laughs uneasily. "Sounds professional, doesn't it?"

"It's just a story—can't you let it go?"

"I can't do that," she says, reluctant to pull away. "It's about my family, too. I want to know the truth about Vita, and Gabriel's the only one who can tell me that."

"But he's an old man, and now . . ." Harry settles back. He won't look at her. Emotions pass over his face like cloud shadows scudding over hills. He points toward a rough track up ahead. "Head down there. When you get to the end . . ." He pauses. "Turn left. Keep on walking up the beach, you can't miss it."

"Thanks for the ride. Once you've built that gallery, why don't you give me a call?"

"Hope you're patient." Harry raises his hand in farewell as she closes the door and steps back. "See you around?"

"Sure," Sophie says, and watches as the truck drives away. A line from her research comes to her: *I'll see you soon, in New York.*

FIVE

Flying Point, Long Island

~~~~~

2000

Gabriel

This year, for Annie, we had Christmas a little early as a surprise for her. I can see Tom and his brother, Albie, dragging the tree across the yard to the trash, a thin line of green needles trailing them like a file of ants. Some days it still surprises me to see my boys grown men, with sons of their own. I still remember the pair of them running across the beach in the summertime after school, their hair bleached white, their beautiful tan bodies thin and flexible as reeds, lambent, full of sap and new life. The yellow school bus would drop them at the end of the lane, and they'd race straight through the house, flinging their bags down on the way to the beach. In and out, and gone. Damn, it goes by so fast.

A strand of silver tinsel catches the light as the bare branches sweep along the sand. I can see Tom pointing at the studio and saying something to Albie. He's probably telling the boy to keep an eye on me while he finishes up outside, but there's no need for that. Tom always was the stubborn, bossy one, as most eldest kids are, but then so was the man he was named for.

We set up the crèche just the way Annie likes it, too, with the cradle empty until the day. The girls are packing it away in the house now, but I've taken the little Santon figure Annie bought me in Marseille in November 1940 with me. The little clay figure of a shepherd facing the mistral is worn and chipped now, but then so am I. I remember the market, the lamps strung from the stalls, the crush of bodies, and the warmth of Annie's hand in mine. There was little food by then, but they were roasting chestnuts on braziers, and sweet smoke filled the air. She chose him for me, her gloved fingers dancing over the identical heads until she saw just the right one for us, and she wrapped it in her lace-edged handkerchief, pressed it into my palm. "One day," she said, "this will be in our home."

Now, my littlest great-grandchild holds it in her tiny fist. She's curled up asleep on my lap in the studio. The guileless sleep of children moves me. The child's fontanel is pulsing in her sleep, and her perfection, her peace, awes me. I think I've slept with one eye open since 1940.

The girls shooed me out of the way while they tidied up the lunch, told me to stop the little one from crying. Her first teeth are coming in and her cheeks are flushed. I'm not use for much these days, but I can still soothe a baby to sleep, rocking in my old Shaker chair looking out to sea. In her sleep, her fingers extend like a starfish, her perfect little mother-of-pearl nails shining in the autumn light. The shepherd tumbles from her palm to my lap, and I put him away safely in my pocket as I carry her back to the house to tuck her up in her cradle in the kids' old bedroom.

My daughter glances up as I close the screen door behind me, and I raise my finger to my lips. She smiles and bends her golden head to scrub the old wood table clean, her sleeves rolled up, her hands soft and pink from the hot water. A chain of silver stars and shells glimmers on her wrist.

One of the toddlers is napping on the bottom bunk already, and the midday sun is diffuse and warm through the orange curtains. I lay the baby down in her cradle and switch on the little lamp at her side. Her eyes open lazily, register the familiar stars and shells rotating slowly around the room, then close, contented, and I pull the door to, silently.

How many nights did I do that for my kids when the wind raged outside? My throat is tight, suddenly, at the thought of all the days, the thousands of nights, that have gone by unremarked, and I lay my head against the door. The sand is running over the smooth hip of the hourglass. I know the creak of this particular door and the click of the latch by heart. I know every breath and sigh of this house that I built with my own hands.

I wait at the porch for the girl to come and turn the shepherd over in my fingers in my pocket, the old clay smooth and good to the touch. The little figure *Le Coup de Mistral,* this man battling against the gods, holding on to his hat as he soldiers on, leading his sheep out of the storm, always makes me think of Varian. I find I think of him more often now. I owe him, I owe them, all of this, and I never had the chance to thank him. Because of him, we are here.

Sometimes I think I left my heart at the Villa Air-Bel in Marseille. When I think back to the war, my memories are all of the house of dreams. Our greatest joys and tragedies played out there. Ask Varian, ask any of them, and they'd have said the same. We knew, even then, that life would never be as vivid as this again, felt guilty, even, that we found such unexpected happiness.

Air-Bel was a sanctuary. There, I saw André Breton conjure a court of miracles. Perhaps when the horror of war surrounds you, when everything—life itself—could be taken from you in an instant, this is what men like André and Varian do. They become gods, fight back any way they can. Some of us—artists and writers, lovers and children—well, while others give up and wait to die, some of us fight the only way we can and create something marvelous.

I still see them walking down the driveway of the château for the last time: Varian, the police at his shoulder, and his loyal dog, Clovis, at his side. After the rain, even the cedar trees seemed to be weeping. In a year, Varian said, we lived twenty. I have never been so afraid and yet so alive.

When he wrote his memoir, Varian said he had to exorcise his ghosts. Maybe that's what I have to do today. He reckoned he couldn't lay them to rest until he'd told his story—all of it. Well, this is my story. I don't want anyone to feel sorry for me—the world is full of miserable childhoods, it's incredible any of us survive. It's where you go, not where you're from, that counts in life. You're dealt a bad hand—make something of it. Every day I thank the stars for my luck. I made a living, made a life doing something I love, with someone I love at my side, and I gave my kids the childhood I never had. Maybe I had a lucky star guiding me home to Annie. I've lived with guilt my whole life, but I am a fortunate man.

For fifty years of peaceful tides and stars, I've waited for this day to come, and now it's here. I close my eyes. The girl, Sophie, is near, walking along the road toward me, her slender dark figure growing closer, and I am afraid again. Bring on the ghosts. It's time.

SIX

Flying Point, Long Island

❦

2000

Gabriel

"Are you Gabriel Lambert?"

"No. Go away." Well, it's worth a try. *I'm ready for you, missy.* No one has seen me in public for years, and it might just fool her. I squint my eyes against the clear autumn light and try to close the screen door, but the girl slings her fancy suede bag up against the jamb. It thuds on the deck with the weight of a brick, and the door gets stuck on a silver laptop I can see poking out the side like a knife. "I said, go away. This is private property. Didn't you see the sign up on the track?"

"Yes." She folds her arms. What is it with girls today, they try to make themselves so deliberately plain? Not a scrap of makeup. I used to love watching Annie making up her face in the morning. It was like she was joining the dots, clearly defining the beauty in her face. I loved it when our kisses smudged her lips, when her eyelids grew smoky with kohl. Nothing like that with this girl, no sir. Even the heavy black-framed glasses are some kind of statement: *Listen, buddy, I know I'm young, and my limbs have the refinement of a gazelle, but I wear this beauty lightly, with a sense of irony.* Jeez, the things we take for granted—if I knew how swiftly the power of my body would desert me, I would have spent the first decades of my life on a beach like my kids, just enjoying the grace, the luck of being alive and young. These days, when I wake in the warm, familiar nest of my bed with Annie at my side, there's a weightless moment when I am still as fresh as this girl. Then—I always think of it like a white-haired janitor in brown overalls walking through a dusty warehouse flicking on strip lights—my old body crackles into life and all the aches and pains fire up, one by one. I'm useless now, before my shower in the mornings. The hot water eases my old limbs, and I've always had my best ideas in the shower. Annie gave me some whiteboard markers for my birthday a while back, and now it's the best time of the day for me—I can shower, and think, and sketch out my ideas on the glass of the stall and the tiles. If it's going well, I stay in there for ages, whistling tunelessly, through the gap where my pipe stem has worn down my teeth like an old limestone doorstep over the years.

But look at this girl, with her sharp black suit and her attitude. Just in case that's too sexy, she's got her hair scraped back so hard, it's like she's had a face-lift, and her jacket's buttoned up tighter than a preacher's pants.

"You don't take any notice of signs?" I say.

"You don't take any notice of e-mails. Or your lawyer doesn't." She smiles sweetly, but there's clarity to her speech that makes me feel she doesn't take any nonsense, and a toughness to her eyes that says: *Come on, give it your best, big shot. I'm not afraid of you. I'm not impressed by your so-called reputation.* I can see her weighing me up, how I've changed from the most recent catalog photograph, which is thirty years old now. I never did like having my picture taken. What does she see? The thick hair in need of a cut turned from black to white. The hollow cheeks tanned and burnished like driftwood, the silver scar above my jaw. Faded blue jeans and espadrilles, a billowing white shirt, untucked. Maybe she notices the cerulean-blue paint under my fingernails and wonders what I'm painting now. "You gave me no choice. . . ."

There have been a lot of girls like this over the years, journalists or students from Parsons or Columbia, come to kiss the hem of the great man or to try to dig up some dirt. I live at the end of an unmarked coast road on Long Island, well away from the chichi villages and "cottages" the size of civic buildings, but still the most determined find me. Sometimes I think it would be easier if they just stuck me in formaldehyde like the sharks and cows the young guns are showing and exhibited me in MoMA under a flashing red arrow with a neat Perspex sign saying, *Gabriel Lambert, artist,* next to some of the big abstract expressionist pieces that made my name way back in the fifties.

Annie used to field the girls for me, kill them with kindness—cookies and milk at the old pine table in the kitchen or chicken soup in the winter. If they had any romantic illusions, she soon sorted them out. They were out of the house and on the bus back to New York before they realized they hadn't seen me or my studio. Annie never had any cause to worry, there was only one girl for me. Is only one girl. I've loved only two women in my life—not much, I know, in all my years, but enough for me. The first, well, that didn't end so well. Annie was different. *We're like swans,* she'd say, *bobbing along side by side whatever the current throws at us.* There were often a few girls sniffing around, but none for a while. The aphrodisiac power of fame and money never ceases to amaze me—they can make a twenty-year-old girl overlook white hair and haunches sagging like an old sofa. But this one isn't looking at me like that. She's different, I can tell. She looks determined, in spite of her lips, lips that remind me of someone. The bottom one is fuller than the top. It has a crease in it like the indentation of a head on a plump pillow.

"E-mails?" I say. "I don't use a computer."

"What about my letters?"

I think guiltily of the endless letters on creamy laid paper, her looping script. Who uses a fountain pen these days? When she kept on writing, I got my lawyer to scare her off, but that didn't work either.

"I assume you got my last letter?" She's talking slower now, like she's thinking maybe I'm deaf or doolally. Well, I can use that to my advantage. I got your letter, sure I got it. Saved your ace till last, didn't you, missy. I hear the sounds of them tidying up the lunch behind me, my great-grandchildren's laughter a bubbling brook, Tom ragging on his brother, the soothing tones of my granddaughter trying to smooth things over.

"Letter?" I make my hand tremble as I rub my brow. "I'm sorry, dear. I get a little confused these days. . . ." It's working. I see her face soften. She was expecting an angry old man of art, but I've got a few surprises of my own.

"This isn't personal, Mr. Lambert, I want you to know that. The editor commissioned me to write the article because of my great-aunt Vita."

"Vita?" I say vaguely.

She bites her lip in impatience, but her voice is steady. "I just want to get my facts one hundred percent straight. I promise, I won't take much of your time."

Facts? Silly girl, there are no facts in a situation like this, only opinions, old memories, and they change over time like a painting fading in sunlight. The girl tries to peer through to the shadows of the cottage, but everything is thrown into darkness by the bright rectangle of light from the open terrace overlooking the sea. Maybe she can make out the Flos Arco lamp curving over the table like an attentive servant or our two old Jacobsen chairs overlooking the sea, the tan leather shaped to our bodies like eggs to chicks. Annie is there. I feel the certain, reassuring weight of her presence behind me, the south to my north like the counterweight of a compass needle.

"You *are* Gabriel Lambert?"

I hesitate. The trouble with telling lies is you have to remember them. They don't come naturally to you like the truth. You have to hold all the strands together. "Who wants to know?"

"I'm Dr. Cass." She offers me her hand, and grudgingly I take it. It's as slight as a bundle of reeds. "But please, call me Sophie." Of course. Sophia, the wise one. She thinks she's wise, you can see that. She's young enough to think she knows everything still. Life hasn't knocked her edges off yet. Give her time. Pretty soon she'll realize that true wisdom is knowing that the more you learn about life, the less you realize you know. I feel stupider now than I ever did at twenty, and she can't be much more than that.

"Well, 'call me Sophie,' you don't look like a doctor."

"Of art history," she says. "I write arts and culture stories for *The New York Times*."

"So you're a hack?"

"I prefer investigative journalist."

"Do you have a card? You can't be too careful."

"Of course." I was hoping she'd pick her bag up so I could lock the door in her face, but she doesn't budge. "As you know, the paper plans to run my piece on you . . ." Her voice trails off as she squats down and shuffles through her bag. She hands me her personal business card—expensive, engraved, naturally. The letters of her name are like Braille beneath my fingertip. As she looks up at me, I notice her knee is poking through a hole in her black stockings, I see smooth white skin and torn flesh.

"What did you do?"

"Sorry?" She hooks a hank of blond hair behind her ear. There's a sharp chrome spike pinning it in a bun at the nape of her neck. "Oh, my knee? It's nothing. I fell over on the road up there."

"You should take them off."

"I beg your pardon?" She squares up to me, full of righteous indignation.

"I only meant you should get some sea air on your skin, wash off the blood." I kick her bag clear and pull the screen door shut. "You've had a wasted journey."

She slams a manila envelope up against the screen. She's written on it: *Vita, last paintings*. "Like I said. I won't take up much of your time."

Fear chills me, I feel goose bumps as the hair rises at the nape of my neck, on my arms. Vita. One glance at the triumphant look on the girl's face and I know if I shut the door on her, she'll still be there on the porch come twilight, so I edge the screen open and take it from her.

"I just want to ask you what you remember about these photographs," she's saying as I slip the thick, glossy black-and-white images she's probably sneaked out of some art history library from the envelope. Sure enough, there's an official-looking stamp on the back: *Do Not Remove*. Naughty girl. "All I know for sure is that Vita was with you in the Languedoc during 1939 to '40, and these photos were taken before the fire. . . ." She's clever, this kid, coming at the subject sideways, not saying overtly what she knows and I know.

An old drinking buddy of mine told me a story once about a guy who turned around to him in a bar on Canal Street and punched him in the throat. No rhyme or reason, no warning, just wham. That's how I feel right now as I turn over the photographs and see what Sophie must have seen. Oh, dear God, it's happened. I close my eyes. I've feared this moment my whole life.

"So, I was right." Sophie smiles, her gaze clear and sly. I see it, shimmering there in my mind's eye like the Cheshire Cat's. "Where shall we begin, Mr. Lambert? The Château d'Oc?"

"I can't . . . I don't want to talk about that, not yet."

"We can come back to Vita." Her words whisper around my mind the way the wind runs its invisible fingers through the trees. The years tumble away like dry leaves on the breeze.

"Why don't we begin with Marseille, then? Tell me about Varian Fry, Gabriel. Tell the story of how you met Annie."

Marseille, of course. It all began in Marseille.

SEVEN

Marseille

October 1940

Gabriel

It was October 1940 when I arrived. As I close my eyes, I can see it again, the gray hills, the lush green of the palms. I'd paid some guy in Arles for the name and address of the American angel all the refugees were talking about. When I got to Marseille, I discovered I could have found him for free—everyone knew Varian Fry. Someone told me he had moved offices. He said I should head up to the American consulate and ask there. So I did. It looked like a castle. You could tell you were heading in the right direction because the closer you got, the fuller the tram became of refugees. I'd sold Vita's car the morning I arrived, because I didn't want to draw any attention to myself, driving around in some cute little red cabriolet. How I made it from the Languedoc to Marseille without having an accident, heaven knows. Sometimes I think I have a guardian angel watching over me.

I stood up to give my seat to an old woman on the tram. It was packed by the time we reached the consulate, people hanging on to one another. There's nothing more pitiful than seeing good folks trying to keep their standards up. Men and women who haven't had a decent bath or meal for weeks, who still button up filthy shirts and pin down crushed hats on hair that needs a wash. I don't suppose I looked any better.

It was beautiful out there, with the plane trees and the sound of the sea. There was water rushing through the ditches. To be surrounded by such beauty in such desperate circumstances was worse, almost. The consulate was like a castle in a fairy tale, and you could see the hope in people's eyes as they traipsed up the white steps. I stood in the blue shade of a café awning—I think it was called the Pelikan—and let the crowds go ahead. Each face bore the same expression. Everything—all the fear of arrest, of concentration camps and the Gestapo, of every machine-gun bullet dodged on the hundreds of miles they had walked—had led to this. They were paralyzed with fear at the thought of staying in France and terrified by the notion of leaving.

As luck would have it, just as I was asking some hard-looking receptionist at the front desk for information about Fry's organization, the American Relief Center, I noticed a tall, kindly-looking man watching me. The ARC had a near mythical reputation for the way they could help refugees escape to safety, and my desperation to get there must have been written all over my face.

"The consulate has no connection with the ARC," the blonde was saying. She was chewing gum and I caught a glimpse of bubblegum pink between her canine teeth. Her hair was brittle and bleached. Blue streaked her eyelids—she couldn't even be bothered to look me in the eye. She wore a tight sweater, and she had the kind of conical breasts that looked like they could do you an injury if you dared go in for a clinch.

"I'm sorry to bother you," I said, and started to walk away.

"Say . . ." The man pointed a sheaf of papers at the folding easel strapped to my bag. "Are you an artist?"

"Yes, sir."

He ushered me outside, past the snaking queues of people. "Pay no notice to her," he said. "Miss Delapré does a hard job fielding all these people day after day." He smiled down at me. He had an unusual face for such a big guy—apple cheeked and radiant. Stick a white beard on him and he could have been Santa Claus. I guessed he must be around six feet four, six five. His thick, round glasses caught the sunlight as he turned and pointed back down the hill. "Why don't you head down to rue Grignan? You can't miss the ARC—"

"Just follow the queues?"

He smiled and shook my hand. "You're catching on. The reception is open Monday, Wednesday, and Friday mornings. Tell them the vice-consul, Bingham, sent you. Good luck."

It's amazing, looking back, how people queued without question. We were all terrified, jittery, and yet everyone waited with the dull resignation of sheep. I've seen animals herded into stalls on the way to a slaughterhouse—one whiff of blood and they panic, scrambling over barriers, crushing the weaker ones beneath their feet. It wasn't like that at all, not yet. People queued to save their lives like they were waiting in line at the baker's. I waited all morning to get an interview at the ARC office, and I can tell you the atmosphere was benign, even calm. There was a young American guy on the door. He had some uniform on, but he looked more like a matinee idol. When there was a bit of pushing and shoving, he'd hold up his hands and say in a southern drawl: "They-ah now. Take it eas-eh, fellah. Evrabody gets his turn." His French was worse than my English at that time, but he made himself understood, and his uniform looked official enough. He was charming and at ease with himself—the French say *bien dans sa peau*. Once in a while he'd step out onto the pavement for a cigarette or to blow a few bars on his trumpet. Just as I shuffled to the head of the queue, he appeared, the mouth of the instrument swinging into view from the dark doorway like a golden halo. He leaned back against the doorjamb and crossed his right leg at the ankle. I nodded along as he played, and he glanced across at me, his fingers working the valves.

"Cigarette?" I said, offering him one when the tune finished.

"Thanks." He cupped his palm around the flame of my lighter. "You play?"

"Me? No, I just like jazz."

"Man, I've played with some of the greats. . . ." I liked Charlie—that was his name. One of nature's gentlemen. I found out later he'd been a professional wrestler in the States, so when he ended up in Marseille after leaving the American volunteer ambulance corps, Fry took him on to keep order at the ARC. Seemed to me he could just as easily have earned a living as a performer. He told me about jamming with musicians who were like idols to me. "And Louis Armstrong said to me: 'Charlie—'"

"Blow, man, blow," a blond girl cut him off. She stepped out onto the pavement with a clipboard.

"Heck, Mary Jayne." He frowned. "That's the best bit of the story."

"And we've all heard it a hundred times," she said. "Are you next?" Her gaze was direct and unnerving. I noticed her hands—they were surprisingly large and strong for a young woman. I had the feeling she didn't suffer fools.

"Yes," I said, and stubbed out my cigarette on the pavement. I slung the bag over my shoulder and followed her inside. Each desk was full, young men and women talking in hushed voices to refugees. The office was cramped, but through the door at the end I could see a farther room. A young man, taller than the rest, with thick dark hair was pacing up and down. He was one of those people who seem to spark with energy. In a chair at his side, a blond man lounged, his arm resting on the desk, his fingers leisurely tracing the pattern of the wood as he talked.

"Please sit down," the girl said. "Why don't you start by telling me your name?"

"My name?" I blinked. "Gabriel Lambert." She wrote it down. "I need to see Varian Fry."

"So does everyone," she said with an edge to her voice. "May I see your papers?" From my jacket pocket I pulled out my documents. She flicked through them, her gaze traveling from the photograph to my face. I felt the saliva in my throat dry. "Fine," she said, jotting down some notes. She handed them back to me, and I took a breath.

"Now, what makes you think you qualify as a client of the ARC?"

"I am an artist," I said. "Perhaps you have heard of my work?"

She shook her head. "Unfortunately, my colleague Miss Davenport is not here." She leaned toward me. "Miriam has the best eye around here. She was studying art history, you see." She sat back and folded her arms. "Do you have some work you can show us, perhaps?"

"Of course." I had taken the precaution of bringing a few satirical sketches and clippings from an exhibition catalog. I handed these to her.

"These are lovely," she said, looking at the paintings. I saw her smile grimly as she looked at a cartoon of Hitler. "Forgive me, though." I caught the tiredness and impatience in her voice as she tossed the clippings onto the table. "We have rather a lot of people coming through here, pretending to be who they are not. Would you mind terribly doing a quick sketch? The Vieux-Port, perhaps? Miriam always asks people to go and sketch the boats."

"May I?" I said, taking the pen from her. She offered me a sheet of paper. "I am known for my figurative work," I said, glancing at her before deftly sketching her face. My hand was shaking. "I don't do boats."

"Really?" She bridled at my arrogance, but I saw her lift her chin a little as she realized I was sketching her.

"Does everyone have to do this?"

"There are many people pretending to be artists, desperate for our help. We can't assist everyone. I mean, our remit changed somewhat. Originally we were helping only artists and intellectuals. That is still our priority, but my colleague Monsieur Hermant suggested we should give aid to a few of the most deserving ordinary relief cases as well." I liked that about Mary Jayne. I found out later it was she who was helping the so-called ordinary refugees by bankrolling what they called the Gold List, but she never bragged about it, not once. She was a wealthy young woman who had been swanning around Europe in her own plane, so when France fell to the Nazis, Mary Jayne could have left Paris and run on home to the States, just carried on living her charmed life. But she made her way to Marseille and stayed around to help.

"So, which am I?" I asked her, handing over the sketch. In a couple of minutes, I had produced something good enough to fool the girl, anyway.

"An artist, clearly." She flashed those big old blue eyes at me. "Very flattering, Mr. Lambert," she said, glancing from the sketch I handed her to the black-and-white clipping from the exhibition catalog. "May I keep this?"

"Of course," I said, inclining my head. "I really would appreciate your help, Miss . . ."

"Gold. My name is Gold." Of course it was. Everything about this girl was clearly a cut above. I wouldn't have been at all surprised if she had a hallmark stamped on her somewhere. I shook her hand. "I will discuss your case with my colleagues. Perhaps you would be kind enough to come back on Monday morning?"

"As I said, I have enough money to pay for my passage to America, I just need your assistance with visas. . . ."

"Yes, I've noted it all down. There is one other thing," she said.

My heart fell to my boots. "Yes?"

"We only help people who are known and trusted by us or our clients.

We have to be on the alert for Nazi and Vichy agents, you do understand? Do you have anyone who can vouch for you in Marseille?"

Oh God, so close, so close. I thought frantically. "Vice-Consul Bingham," I lied.

She looked up in surprise. "You're a friend of Harry's?"

"More of an acquaintance." I leaned toward her and fixed her with my gaze. "I can't say too much. It really is imperative I leave France immediately," I said. "I've been an outspoken critic of Nazism for many years." I pointed at the political cartoon.

"I do understand, Mr. Lambert," she said, lacing her fingers together. She leaned toward me. "But you must understand, too. Every person who walks through this door is scared for his, or her, life. We have to choose who we help very, very carefully."

I saw Miss Gold again late Sunday night, in a bar in the Vieux-Port. I was surprised to see her in a joint like that, but she looked as happy as a debutante at the Ritz. A slim, dark guy with round glasses escorted her onto the dance floor. Her face was all lit up with love like Christmas as they danced, but he looked hard, I can tell you, lean and mean, not the kind of fellow you'd expect a rich girl like her to go for. But then, people can be funny like that sometimes. The bar was noisy with voices and laughter, and the band had to fight to be heard. Miss Gold and her man were dancing in the middle of the old parquet dance floor, dark figures moving around them. The dim red light lit up her blond waves, blushed her cheeks like a fallen angel's. When I think of Mary Jayne, that's how I remember her, with a smile on her lips as they turned slowly on the spot, lost in one another.

EIGHT

Marseille

1940

Varian

Varian Fry struck his gold Dunhill lighter. The flame licked the soupy night air east of the Vieux-Port, illuminated his horn-rimmed glasses beneath the brim of his dark homburg. The signet ring on his finger glinted. The last warm evenings of a Saint Martin's summer had lingered, but now the mistral swept down from the Vaucluse mountains, a chill whisper in the ear of the gilded Virgin of sinners and sailors atop Notre-Dame de la Garde on its way down to the city and the sea. The wind rustled through palm and plane trees, bringing the metallic tang of the week's catch from the sluiced-off market stalls on the Quai des Belges. That night they were undertaking the third attempt to help a number of the refugees in greatest danger escape to Gibraltar by boat, and it was the biggest risk they had taken yet. *After two failures, this has to work. It will work,* he told himself again, his stomach knotting with fear at the thought of discovery by Vichy troops or the Gestapo.

"Thanks." Beamish leaned in to the flame, lighting his cigarette. His calm impressed Varian. You would not want to play poker with Beamish. The way he leisurely flicked his cigarette with long, dismissive fingers reminded Varian more of the studied nonchalance of a boy at a dance than of a man arranging one of the most daring escapes of the war. Varian wondered if he was scared, too.

"Are you sure you weren't followed?" Beamish said.

"Of course. I may not be as sharp—"

"*Je me débrouille.*" I look after myself. A grin illuminated his face. That smile was why Varian had nicknamed Albert Hermant—aka Hermant the varmint, as Miriam and Mary Jayne called him—Beamish. *A demon of ingenuity with Puck's smile*, that was how Varian described his best friend and right-hand man in Marseille. Who would guess that Beamish had been born in Berlin and arrived in Marseille via the Sorbonne, the London School of Economics, and a doctorate at the University of Trieste? He had fought for the Republicans in the Spanish Civil War, but when Spain fell to Franco's fascist forces, Beamish ended up in France, a refugee himself. Now, he was putting his intellect and battle-hardened street smarts to good use helping the ARC. Bound by a common intelligence and drive to save as many refugees as they could, Varian and Beamish had become fast friends.

"I'm not a fool, though. No one was tailing me." But it would have been easy enough. Varian had strolled beneath the blue-painted streetlights of La Canebière with the natural assurance of a Harvard man. His long-legged, confident stride, even his height, marked him out among the teeming crowds of refugees clogging the dark arteries of the city. His anxiety was hidden deep. He wore his learning like armor, a sword and a shield, his nationality like a cloak—*I am untouchable. I am the child of a great and neutral country. I am an American.*

Now, as he sheltered with Beamish in the shadows on the pier, he had a small valise at his side. Somewhere in the darkness, a ship's foghorn sounded. Until this evening, it had always amused him that the cannons of Fort Saint-Jean pointed inward, as if to keep the inhabitants at bay. Now, he felt the harbor had him at gunpoint, and the dark bulk of the Île d'If made him think of the Count of Monte Cristo, of capture. His gut instinct told him something was wrong. Varian slipped his hand inside his coat and winced.

"You need a holiday," Beamish said. "At least you look like a tourist on vacation."

"Good, that's the idea." Varian checked his Patek Philippe. "The train leaves for Tarascon at midnight."

"Make sure you're on it. The flics can't hear you were anywhere near here tonight." As he spoke, Beamish's gaze followed a group of figures lurching along the dock. "Don't worry, it's nothing."

The door of a shed on the quay near the lighthouse eased open a crack, and Charlie poked his head out. "Hey, boss, we're all set," he called quietly. His warm southern drawl was reassuring, but his fingers worked nervously, as if he were playing his trumpet.

Varian looked around, then strode over and slipped inside, his eyes adjusting to the darkness. He made out the shadowy figures of the refugees, the pale, exhausted faces of British prisoners of war on the run, Spanish and Italian Republicans, writers, artists, and among them the towering figure of Georg Bernhard, his white hair like a cloud on a mountaintop. He stepped forward and shook his hand. "Good luck, Bernhard."

"Thank you, Fry."

"I'll leave you in Charlie and Beamish's capable hands. The boat will be here in an hour. You'll be in Gibraltar before you know it." The man's intelligent, haunted face touched him. For once, the editor of the anti-Nazi newspaper *Pariser Tageblatt* had lost his natural assurance. *Number three on Hitler's Most Wanted list,* Varian thought. *I'd be worried, too.* Two other ARC clients—the German politicians Rudolf Breitscheid and Rudolf Hilferding—were numbers one and two. As leading members of the Social Democratic Party, they were in grave danger. *They think they are untouchable, sitting leisurely in the same café every day when they should be in hiding,* Varian thought. He had given up trying to warn them to be more careful. These great men believed the so-called unoccupied zone was safe, but Varian knew better. *No one is safe.* "That couple ah sons ah bitches ah just asking for trouble," that's what Charlie said the other day about the pair of them. *But it's up to us to get them out, too,* Varian thought.

The hot bovine bulk of the dark figures in their winter coats, the muffled sound of shallow breathing in the claustrophobic shack, unnerved him. "I'll see you soon, in New York," he said, and stepped out onto the dock, closing the door.

"Sometimes," Beamish said quietly, "I think you say that as much to give yourself confidence as them."

⁓ঌ⁓

Striding on through the Vieux-Port, Varian imagined the cellars and subterranean smugglers' tunnels beneath the steps of his polished brogues. He sensed the hidden layers of the ancient city, the Phoenician foundations and Roman walls buried below. He glimpsed the gilded Madonna on top of Notre-Dame de la Garde. *Once this city worshipped Astarte, Venus*, he thought, gazing up at the night sky, trying to locate the planet as he walked on. He loved the age of the place, the sense of history. He had taken a boat out before the weather turned cold to try to look for the cave of Mary Magdalene in the cliffs near the city. *"I have found him whom my soul loves,"* that's what she said.

Varian glanced up at a cry from an alleyway, the heavy thud of a man's body hitting the pavement. He heard footsteps racing away, splashing through dark puddles oily with gasoline. Lines of washing festooned the alleyway, like dark flags in the moonlight. Varian paused, wary of getting involved. It seemed to him that half the people in Marseille were gangsters and the other half wanted to be. The man was already on all fours, shaking his head as he struggled to his feet, silhouetted against the green light seeping from a bar.

Varian slipped the hip flask from the pocket of his overcoat and knocked back a slug of cognac. For a moment he longed to be back home, in New York, with his wife, Eileen, just reading a book by the fire or in the comfort of his own bed. *My old poo-dog*, he thought. His face softened with sadness at the thought of the letter she had posted to him in Marseille the day before he'd left America. She hadn't the nerve to talk to him face-to-face. Eileen had asked him to bring back a war orphan with him, a child they could adopt and raise as their own. *What does that say about us that she couldn't talk to me, and I've been unable to reply? She'll think I've just ignored her.* Varian walked on and took another hit of cognac. *She doesn't understand, can't possibly understand what I am going through here, how it's changing me.* He was so caught up in work, he hadn't even noticed he had missed the day planned for his return flight to New York. He thought of Eileen's latest letter, coolly asking if he was ever planning to come home. *I can't leave*, he thought. *Not yet. They need me. They all need me.* He raised his hip flask and hesitated. *Or do I need them?*

Varian felt as if he had lived a lifetime in Marseille already, but it was only a couple of months since he'd arrived at the Gare Saint-Charles with $3,000 strapped to his calf and a list of two hundred of the greatest creative minds in Europe to rescue. The newly established Emergency Rescue Committee in New York had needed someone on the ground in France to help the refugees to safety. When no one else stepped forward,

Varian volunteered. He was an able multilingual journalist and editor, but he had no experience of relief work. Alfred Barr, an old Harvard classmate and now director of the Museum of Modern Art in New York, had helped compile the list of the most important refugees in danger. Varian's was matched almost name for name by the Nazis' blacklist of targets, a deadly mirror image. *How many have we ticked off so far?* he thought, totting them up as he walked. *Not enough. Not nearly enough.* He had thought it would take a couple of weeks to spirit his clients out of Marseille, but his work was only just beginning. With no official help from the U.S. consulate, Varian had soon realized the only way out of France for his clients was through illegal and secret routes.

The endless stream of hopeful, desperate faces filled his mind, the refugees queuing outside his cramped hotel room at the Splendide and now at the ARC. *I feel like a doctor during an earthquake half the time.* The threat of Article 19, which directed the French to "surrender on demand" anyone sought by the Nazis, hung over Marseille like the sword of Damocles. Fry thought of some of the petty crooks and gangsters they had no choice but to work with to keep the ARC afloat. *Dealing with people like that, it's only a matter of time till someone betrays us.* It felt to Fry like the very air of the city was alive, crackling with fear and suspicion. *Thank God for my team,* he thought, secure in his trust for them, at least, and that the outwardly respectable relief center's activities giving subsistence allowances and advice about visas to refugees was hiding their more clandestine work, spiriting people out of the country.

"It's essential that we help André Breton and his family," Miriam Davenport had said during the last meeting, leaning forward into the lamplight. "He's more than a poet, and the leader of the surrealists. He's the epicenter of an entire generation of European intellectuals. . . ." Varian listened quietly as she argued André Breton's case with passion, her left hand beating the palm of her right. He was proud of Miriam, how the young art history student had learned to make her voice heard among the men. She had been one of the first to join his staff, only two weeks after he arrived. When the Paris universities had closed their doors after the German invasion, she had made her way to Toulouse. There, a refugee had told her the only chance for them was "to be wrapped in the American flag." Miriam resolved to do just this and hurried to Marseille to help any way she could. Her good nature and intelligence had proved invaluable to Varian, and it was thanks to her introductions that he had recruited several key staff, including Mary Jayne. Miriam had been afraid to speak up at first, until Beamish took her aside one night and said, "Listen, these guys don't know any more about relief work than you do. If you don't argue for your clients, they are going to be shipped off to the concentration camps or killed." After that, she fought for every case. *Meeting her was a lucky break,* Varian thought. He had needed someone with languages to help with secretarial work and interviewing refugees. Now, she was indispensable, even putting her academic skills to work discerning which of the would-be clients really were artists and which were hoping for a lucky break.

As Miriam read on from Breton's letters of recommendation, Varian looked around the crowded table. Among the many faces, he searched out those he relied on the most. Daniel Bénédite handed the secretary a pile of files as she tidied up for the day; Danny's attention was on Miriam, and Varian could see he was digesting her case with the sharp focus of a man used to working in the prefecture of police in Paris. The Bénédite family were friends of Mary Jayne's, and she looked on Danny as a brother. When the Bénédites had fled to the south of France after the Occupation, Danny, his wife, Théo, and their small son headed to Marseille. Tall, slim, and dark, with intelligent, kind eyes that missed nothing behind his thick glasses, Danny ran the ARC with incredible efficiency. Just as Beamish was Varian's closest friend and ally in the more clandestine work of the organization, Danny was relied on to run the official work of the center, giving aid and advice to refugees. Behind him, Varian could see another of Mary Jayne and Miriam's recruits. Justus Rosenberg, or "Gussie," as they affectionately called him, was the fourteen-year-old office boy the girls "adopted" as they fled south to Marseille. His innocent face had proved useful messengering documents across the city. Now he sat guarding the entrance door with Charlie.

They were all adrift, Varian realized, all on the run themselves, yet they were risking everything to help people whose work had changed the world. *Whose work* will *change the world,* he corrected himself. *I'm going to get every name on that list out of France if it kills me.* Some days it felt as though it just might. But then, with his team, every day miracles seemed possible.

"I have another recommendation," Miriam said, sorting through the files. "Mary Jayne interviewed a chap—Gabriel Lambert. A highly respected painter, more art deco than avant garde...."

Even Mary Jayne, he thought now, *whose sheer privilege and* ... Varian frowned as he tried to pin down what it was that annoyed him so much about the beautiful young American heiress. Was it her money? Her taste in men? *Goddamn that punk Couraud.* The thought that Mary Jayne's boyfriend could betray them at any moment, could bring too much police attention to the organization, troubled him. He bit the inside of his lip as he walked on. He had to admit, even Mary Jayne had been invaluable. *She's given freely of her fortune and her time.* Thanks to her, a second list—the Gold List—had been drawn up, and the $7,000 she had given to the rescue committee had saved hundreds of lives already. *She risked her own, too,* Varian had to admit. He had been impressed that she managed to get four prisoners of war out of the camp at Vernet. *Though I'd rather not think how she persuaded the camp commander.*

Now, as he wove through the back streets toward the station, he thought not for the first time that the city was half cesspool, half asylum. Varian marked off in his mind the brothels and fleabag hotels where their refugees were hiding out, waiting for visas and passports. Brothels were safe because the police were bribed not to raid them. Elsewhere in the city, the refugees had to take their chances.

Varian switched his suitcase to his other hand and shouldered his way through the crowd outside a bar. Demobbed soldiers jostled on the pavement—a group of Zouaves in Turkish trousers and Senegalese fighters in bright turbans was arguing. He saw the flash of a knife and skirted around, adrenaline pulsing through him. His stomach lurched with hunger at the sight of a woman spooning bouillabaisse from her bowl. He thought of his empty hip flask and checked his watch. There was just time to get it refilled, so he pushed his way through to the bar.

Nine

Marseille

1940

Mary Jayne

Mary Jayne Gold and Raymond Couraud danced close, lost in one another on the crowded dance floor. She felt the pressure of his hand at the base of her spine, the warmth of his palm through the thin silk of her blouse. His cheek was smooth against hers, freshly shaven, and she breathed in the scent of him. The small room was dark and busy, figures pressed up against the bar, a hum of conversation, the chink of glasses and bottles punctuating the jazz.

"Don't let's ever get old, Raymond," Mary Jayne said, watching a gray-haired couple sitting in silence at the edge of the dance floor, their slumped backs twin c's of defeat.

Raymond followed her gaze. "We won't ever be like that, *bébé*." He glared at a young man with black hair and pale blue eyes watching them from the bar, staring at him until the man downed his drink and left. Raymond eased her closer to him, his lips grazing her jaw, her neck. "We'll still laugh, and fight, and make love. There will always be passion. I'll love you forever with all my black heart."

"Forever is a terribly long time," Mary Jayne murmured. "What if we don't have forever, Raymond?"

"Then we have now, we have tonight."

"Sometimes I think that's all I am to you. A good time, a meal ticket—"

"You're my girl, it's as simple as that."

"And you're my bad, bad boy?" Her laugh was rich, throaty.

"I think you like that, Mary Jayne. I think you like it that your friends say I'm no good for you. You like a little danger, no? Something your money can't buy." She felt the lean muscles of his shoulder, his back, flex beneath her hand. "Tell me you love me."

"You underestimate me, Raymond. I see what you are capable of, I see the strength and the bravery hiding in that black heart of yours. You're my 'diamond in the rough,' and I know plenty about diamonds, trust me." Mary Jayne laid her head against his collarbone. "I adore you, darling boy."

"Tell me you love me."

"Not here. . . ."

"Why won't you ever say it?"

She lifted her head, gazing into his eyes. "Darling, it's impossible for us to be together, you know that. Now you've left the Foreign Legion, you shall go off to Britain with de Gaulle and fight with the Free French, and I shall . . ." She paused, wondering what the future held for her, for them. It was such a short time since she had met Miriam in Toulouse, since they had traveled to Marseille together and met some young Americans, and Raymond. There was a dangerous, masculine energy to him that had drawn her the moment they met, a self-assurance verging on arrogance. She felt the intensity of his gaze now, as he waited for her answer, and a heat rose in her, responding, helpless to resist him.

"You will go back to America, and forget me." Raymond pulled away from her, the dim light gleaming on his dark hair, glinting on his round glasses.

"You can write to me," she said, stepping close in the crush of the dancers. Her lips brushed his ear. "You can tell me about all the battles you have won, and all the hearts you have broken."

"You will marry some rich idiot—" He wouldn't look at her, his hands clenching into fists.

"Why would I marry?" Mary Jayne laughed, a breath against his neck. "I don't need a husband. I have money of my own."

"Then marry me, for love." The raw passion in his gaze caught her off guard, and Mary Jayne felt her stomach free-fall.

"I told you, I don't plan ever to marry," she said lightly, hiding the effect he had on her. "I shall travel the world with Dagobert for company."

"You love that dog more than you love me."

"You dear, sweet boy." She pouted, imitating him. "Don't sulk." He kissed her then, claiming her, his hands in her hair. Mary Jayne broke away, placed her fingertips on his lips as she glanced around, self-conscious. "Darling, stop. Not here."

"I want you," he said, holding her close. "And you want me, I know you do." Raymond took her hand in his, kissed the palm, his gaze not leaving her. He laced their fingers together, and they danced on, cheek to cheek. She felt alive with him, her body coursing with desire. "Will you forget me? Will you forget what we have?"

"Never. How could I?"

"Stay with me tonight." His lips brushed her ear, but Mary Jayne didn't answer. She was looking toward the bar, where the waiter was handing Varian his filled hip flask.

"Good heavens, what's he doing slumming it down here?"

Raymond frowned. "Probably looking for a whore."

"Don't be so beastly." Mary Jayne sauntered over to Varian.

"Mary Jayne?" he said in surprise. "What are you doing here? It's not safe. . . ."

"She is safe with me," Raymond said, slinging his arm over her shoulder.

"Good evening, Couraud," Varian said. The silence strained between them like an overtightened violin string.

"Darling, would you get me a glass of wine?" Mary Jayne said finally to Raymond.

"Sure, *bébé*." His eyes narrowed. "Dance with my girl, Monsieur Fry, feel free. I will look after your little bag." He gestured toward the dance floor and took Varian's valise and hat, tilting the homburg onto his own head. Varian clenched his jaw.

"Don't," Mary Jayne whispered, pulling him toward the dancers.

"Why do you let him talk to you like that, like he owns you?"

"No one owns me."

"Bet that's the last I'll see of my case," Varian said, taking her in his arms. They moved easily to the music, his hand resting lightly on her waist.

"Oh, stop it." Mary Jayne sighed. She was pleased to see him. At least with Varian she was on home ground. She knew him, knew his type, there was no need for explanation. In spite of their differences, they were both Americans abroad, and his directness was a relief. *There are cat and dog people*, she thought, glancing over Varian's shoulder to watch that Raymond still had the suitcase. *Raymond is a cat, and Varian is a dog, definitely. Confident, direct* . . . She watched Raymond chatting to a pretty young brunette at the bar. *Loyal.*

"What are you doing in the Vieux-Port?" she said.

"Just felt like a stroll before my train to Tarascon."

"Nonsense. I know you boys are up to something. You think you're all being so cloak-and-dagger, and trying to keep Miriam and me out of it, but we could be useful, Varian. I mean with the clandestine work, not just the ordinary relief cases."

Varian glanced around him to see if anyone was listening. "Keep your voice down. You and Miriam are doing excellent work, but there are some things that are just too dangerous—"

"For a woman? What about Vernet? Wasn't that dangerous?"

"Mary Jayne, I'm grateful for all you are doing for the ARC."

"But?"

"But I can't in good conscience involve you with some of the more delicate work while you are . . . while you're . . ."

Mary Jayne realized he was talking about Raymond. "While I'm sleeping with Killer?" She wanted to shock Varian, provoke him. She saw a slight tremor pass over his face, but he didn't rise to the bait.

"What do you see in him?"

"Something that everyone else doesn't."

"He's a hoodlum, Mary Jayne, a petty crook, and God knows I bet he got his nickname for killing more than the English language."

"It's just a joke that Miriam and I came up with. His accent's appalling."

"You could do—"

"I could do better? You really are trotting out all the bourgeois clichés tonight, aren't you, Varian?" She tossed her blond hair back and looked him straight in the eye. "You want me to be with someone suitable, like you?"

"Would that be such a disaster?"

"Careful, Varian, you're a married man. Anyone would think you're making a pass at me."

"I didn't mean me, you silly girl."

"Girl? We're practically the same age."

"Do you ever take anything seriously?"

"Not if I can help it."

"You need to consider your position. Who's buying dinner tonight, Mary Jayne? Who's going to pay for the hotel room?"

"Stop it." Varian's words had shaken her, but she wasn't going to show it. "Just stop it."

"Be careful," he said as Raymond approached.

"I'm a big girl, Varian." She smiled up at Raymond as he handed her a glass of red wine. "Thank you, darling."

"I have a train to catch. I'll bid you good night," Varian said, taking his case and hat. He pushed his way past Raymond and out of the bar.

"I wish you two would get along," Mary Jayne said, settling at a small table with a red lamp. Raymond took out a silver case and lit two cigarettes, passing one to her.

"Play nicely, you mean?"

Mary Jayne kicked him gently under the table. "It would just make things a lot easier. I . . ." The words died on her lips as three policemen walked into the bar. They spoke to the bartender and showed him some papers. "Raymond," she said quietly. "We should get out of here. Something's going on. There's going to be a raid."

Raymond exhaled a plume of blue smoke, his eyes closing as he tilted his head back. "We will be fine, *bébé*."

One of the policemen strode over to their table. "Raymond Couraud?"

"Who wants to know?" he said, taking another drag of his cigarette.

"Are you Raymond Couraud?"

"I might be."

"Papers." The policeman snapped his fingers. Raymond leisurely pulled out his wallet and handed over his identity card. "This is him." He beckoned over his colleagues, and they blocked his escape as Raymond made a break for it.

Mary Jayne cried out as the table went flying, the glass of wine smashing on the floor, the red lamp rolling in an arc, light swinging across their shoes as they scuffled. "Raymond!"

"We have a warrant for your arrest. You are absent without leave from the Foreign Legion," the policeman said, snapping the handcuffs closed.

"No! There's a mistake!" Mary Jayne clung to Raymond, who was panting, his arms held firmly by the other two policemen. "He has his demobilization papers, I've seen them."

Raymond leaned down to kiss her and whispered in her ear, "Forged."

The color drained from her face. "What can I do?"

"Money," Raymond said, "and get a good lawyer."

TEN

Rue Grignan, Marseille

1940

Gabriel

Mary Jayne wasn't at the office the next morning. When they told me to come back on Wednesday to see Fry, who was out of town, I made sure I was first in the queue. I hadn't gotten a whole lot of sleep in my cold, pestilential room anyway. Bedbugs, or fleas, or both, had kept me awake all night, and I was scratching at a bite on my wrist as a kid with sleep-mussed eyes unlocked the door.

"No one's here yet," he said. There was something about his face, an innocence, that touched me. He must have been only a couple of years younger than me, but there was a goodness to him that I'd lost somewhere along the way.

"Hey, Gussie," Charlie said as he squeezed past into the office. "Good night?"

"All quiet, Charlie."

I glanced along the pavement and saw a tall, dark-haired man striding down the road, his overcoat flapping around him. A little black puppy was trotting along at his side, pulling on the leash. "Good morning," he said cheerily, holding on to his hat as they blew into the office. A few people were gathering behind me now, and it wasn't even light yet. It seemed to take hours for the office to open up. I couldn't bear to think what it would mean if they couldn't help me. How else was I going to get away? My mind filled with visions of police cars, cells, the Gestapo. I could be hauled up for manslaughter, murder, even. . . . I screwed my eyes shut as I thought of the fire. *Vita,* I thought, my guts twisting with guilt and sorrow.

"Lambert," Charlie called out, reading from his clipboard. There was no answer. "Gabriel Lambert?"

Something inside me registered he was calling my name. "That's me," I said.

"Say, I remember you. The jazz fan. Well, come on in, fellah," he said, and clapped me on the back. The queue shuffled forward behind me as I stepped into the office. "Head right on through," he said, pointing to the room at the end. I smoothed down my hair and knocked.

"Come in," a voice said. I pushed the door open and found the dark-haired man sitting behind the desk.

"I am Lambert," I said. "I am . . . I . . ." My faltering grasp of English deserted me.

"We can talk in French," Fry said with perfect fluency. A young woman stood at his side, handing him paper after paper to sign. "I won't be a moment, do take a seat." He glanced at me and smiled. In the silence, my breath seemed loud. My heart was jolting so hard, I could feel it pulsing in my throat. The puppy yawned and turned a couple of circles before flopping down into a wicker basket by the fireplace. "There," he said finally. "Thank you, Lena. Would you mind closing the door?" He stood and offered me his hand. "I'm Varian Fry. Pleased to meet you, Monsieur Lambert."

"Likewise," I said, horribly aware that my palm was sweating. I quickly wiped it on my thigh before shaking his hand. I was so nervous to finally meet the fabled Varian Fry that as I tried to smile my lips trembled, and I saw a flicker of concern on his face. I tried to calm myself. The ARC was my gateway to freedom, and Fry held the key. It wouldn't look good to be too scared.

"Well," he said, scanning quickly through the file on his desk. I could see my name on the tag: *Lambert, Gabriel.* "You made quite an impression on Miss Gold." He held up the ink portrait. "This may have had something to do with it. Most charming."

"Thank you."

"But, I checked with Bingham." Fry made a steeple with his fingers, pressed them to his lips. I held my nerve, stayed silent. "As you know, we only help people we can trust."

"You can trust me."

Fry stared me down. "Bingham couldn't place you—"

"We met only briefly." Panic chilled my stomach, and sweat trickled down my spine. "I assure you—"

Fry raised his hand to stop me. "Fortunately, a couple of my colleagues had come across your work in Paris, too."

"I had a certain amount of celebrity," I said, glancing down in a way I hoped looked modest.

"Ordinarily, your case would not be a priority."

"But I must leave, at once!" I cried. "I have spoken out against Nazism."

"So has any sane person," Fry said calmly. "The thing is, you are not, I believe, classed as a 'degenerate' artist by the Nazis. In fact, your glamorous art deco work is—forgive me . . ."

"Decorative?" I said, challenging him.

"Admired. And the authorship of your political cartoons is not known generally. You're not on the Emergency Rescue Committee's lists."

"I don't understand. I thought this was the American Relief Center."

"It is." Varian pressed his fingertips together. "The committee is our parent organization in New York. It was established to help refugees displaced by the war in Europe. My remit in setting up the ARC in Marseille was to help specific clients in grave danger." Fry glanced up at a noise from the outer office. "Our work has expanded somewhat, as you can see from the queues, but the American Relief Center's priority is to sort through the thousands of applicants and help those in immediate danger. . . ."

Decorative, degenerate? Who cares? I thought as he talked on, desperately concocting any number of degenerate artworks in my mind. "Please, you must help me." My throat was tight. "I lost . . . I lost everything, you see?"

"Yes, yes," Fry said, pulling a clean handkerchief from his pocket and offering it to me. "There, there, old boy. Don't upset yourself." Was I crying? I felt hot, and dizzy with hunger and emotion. "I understand you have funds for your ticket, and the ARC will help you obtain the paperwork and visas—"

"Oh, thank God!" I leapt forward, and clasped his hand. "Thank you!"

"Please, calm yourself, Mr. Lambert," he said. "Listen, all we can do is wrap anti-Nazis like you in the American flag. It's your only chance."

He leaned toward me. "Someone said to me the other day that we are in the export business, pure and simple. We are exporting men and women." He made it sound so easy. "Now, I understand from Miss Gold that you have the finances to take care of your ticket," he went on, "which is a big help. All we have to do is guide you through the lengthy process of obtaining the correct papers. I'm going to assign your case to one of my colleagues. You'll like him, he's a good, steady chap and he'll get you sorted out." Fry leaned forward and tapped the side of his nose. "Don't you worry. We have ways of getting you out of France."

I could have embraced him. What it meant, after all the weeks on the road, after everything that had happened to me, to have this American angel talking so confidently to me, I can't explain. There was something, of course, a small voice of conscience in me that said: *You have no right to this kindness*. But to be honest, my heart was broken and gone. Then, I was thinking only of myself, and it's only now, after decades of guilt for the way that I deceived that good man; that I will make amends.

ELEVEN

Rue Grignan, Marseille

1940

Varian

Varian knew the moment Beamish walked into the American Relief Center that the poet Walter Mehring hadn't been exaggerating. "Baby," as they all called the writer who looked more like a vagabond than a man of letters, had appeared at Varian's hotel room the night before, shaken and terrified. Varian had last seen him in the dark shack near the lighthouse, peering around the bulk of Bernhard's shoulder like a bird with its head tucked down behind a cliff against a storm. Baby should have been in Gibraltar by now, but he told Varian that the boat had failed to materialize, and at two A.M. Beamish had sent them back to their hiding places in small groups so they wouldn't attract too much attention.

Varian couldn't let the refugees trailing out of the waiting room see how exhausted he felt. "I'm sorry," he said brightly, "we've just run out of time for today. Please come back tomorrow."

Lena, Varian's secretary, was still hard at work, her head bent over her desk by the white marble fireplace, blown tulips in a blue vase nodding toward the ledger she was writing in as she handed out meal tokens and a subsistence allowance to a couple whose desperation was etched in every line on their gray faces. She talked calmly to them, as you might to a frightened animal. As the man began to babble, to plead, she looked up and tucked a strand of dark hair behind her ear.

"*Il ne faut pas exagérer,*" she said, smiling at them. You must not go too far.

Good old Lena, Varian thought. She was another one who seemed to have arrived like a miracle. *How many professional social workers who speak six languages fluently are there around when you need them?*

"Everyone's ready, boss," Charlie said quietly. He seemed cheerful enough, but there was something in his gaze that made Varian uncomfortable. *Sharlee* looked more like a matinee idol than a doorman, he'd always thought, but his old ambulance uniform gave him something of an official air, and he did a good job of keeping the refugees in order and good spirits as they waited on the steps up to the second-floor offices. The ARC had set up camp above a leather and pocketbook store abandoned by the shopkeeper when the October 3 Jewish Statute forced him out of his job and his home. The man had suggested they use it until they found somewhere larger, and in the early days they did their work surrounded by cases of stock, the warm scent of leather and polish filling the air. A six-foot flagpole with the Stars and Stripes stood in the center of the office like a beacon of hope. Varian knew he was the eye of the storm, that for many of these people he was their only chance, and all he could do was try to look as confident as possible. Once the last of the refugees had gone, Varian walked briskly to his office. One glance at the faces of the men ranged around the table confirmed his fears.

He handed Lena a couple of files with handwritten notes to be typed up and closed the door after her. Varian allowed his head to fall forward and rest against the door a moment. He slid his thumb and forefinger beneath his glasses and rubbed the bridge of his nose. "So?"

"The situation's hopeless but not serious," Beamish said, a line, a joke, from the trenches of World War I they often threw around. He balanced a paper knife on the blotter, spun it on its point beneath his index finger.

"What the hell happened?" Varian burst out.

Beamish sat back in his chair and calmly folded his arms. "It looked like it was going to work, right up to the last minute. We met the captain in Snappy's bar like it had been arranged." Fry knew it well, a seedy joint in the Vieux-Port, a favored haunt of British officers hiding out in Marseille. "Even the Brits thought it was a sure thing. There's no way they would have risked trying to get so many of their prisoners out on the boat if they'd thought the deal was crooked." Beamish paused. "The bastard wouldn't budge without the cash up front."

"The captain took the money? All of it?" Varian felt nauseated.

"He told our man he'd go to get the boat—"

"Forty-five hundred dollars. I thought we agreed—no money until the boat was safely at sea."

"It wasn't our contact's fault." Beamish looked impassive, bored, even, but Varian knew him well enough by now to see how shaken he was. "We both tried reasoning with the skipper. He wouldn't budge until we paid up front. He's probably halfway to Morocco by now." He pursed his lips. "Some of the soldiers tracked down the hoods who set this up for us. They won't be doing any more deals for a while, but there's no sign of the money."

"I'm sure that made them feel better, but it hardly helps us."

"We took a gamble."

"And lost." Varian slumped in the chair at his desk. "Where are the rest of the refugees? Mehring is in my hotel room and refusing to budge."

"Back in hiding," Beamish said.

"And Bernhard?"

"He's safe for now. We have him and his wife hiding out in a *maison de passe*. The owner believes they are a middle-aged couple having an affair."

"Good. Getting him out of Marseille as quickly as possible is our priority. We could try the F route. . . ."

"I agree, Spain is the best plan, but not quite yet."

Miriam knocked on the door and looked in. "*Quel pagaille*, it was crazy out there today. Are you going to lock up—" Her voice broke off into a hacking cough.

"I wish you'd get that looked at," Varian said.

"Me? Oh, I'm just tickety-boo," she said, catching her breath. "Varian, I've written to the Bretons to say the ARC is going to help them, and asked them to come to Marseille."

"Excellent. I'll make a note to chase up Peggy Guggenheim about helping them with their passage to New York."

"Say, Mary Jayne and I are going house hunting tomorrow. Any of you want to come?"

"You're still going ahead with that harebrained plan?" Varian rolled his sleeves up.

"I just think it would be a good idea for a few of us to find a little cottage somewhere, out in the country."

"This isn't a vacation, Miriam," Beamish said.

"You think I don't know that?" She folded her arms. "Everyone's exhausted, that's all. It would do us good to get out of the city, and I want to get out of my fleabag hotel."

"Hey, it's not so bad," Gussie said as he sidled past loaded down with client files and dumped them on Fry's desk. "Anyway, you gave me the best room. Oh, the view from that garret."

Miriam burst out laughing and dug him in the ribs. "At least the bedbugs can't be bothered to walk up all those flights of stairs." She scratched vaguely at her wrist. "Are you working late?" she said to Varian.

"There are a couple of things to sort out."

"Don't do anything I wouldn't do. See you in the morning." The lightness of her tone belied her shrewd expression.

Once the door closed behind her, Varian beckoned to Beamish. They spoke quietly, heads close together, as the other men chatted. "We need more funds, urgently."

"I'll go and see Kourillo. He always has a few associates who need to shift their francs out of the country."

"That hood? Can we trust him?" Varian frowned as he thought of the White Russian. Five feet tall at a stretch and with a handshake that always reminded him of an empty glove, he made Varian's skin crawl.

"Do you have any better ideas?"

❧

Varian unplugged the phone cord after his final call of the day to Harry Bingham at the U.S. consulate and poured a large brandy. You couldn't be too careful. If they were connected all the time, their conversations could be listened in to. *That was something I hadn't bargained on adding to my résumé,* Varian thought. *Classicist, journalist, editor, spy.* His task seemed Herculean sometimes. For each person, each family, they helped, several more appeared who were equally deserving. Varian ran through the usual litany of paperwork that each client needed: Passport. Transit visa from

Vichy. French exit visa. Entry visa for Spain. Transit visa for Spain. Travel visa for Portugal. Transit visa from Portugal. Travel visa for any other country. The list went on and on. Then they needed a ticket paid in full and a firm sailing date. Varian knocked back his drink. Even his dreams were filled with an endless paper chase.

"Are you ready?" Beamish buttoned up his jacket, and Varian scooped up the papers for the last cable of the day to New York with the list of clients' names they had taken on that day for the ERC to request visas from the State Department. The names of any clients too high profile to risk sending by telegram would be concealed in tubes of toothpaste and smuggled out by escaping refugees to send on to New York.

They talked in low voices as they walked along the dark rue des Dominicaines, their footsteps echoing down the empty street.

"What's the latest with Bernhard?" Varian said.

"I sent a message to our people on the French border today."

"Good." They paused as the blue lamps of the police station came into view. A large rat scuttled along the damp pavement into the gloom of the alleyway. "It seemed so easy a couple of months ago. I just assumed it would go on like that. Those boobs in New York have no idea what we are up against."

"We had a few lucky breaks. We've managed to get several groups out over the mountain passes."

"Not counting poor Walter Benjamin."

"None of us knew he'd kill himself rather than risk arrest on the other side." Beamish paused and listened for footsteps, signaled Varian to walk on.

"Christ, it's unbearable," Varian said. "Any one of the names on my list is a man or a woman who can change the whole course of human history for the better."

"We'll get them out. The rules will change again, you watch. The Nazis have everyone right where they want them. France is the biggest man-trap in history."

"As long as they believe all we are doing is giving refugees pin money to live on, and helping them to obtain official visas . . ." Varian paused as a car swept past the end of the road. "We've just got to do what we can in the time we have. I'm glad that you suggested we take on ordinary relief cases."

Beamish laughed softly. "Ordinary people, ordinary soldiers, ordinary Jews?"

"You know what I mean."

They had the *visa de télégramme* stamped and took the cable to the post office near the stock exchange. Varian filled out the cable address—Emerescue for New York. He thought of it as the answering echo to their "Amesecours" in Marseille, two tin cans on a very long string.

It's not Hercules I feel like, Varian thought as he walked in weary silence at his friend's side toward his hotel. *I feel more like Sisyphus. Each day we push the boulder up the mountain, and each day it rolls back down again.* Beamish pointed ahead. "There you go, home safely."

"Thanks, Beamish." Varian shook his hand. "You know you don't have to walk me home every night. I feel like a blushing girl."

Beamish shrugged. "It's safer if there are two of us." He glanced over Varian's shoulder and pulled him into the shadows of the side street. Varian turned to see a dark Mercedes pulling up outside his hotel and a group of five Nazi officers climbing out, the blue streetlights gleaming on the insignia on their caps. "Give them time to get inside and to their rooms before you go in."

Varian felt his stomach drop with fear. He remembered a conversation with Charlie:

Say, Varian . . .

Yes, Charlie?

I'm scared as hell all the time.

So am I.

Had they come for him or someone else this time? A knock on your hotel door had always meant room service to him. Now he knew it could mean the end of the world. "I think perhaps Miriam is right," he said. "It's time to find a new place to stay."

TWELVE

Flying Point, Long Island

2000

Gabriel

"Mr. Lambert? Tell me about the photographs." The girl won't give up. I have to be ready for her. Dragging myself back from the past to the present, to her unflinching gaze, feels like swimming against the tide.

"Look," I say. "I've never seen these pictures before." But of course I have. Quimby took them just before he left the Languedoc in the summer of 1940. I thought I'd destroyed the only copies in Marseille. Trust Quimby to have more tucked away somewhere, the blackmailing son of a bitch. "Where did you find them?"

"It was luck, really. A friend of Dad's in London knew about my family connection to Vita, and he spotted them in an archive among Quimby's papers."

"He stole them, for you?"

"Borrowed, Mr. Lambert," she says firmly.

Nonsense, I know those places, you can't turn a page without a pair of white gloves. As if they'd let this girl bring them halfway around the world. Christ, all this time, these photos have been floating around? "It was just a—well, it was a shock to see Vita's face again after all this time. I can't help you. . . ."

"But you must!" The color rises in her cheeks, a gorgeous bloom. "I'm going ahead with the story whether you like it or not."

"Not."

"Please, Mr. Lambert." She tries to control her frustration. "For me it is about family, as much as anything else. You're the only one who was there with Vita—" She stumbles, realizes what she's said.

"I'm the only one alive, you mean?"

"I don't mean to be tactless." She's too young to know how to handle this. "It must have been a terrible time for you. Everyone knows..." She chooses her words carefully now. "Everyone has heard how you lost your son, and Vita. I just hoped you'd be able to help me find the truth."

I close my eyes for a moment and rub the bridge of my nose. The afternoon sun has burned a vivid red-and-gold corona behind my lids. The truth? I don't even know what this is anymore. Vita, Vita, Vita... Christ. Days go by now, weeks, even, when I don't think of that name.

"I can't help you."

"Can't or won't?"

Damn, she's cocky. "Why don't you just clear off back to the city?"

Good, I've shocked her. "That's not very nice."

"Nice?" I rail on her, then lower my voice. "Who the hell said artists were supposed to be *nice*?" Look at Varian, at everything he did for the artists whose work he loved. How did they repay him? Sure, there was the odd exception—like Lipchitz, he was the best of the lot and a good friend to Varian—but most of them turned their back on him once they didn't need him. Lipchitz never forgot what Fry did for him, but Chagall wouldn't even sign the print Varian practically had to beg him to put into the *Flight* portfolio. After all Varian had done for him. I stare at the girl, and she flinches. Maybe there's still something in my gaze after all. I've rattled her. "Let's take a walk."

I usher her on around the house toward the beach. I follow the trail of pine needles to the lean-to where we stack split logs every autumn and the boys have left the Christmas tree. Her high heels are sinking in the sand, and as she pauses to slip them off, I see their red soles flash like a warning. My chest is tight, and once she's walked on ahead, I search in my pocket for my inhaler. I've left it in the studio. I start to panic, but Annie's voice comes to me: *Easy, Gabe. That's it, try and relax. Easy now. Breathe.* Once my lungs have eased, I catch up with the girl and she turns. "It's beautiful here," she says. "I can see why you love it."

I hesitate. She can't sweet-talk me, oh no. "You came out here alone?" What I want to say is: *Who knows you're here?*

"I'm a big girl." She takes a deep breath of cold sea air, guileless, and shrugs off her jacket. "When I heard you had a cottage down here on the beach, I was expecting something . . ." Her voice trails off, aware that she's said the wrong thing again.

"Something grander?"

"I just meant," she says carefully, "something different, what with your success, and reputation."

"It's not much, but Annie and I built this place ourselves the summer we moved out here, 1951." I run my fingertips along the flaking white clapboard as we skirt around the side to the beach path. Every time we had a few bucks, or a new baby, we added on a room. It's higgledy-piggledy, as Vita used to say, but we love it. Now, the house and I have both seen better days. I glance up at the terrace where Annie, my Annie, sits gazing out at the sea, a smile on her lips. Our home, the place we chose to plant our flag. Gabe and Annie, a couple of kids playing house. I always expected at some point it would feel like we were grown-ups, but it never did. Still doesn't. Sometimes it still surprises me to look in my shaving mirror and see an old guy staring back. My hip twinges as I climb gingerly down the wooden steps and shuffle onto the beach. I pick up the stick I turned one winter from its place beside the steps, and we walk down toward the hard-packed shore, where it's easier walking. "We lost everything in France. Once that's happened to you, you realize how little things matter. We never needed anything more than one another." I wave my stick at the sea. "Than this."

"How many kids do you have?"

"Kids?" I laugh. "Our babies are old crones now. My youngest grandson Harry's about your age." Come to think of it, this girl would be just his type. He likes these city girls, tough and polished as hazelnuts, sweet and yielding inside. Maybe I'll get him to drive her back to the station, work his magic. Maybe a distraction will make her forget she hasn't found out what she came here for.

"Harry?" She sounds wistful. Perhaps luck's on my side and she's alone or lonely. "You're lucky, having family nearby. Are they all painters too?"

"My kids? No, they took after their mother, far too sensible. I didn't care as long as they did something vaguely creative. I couldn't have borne it if they'd become bankers and lawyers." I throw her a bone. "My grandson's a painter, though." I know you shouldn't have favorites, but I love that kid. He looks just like me at that age. All our children turned out blond and fair, just like Annie, but he has my olive skin and dark hair.

"Is he any good?"

"It's too soon to tell if he has it in him."

"So how did you and Annie end up here, from France, I mean?" She hesitates, wary now, trying to hide how much she wants her answers. "I'm surprised. You don't even sound French."

At that, I laugh. "It was a long time ago, and it's a long story." I turn to her, the surf crashing against the shore, the sunlight glancing off a mirror mobile spinning in the breeze on the porch. The infernal tinkling of Annie's wind chimes drifts across to us. "Listen, I'll cut you a deal. If you leave me and Annie out of the story, I'll tell you anything you want to know about Vita." She waits silently, until I give in. Patience will serve this Sophie well. It's amazing how many people will talk to fill a silence and say more than they intend. "Damn it. You want me to tell you everything, don't you?"

She nods. "Tell me about France. Start at the beginning."

THIRTEEN

Marseille

1940

Mary Jayne

Mary Jayne and Miriam settled into their seats as the blue-and-cream tram lurched away along La Canebière toward Aubagne, sounding its foghorn. Dagobert, Mary Jayne's large black poodle, circled once, twice, then flopped down in the aisle beside them, his snout on his paws. The landscape opened up as they headed east toward the suburbs; gray limestone hills, palm trees, and the dancing light of autumn sun on the water trundled past. "I do love the smell of these old things," Mary Jayne said, checking her reflection in a platinum compact. The air was rich with the scent of charcoal burning. Sometimes the city seemed to smell like one big fireplace, so many people had fitted charcoal burners to their vehicles now there was little gasoline. She dabbed at her nose, clicked the compact shut, and slipped it into her handbag.

"Boy, what a swell day for a trip to the countryside," Miriam said. There was a fresh breeze from the sea, teasing gold leaves from the trees. The Cimetière Saint-Pierre passed by, and the tram headed for the hills.

"It's just good to get out of that place."

"You're not still smarting about Varian, are you?"

"Varian? I couldn't give a damn about him." Mary Jayne snapped her bag closed, and her husky voice lowered to a growl. "You'd think after I managed to spring those four guys from the Vernet camp he'd treat me with a little respect by now." She bit her lip. *I know men like him,* she thought.

I bet he reinvented himself at Harvard, started eating burgers with a knife and fork and took up smoking just because it looked elegant. To hell with him. Stuck-up dilettante, that's what he thinks I am. Spoiled little rich girl.

"I'm sure he does respect you, he just doesn't show it. I know some of the refugees think he's buttoned up, but it's just a front to give them confidence—"

"Jeez, Miriam. Respect? Don't you get it? Men like him don't know what to do with a woman if you're not in their bed, typing their letters, or keeping their house. The ARC is an all boys' club. I said as much to his face the other night."

"Oh, Mary Jayne, you didn't?"

"Well, why not? They think they are being so clever hiding what they are up to from the girls, but we all know they are doing something crooked."

"I think he's rather wonderful. Don't you think he's attractive?"

Mary Jayne laughed briskly through her nose. "Not at all, my dear. I prefer more macho types."

"Like Killer?"

"Raymond is . . . He's not what he seems."

"Well, neither are you," Miriam said. "You succeeded where letters from the ERC and the American consulate failed. You still haven't told me exactly how you persuaded the commandant to let those four prisoners out of Vernet."

"A lady never tells." A smile twitched at the corners of Mary Jayne's mouth. "As Beamish said, I have the most innocent face in the world, and let's just say the commandant wasn't immune to my feminine charms." *I felt more like the Trojan horse than Helen.* Mary Jayne had been their last chance. Emergency U.S. visas had been issued for four of the political prisoners in greatest danger, but all diplomatic requests to bring the men to Marseille under guard to collect them had been refused. Mary Jayne had dressed carefully in her best blue suit with yellow piping and all her grandmother's diamonds. When she'd looked at the reflection in her hotel room mirror, she'd thought, *Good, I look exactly how they want me to look—like a pretty, rich American girl.* She remembered how, when the commandant offered her a cigarette, Chanel No. 5 wafted from the cuff of her blouse as she leaned in to the flame cupped in his palm. "God, I was glad to get out of that place. They've got the whole camp penned up behind two barbed-wire fences, and the guards are told to shoot to kill." She looked down at her hand and twisted the ring on her finger. She could hardly bear to remember the sight of the shaven-headed men, their emaciated faces. *They smiled at me the way poor kids light up at the sight of a Christmas tree.*

"I hate it," she said, "it's inhumane seeing people penned up like that. Everyone knows the Gestapo are just going around cherry-picking whoever they want. The Vichy lot are just doing their dirty work for them."

Miriam squeezed her hand. "What you did was very brave."

"The guys did as much as me. If Beamish and the boys hadn't plied the camp guards with wine and women at some brothel when they brought the prisoners into town, they would never have been able to disappear."

"Promise you won't let Varian get to you?"

"Don't give it any more thought. *Il est un emmerdeur.*"

"Mary Jayne!"

"Well, he is. He drives you nuts and he's a pain in the ass. I love that word *emmerdeur.*"

"The only way you get anything done around here is by being a pain in the ass."

"Oh, I can handle him, and if your visa for Yugoslavia comes through, someone's going to have to keep him on his toes."

"Good. You know, if we do find a house . . ."

"No way." Mary Jayne folded her arms. "I told you, I'd rather go sleep in a *maison de passe* with the hookers in the Vieux-Port than share a house with him."

"Okay, okay." Miriam laughed. "It's just he's working so hard."

"We all are."

"I still can't figure him out." It was one of their favorite games, trying to decipher their boss. "One minute he's sitting there in his Blackwatch boxer shorts, knocking back the Armagnac in our late-night meetings, and the next he's all buttoned up again."

"A regular sphinx, our Varian," Mary Jayne drawled.

"Don't be like that."

"It's okay for you. You have a role. I just wish he'd let me do more than interviewing the odd client." Mary Jayne gazed out across the sea. "I can do a lot to help, and he just . . . well, he's just *Varian.*"

"Listen, you've got to realize with Varian that his way is the right way.

There's no point in trying to fight against him. He's the reason the ARC has been so effective."

"God, you're loyal, aren't you? He's lucky to have you." After half an hour the tram pulled into La Pomme, and Mary Jayne craned around, pointing out the window. "Look, there's a café back there. Why don't we jump out and see if they know of anywhere to rent?" She rubbed her hands together. "I'm freezing. I could do with a coffee to warm up." The girls held on to the straps as the tram shuddered to a halt. "Come, Dago!" she called, tugging on the dog's lead.

Miriam jumped down and looked around her. "This is great, it's perfect!" As the tram pulled away into the distance, she cupped her ear. "Listen."

"I can't hear a thing," Mary Jayne said, heading to the café.

"Exactly!" Miriam hugged herself. "It's perfect. Peace, quiet . . ."

"Don't you dare say 'Varian will love it.'" Mary Jayne turned and wagged a finger at her. "Excuse me!" she called, waving at a young girl with long blond hair walking along the opposite side of the road. "How do you do? I'm Mary Jayne Gold of the American Relief Center."

"Bonjour." The girl smiled. "I am Marianne Bouchard."

"Tell me, are there any houses to rent here?"

Marianne shrugged. "You could try our neighbor, old Thumin." She gestured toward a driveway beside the road. "Air-Bel has been empty for years."

"Thank you!" Mary Jayne waved in farewell. "Perhaps we shall be neighbors."

"Look, I can see someone in the grounds over there," Miriam said. "Why don't we ask him if he knows this Thumin fellow?" The girls stopped at the entrance to 63, avenue Jean Lombard, where two redbrick pillars with white stone tops and iron gates marked the entrance to the estate. In the distance, they saw a small man in a black bowler hat raking leaves. His wide black trousers flapped in the wind.

"I'll be damned!" Miriam gazed upward at the engraved white stone capitals on the pillars. "Look at that: Villa Air-Bel. That's the name of my fleapit hotel!"

"Hotel Bel Air?" Mary Jayne peered through the gate.

"It's meant to be. I'm sure of it."

"I don't know, Miriam. This place is huge. It'd be crazy, much too big for us." At the end of the leafy drive, she could just see the corner of a great block of a house, three stories high. Gold and copper leaves fell in slow motion onto the white stones of the driveway, settled on the low slope of the pink-tiled roof. "It's like something from a fairy tale, a sleeping château. We just need a little cottage."

Miriam called and waved to the old man. *"Bonjour!"* He paused in his raking and limped toward them.

"He won't know anything, he's just the gardener."

"Bonjour." The old man eyed them suspiciously through the bars of the gate. Mary Jayne turned her back as Miriam spoke to him in French, and her breath caught. *It's heaven,* she thought, captivated by the view framed by plane trees and cedars, sweeping down over terra-cotta rooftops to the sparkling sea beyond.

"He says there's nothing for rent here."

"This house," Mary Jayne said clearly in French to Thumin, and pointed at Air-Bel. "Is this house for rent?"

"Non, non, non," the old man grumbled, and started to walk away.

"We are Americans," Mary Jayne said, and he stopped and turned to her, chewing on his gums as he ambled back. "Americans," she said again, just to make sure he heard her.

"Bon," he said, and took a hoop of keys from his pocket and unlocked the gate. He ushered the girls ahead. "This is my house," he said.

"Your house?" Mary Jayne tried unsuccessfully to keep the surprise out of her voice.

"I am Dr. Thumin. I live with my sister, over there at La Castellane. Air-Bel is too big for us."

"The other neighbors?" Miriam asked. She had a broad smile on her face, watching Dagobert race ahead, kicking through the piles of burnished leaves. The crisp air was perfumed with the smell of bonfires. "We met a charming girl—"

"Marianne? The Bouchards are good people. Quiet, conservative," he said, shuffling along the drive, sorting through the keys. "They wouldn't bother you."

"Tell me, how long has the house been empty?" Mary Jayne's gaze traveled upward as they reached the large terrace overlooking the formal garden with its boxwood hedges and pond. Huge plane and cedar trees marked the boundary of the gardens.

"A while. It is perfectly habitable, though."

"These grounds are lovely . . . ," Mary Jayne said, "but there's too much to do."

"*Non,*" Dr. Thumin said forcefully. "I rent the house, not the grounds. There are eighty-five acres of land that you can enjoy looking at—the magnolias, the olives, the acacias, but everything in them is mine." He stepped toward her. "Including the firewood."

"Okay," she said, and threw a wide-eyed look at Miriam once he turned to the door. The key creaked in the lock, and the door swung open.

"Come," he said, beckoning over his shoulder. "We are a quarter of a mile off the main road, and the house is quiet and peaceful, as you will see."

The house cast its spell on them the moment they walked through the great doors into the black-and-white-tiled entrance hall. Dr. Thumin shuffled ahead, throwing open the metal shutters. Mary Jayne thought of a stately old woman, loosening her stays and sighing with relief. Sunlight poured into the house, waking the rooms, chasing shadows from the high ceilings. She walked in silence from room to room, only vaguely aware of Dr. Thumin telling them about the Louis Quinze tables, the refinement of the Second Empire furniture, the classical frescoes in the library. The atmosphere struck her as unmistakably French—somber and obscure, caught in time. Her reflection in the antique mirror over the marble fireplace in the living room was opaque, the clock beneath stuck permanently at a quarter to twelve.

"It's wonderful," Miriam whispered, taking her arm. "Can you imagine the cozy winter nights in here with a big fire roaring in the hearth?" She ran her fingertips along the keyboard of the old piano. Ornate candlesticks stood ready to illuminate sheet music.

"Just think, if all your plans go well to rescue that handsome fiancé of yours from Yugoslavia, you could be dancing cheek to cheek here by Christmas."

Miriam's smile faltered just for a moment, and her eyes grew soft. "Do you really think so?" She hugged herself with her free arm. "It's too much to hope for, to be together, here."

"Sweetie, after all you've done to save him, he'd better make you the happiest woman alive or he'll have me to answer to."

"I will. I'll make it safely back with Rudolf."

"Attagirl." Mary Jayne leaned in to her friend, nudging her gently. She hated the idea of Miriam leaving and realized at that moment how much she would miss her. She glanced at her, worried suddenly at the risk she was taking for the man she loved. "You will take care, won't you, Davenport?"

Miriam grinned. "You? You are telling me to be careful?" She lifted her arms as if she were dancing with a partner and waltzed away across the echoing room. "Imagine it. Christmas . . . music, dancing . . ."

"I don't know. It's too big," Mary Jayne said again, catching Thumin's cunning expression at their excitement. *And yet, and yet,* she thought as Dr. Thumin pointed out the six-meter-long range in the kitchen and the château's only bath next door. "It's like the one Marat was murdered in," she whispered to Miriam, and the girls stifled their laughter.

They followed Thumin upstairs, through suite after suite of rooms. "There are fifteen rooms up here," he said. "Each bedroom has its own fireplace, so you won't be cold."

"Want to bet," Mary Jayne said under her breath. On the top floor, they gazed out of the windows across the lawns to the sea.

"Look!" Miriam said. "There's a marvelous palm shading the table out there, and acacias and magnolias. Can you imagine how beautiful it will be in the spring?"

"It's the worst kind of dubious, bourgeois elegance." She raised her hand as Miriam began to speak. "Yes, I know. Varian will love it, but he's a snob." Mary Jayne traced her fingertip in the years of dust on the sill. "How much?" she said abruptly, halting Dr. Thumin's monologue. He sucked his teeth.

"It is very expensive."

"How expensive?" she said.

"Thirteen hundred francs."

"A month?" Mary Jayne pursed her lips. "We'll have to think about it." Miriam joined her, and they talked in low voices as Dr. Thumin pretended to check the shutters at the far side of the room.

Miriam did a quick calculation. "That's about thirteen dollars! The smallest hotel room costs fifteen francs a night. Listen, if we were to share this place . . . ," she whispered.

"Like some kind of commune?" Mary Jayne wrinkled her nose.

"It would be a blast, like at college. It would be more like a swank private hotel. We can invite some of my clients like the Bretons to share with us. Split a few ways, we could pay for a cook, and maid, and this place would still cost us less than the ratty hotels we're all staying in." She squeezed Mary Jayne's hand. "Imagine it! Imagine the space, and the freedom . . ." They heard Dagobert's footsteps echoing down the staircase through the empty house.

"It would be wonderful to have somewhere for us to escape to," Mary Jayne said. "And it would be so much better for the families like Danny's with children." She frowned. "But who else? That's not enough to fill this place. We were only looking for somewhere big enough for us and Danny."

"There's Var—" Miriam began to say.

"No," Mary Jayne said firmly.

"I know he'd love it."

"Then tough luck to him. As I'm bankrolling this whole jolly adventure, maybe he should have been more civil." Mary Jayne stuck her chin out.

"What about Beamish?"

"No, if I know him, he'll want to stay in town." Mary Jayne did a quick head count. "But I reckon we can swing it." She nodded at Dr. Thumin. "We'll take it." She could tell from the confusion on his face that he was expecting to negotiate and now wished he had asked a higher price. "When can we move in?"

FOURTEEN

Flying Point, Long Island

2000

Gabriel

I watch Sophie bend with the grace of a ballet dancer and scoop up a white oval stone from the shore. What I wouldn't give to be that lithe still. Sometimes when I'm pottering along the shoreline here, I imagine my younger self powering through the surf on my daily run. Day after day for years in all weathers until it suddenly became a chore, not so easy. When was that, 1980-something? Years and decades run into one another now. There was always a dog or two running at my heels. When our last old fella died, we didn't replace him. I won't be long for the happy hunting ground myself, and I didn't want to leave some young dog brokenhearted. It's easier that way, though I miss the clatter of paws on the deck, the sure weight of a dog on the bed at night.

"It sounds like *Casablanca*," Sophie says.

I glance over at her. "Sorry?"

"I was saying, it sounds like *Casablanca*."

She's smart, this girl. "That's what some people say, 'the real *Casablanca*,' or that Varian was the artists' Schindler." I want to say: *Life was already over for me when I met him. Then along came this American—tall, kind, talking with quiet confidence like some actor in a gangster B movie: "Don't worry. We have ways to get you out of this mess."*

"What was he like as a person?"

"Varian? Have you ever heard something's like a riddle wrapped up in a mystery inside an enigma? That was Varian. None of us could figure him out. But he was an extraordinary man. Courageous, tenacious, and permanently good-humored. He was kind, too, so kind." My eyes prick now, just thinking of it. "After everything I went through, when I landed at his desk and he said he'd help, I cried hot, stupid tears. I couldn't help myself. He handed me a clean red-and-white handkerchief from his breast pocket, and clapped me on the back. I guess he saw scenes like that every day. When people made it as far as Marseille, there was a sense of relief—that you were home free. Then the reality set in—going door-to-door with the hotel concierges all saying, *'Nous sommes complets,'* discovering that thousands of other souls had had exactly the same bright idea as you." When I think of Marseille, I remember the smell of wine, and pissoirs, and fish, and ink from the newspaper stalls, and the sea, always, the sea. The place was bedlam. People wandered the streets with all their worldly goods piled up on handcarts. You couldn't get a room anywhere. Then the realization that you were trapped here dawned—that Marseille was like a holding pen, really. You had got this far, but could go no further without your papers being *en règle*. That's what Varian realized, and calmly set about overcoming it all. What is it they say? Tears may be the path to grace, a way for women to become angels. What of men? "Fry was like an angel of deliverance to us. A regular miracle."

"Well, that's all fascinating, but can we backtrack a bit? I don't want to waste your time when you could be with your family." She smiles, cocks her head, all charm. I'm on my guard now, missy. "Tell me about the first time you saw Vita."

Vita. I have to think for a moment, scroll back through the years like the pages of a photograph album. There she is. I check I have the right page, the right line of the story. There are many ways to tell the same tale. "Yes, now, let me think . . . ," I say, buying some time. The light is dazzling on the white sand, and I shield my eyes, rubbing at my brow.

Sophie butts in, impatient. "The official story is that Gabriel Lambert, enfant terrible of the art deco crowd, met a young British art student, Vita, at a party in Montmartre in 1938. Lambert was quite the catch—rich, talented, and brave. He'd fought with the Republicans in Spain, and entertained his friends by firing off satirical sketches of Hitler, Franco, and Mussolini. He was, in other words, sexy and dangerous and catnip to a girl like Vita."

"Thank you. Go on," I say.

"Most people never knew if she had a second name—she was always only Vita, decades before Madonna or Cher thought of it. It was love at first sight. You were thirty-three, she was younger, closer to twenty, though she never let on her real age. She could have been seventeen or twenty-seven, you never knew with Vita."

"If you know all this, what are you bothering me for?"

"I'm trying to track down her history between leaving England and arriving in Paris, but it's like my great-aunt appeared there out of nowhere. I don't get how someone's history can disappear."

"People disappear all the time, particularly when there's a war on." Or if they don't want to be found.

"Tell me what she was like."

"She was . . ." I search for the right word to describe her. Passionate. Crazy. A messed-up, beautiful kid. "She was dazzling."

Sophie smiles, reassured. "And her work? Was that *dazzling*, too?" She labors the word, mimics my drawling pronunciation.

I stop dead. "You want to know the truth? Vita had more of a talent for living than she did for painting."

Her eyes damn near pop out of her head. "How can you say that?"

"Have you even seen her work?"

She flounders. "No, of course I haven't. I mean, a few early sketches attributed to her, but you know that none of her later work survives, only these photos of her studio." She taps her bag. Oh God, the photos. Clever girl, slipping in a reminder that she's just warming up for the knockout blow. I wonder if she's been smart enough to make copies?

"So if this article is about me, why are you writing about her?"

"It's the story, Gabriel." Sophie speaks slowly, as if she's talking to a sulking toddler. "The discourse . . ."

"Phooey."

"Vita was just starting out when she was killed," she says defensively. "She could have been great."

"Could have been, might have been . . . who gives a damn about all the what-ifs? It's what you do in life that counts, not what you might have done." I kick at the sand with my espadrille and walk on. "You're running up a blind alley, kid. The truth is, she never progressed."

"I don't believe you."

"Sweetheart, Vita told me herself. She reached a point with her painting, and couldn't get any further. Some people don't. She wasn't satisfied with being second-rate. When she died, she was thinking of going back to acting."

"Acting?" Sophie's voice shoots up an octave.

"You didn't know that about her?" Good. If she didn't know that, hopefully she's missing a few other vital details. "Listen, Vita's life was her art, her best creation."

Sophie is quiet for a moment, processing my revelation. "Let's go back. I'm trying to picture Lambert and Vita on the night they met. In all the biographies they say he—"

"I."

"They say you insulted her dress—a revealing gold-beaded shift, by all accounts, and from what I can make out of the photographs. Apparently you said she hadn't got the figure to wear it. Anyway, she poured an entire bottle of champagne over you. The rest is history. Vita became your most celebrated muse—she had just the right liquid grace for those art deco girls, like a greyhound at full stretch or a chiffon scarf in the breeze."

Vita was beautiful, for sure. She would have been a good actress, I think, her voice was wonderful, too—it poured out of her as naturally as a draft of cold water from a crystal jug. Half the faces are forgotten, but Vita stands out. She had some kind of mirrored band around her forehead, a plume of ostrich feathers. She looked like a queen. Dazzling.

"I've read about the costume party, of course," Sophie says. "It was legendary. I've read how you all danced madly," she says as we walk on, and I imagine the screeching horns of the jazz band.

"Like I say, it was a lifetime ago, I don't remember." But I do. I remember it all.

The question is: How much can I tell her?

FIFTEEN

Marseille

1940

Mary Jayne

Mary Jayne lay on her narrow bed in the Continental Hotel, her feet resting against Dagobert's stomach. Pink blown roses on the faded wallpaper trailed up toward the ceiling from the brass bedstead, and her golden hair spilled around her on the white pillows. She wore men's blue-striped pajamas, with the legs rolled up around her slender ankles, and she hummed along to the swing tune drifting up from the bar below, tapping her foot to the beat as she read her book. An alarm clock on the nightstand ticked contentedly.

"Last night in this joint, Dago," she said, tossing the book aside and stretching. He raised his head and laid it on her leg, gazing up at her. "You don't care, do you, dear dog?" She ruffled the springy fur on his crown. "You're just glad to be along for the ride." Mary Jayne looked up as someone knocked on the door. "Who is it?" she called.

"It's me, Miriam."

"Just a minute." She swung her legs down and opened the door. "Hello, darling."

"Aren't you packed yet?" Miriam laughed, gesturing at the clothes and lingerie hanging from every surface. "How much stuff did you have in those two suitcases of yours?"

"Oh, there's plenty of time for packing."

"I'm so excited about moving into Air-Bel tomorrow, I'm sure I shan't sleep a wink. The fun we'll have out there! All the artists are coming out this weekend to welcome Breton." Miriam hugged herself. "Danny signed all the papers this afternoon."

"Did Thumin try and up the rent?"

"Don't be such a cynic."

Mary Jayne closed the bedroom door and padded across to the nightstand. "Whiskey?"

"What a treat." Miriam flung herself down in the armchair.

"I've been saving it for a special occasion. We may as well toast our new home." She poured two fingers into each glass. "To new beginnings, and old friends."

"I'll drink to that." Miriam sipped her whiskey. "I thought you might be out with Raymond."

"No, we just felt like a quiet night in, didn't we, Dagobert?" The dog pricked up his ears at the mention of his name. "It amuses me that Varian thinks I am such a good-time girl. I'm never happier than when I'm by myself." She shrugged and swirled the drink in her glass. "Besides, Raymond has been arrested."

"Arrested?" Miriam sat up in her chair. "What for?"

"Desertion. Forging his demob papers—"

"Oh no, Mary Jayne, I warned you!"

"Please don't say you told me so." She couldn't look Miriam in the eye. "I can't bear it. They have him locked up in the Fort Saint-Nicolas awaiting trial."

"What will happen to him?"

"I can't let him rot in jail."

"Please think clearly, darling—"

"I don't care what any of you think of him," Mary Jayne challenged her. "I don't care that he's done wrong."

Miriam whistled softly. "You're in love with him, aren't you?"

"No. I . . . It's madness, I know, to fall for someone like Raymond." She sat on the edge of the bed and held her glass to her cheek. "I can't see us settling down with a white picket fence anytime soon, can you?"

"Oh, Mary Jayne . . ."

"I know what I'm doing."

"No, you don't."

Mary Jayne's mouth twitched, a small smile. "He makes me feel alive. Really alive, for the first time in years." She took a sip of her drink. "Perhaps I've met my match."

"No, you're better than that."

"You are a darling." Mary Jayne looked at her. "I know it's crazy. I feel quite mad, having sleepless nights over some boy...." She stared down at her hands. "I can't abandon him. There's a side to him he never shows, you know. Beneath that tough-guy exterior there's a good and brave heart. I believe in him. When we are alone together..." Her words trailed off as she thought of Raymond. She felt a warmth bloom deep in her, a heat rising. Mary Jayne shook her head and laughed. "Don't you dare tell him any of this."

"Okay, okay," Miriam said, backing down. "You're going to need to hire a damn good lawyer."

"I've done it already."

"Does he know who to bribe?"

"Of course," Mary Jayne said. "Come on. Why don't you give me a hand to squeeze this lot into my suitcases, and then I'll take you out for a late supper."

"Wonderful. I haven't had a chance to stop for a bite all day. The office has been bedlam." She began to neatly fold Mary Jayne's clothes, handing them to her. "Is the chest of drawers empty?"

"Yes, I think so. I never really settled in."

"Do you ever?" Miriam laughed. "You're like a wild bird, following the snow and the sun in your little airplane."

"God, I miss that freedom."

Miriam slid open the top drawer. "Look, all your jewelry, and you've got a new pack of silk stockings in here!" She offered the stockings to Mary Jayne as if she were holding a priceless work of art. Mary Jayne saw the longing in her eyes.

"You take them, darling."

"I couldn't!"

"Take them for your trousseau. Give Rudolf a thrill." She quickly cleared the drawers, tossing jewelry boxes carelessly onto the top of the suitcase.

"If I ever get to Yugoslavia."

"You will," Mary Jayne said, embracing her. "Your visas will come through, and you will rescue that man of yours, and live happily ever after when you escape to America."

"It all seems impossible sometimes." Miriam hugged the packet of stockings to her chest. "Thank you. I love them."

"And I'm sure Rudolf will appreciate your wedding present. Now, what am I going to wear out?" Mary Jayne looked down at her pajamas.

Miriam clipped on Dagobert's lead as Mary Jayne dressed. "Do you feel like heading out to the Pelikan to see who's around?"

"Sure. We might get a bit of news from the U.S. consulate."

Miriam sat on the bed and opened one of the red leather jewelry boxes. A diamond brooch gleamed, light refracting across the wall. "This is lovely."

"My grandmother's."

"Is it safe, darling, leaving all these lying around?"

"You mean with Raymond?"

"I don't mean to pry. I'm just worried about you." Miriam clicked the box shut and tucked it into the suitcase.

"They have sentimental value, more than anything." Mary Jayne looked at her reflection in the mirror. "Daddy gave me most of them, before he died." She adjusted the neckline of the blue wool dress she had chosen, tucking the silk strap of her slip away. "It's funny, isn't it, how unimportant things become when you are running for your life. When we fled Paris after the invasion, I left most of my luggage on the side of the road to Toulouse. I can't even remember now what was in the trunks."

"Some of us didn't have much to leave behind in the first place."

"Just you wait, once all this is over I'm sure you will have a darling home full of beautiful things, and hordes of children."

"So will you."

"Me?" Mary Jayne picked up a hairbrush. "No, I don't think so. I can't imagine choosing a life like that."

"You know you're going to have to make a choice, though, don't you?"

Mary Jayne brushed out her golden hair and put a slick of red lipstick on, rubbing her lips together. "A choice?" she said, spritzing Chanel No. 5 into the air and walking through the mist. "Come, Dago," she said, taking the lead from Miriam.

"Varian and the committee can't risk someone like Raymond having any connection with their work here. It's too dangerous."

"You mean I'll have to choose between Raymond and the ARC?" Mary Jayne locked the door and tossed the key into her clutch bag.

"Darling, it's extraordinary how much you have helped with the Gold List, but if you stay with Raymond, you know the committee will just see you as some kind of gangster's moll. You know the types he's involved with."

"I'd rather that than be at Varian's beck and call." She marched ahead, Dagobert trotting at her heels as they walked out into the corridor and down the sweeping staircase to the lobby.

"Do think about it. The work we are doing here counts. It really counts. I'd just hate to see someone like Raymond taking advantage of you." Miriam took her arm as they reached the lobby. "Do you really love him that much?"

"Perhaps I don't know what love is," Mary Jayne said finally. "But this is turning out to be quite some year for a nice girl from Evanston."

SIXTEEN

Flying Point, Long Island

2000

Gabriel

"Gabriel," Sophie says. "Gabriel." She tugs at my sleeve and I snap back to now, to the clear blue sky above me and the white sand beneath my feet. "I read that after the New Year's party in Paris you and Vita were inseparable. Is that when your relationship started?"

"I suppose you could say it was." See, it's not a lie, as such.

"You don't look so good. Are you getting tired?" Sophie asks me.

"A little." My hand's shaking as I reach for my breast pocket. Damn, I've forgotten my tablets, too. I'd wanted to enjoy a last lunch with a clear head before we closed up the house for the season, and I didn't want to feel woozy looking after the little one. The kids have decided that we are too old to spend another winter out here. What do they know? I can still walk to Marv's place or heat up a can of soup when we're hungry. Which isn't often these days.

The sun is dazzling on the sea, the white deserted sand. We must look like a couple of chess pieces walking along—the white king facing the black queen. Some days, when the beach is empty like this, the sense of space is so infinite, I swear you can see the curvature of the earth on the horizon, the suggestion of a perfect circle. Maybe that's why my paintings lately have all been arcs and lines inscribed on empty fields of blue. It takes me days to prepare just one canvas, finishing each with a single white dot in a fractionally different place from last time. There is every color in white light, did you know that? To capture this luminosity, that's what I've been chasing, the weightless sensation of being on our deserted beach, the white sand beneath your feet, the limitless cold blue air arcing over you.

Once photography came along, there was no point in rendering real life. I wanted to capture raw experience, sensation, to make people feel. There is nothing more difficult than simplicity. Oh, the critics will have a field day with my new work, coming up with some theory or other, when the reason, the inspiration, is here in front of them. I love this place. It's breaking my heart thinking of leaving, of being a guest in my son's home in the city. This is ours. All of this is ours.

Sophie notices the sign by the steps. "Why don't we head up to the café?"

"Good idea. I'll buy you a soda."

"I'll pay, Mr. Lambert." She folds her arms across her rib cage.

I wave my hand dismissively, that word my great-grandchildren seem to love so much on my lips: *Whatever.* This girl has destroyed my peace, and now she's getting smart with me? I'm not going to show her that she has me rattled. I'm going to stick with the "angry old man of art" act and hope she won't see past that.

"I'm sorry," she says, at my side again as we walk up the next flight of wooden steps and head across a half-empty car park toward the small café. It hasn't changed in thirty years. Marv's only concession to progress is the satellite dish up on the roof of the old cabin for the cable TV and Internet for all the whiz kids who can't leave their work behind on their summer weekends. I catch a couple of surfers, wet suits peeled down from their torsos, staring at us as we talk, checking her out. Perhaps she's cuter than I first assumed.

"Hey, Marv," I call across to the owner, and settle with relief into the booth by the window, my booth. Most places are already closing for the season around these parts, but Marv stays open all year. He says the locals and the odd surfer or dog walker are enough to keep him ticking over through the winter, and what else would he do? This place is his life.

"Haven't seen you for a few days, Gabe. You okay?"

"Me? I'm fine," I say.

"Okay, okay. Just asking." He sets a jug of ice water down on the chipped yellow Formica. As he leans down, the lamplight gleams on his bald head like polished mahogany. "D'you hear the Knicks have traded Ewing?"

"Yeah. I remember when he came in as the number one pick in the '85 draft," I say, pouring two glasses.

"Fifteen years, man. It's sure a good trade for Seattle," Marv says as he shuffles away, shaking his head.

"You like basketball?" Sophie asks as she sips her water.

"What, you mean just like a regular guy?"

"You're kind of touchy, aren't you?"

"Just had my fill of people who seem to think all artists live on ambrosia." The water is good, I'm thirsty. "It's a mistake to think artists only want that." I lean toward her. "You really want friends who'll talk about the weather, or how they're building their boat, or trade you recipes for beans."

"Don't disillusion me." A smile is playing across her lips. "Next thing you'll be telling me is you do your own tax returns, and the washing up...."

"And diapers. I've changed more diapers than you can imagine." I try not to smile at the disbelief on her face. "Between all the years of kids and grandkids, and puppies and kittens, I seem to have spent half my adult life picking up caca."

She laughs and settles back into the booth. "Maybe people waste a lot of time trying to pin their ideas on artists."

"Are you talking about yourself?"

"I was thinking about a book I'm reading on Duchamp."

"Ah, the master. He taught me that your life can be a work of art, kiddo."

"Do you always talk like a bad gangster movie?"

"I learned English watching Humphrey Bogart and Jimmy Stewart."

"It shows."

Back in the day, I'd have snapped at her for being so bold. Now it doesn't seem to matter. "You hungry?"

"Oh, no. I haven't—"

"My treat." My guess is she's one of those career girls who don't even stop for breakfast, just tank up on coffee. "Do you like pancakes? Marv, get us some of your blueberry specials."

"Whatever you say, Gabe." Marv slings a white cloth over his shoulder and goes through to the kitchen, whistling along to the Shirelles on the jukebox: "Will You Love Me Tomorrow."

"How long have you been coming here?" she says.

"Forever."

"Tell me what you like about it."

"Listen, kid, I like normal. Jeez, if you had to live with my mind . . ." I rake the heels of my hands across my temples. "If you had to live with that, you'd like normal, too. I like logs piled up for the winter, and Annie's laundry room, and this beach when it's empty. I like a pile of clean white plates on the kitchen table, and the tick of the longcase clock in our hall." I look her in the eye. "I like order, and peace. God knows that's not what I have in my head."

See, I have a theory about artists—their heads are like a basin with the tap running. Once in a while they have to let the plug out and set free a painting or a book, or there'll be a hell of a mess. When you get to my age you are better at regulating the flow, but it hasn't always been so easy. Maybe that's where my reputation comes from.

"Have you always lived here?" she says, tracing a line in the condensation on her glass.

"Always? Pretty much a lifetime. Annie and I shared a studio in Brooklyn for a while, but as soon as we could we headed out to the coast."

"She's an artist? I thought you said—"

"She was . . . well, she calls herself a crafter. Maybe you've seen some of her textiles. She did beautiful work, but then her hands got bad."

"I'm sorry." She pauses. "I've been wondering. You two never wanted to go back—to France, I mean? A lot of the artists did."

I shake my head. Sure, there are still days when I wake from dreaming about France and I wonder if we should have gone back. The dreams are fragments, really—the color of pale blue shutters changing chromatically with the light. Beneath a slate sky when the mistral is whipping through the olive trees, they seem gray. Beneath a cloudless blue sky they are bleached like the firmament above them, the perfect shade of old denim. I miss stone walls that radiate the heat of the day at night. I miss the smell of rosemary on a bonfire, the taste of a cold *pression*, and the soft light and shade of a plane tree in a market square. I miss great cheese, and geckos, and those mad, sun-blind dogs they have in the south of France with amber eyes. I miss, I miss . . . oh, avenues of lime trees like bleached bones along the roadsides, and fat asparagus and peaches. I miss the age of the place—how old villas with lime smudged onto their wall like ocher pastels look at sunset, with their rusted eau de nil gates, and deep indigo convolvulus on glorious mornings. The hardest thing of all, for many, was leaving behind family graves, of course. But I'm not going to tell her that. Too many of us had to do the same thing. Meyerhof said to me once, "You pick up your life and you don't think back." That's the secret. Never look back. Your home, your birthright, is tied to you but lost forever.

"The thing you've got to remember is that some of us dreamed about America, even before the war."

"Really?"

"Sure. At least I did. Jacqueline, André Breton's wife, said it was the Christmas tree of the world. Chagall worried there would be no cows here. But I wanted this my whole life, the possibility of it, this new world. I still get a kick every time I take the train into the city and see the Statue of Liberty, the Empire State."

"But it must have been incredible, your life with Vita?"

"It's another lifetime. I was a different person."

"That's what I want to talk to you about," Sophie says. She slips a tape recorder from her bag of tricks and nudges it on the table. "Do you mind?"

It's on the tip of my tongue to tell her this was a mistake, but then Marv rolls over with a stack of pancakes and the coffee.

"Gabriel . . . ," she says.

"You can call me Mr. Lambert."

"Well, that's kind of formal, considering how long we've been friends," Marv says.

"I wasn't talking to you," I say, the breath rattling in my chest, "I was talking to her." I wave my hand at Sophie. She jumps, knocking the coffee, and I snatch at the napkins in the chrome holder, mopping at the table.

"I can't stand mess," I snap at her.

"I'm sorry." There it is again, that bloom in her cheeks.

"Sure," Marv says, backing away. "Sure thing, Gabe. Enjoy your pancakes." I watch him go out back and pick up the phone.

"Mr. Lambert," Sophie says, "I'm sorry. We got off on the wrong foot. I'm not just a journalist. Think of me as an old family friend, like Vita." Phooey. There's no one on earth like me and Vita, believe me. I can almost see the radiance of Sophie's halo gilding her eyelids as she looks down at the plate in front of her. I don't trust her an inch. While I'm busy watching Marv, I hear Sophie quietly click on her little mumble machine.

"Why are you kids so hung up on the old stories?" I round on her. "You should be making history, not rehashing it."

"How can we learn if we forget the lessons of the past?"

"Listen, kid. There is only now. The past is a fabrication." I wave my hand as if I'm sewing. "It's a patchwork quilt of so-called facts and hearsay. History is up for grabs, a fiction spun by whoever has the strongest voice." I try to catch my breath, bunch my fist under the table. "The future is conjecture. All I want is now. The paint beneath my fingernails, to eat, to sleep, to fuck."

"At your age?" she says without looking up from her notebook.

"Yeah. It had more effect when I used to say it."

She settles back in the booth and folds her arms. "I've read that line in at least three of your biographies."

"That's what happens when you get to my age. You start repeating yourself."

"You're a walking cliché."

"Maybe. But I'm a happy one." I play with the coaster under my water. "So you've read them, then?"

"I need to put my article in context. If I'm honest, I'm more interested in Vita."

How amusing. I'm just the frame, not the picture.

"To lose one wife tragically is heartbreaking," she says quietly. "To lose more smacks of carelessness."

I have to think for a moment or two, it's all so long ago. My life here with Annie has been everything, is everything. All that went before—it's like trying to read a letter that's been left out in the rain. I hope the expression on my face reads as tragic rather than confused. "You're wrong there. I was never married to Vita."

"I know that." Good, she's getting exasperated. With any luck, if I play the old, doddering fool card, she'll get frustrated and start making mistakes soon. "But she was as good as, common law and all that. I'm talking about Rachel. She was your model, too, wasn't she?" She checks her notes. "She died just after you met Vita."

There's her first mistake. Rachel died before Vita was ever on the scene.

"Are you saying that was convenient in some way?"

"You tell me."

"There was a car crash. She was driving."

"Presumably heartbroken...."

If only you knew the truth. "People die for more stupid reasons than love all the time." I run my hand across my brow. "Does it really matter?"

"Yes, it matters. It's part of your story, of Vita's." She leans toward me. "In history, anonymity is the enemy. It reduces everyone to no one. It's my job to put names to the people that we have forgotten."

"You're wrong. It's an artist's job to name."

"Like God?" she says.

"Don't be cute. Besides, he's the greatest artist."

She taps her pen on the table. She's nervous. Good. "You don't want to talk about Vita yet?"

"No." I recognize that voice. Like my sons when they were toddlers, throwing their toys out of the stroller.

"Fine." Her voice is placatory. She's going to humor me. "Then tell me about Air-Bel. Tell me about Annie."

SEVENTEEN

Villa Air-Bel, Marseille

November 1940

Gabriel

"Say, Gabriel, good to see you." Varian shook my hand. He had been deep in thought, staring at the murals in the library, but he turned to me now and smiled warmly. "Have you come to welcome André Breton? Do you know him?"

"Of course, by reputation," I said. "I admire him greatly."

In my pocket I still had Fry's scribbled note with the address: *Villa Air-Bel, La Pomme.* I fingered the paper nervously. It was too much to hope for, that I should meet Breton, too. It felt like the world had tilted on its axis, and after the horror of the last months I had arrived in a place where your wildest dreams could come true. I wanted desperately to belong here, with this crazy group of nomads and artists. I felt awkward around Fry, still, his confidence awed me, and the way I'd seen him slip easily and fluently between English, French, and German as he chatted with his friends and clients. I felt tongue-tied in comparison.

"How is everything? Do you have money for food? We can give you some meal vouchers if you're having trouble with cash. You have somewhere safe to stay?" I nodded. "Good. Now you stay out of trouble, okay?" Fry shook my hand. "Don't you worry. We'll get you out of here just as quickly as we can. It may take a couple of months, but be sure we'll do our best for you." He smiled reassuringly. "Meanwhile you're welcome at Air-Bel whenever you want. We're planning a little get-together on

Sunday." Varian glanced up at the sound of Mary Jayne's voice drifting through from the first-floor landing, the sound of her heels clicking down the staircase to the entrance hall. At her side trotted Dagobert, the poodle an ever-present shadow, his claws tapping on the wooden steps. We followed her downstairs to wait for the Bretons.

"He's a smart dog, old Dago," Varian said. "Have you seen his party trick?"

"No."

"If you say 'Hitler, Hitler,' he'll bark ferociously." Varian laughed. "Maybe I can train Clovis to do the same."

"There you are!" Miriam skipped down the steps beside us. "The Bretons will be here any minute."

"This place is swell, Miriam. I was just enjoying the murals," Varian said, gesturing at the library.

"They're beautiful, aren't they?" Miriam hugged herself in delight. "I just knew you'd love this place. Do you know what they are of?"

"Sure. I'll show you later. There's even one of Aeneas, son of Venus, carrying his father, Anchises, from the flames of Troy."

"Well, that's appropriate."

"The original refugee," Varian said. "When he fled Troy, carrying his father on his back, he set a precedent for us all, didn't he?"

"Listen, Varian, I'm glad I've caught you," Miriam said. I walked on ahead, but I could still hear them.

"Is something up?"

"When I left the office tonight, I found out my visas for Yugoslavia have come through."

"Oh." Varian couldn't hide his shock and disappointment. "Of course, I'm delighted for you and Rudolf. Will you marry now?"

"That's the idea, and then I hope I can get us safely back here before going on to the States."

Varian took his glasses off and polished them with his handkerchief. "It's funny. I mean, I know the deal all along was that each of you would escape yourselves just as soon as you could, but I hate to see you go." He looked at Miriam. "You've done great work, Davenport. Thank you. People like the Bretons are safer because of you."

"Oh, stop it. You're making me blush."

"You will take care, won't you?"

Miriam hugged him. "I'm going to miss you, too, boss."

"When do you leave?"

"Four days."

"So soon?" At the sound of voices in the hallway below, he slung his arm around her, squeezing her shoulder affectionately as they caught up with me. "What a shame you're leaving just as you've found this place. I can't think of a better refuge from the center than this...." His voice trailed off.

"I'm hoping Mary Jayne will come round," she said as they paused on the landing and looked down into the black-and-white hallway. Mary Jayne stood at the open doorway, and Dagobert bounded out onto the terrace at the sound of tires stopping on the gravel drive. "It would do you good to live here, too."

"I wouldn't want to put Miss Gold out," Varian said.

"Don't be like that," she said. "If you think I'm going off to Yugoslavia while you two are still at one another's throats—"

"We'll be fine. She thinks I'm a stubborn ass, and I think she's a highly strung little rich girl."

"Just wait and see," she said. "One day you two'll look back at all of this as the best of friends."

"Like a donkey and a racehorse put out to pasture?" he said doubtfully. "Have you told her yet?"

Miriam shook her head. "I will, later. I just didn't want to spoil everything, not yet."

I glanced downstairs as a tall man with a chestnut mane of hair strode into the hallway. A slender blond woman walked at his side, holding the hand of a young girl. The woman moved with the grace and certainty of a dancer, and her full black-and-white-striped skirt swung as she stepped into the hall. She stood with her hand on her hip, chin raised. *A woman who is used to making an entrance,* that was the first thing I thought. The lights of the chandelier gilded their hair, danced from the mirrored clips in the woman's hair.

"Monsieur and Madame Breton," Mary Jayne said, stepping forward from the crowd gathering in the hall to greet them. "Welcome to Air-Bel." André Breton shook her hand and introduced his wife, Jacqueline, and daughter, Aube, to the welcoming group. As they talked among themselves, André's gaze traveled around the house. I thought of photographs

I had seen of lions gazing out across the plains of Africa, how they always seemed to be part of the world and yet somewhere else, too. *Perhaps they see something we don't*, I thought. Just then, André looked up at me, his hair a blazing halo above his dark green suit and red tie, and raised his hand in greeting like a blessing.

If you look really closely at the photos they took that night, you can see me hanging around in the shadows. I can never figure out why we all looked so much older than we were in the photographs taken at Air-Bel. Maybe it's the formal clothes—we all wore a shirt and tie every day back then. Kids of sixteen looked like old men. Perhaps it's not your calendar age but what you've experienced that shows up in a photograph. Annie says I'm an old soul. Me, I just think I went through a lot in 1940.

I was introduced to Breton and his wife but hadn't the guts to talk to him properly. I was still feeling pretty nervous when I headed out to La Pomme on the tram that Sunday. Almost turned back a few times at the thought of this house full of people I had admired my whole life. Sundays at Air-Bel became legendary in Marseille—all the young artists and writers were talking about it, and here I was waiting on La Canebière for a tram to La Pomme. The city looked beautiful in the snow. To talk to a resident of Marseille, you'd think it was never cold, never snowed, but this was the first indication of how bitterly cold that winter would be, and my feet were soaked through already. But the snow covered up the worst of the dross and the filth in the city and made everything feel brand new, including myself.

You wouldn't be going to meet Breton if Fry knew the truth, I told myself. I'd already come to picture my conscience as me as a schoolboy. I imagine the little fellow even now, sitting on my right shoulder, swinging his legs, his shoes shined. *You're a bad boy, Gabriel*, he says. But it's not my voice. Who said that to me, and when? My mother, perhaps? I don't know whose voice it is, but I know that sense of mortifying shame only too well, the sickening feeling of having been caught.

To hell with them, another voice piped up as I gazed out of the tram window, squinting at the bright light bouncing off the distant waves. This voice is more like my father, lounging around on my left shoulder with a glass in his hand. I have him under control most of the time now, but then . . . well. I was so messed up and broken inside, most of the time he made his voice heard.

You go out there, and you have a good time, he said. *Drink their wine, soak up their ideas, suck them dry. Don't let them give you any nonsense. You can hold your own with them.* "I am Gabriel Lambert," I said under my breath.

A few people jumped down from the tram at La Pomme, just before the railway bridge, and I followed them at a distance. I turned up the collar of my overcoat and tucked my head down, the wind whipping through my hair. They chatted among themselves—they were obviously friends, relaxed in one another's company. They turned into a long driveway, and the last of them—a tall, good-looking fellow with a beautiful woman on his arm, held open the iron gate for me.

He had fine features, and his hand on the gate was slender, long fingered, his skin the color of burnished teak.

"Are you here for the salon?" he asked.

"Yes. I'm Gabriel Lambert," I said, offering him my hand.

"Wifredo Lam," he said. "This is Helena." The girl smiled at me and walked on.

"Are you a painter?"

"Yes. I've been studying with Picasso."

"Picasso?" The name of the great man stuck in my throat like a fishbone. I almost ran at that point, I felt so out of my depth.

"Are you managing to work at all?"

"A little." My voice sounded unnaturally high.

"It's the only way," he said, walking up the drive to the house. "I feel my drawings are changing here. I'm illustrating André's new poem."

"André?"

"Breton," Wifredo said, laughing. He chatted on about the poem, *Fata Morgana,* and introduced me to the others on the terrace, to Óscar Domínguez, and André Masson. I was so relieved that Wifredo had taken me under his wing, I have no recollection of what we talked of at all. I do remember him saying that he had fought with the Republicans in the Spanish Civil War, and thinking how unlikely it was that this tall, gentle man should be caught up again in conflict. I was just happy to listen to them all talk, happy to blend into the group. I could hear music drifting from the house, some wild Count Basie jazz tune with screeching trumpets and thundering drums on the radio. I began to sweat, thinking of that night only a few months before with Vita, the sound of the band and the pounding beat.

"Lambert!" I heard Varian call, but I could not see him. Through the open French window, I saw André Breton dancing with Jacqueline. His head was lowered, his cheek resting tenderly against her temple. They were surrounded by people but seemed lost in each other. "Up here!" Varian called, laughing. I turned and looked back across the terrace to the trees.

"Good heavens," I said, "what on earth are you doing?"

"We're having a little auction," he said, waving from the branches. "Would you mind passing me that last canvas?" I flipped it around and handed it carefully to him. I whistled softly, realizing I had a Max Ernst in my hands. Varian casually swept it up into the branches. He took a length of string and tied the wire on the back of the picture to the tree, holding one end of the string in his teeth as he tightened it. "There," he said, and scrambled down. The paintings spun in the breeze, bright paint glimmering against the trees, the air like flowers in the park.

I could hear the sound of voices behind me, exclamations and greetings as Breton welcomed his friends. I was too nervous to turn around and introduce myself.

"What do you think?" Varian asked me.

"It's incredible . . . ," I started to say.

"It is marvelous!" Breton cried, and clapped his hands. The trees on the terrace were strung with thirty, forty paintings. Looking back now, I realize that it was a collection any fine-art museum would kill to have. "We shall hold the auction later, but first, we play!" I trailed inside, following the young boys I had seen at the ARC office, too shy to introduce myself to Breton.

I hung back, observing the artists from the edge of the room. It was freezing cold—they say 1940–41 was the coldest winter on record—and everyone was done up in their overcoats and scarves, sitting around the huge polished wood table. It was impossible to stay still for more than five minutes without the cold becoming unbearable, and everyone was restless, blowing on their hands. Breton had put magazines, scissors, paper, and glue at the center of the table, and glasses with pencils and crayons. I couldn't make out what was going on. A single sheet of paper was passed from artist to artist, and they folded down the section they had drawn before passing it on to the next person.

"What are they doing?" I whispered to Varian.

"They are playing games," he said. "They call this one *cadavre exquis*. I think before now, they have used words, made chance sentences. Now they seem to be experimenting with images. Breton calls them *les petits personnages*. After they have drawn a few pictures, he decides the best."

It's rare that people surpass your expectations, but André was magnificent—every bit as provocative and extraordinary as his writings had led me to hope. He presided over the gathering, stooping occasionally to murmur words of encouragement to the artists. When they had finished, he sorted through a sheaf of papers and raised a drawing of a head in the air. *"Stupéfiant!"* he cried. "A true collaboration. We shall call this 'The Last Romantic Has Been Buggered by Marshal Pétain'!" The table erupted in cheers and laughter. *"Formidable."*

"Do you not want to join in?" Varian asked me.

"No, no," I said. "I'm happy to watch."

"You should! A lot of the games they play seem to be collaborative."

Only now do I realize what those games meant. When all around us the world was turning dark, the surrealists were focused on the light. They believed in absolute freedom, and this is what those crazy-looking games were all about. They wanted to free the unconscious mind. They showed us the luminous, random beauty around us and in our dreams, and everything Breton and the others did has changed the way we look at the world forever. Air-Bel became the house of dreams. In that little room in the falling winter light, I watched men and women who, for an afternoon a week, put aside their fear and hunger and created, and at the beating heart of them was Breton. I still wish I'd had the nerve to talk to him, but the greatest lesson Breton taught me was that the most effective course against despair is to preserve your freedom of mind.

"As I have said many times before," Breton said to one of the men, raising his voice above the crowd. "When one ceases to feel, I am of the opinion one should keep quiet, my friend." The group dissolved into laughter, and one of the artists loped off, red faced. It was like seeing a badly behaved cub get a clip around the ear from the head of the pride. I opened my mouth to ask him what he meant, what was this "pure psychic automatism" they kept talking about, but the words tightened in my throat. I was afraid of getting the same treatment.

I felt completely out of my depth around them all, like the new kid at school. I wanted to belong here, in this beautiful house, with these incredible people, but I felt like a phony. I pushed my way out onto the terrace and gulped down the cold air. The hum of voices, the clear notes of the music, fell away as I walked across the lawns. Yet more people were heading up the driveway with their heads bent against the wind like pilgrims. I turned away toward the parkland at the back of the house and walked on.

I heard children laughing up ahead, and I followed the sound. There was a little blond girl with a red ribbon in her hair, and a small boy about the same age, five or six, I guess. They were on the ground, arcing their arms and legs, making snow angels. It looked like fun, so I lay down beside them and started kicking and swinging my arms. The milk sky was heavy with snow above me, and sound was muffled, so when I heard a girl laughing beyond the garden wall, the note of her voice was clear and pure as a bell. "Who's there?" I said, turning my head. The snow was cold against my cheek. "I said, who's there?"

A snowball arced over the wall and hit me squarely on the chest. I blinked, flakes wet in my lashes, on my lips. "Hey!" I cried out, and scrambled up. I could hear footsteps crunching through the snow on the other side of the wall, running away. I chased her, deeper into the woods where the wall began to fall away and a tall, dark hedge marked the boundary. I was breathless, my heart pounding. The grounds weren't tended well this far away from the house, and the hedge was old and patchy. I caught a glimpse of her once or twice—a flash of blond hair between the dark leaves, a pale hand or cheek. I squatted down and breathed deeply, the cold air hurting my lungs, my breath a pale cloud in front of my face. I could see her slender legs between the trunks of the hedge—her dark stockings and boots, the hem of her dress. She had her back up against the leaves, hiding against the trunk of a tree. I crept forward on my belly, silently, pushed my way through a gap in the hedge a little farther up. Everything seemed to slow down. My breath trembled in my throat. Then, just as I poked my head through into the light, my foot must have caught on a dry branch. A twig snapped, and she spun around, startled, her eyes wide and alert like a fawn. You hear people talk about love at first sight in songs, but that was it for me. Looking back over my life, I see that there are a handful of moments like that, which I can recall with perfect clarity. Not all the in-between times we lose along the way, but the moments that matter. The first time I saw Annie, I was absolutely present. Not thinking about the past or worrying about the future, but there, with her. Too often when you're young, you fall in love with your idea of a person. I always reckon people stay happy just as long as their idea of each other fits. Annie's never wavered for me, not once. I saw her for the first time, and I knew her—recognized her, even—and she knew me.

Annie's hair swung after her, pale and luminous. Her face registered fear, then amusement when she saw me, and she scooped up a handful of snow, molded it into a ball as she backed away from me. Just as I scrambled clear of the roots, she swung her arm back. She was grinning now, and I saw she had a little gap between her front teeth. Her lips were unnaturally bright, full and red in the cold, her cheeks flushed pink. She was, she is, the most beautiful girl I had ever seen. I was unmanned, and she knew it. She threw the snowball with the aim of a marksman and it clocked me between the eyes.

"That does it," I yelled, scooping up a big handful of snow. On open ground she was no match for me, and I sprinted after her, stumbling. The snowball hit her on the back of the head. She shrieked, fearful and excited as I grabbed her by the waist and we fell into the snow. "Now, we're even." We lay in silence, face-to-face—aware, I guess, that we had never met. She looked uncertain, suddenly. "My name is Gabriel," I said. Her blue eyes gazed at me. The truth is, it felt as though I'd known her, had been waiting for her, my whole life.

"I'm Marianne," she said.

Like an echo, I heard a woman's voice calling, "Marianne! . . . Marianne!" She sat up quickly and glanced back over her shoulder at me, smiling. "But you can call me Annie. I have to go." She leapt to her feet, looking down the woods to the little stone house by the road. I could make out a plump, shrewish-looking woman dressed in a black coat bustling through the back garden gate.

"Wait!" I caught at her hand. "Who are you? Where do you live?"

"I'm always here," she said, slipping away.

"Can I see you again?"

She laughed, as if it were the most natural question in the world. She glanced down the hill; the woman—her mother, I guessed—was steaming up the hill, her breath puffing out of her like a train. "Do you live there, with all those crazy people?"

"Me? No. I'm an artist, though. I'm just . . . I'm visiting."

"Good." She inclined her head toward her mother. "She would not like it if you did. My parents think Air-Bel is full of Communists and sex maniacs," she said. "It's quite the scandal in the village that the old miser Thumin has rented the villa to them. Who is the woman who goes shopping with bracelets around her ankle and a stuffed bird in her hair?"

"That must be Madame Breton."

"People are talking. They do not like things that are different around here."

"Do you care about that?" I asked, pulling myself up from the snow. I was about a head taller than her, and as I looked down at her all I wanted to do was take her hand and keep on running, away from her parents, the village, the war, away from everything.

"Of course not." She glanced quickly over her shoulder. "I love art, in fact I want to study, after school." It was impossible to tell how old she was. Sixteen or seventeen, perhaps. She seemed older. I think sometimes now that young people like that who have grown up in one place, who have only ever known certainty, the sureness of where they belong in the world, have a confidence I'll never possess, even as children. Of course she was beautiful, and exhilarating, but I think that is what drew me to her as surely as north follows south. When people ask how we met, she always says it was love at first sight—and that's true. But there was more to it than desire. I recognized something in her that I needed like air, like water. I coveted her roots—how real she was. Marianne, my Annie, has always only ever been herself. Unlike me.

"I'd be happy to take a look at your work," I said.

She weighed me up with that clear blue stare of hers. "I will meet you in town next weekend. I have my ballet class in a hall near La Vieille Charité at two o'clock on Saturday. There is a little café with red shutters just down the road." She backed away, raised her arms to a graceful fifth position, her pointed foot arcing the snow. "I'm meeting a friend there after the class."

"A boyfriend?"

She grinned. "No, a girl if you must know." She looked back over her shoulder as she walked away. "You'd better go, my mother doesn't like trespassers."

I crawled back through the gap in the hedge and jogged along until I caught up with Annie. She was trailing her hand against the branches again, and I reached up and did the same. I caught her, once or twice, looking at me—a glimpse of her eye, her lips. I could hear her mother coming, a tirade of complaints rattling from her lips like keys in a tin can. As I neared the garden, I could hear the auction beginning on the terrace. "Annie," I whispered to her, and she stopped walking and turned. I reached through the leaves to her, bobbed my head until I found her, her gaze, her smile. I pushed aside the branches and touched her fingertips. Then, as her mother's voice reached me clearly, she turned and was gone, as swift and silent as a bird in flight.

EIGHTEEN

Flying Point, Long Island

2000

Gabriel

"Annie...," I say quietly. The girl is watching me. I have to be careful. "You made short work of those," I say to her.

"I was starving," Sophie says. She runs her finger through the last of the blueberry juice and sucks it clean. That's the kind of thing that would have got me going a few years back, but now, nothing. "Thank you," she says, dabbing her mouth with her napkin. "They were very, very good." She checks the recorder still has tape left and reaches into her bag for a pen and notebook. As she flips through the pages, words jump out at me: *Vita. Gabriel. Why?* "Let me just check something," she says.

"Sure."

Sophie flicks through her notes. "According to the research I've done, you moved to the Château d'Oc, which is near..."

"Carcassonne."

"Yes, you were near Carcassonne in 1938, correct?"

"Yes." Which way is this heading?

"And in the summer of 1940, you were living alone there with Vita?"

"Most of the time."

"What do you mean?"

"I mean, people came and went."

"Such as?"

"Quimby, my dealer. Friends," I say vaguely. She's not buying it.

"I heard you were a recluse by then."

I pick up the sugar shaker and stir a slow stream into my coffee before I remember the doctor had told me to cut it out. "Did you now?" I look directly into her eyes as I put it down. "As you can see, I don't much like company, still."

"You seem to have a houseful today."

"Family. That's different."

"Talking of family . . ."

Oh God, here it comes.

"Tell me about your son." She has the good grace to blush slightly. "I mean, if it's not too painful?" Her eyes flicker down to her page and she unscrews her ink pen.

"Who the hell uses a fountain pen these days?"

"I do. At least for important things."

"Like writing to me?"

"So you *did* get the letters."

"And about me," I say, reading her notebook upside down. I tap it with my dry old finger. My nails are curved and hard, more like claws these days.

Sophie hesitates, looks from her notes to me. "I thought you're dyslexic."

Clever girl. I'm going to have to be careful. "Maybe I struggled with *War and Peace,* but I get by." I wait for her confidence to waver and hope she doesn't push that line of inquiry. "I don't give a crap what people say about my work, but you're not concocting some fairy tale about me and Vita just to suit the story you're trying to conjure up. You're wrong about that, I told you. I never stopped Vita doing anything."

"But these photos of Vita's studio . . . ," she says, sliding the black-and-white photos onto the table. Oh God, my heart's racing again. It's there, staring her in the face. Maybe I'm in luck, maybe she's not noticed, not seen? But then, I know in my gut she has. She hinted as much in her letter. Perhaps if I can get her to focus on Vita, she'll forget. "Lambert?"

"Quimby took them."

She checks her notes. "You say he was your dealer?"

"For a time."

"Look, I don't believe you when you say Vita was no good. I mean, it's hard to make out, but these paintings look . . . well, to use your word about her, dazzling. Why did she never show them?"

My gaze falls to the images. I know them like the lines on my palm. Vita didn't paint them. I did. "They were the beginning of something," I say to the girl. Or maybe the end.

Memory is a funny thing. I spend more time thinking of the past than the present these days. It is more detailed, more full of life, than the days I drift through now. Just like that, I'm back in the Château d'Oc. I am more there than here in the café with the girl. I can still hear myself, my old voice worn out by years of sea air and pipe tobacco, rabbiting on to Sophie, weaving a string of lies, the story she wants to hear, but I'm long gone.

Here is the beat of my heart, racing in my chest as I follow Quimby into the house. Here is the thrum of hooves on the hard earth as Vita rode into the party. Here is the pulse and the rush and the pull of the past. I'm back, I'm back, and I can't bear it. I close my eyes, push on, past the fire. The days, the months, fast-forward, and the memories kaleidoscope until I am safe again at Air-Bel, the night I met Annie and my life changed track forever.

NINETEEN

Villa Air-Bel, Marseille

1940

Varian

That night, Air-Bel swung to the tinny sound of American jazz, picked up on the shortwave radio. The reception rooms hummed with conversation and laughter, and blazing fires danced in the hearths. From the kitchen drifted the sound of pots clattering on the stove and the voice of the chef, Madame Nouguet, shouting orders to the housemaid, Rose. Above, children's footsteps clattered across the wooden boards, muffling for a moment as they ran across a rug, then racing on, their excited voices pealing like bells through the old villa.

"We shall christen this house Château Espère Visa," Varian said, raising his glass of wine. He stood before the crackling hearth, his hand resting by the stopped clock.

"Perfect!" Mary Jayne cried. "Haven't we been calling this old place the château?" she said to Miriam. They sat beside each other on the sofa, legs curled beneath them. Their cheeks were flushed with wine and the warmth of the fire. "Of course, 'château' is a bit grand."

"Well, I think it's a swell place," Varian said as he joined them. He placed his glass of red wine on the marble fireplace and reached for the bottle to top up the girls' glasses.

"Thanks," Miriam said, smiling up at him.

"So, has Miriam told you the good news?" he said to Mary Jayne. "Her visas have come through. Miriam is getting married." He raised his glass. "We should make a toast. To Miriam and Rudolf!" He chinked his glass against hers.

"Why didn't you tell me?" Mary Jayne said quietly to Miriam.

"I didn't want to spoil tonight." Miriam looked crestfallen. "I told you not to say anything, Varian."

"Typical," Mary Jayne said under her breath. "Damn it, Davenport. I knew you'd get your papers sooner or later, but I'm going to miss you." She squeezed her friend's hand. "And it's just as we've found all this." She pointed across the room. "Tell me again, Varian, who are these people?"

"That chap's a writer. Well . . . a writer and a revolutionary," Varian said quietly. "He's in great danger because he's spoken out against Stalin. In fact, he was the first writer to call the regime 'totalitarian.' He's been in and out of prison for years, and he's stateless and penniless now. I believe a lot of his family are either imprisoned or in gulags."

"How terrible."

"I hope this old place is a refuge for him."

"Varian certainly loves it—you should have seen him!" Miriam said. "He's been like a child all afternoon, going from room to room, looking in all the drawers." She glanced up as the children raced through, running after Dagobert and Clovis. "I don't know who's had more fun, Varian or that lot."

"I said you'd love it." Mary Jayne sipped her drink.

Madame Nouguet appeared at the door. "Dinner is ready to be served."

The table was laid for twelve in the heavy, Spanish-decorated dining room. The room had the natural exuberance of a funeral parlor, with faux Córdoba leather walls and heavy mahogany table and chairs. As the group filtered through, Mary Jayne directed everyone to their places. "I'm so glad you could join us for dinner," she said pointedly to Varian.

"Thank you for inviting me," he said.

"I'm not sure what Madame Nou . . ." Her voice trailed off as she saw André whisk away a red cloth from the center of the table. "What on earth?"

Varian pulled back her chair. "Thank you," she said, craning forward to look at the pile of leaves arranged in front of her.

Varian adjusted his horn-rimmed glasses and squinted at the arrangement. Just then, one of the twigs moved and swiveled a triangular head toward him. "Ha!" he cried in delight. "A praying mantis."

"Two, male and female," André said, settling in the chair opposite Varian. "Just watch."

The dinner continued late into the night, long after the sparse meal had been eaten and the servants had retired to bed. People danced in the hall, swinging to the jazz tune crackling through the ether from Boston, and the air in the dining room swirled with wood and cigarette smoke, the table littered with empty wine bottles and overflowing ashtrays. For the first time in months, Varian felt truly at ease—he lounged back in his chair, shirtsleeves rolled up, tie loose around his throat. He smiled benevolently as he looked around, at Miriam with her head thrown back, laughing as she danced; at Mary Jayne admiring the tiger's-tooth necklace Jacqueline had strung around her neck; at Danny, who sat with his arm slung over his wife's shoulders as he debated with the men. For the first time in his life, Varian had the feeling that he had come home. It felt almost indecent to be this contented, enjoying a simple dinner with friends in a setting as perfect as this. *And yet,* he thought, his eye caught by a movement at the center of the table. How long could this last? How long until they were kicked out of the country, arrested, or worse? Varian reached for the bottle of wine as Gussie passed it to him and nodded his thanks. *How long will we be safe?* he thought as yet again, Varian's attention returned to the two praying mantises stalking each other at the center of the table. It was how he felt every minute of every day—under threat, from the gangsters, the cops, the Gestapo. He glanced at Mary Jayne. Even her relationship with Killer put them at risk.

"Aren't they marvelous?" Breton said, interrupting his thoughts.

"Where did you find them?" Varian asked André.

"In the greenhouse," he said, peering closely at them. "It's almost time." He sat back. "Have you seen the garden yet? Old Dr. Thumin's greenhouse is quite marvelous. I think I shall work in there."

"Are you managing to write, in spite of it all?"

"One must always write." André drained his glass.

"What are you working on?" Varian said, and hesitated. "If I may ask?"

"Something new." He reached into his breast pocket, and Varian glimpsed a folded sheet of paper scored with looping green handwriting. "A new poem." Then he lunged forward, pointing at the center of the table, his eyes glittering with satisfaction. "There!"

It seemed to Varian that the flames, the candles in the dining room, the firelight, flared and glowed in André's eyes the very moment that the praying mantis bit down on the head of its mate.

TWENTY

Flying Point, Long Island

2000

Gabriel

Whenever I see one of those lumps of amber fashioned into a paperweight in those fancy decorator's stores that Annie likes browsing in, I think of the summer of 1940. I stopped in the street to look at one in the window of a store last time we went to town. Annie had on that old blue dress of hers I love so much, and she was laughing, chatting to an old friend about the grandkids. I could hear her talking, and the thrum of the convertibles driving nose to tail up the main street with their identical cargoes of guys in Ralph Lauren polo shirts and khakis and their expensively blond wives and kids who look like they are out of a catalog. The light was bright and clear, but as I looked at that amber, it seemed to darken and I felt again the heat, the weight of the Château d'Oc, and the taste of the dust in my mouth, and I saw the sulfurous yellow tang of the sky over the hills. I can't remember what the paperweight was sitting on, some flimsy-looking desk or writer's table or something too small to ever be a useful working surface, but it was the quality of the light caught in it that stopped me. It reminded me of looking into a tin of golden syrup. I didn't buy it, of course. What is it they call that style the decorators are all crazy for now? Shabby chic. I don't get that at all, the fakery and faux finishes. Something should be what it is, of its time. It should have heart and authenticity. Everything I have in my life is shabby, but it's beautiful and useful and real, and it's grown shabby because I've loved it and used it. Why is everyone looking backward, instead of creating something new and marvelous now, hey? These decorators just get some kid in a garage to beat up some piece of pine junk, triple the price, and stick it in the window of one of their little chichi shops in East Hampton, artfully scatter a few magazines or papers around, and then hold it all together with a great piece of amber. What do I know—that's probably plastic, too. Anyway, you can guarantee that stuck at the heart of the amber there's some hapless insect. That's how I felt before I met Annie—trapped. Even thinking of it now, my breath tightens.

There have been times when I wasn't sure I'd make it through one of my attacks. Annie's always been good at calming me down, but when I was younger, before the meds got better, there were days when each breath had to be torn out of the air. I had an old mirror in the studio, and I'd stare at myself, trying to still my chest, thinking over and over: *I am Gabriel Lambert.*

"Say, Gabe, I know who you are, buddy."

"Hm? What?" I say. I look up to find Marv standing over me.

"I'm sorry, man," he says. "I've got to close up early today. Lil wants me to take her into town."

"Ain't that just the way," I say. "Annie's always on at me to take her into town more. I say, 'What do you want to go to town for when we have everything we need here?' She says she just likes to look." I search in my pocket for some change and catch Marv watching me.

"No, you're all right, Gabe," he says, and pats me gently on the shoulder. "It's on the tab. In fact, this is on me."

I laugh out loud. "It must be Christmas."

"Soon enough, Gabe," he says, shuffling away. "Soon enough." He pauses as he flicks out the lights in the café one by one. "You sure you're okay?"

"Never better," I say.

"You want me to drop you back at the house?"

"No, it's a beautiful day for a walk." The sun is sinking already, washing the windows apricot and gold.

"Gabe . . ."

I can see the way he's looking at me. I'm choked up suddenly. "Now, Marv, don't go getting all sentimental on me." We slap each other on the back awkwardly, half hug, half tussle.

"Don't be a stranger, you hear?"

"I'll be around," I say, and wink. I step aside to let Sophie walk ahead of me, out onto the deck overlooking the beach, and as I turn from Marv my face sets hard. There's no one on the beach now, it's a strip of perfect white sand arcing beneath clear sky. The sunset is seeping up into the blue like rinsing Rose Doré from your brush in a jar of cold water.

I can't see her face, but the wind is whipping the girl's blond hair free as she walks ahead of me down the wooden steps to the beach. I glance behind me. Marv's car is just pulling out of the car park, and the surfers are long gone. The cottages are deserted. We are alone.

The stick is heavy in my hand, the end round like a cudgel. For a split second, I imagine bringing it down on her head. I wouldn't be able to take her down hand on hand anymore, but if I were to catch her unawares . . . One blow to the temple, I think, would do it, and then I'd just set her loose in the sea. My heart is jolting in my chest, my ribs a taut xylophone beneath the skin. I've killed before, I could do it again, if I had to, to protect Annie, my children.

The guilt has never left me. I've never been able to forgive myself. I've asked myself so many times if leading a good life redeems your soul. Do thousands of ordinary days atone for one deadly act? You'd think you would forget how it feels to kill, but it is always there, tainting everything. I look down at my hands, with their long fingers and wide, full palm. They look innocent enough, but it's always there, beneath all the tenderness, the touches that have created, and healed, and aroused.

She knows too much, this girl. Why now, after all these years, so close to the end, so close to getting away with it? I will do anything to protect my family. If she pushes me . . . I'm just waiting for her to turn and point her finger at me and say the words I've waited sixty-odd years to hear.

But she doesn't, she just keeps on walking, her steps so light and free they barely leave a trace in the sand, just licks of wind. No matter how fast I walk, she is just out of reach. "So after Vita and your son were killed, you just upped and left for Marseille? You never looked back?"

Never look back. Like I always say, the ones in the myths who look back are the ones they turn to stone or pillars of salt. Always look forward. "Yep." I have to shift my weight and tighten my grip on the carved wooden stick as we hit the soft sand. "Gabriel Lambert left for Marseille."

TWENTY-ONE

Marseille

1940

Varian

"Well done, Bill. These are perfect." Varian held the visas up to the window in the artist's studio, then placed them carefully on the drawing board, peering down through a magnifying glass at the papers, one bespectacled eye magnified, blinking in the bright lamplight. Bill Freier pulled the light closer and pointed at the stamp he had forged on the document.

"Not too perfect," he said, pointing at a smudged edge. "That would be suspicious." Part of his skill was turning the brand-new identification cards he could still pick up in *tabacs* into convincingly battered documents. "A few thumbprints and dog-ears help to pass them off."

Varian stood and reached into his breast pocket for his wallet. "What do I owe you?" He glanced up at the sound of quick footsteps on the wooden stairs leading to the attic room.

"Pfft," Bill said, waving him away. "Fifty cents apiece, call it five bucks."

"Hello, Varian," a slender brunette said as she walked in. She slung an empty-looking basket onto the kitchen counter.

"How are you, Mina?"

"Cold, hungry . . . ," she said. Bill wandered over and kissed her. Varian smiled indulgently—the young couple's love was clear to see. It radiated from them, a heat that even the chill mistral couldn't destroy. *When was the last time Eileen and I looked at one another like that?* he thought. Mina gazed up at Bill, giggled as he whispered something in her ear. *Have we ever looked at one another like that?* They were still at the stage where their hands danced around each other like butterflies, never still, full of the novelty and joy of being young and in love.

Mina unpacked her basket as Varian paid Bill. He glanced over and saw a single onion, a half loaf of bread. "Thank you, Bill," he said, slipping an extra note to him. "You are being careful?"

"Of course. Why would they be interested in a little fellow like me?" Bill tossed the roll of money onto his desk, where it landed among the brushes and inks, the piles of blank visas and passports waiting for his attention. "Do you have anything for me today?"

"As always." Varian clicked open his polished brown leather briefcase and slipped the documents Bill had given him inside a copy of Virgil's *Aeneid*.

"Say, I just saw your friend Hermant outside the café Au Brûleur de Loups," Mina said.

"Beamish? Did you?" Varian said, glancing at his watch. He handed Bill a file of documents, each with black-and-white passport photographs pinned to them. He shook Bill's hand. "Take care now, both of you."

"There you are, Buster," Beamish said as Varian walked toward his table. "Shall we move inside?" The café Au Brûleur de Loups was quiet at this time of the day, and Varian spotted the man they were meeting immediately. The gangster Kourillo sat at the back of the empty café, hidden from the road by a large pillar. Varian recognized him from his hand, the fluid way he reached again and again, flicking his cigarette impatiently into a rectangular yellow ceramic ashtray stamped *Ricard Pastis*. He followed Beamish in silence. Varian disliked Kourillo, distrusted him on gut instinct. *But yet again, we have little choice but to deal with men like him if we are to fund the ARC.*

"Monsieur Fry," Kourillo said, shaking his hand limply. "Monsieur Hermant."

"Kourillo." Varian sat opposite and folded his arms. He nodded as Beamish ordered a carafe of red wine for them.

"How is the relief business?"

Varian folded his arms. "I wouldn't call it a business."

Beamish glanced at him, warning him.

"We are all in business, my friend." Kourillo laughed softly. Varian noticed he had tiny teeth, like a child. "Now, I have a proposal to discuss." He poured water from a carafe into his pastis and watched the glass grow opaque, opalescent.

"Go ahead," Varian said, trying to conceal his impatience.

"No, no, no." Kourillo sipped his drink. "Not here. I just wished to see if you were open to . . . ideas."

Varian bit down hard on the inside of his lip. "Monsieur Kourillo—"

"Of course we are," Beamish said smoothly. "Shall we meet you at the Dorade tomorrow? I imagine Charles is involved?"

"Naturally. Vinciléoni is involved with everything." Kourillo rose and put his hat on his head. "Until tomorrow."

Varian waited until Kourillo had left the café before he spoke again. "That man," he said, his words clear and quiet. "Wasting our time like this—"

Beamish knew the signs. "Calm down."

"Don't tell me to calm down." Varian glanced up as a couple took a table not far from them. He lowered his voice. "What the hell do you think he is talking about?"

Beamish shrugged. "I've heard rumors about gold."

"Gold?" Varian whispered. "Jesus, Beamish. Laundering francs is one thing, but if we get caught trading in gold, we'll all be locked up."

"We need money, urgently. You said so yourself."

"I know, I know. If only we didn't have to do business with men like him."

"You don't get it yet, do you? Men like him are running this city." Beamish drained his glass and pulled on his knitted woolen hat. "We have no choice but to do business with crooks. It's the only way we are going to get the good guys out of here."

TWENTY-TWO

Villa Air-Bel, Marseille

1940

Mary Jayne

"Well, our little friend has settled in," Mary Jayne drawled. She was sitting with Miriam at the table on the terrace in the evening sun, the slatted shadows cast by the great palms shifting over them like the pelt of a wild animal. Dagobert ran across the terrace, a yapping black poodle puppy at his heels. "I can't believe you twisted my arm about Varian."

"Clovis!" Varian yelled, racing after the dogs, a lead flapping in his hand. "Clovis!"

"Think of it as a parting gift to me," Miriam said, laughing, pulling her coat tighter around her against the cold. "It is good to see Varian looking so relaxed. I think the puppy is good for him. Maybe he's been lonely. I've been worried about him."

"I'm still surprised he chose a poodle," Mary Jayne said.

"I'm not, he adores Dagobert." Miriam nudged her.

"He likes my dog well enough. It's just me he can't stand."

"Phooey," Miriam said, and laughed, watching the children run after the dogs hand in hand, chattering excitedly. "Oh, I'm going to miss this place." She closed her eyes as she turned her face to the sun. In the distance, the Mediterranean shimmered, light sparkling on the rose-gold surface like crystals on a gown. "I do hope I can bring Rudolf back from Ljubljana with me, he'd love it here." She laughed uneasily, and her voice shook. "I don't know what I'm going to do if they won't let us back into France."

"Don't you dare. We promised, remember? No tears," Mary Jayne said firmly, her voice throatier than usual. She took Miriam's hand, rubbing some warmth into it. "If they won't let you back in, then you just get the hell out of Europe some other way, you hear? We all know this isn't forever. The château is just . . . well, it's just a wonderful adventure, that's all. And you're not leaving yet, there's still tonight," she added, nudging her.

"You should ask one of the artists to take my room," Miriam said. "What about that chap Lambert?"

Mary Jayne narrowed her eyes. "I don't know that I trust him. There's something 'off' about him."

"Do you think so? He's been through a terrible ordeal."

"Really?"

"I found out that his wife and son were killed."

"God, how terrible. He never talks about it."

"My dear, we are all men and women of mystery these days." Miriam sighed wearily. "Too many secrets, too much to hide." She smiled at her friend. "Think about it, at least. He spends most of his time here anyway."

"I think hoping to see Marianne Bouchard has as much to do with that as paying court to Breton and the gang."

"I am glad you agreed to let Varian stay," Miriam said. She smiled as she watched him tossing a red ball for the dogs, the children racing to and fro across the lawn. "He's so happy here."

"I've certainly seen a different side to him." Mary Jayne's gaze followed three men walking up the driveway. "Who are they?"

Miriam shielded her eyes with her hand. "More surrealists, I imagine. Now Breton has arrived, they are flocking here like homing pigeons." Birdsong sparkling across the grounds melded on the air with music drifting from the house. The girls heard someone's fine baritone voice singing a barrack-room song, then laughter before others joined in with the chorus.

"It's more like Breton is a king, or pope and they're all coming to pay court to him."

"That's what this place is." Miriam laughed. "A court of miracles. I'm so glad I've had the chance to see a little of it. I'll never forget meeting men like Masson, and Breton . . ."

At that moment, André appeared at the French windows leading to the terrace, closely followed by Jacqueline. They were too far away for the girls to hear their conversation, but it was obvious they were arguing.

"I am thirty," she yelled suddenly. "My life is over!" A string of curses fell from Jacqueline's lips, her hands clutching at the air. "You see in me what you want to see, but you don't see me, André, you don't see me." Finally, she tossed her head and stalked away across the garden to where she had strung a trapeze from the branches of one of the trees. André's chin fell to his chest, and he gazed at the ground, his hands in the pockets of his green tweed jacket.

"What do you think is going on?" Miriam whispered.

"I don't know," Mary Jayne said. "I talked a little with her last night. She was happy, it seems, in Martigues. She loved the freedom and how beautiful it is there."

"Is she not happy at Air-Bel?"

"I think she loves the intellectual vibrancy of the place, but . . ." She hesitated. "It must be hard, sharing your husband with so many people." She slipped a pack of playing cards from their case and began to shuffle them.

Miriam thought of the line from Job: *If I beheld the sun when it shined, or the moon moving in brightness.* "They both have such presence. Maybe it's inevitable they clash sometimes."

"They are obviously in love. I overheard him calling her his little squirrel yesterday."

"It can't be easy, being married to a man like Breton," Miriam said quietly. "I've heard all about his reputation, the disturbances . . ."

"Oh, he's a pussycat," Mary Jayne said, laying out the cards for solitaire. "Quite charming, and so charismatic when he's talking at night, or reading from Duchamp's letters . . ." She paused, the ace of hearts in her hand. "Don't you think he is like the magnetic core of the château? He never shows off, he's just fascinating. I love it when he produces some rare copy of *Minotaure* or one of his books from those cases of his. It's like he is presenting treasure to us. His words are enchanted. . . ." She smiled, glanced quickly at Miriam. "When he says, '*Alors, on joue* . . .'"

"Don't go getting any ideas!" Miriam laughed. She looked over to where Jacqueline was swinging to and fro on the trapeze with the ease of a gymnast, her slender body flipping upside down, flexing in a smooth curve, arms outstretched to the ground. "I daren't think of the consequences." Jacqueline's seductive presence seemed to permeate the house. Whether she was working on her paintings or sitting in quiet reflection with a halo of cigarette smoke around her head, there was a refinement to her, a magic.

"I'm not interested in him like that. I just wish I understood more—I mean, what are all the games the surrealists are playing? Is it some kind of catharsis? I know humor is a great antidote to fear, but I just don't get the subtleties of what they are doing."

"I don't know. I heard André say the other night that they believe that love is a fundamental principle of moral and cultural progression." She paused.

"Love?" Mary Jayne said, her brow furrowed. "I know Breton was extolling the importance of monogamy and exclusivity the other night. It surprised me. One tends to think artists are all at it like mad."

Miriam laughed. "Why don't you ask him about it? I have no idea either—it all seems rather racy."

"You need to loosen up."

"Unlike you," Miriam said.

"I don't know what you mean."

"Mary Jayne, you will be careful, won't you?" Miriam turned to her.

"I know what I'm doing."

"Do you? What do you really know about Killer?"

"I know that I adore him, I told you," she said, smiling to herself. "I know that he makes me feel alive...."

"He's dangerous," Miriam said firmly. "How old is he? Twenty-eight, twenty-nine?"

"Actually, I found out the other day he's twenty."

"Twenty! And you are?" Miriam insisted.

"Old enough to know better, I know." Mary Jayne gave up on the game and spread the cards in her hand into a fan.

"You're thirty-one, Mary Jayne. You're nuts to be mixed up with someone like him. We don't know why he left the Foreign Legion, or what he's mixed up with here. He's trouble. Varian doesn't trust him...."

"Varian can go to hell."

"If Killer compromises the safety of our clients, of the ARC..."

"Not this again." Mary Jayne threw down the cards, scattering them on the table. "He won't. You have my word. Nothing I do will reflect badly on the ARC. Just as soon as Raymond gets out of jail, I'm going to help him get to England to fight with de Gaulle, and Varian and the precious committee won't have to fret about a thing. Honestly, they're like a bunch of old women."

"Let's not fight," Miriam said, putting her hand on her friend's arm.

"It just drives me crazy. Here I am gladly giving thousands of dollars, and I get treated like some dumb blonde." She scowled for a moment, then smiled as Miriam caught her eye.

"Danny says even when you stayed with his family in Paris, you liked the bad boys."

"Oh, Danny was forever teasing me."

"I think you just like danger. Look at the way you used to tool around Europe piloting your Vega Gull."

"My feelings for Raymond scare me, but the plane never did. I was in control." Mary Jayne's face clouded. "Perhaps I should have hung on to the plane. It would be rather useful down here, but I thought the French forces could make better use of it." She gazed into the distance, imagining how it would feel to pilot herself and Killer to freedom. She pictured her plane swooping low over the dazzling sea, flying free with him at her side. They could go anywhere—west to Lisbon or London, perhaps, then on to New York. *He'd hate it,* she thought, trying to imagine Killer in America. *He'd never come. He says he loves me, but he just wants to get back in the war, to fight. I adore him, but I have to let him go. He'll be a hero one day. That'll show them. That'll show them all.* She sensed Miriam's concern and looked at her. "You know, I've always been able to have pretty much anything I wanted in the world," she said. "But I can't have him. At least, not for long. I know that."

"Oh, Mary Jayne." Miriam took her hand.

"No, it's fine. I've quite come to terms with it." Mary Jayne lifted her chin. "I've always thought that no one and nothing can contain you," she said quietly. "Whatever stops you living your best life is your own fault—the bars are inside of ourselves, and I'm going to help set Raymond free."

The next morning, as the rest of the house slept, Mary Jayne joined Miriam in the dining room. The fire's embers still glowed in the hearth from the night before, and their eyes were red with exhaustion.

"Coffee?" Mary Jayne said, pouring a cup for Miriam. She slipped on the jacket of her pink suit and perched on the edge of the table, her feet in their white ankle socks and sandals swinging above the floor.

"So-called coffee." Her laugh was flat. Miriam gulped down her drink, scalding her mouth. "Listen, Mary Jayne, I—"

"Stop it." Mary Jayne smiled, blinking, unable to speak for a moment. "No grand farewells. This isn't good-bye. If luck's on your side, you'll be back here with Rudolf in a couple of weeks." She checked her watch. "We have to go, we mustn't miss your train. Varian and Beamish are going to meet us at the station to say good-bye."

The friends walked in silence, arm in arm along the driveway. The cold gravel was wet with dew, crunching beneath their feet. Melting snow banked on the verges still, and mist rolled among the cedar trees, birds singing their dawn chorus in the branches. At the gates, Miriam turned and took a last look at the house. Her throat was tight, her eyes welling with tears. "I'm going to miss you. I'm going to miss you all so much."

At the Gare Saint-Charles, they raced along the platform. The train was waiting, steam billowing along the roofs of the carriages. Miriam craned her head above the crowd at the sound of Beamish's whistle and saw him halfway down, holding open the door of the train, with Varian at his side.

"Thank you, Albert," she said to him, catching her breath.

Varian embraced her. "Stay safe, Davenport." He pressed his lips to the top of her head. "You stay safe, you hear?"

Miriam hugged him, tears brimming in her eyes as she turned to Mary Jayne. The girls stared at each other, unable to find the words. They fell into each other's arms as the whistle blew. "This damn war," Mary Jayne said. "What if we never find one another again?"

"We will, we will," Miriam said. She hugged her tight and whispered, "Be careful."

"Of course."

"I mean it." She took Mary Jayne by the arms. "Listen, you look out for yourself, do you hear?" Beamish swung Miriam's suitcase into the packed corridor, and Varian helped her up, slamming the door behind her. Miriam lowered the window and stuck her head out as the train pulled away. "Thank you," she said, raising her voice as the whistle blew and the train chugged out of the station. "I'll never forget any of you, any of this." She waved. "Good-bye! Good-bye! I'll see you soon, in New York!" she cried.

TWENTY-THREE

Flying Point, Long Island

2000

Gabriel

I'm struggling to keep up with her now. The girl's walking on ahead, her blond hair tumbling down, free and loose. I remember Annie standing on the shore when she was not much older than this girl, her hair blowing in the wind just like that. After the babies were asleep, she'd come down here once in a while and just stand with the surf lapping her feet, staring out at the horizon. I know she was thinking of France and everything we had left behind, but I never did. I never looked back, not until today.

The sun's going down now and the beach is luminous and empty in the half-light, Venus gleaming above us.

"Something I've always wondered . . . ," the girl says, calling over her shoulder.

I stop and try to catch my breath, but it's rattling around my chest like nickels in a tumble dryer. "Yes?"

"Why was there such a huge change in your work between 1940 and the paintings you did in America?"

Here we go. "How could I not have been affected by meeting men like Breton?"

She stops and gazes out to sea, her hand shielding her eyes against the falling sun. "Is that the best you can do?" she says. "I know a whole generation of American artists like Pollock and Rothko were all deeply affected by the exiled artists over here. I know Duchamp, and Breton, and all those people made a huge difference, but you don't make any sense."

"I'm sorry?"

"It's like you became a different person."

My hackles rise. "That's ridiculous. . . ."

"Did the war really affect you that much? I mean," she says, walking on, "your work before the war was lovely, but . . . well, decorative." She says it like an insult.

"That's the line they always throw at art deco. It was a fashion, that's all. You can't deny the sheer technical skill of my early work."

"After you arrived in America, your painting . . ." She throws her arms out to the sky, fingers extended. "It exploded. The anger, the clarity—"

"Like I said. It changed, because of the war." It changed, I changed . . . what's the difference anymore. The blood is singing in my ears now, and I rock slightly on my feet.

"Say, are you okay?" That voice. I . . .

"I'm fine."

She sits down on an old log that has washed ashore and stares out to sea. I stumble as I join her, my feet tripping in the sand. I end up sitting on the ground, my back against the smooth driftwood. Sophie's sitting behind me, so all I can hear is her voice. I feel the weightlessness of her hand on my shoulder.

"It's time. Tell me everything. What happened in Marseille, Lambert?"

TWENTY-FOUR

Rue Grignan, Marseille

November 13, 1940

Gabriel

"Still no news after your report?" I heard Beamish ask Danny. He was shuffling through the pile of papers in front of him on the desk. "Your tour of the concentration camps has to have had some effect, surely? Tens of thousands of men, women, and children are penned up behind barbed wire like animals." Beamish shook his head as he scanned Danny's meticulously typed document. "Look at this—dysentery, typhus. It's like the Middle Ages, not a modern European country." Eight men sat around the meeting table in the rue Grignan office, a single lamp illuminating the files in front of them. The main office lights had been switched off, and I sat with Charlie and Gussie in silence, guarding the street door. The truth is, I didn't much enjoy my own company in those days, and when I wasn't at Air-Bel hoping to bump into Annie, I was happier around the ARC crowd. They had grown to trust me, and I made myself useful enough around the place. The hours I spent alone dragged, and I lived in fear of bumping into Alistair Quimby. I knew he was in Marseille somewhere, and he haunted me like a specter. I would be walking through the market, my stomach groaning with hunger at the smell of the food on the stalls, and I would see him walking toward me—or at least I'd think I'd seen him, and I would run, doubling back on myself, trying to lose this ghost from my past. At least at the ARC I felt safe and among good people I could trust.

"Not a word, not a damn word from Vichy. They're not budging an inch." Beamish leaned back in his chair, his arms folded. He had his habitual pout on his lips, and though I couldn't see his face clearly in the dim light of the domed chrome lamp on Varian's desk, I knew something was wrong.

"What's up, Beamish?" Danny said.

He shrugged. "Nothing definite. I just . . ." He leaned forward into the lamplight and picked up the model airplane on the blotter. He spun its propeller speculatively. "I think it's time to get as many people out as quickly as we can. Things are changing, for the worse."

"What makes you say that?"

"It's just a feeling. Up until now the Gestapo has been happy to let the Vichy lot do their dirty work, but I think—" He was interrupted by a hammering on the front door, the glass rattling in its frame. As one, we all looked up, alarmed, like a herd of deer sensing a predator.

"Are we expecting anyone?" Danny said quietly.

"No. Varian won't be back from Vichy for a day or two." Beamish jumped up. "Stay there," he said under his breath to the men around the meeting table. "Turn out the light." He pulled the office door to and locked it behind him. "Open up," he said to Charlie. He sat quickly at the table beside me and picked up a pack of cards, dealing four hands. My fingers trembled as I fanned the cards he dealt me. Someone knocked again, harder this time.

"Hey, fellah, keep your hair on," Charlie said, noisily working his way through a hoop of keys until he saw that Beamish had settled back, casually picking through his hand of cards. Charlie ran downstairs and unlocked the main door, opening it to the street. A car rumbled by in the darkness, its dim blue lights sweeping up the staircase wall. "Why, good evening Detective Dubois," I heard Charlie say, loud and clear. "Come in out ah the cold." Charlie walked back up to the office, followed by the policeman. I glanced at Beamish, saw him pause, ready to lay a king down on the table. In the silence, I heard the click of the card on the wood.

"Monsieur Fawcett," Dubois said, taking his hat off. "Hermant, Gussie." He glanced at me. I felt the hair at the nape of my neck prickle. "May I come in for a moment?" He went to the window and lifted the blind a crack, watching the street.

"How can we help you?" Beamish said.

"Is Monsieur Fry here?" Dubois glanced at the locked office.

"No," Beamish said. "He left some time ago, for Vichy."

"No matter. It is you I came to see, Monsieur Fawcett." Dubois turned to Charlie. "It's time for you to leave town."

"Me? Why?" Charlie paled.

"You're going to be picked up in the morning."

"In the morning? But why? I haven't done a thing," Charlie said, his voice tight with anxiety.

"How do you know?" Beamish asked Dubois.

"Because you're going to be picked up," Dubois said, "by me." He put his dark trilby back on his head and stepped toward the door. "Unfortunately, Monsieur Fawcett, your gallant—if bigamous—efforts to free Jewish women from the camps has been uncovered. A couple of days ago, two Mrs. Charlie Fawcetts turned up in Lisbon at the same time." He held Charlie's gaze, his eyes crinkling. "I'll be here at six A.M. sharp."

Charlie held it open for him. "Thank you," he said, shaking his hand.

"I hope I won't be seeing you in the morning."

"You can count on it."

"Alors, bon soir, et bonne chance."

We waited until we heard the street door close behind Dubois, and then we exhaled as one.

"Jeez, Charlie," Gussie said. "You kept that one quiet. Just how many girls have you married?"

"Five or six. I kind of lost count." He raked his hand through his hair. "Darn it, of all the rotten luck. Imagine two ah them turning up on the same day. There was never anything in it for me, you know, it just seemed like a good way to get the girls out of the camps."

"Well, good for you, Charlie." Beamish knocked the table as he went to unlock the office, and the playing cards scattered on the floor.

"Was that Dubois?" Danny marched over. "What did he want?"

"They're coming for Charlie," Beamish said.

"When?"

"Tomorrow."

"Then you must leave tonight." Danny clapped his arm around Charlie's shoulders. "Don't worry, my friend, we'll get you out of here."

The meeting broke up, and one by one the men slipped away into the night. I stayed behind with Danny and Gussie to help Charlie get ready.

We worked through the night. On a small table in the kitchen, Charlie tucked some documents into the hollow center of some of his sculptures, and I helped him reseal them with plaster of Paris. Next, he rolled translucent paper lined with tiny script into narrow tubes and threaded them into the third valve of his trumpet. I knew better than to ask what the documents were—I'm not sure if Charlie knew, either, to be honest. He just wanted to help Varian get information to the United States about some of the clients in greatest danger.

"What if they ask you to play something?" I said.

"It's okay," Charlie said. "I know a few tunes where I only need a couple ah valves." The smile on his face faltered as he looked at the maps on the table. "It sure looks easy, doesn't it, when you just trace a line on a map via Gibraltar or Casablanca. Freedom seems so close." He cleared his throat. "Danny?"

"Hm?"

"It's been crazy, man, hasn't it. . . ."

Danny punched him on the arm. "This isn't good-bye, Charlie."

They glanced up as Beamish tapped out the code on the front door. Gussie ran down and let him in. "Right," Beamish said. "It's all arranged. You're going out through Spain," he said to Charlie, pulling off his woolen hat. "We're going to get you out through the station, and then in Madrid you look for the red-haired porter."

"He's a good chap," Danny said. "He's helped a lot of our clients and he'll get you to the safe house until your train for Lisbon is ready."

"But what about the border, what if I'm stopped?"

Beamish tossed a dozen packs of Gauloises Bleues and Gitanes Grises and Vertes down on the table. "These are for the guards. Just keep your head and you'll be fine. You're simply an art student, heading south. You'll have to get rid of that," Beamish said, pointing at Charlie's ambulance uniform. "Are you packed?" Charlie nodded. Beamish checked that the top of the suitcase was secure. "Good. The border guards are idiots. They never think to check for a false top to a suitcase, they're only ever interested in false bottoms. Did you manage to get everything in the sculptures? We may as well get as much information out with Charlie as we can."

I tapped the base of one. "Just about dry. If they look too closely, they'll guess."

"I know!" Charlie said, pulling a sketchbook out of his case. He dragged over a stool and quickly sketched out a voluptuous woman straight out of a pinup. "Say, Lambert, give me a hand here." He tore off a couple of sheets and handed them over to me. As Danny and Beamish wrapped the sculptures in Charlie's clothes and tucked them in the case, I sketched a leggy art deco beauty, her body entirely Vita's, her face . . . I hesitated. I had drawn Vita so many times, but now her image was fading for me. The face was Annie's. "There we go," I said, tossing the nude casually on top.

Charlie whistled in appreciation, slotting his own sketches underneath. "Hopefully, if they stop me, they'll take one look at these and won't bother searching the rest of the case."

"You know, it might just work," Danny said, tilting his head to look at the drawings. Charlie clicked the case shut and picked up his trumpet.

Beamish looked at his watch. "Come on. We need to go."

Gussie opened the street door and shook hands with Charlie. "Good luck," he said.

"You too, kid," Charlie said.

Danny embraced him. "Stay safe, you hear?"

"Will you say good-bye to Varian and the others for me?"

"Sure."

Charlie shook my hand. "Like Varian always says, I'll see you soon, in New York."

TWENTY-FIVE

Marseille

1940

Gabriel

I never knew for years what happened to Charlie. He made it through the border safely enough, thanks to his cigarettes and our saucy drawings, but it turns out he was arrested in Spain. They brought him back to France to be interrogated by the Gestapo, but the guards can't have been up to much. They left him unattended in the railway waiting room for a moment, and Charlie calmly picked up his trumpet and his little suitcase with all the hidden information and jumped onto a train that was heading down to Madrid. He was one of the golden ones, old Charlie—slipped right through the fingers of death time and time again.

Like I said before, people disappeared all the time in Marseille. It was an easy place to get lost in. The winter days rolled into one another, and I could have been there two days or two months, it felt, as I wandered the streets and waited to see Annie again. I'd taken to hanging around Air-Bel every day in the hope of seeing her, but it had been a week since the Sunday we first met, and I longed to be with her, counting the hours until our arranged meeting after her ballet class.

I was early. Of course I was, I was longing to see her. As the Saturday crowds milled around the pavements, I walked the streets, burning off some of my nervous energy. I happened to see Annie, across the road, jumping down at the tram stop on La Canebière. I raised my hand, about to call to her, but I felt foolish suddenly. I didn't want to come across as too keen. But the sight of her—I couldn't wait another hour to be with her, so I followed her to her ballet lesson like a stray puppy; she was talking and giggling with her friends, completely oblivious. The other girls were like children to me, mousy and unformed, but Annie—she was radiant, the winter sun on her blond ponytail, the sure carriage of her head. They ran up the steps to a hall near La Vieille Charité, and I snuck around the side of the building into the alley. My heart was beating fast as I climbed the old metal fire escape, the treads creaking under my boots. I could hear the piano player warming up in the hall, scales and arpeggios drifting up from an old upright piano. At the top of the fire escape, I settled down on the low wall and leaned across, peering through the clear glass corner of one of the large skylights. The girls must have still been changing, because all I could see was the gray head of the piano player, bent over the keys as his hands swept up and down. Up there, I could see across the terra-cotta tile roofs to the old baroque chapel. The delicate dome and the stonework were falling apart in those days, before Le Corbusier took an interest in the place after the war. The music stopped, and I saw the class lining up at the barre, and the gilded crown of Annie's head. Her arms unfurled like the black stamens of a flower. The girls all wore black leotards, black tights, and shoes. None were as lovely as she. I laid my cheek against the cool glass and watched her for an hour, imagining how it would feel to place my hands around that waist, so slender I was sure my fingers would touch. I think I knew I was in love with her then, as I watched, and I grew self-conscious. I slipped away and walked for a while to give her time to reach the café.

I strolled up, ten minutes late. The red awning flapped and snapped in the breeze. She was sitting outside on a bentwood café chair, her ankles crossed elegantly in front of her. She has beautiful feet still—gorgeous toes, a ballet dancer's arch, slender ankles. She was wearing a gray dress with a full skirt and a white collar. She looked a little like a novice nun, with her hair piled up on her head, but there was something in her gaze as she looked at me that sent my guts falling away like the drop of a roller coaster. Then she smiled. That little gap between her front teeth.

"Mr. Lambert," Annie said. I took her hand and pressed her fingers to my lips, our gazes meeting. From the flush in her cheeks, she felt it, too, the energy flowing between us the way the sky becomes alive before a storm. She introduced me to her friends, but I barely registered them. I felt myself expand, looking at Annie, the world shrink around us to a fine point, to her. I was polite enough, made small talk with her friends—even then I was smart enough to realize their approval would count. I ordered a coffee and cognac, and cordials for them. Annie asked for a tisane of chamomile. Once the waiter had served our table and the other girls were chatting happily over their drinks, Annie cradled the steaming white cup in her hands and blew gently, raising her gaze to mine.

"So," I said, leaning toward her, the old wicker chair creaking beneath me. The table was narrow. I could feel my leg brush lightly against hers, and our elbows were just a hand span apart.

"So," she said, her eyes creasing with amusement. "What did you think of our ballet class?"

"You saw me?"

"Of course." She glanced down the table, making sure her friends weren't listening, a smile playing on her lips. "I saw you crossing the road just after the tram stopped."

"Why didn't you say something?"

"I wanted to see what you would do." She leaned closer. "I don't think you would make a good spy, you stand out in a crowd, Mr. Lambert—"

"Gabriel." I was so close to her, I could smell the sweet herb scent of her tea. The cognac warmed my stomach. I could feel a golden heat thawing the coldness from my torso, my limbs, my fingertips. Or was it Annie made me feel like that?

"I felt you, watching from the skylight like a naughty black cat."

"But you didn't look up once."

Annie shrugged. "Didn't want to spoil your fun."

I pressed my mouth to my knuckles to stop myself laughing in my embarrassment. "I'm sorry. I couldn't resist. You looked so beautiful." She lowered her eyes. "Are you angry with me?"

"No, I'm touched you wanted to see me again so badly." She blinked. "I did, too."

"I've thought of little else all week," I murmured. The space between us seemed to contract. I felt light-headed with longing for her. A raucous shriek from one of the other girls broke the moment. A couple of boys they knew dragged over a table to join them. Annie introduced me to them, and we waited for the table to settle down. She looked from the boys to me.

"How old are you?" she said quietly, leaning toward me again.

"How old do you think I am?"

She cupped her chin on her hand and studied my face. I wondered what she saw. The flecks of gray at my temples, the dark olive skin?

"Too old," she said, a smile playing on her lips.

I folded my arms and leaned in to her. "Too old for what?"

"For me." She laughed. "My father would never allow me to step out with a man like you."

I lowered my voice. "What if I told you I was eighteen years old?"

She threw back her head and laughed. "I'd say you were the biggest liar I had ever met." See, Annie knew me well even then.

"Well, the answer is easy," I said, tracing my finger on the table, achingly close to her hand. "We don't tell him."

"A secret?"

I glanced at the kids at the table with us. They were deep in some conversation about the war, not paying any attention to us. I was dizzy with wanting her, quite sick with desire. My thumb stroked the inside of her wrist, the lightest touch. She didn't take her hand away. "I have to see you alone." I could see from the rise and fall of the small gold crucifix strung around her neck that she was breathing quickly.

"Tomorrow," she whispered. "Meet me at three o'clock on Sunday, under the railway bridge at La Pomme."

TWENTY-SIX

Marseille

1940

Gabriel

I skipped some of Breton's meeting for her, and we met every Sunday from then on in the same place. It was a narrow little bridge, barely a car wide, with elegant stone walls sweeping up the steep embankment to the railway track above. It always felt like entering a grotto as I stepped into the darkness, like something from a fairy tale. I don't know where her parents thought she was, but she brought a little dog with her, and we walked in the woods. It was a greasy-looking terrier that growled every time I went near her and nipped at my ankles. In the end, I had to tie it to a tree so I could kiss her. That first kiss I remember in perfect detail. She leaned back against a bare winter tree and waited for me. The leaves were soft and wet on the ground, my footsteps muffled. The clouds were low, enfolding the trees like a blanket. It was so quiet, I could hear my own breath and the slow drip of water from the branches.

"I saw Madame Breton in the village the other day," she said. "She was like an exotic bird, with feathers in her hair."

"You know she is the wife of André Breton, the famous surrealist?"

"The writer? Even I've heard of his poems." She tilted her head as I put my arms either side of her, trapping her against the tree. "She must have seen us together. She asked me if I was seeing 'that handsome Gabriel Lambert.'"

"Did she now? What did you say?"

"I told her I knew you." Annie shrugged. Her eyes were lowered. "We walked back to the house together."

"What did you talk about?"

"She told me about meeting her husband. She said a love like that is an illness from which you never recover. Do you think she is right?"

"Even geniuses are idiots when they talk about love." I sensed her disappointment and backtracked quickly. My head was swimming with desire for her. "I hope that I never recover from you."

Annie raised her gaze to mine. "She said to me just being pretty isn't enough for a woman to become and remain a part of a great man's life."

"Oh, Annie . . ."

"What if I'm not enough for you? What if you get tired of me? I'm not a great artist, like you, I haven't traveled, or learned things, not like you—"

"Annie," I said, and cupped her jaw in my hand. "If only you knew . . ." I hesitated. "If only you knew how I've loved you from the moment I saw you. My love is . . ." I looked up at the sky, searching for a way to express how I felt about her. "My love is more than the stars. It is like Venus, the morning star. It is there, all the time, night and day, burning brightest of all." I felt her relax; her head fell back. I knew Annie was ready then, waiting. There had been no hurry with her, no urgency, not like Vita, just a slow, deep longing for home. There was an inevitability to us. I remember the roughness of the bark beneath my hands as I leaned in to her, the moment just before my lips touched hers, how the world seemed to dissolve and fall away, a burning light around us as my eyes closed.

Annie may have hidden me from her parents, but they would have been proud of the way she held on to her virginity. I tried everything short of downright begging, but I fell for the only girl not making love during the war. Every Sunday I traveled to La Pomme and walked miles with that damn little terrier snarling at me, all for a kiss and the hope of more. She was beautiful, and mercurial, and I wanted her, so I came each week. By December, Marseille lay under a blanket of slush. My feet were permanently wet or cold, I remember. It's very true: if your feet are comfortable, you can cope with a lot in life. What is it they say, an army marches on its stomach? Stupid saying, it marches on decent boots. Anyway, I was starving hungry *and* my feet were bad. They have been, ever since the war. I endured chilblains and tormented nights for Annie, but it was no more than she deserved.

"I like this," I said one Sunday, touching the embroidered gold scarf she was wearing.

"Do you? I made it." She slipped it from her neck and wrapped it around mine. "Here," she said. "Keep it."

"I couldn't."

"Please, it would make me happy to think of you wearing it when we aren't together." She tucked it into the lapel of my coat. "Besides, I think you need it more than me. Your lips are blue." She kissed me. "Better?"

"I'll treasure it. Thank you." I rubbed the pale gold wool between my fingers. "It's beautifully warm."

"It's cashmere." She had embroidered it with hundreds of stars. Later, when I read Yeats's "Aedh Wishes for the Cloths of Heaven," I thought he had written it for us. That's what we did on those walks—we spread our dreams before each other like an offering.

We talked for hours about everything and nothing. She asked me about Paris, about my family, about art school, and I told her. I lied as little as I could, yet I kept the truth about America from her. I think I was afraid I would lose her. Now that I had found her, it made the knowledge that I would leave soon harder to bear.

One evening—it must have been at the beginning of December—I was heading back to my lonely bed in town after walking her home. We had been to the Santon fair together, and Annie had bought me the little shepherd. It had been the most wonderful afternoon, and I felt a rare contentment as the tram trundled back into town. There was mist in the valley, only the tops of the roofs and umbrella pines poking out as the tram trundled along its route to La Canebière. Everyone huddled up on the tram had the sunken look of cold and hunger. I was no different, but I was lit up inside with love. You can endure anything when you feel like that. I decided to buy her something for Christmas and remembered an old jewelry store I had passed with her on the way to the Vieux-Port.

I stopped in the café Au Brûleur de Loups for a cognac on the way.

"Non, monsieur," the bartender said, pointing at a sign tacked above the bar: *Jour sans alcool.* "I can offer you a glass of champagne instead, perhaps?"

"It doesn't feel like a day for champagne," I said, and ordered an espresso instead. I love that about the French. Once in a while they banned booze, but you could still get a restorative glass of champagne. I hail from a civilized nation. As the bartender cranked the machine for my coffee, steam poured out, hissing and gurgling. I leaned against the zinc bar and looked in the mirror behind the bottles. Above the noise of the coffee machine, I could hear Varian's voice. I sipped at the scalding coffee and listened. I could just see in the mirror that he was sitting at the back of the café with Beamish, talking. I wandered over and greeted them.

"May I join you?" I said.

"Hello, Lambert. Of course." Varian moved aside his overcoat, and I pulled out the wooden chair. "How are things at the hotel?"

I shrugged. "Not bad. It is the waiting that is getting to me."

"You seem to be passing your time constructively," Beamish said, a smile playing across his lips.

"What do you mean?" I said.

"Your girlfriend is very beautiful."

"She's not . . . I mean . . . ," I said, blushing furiously.

"Leave the poor fellow alone, Beamish," Varian said, laughing. "Besides, you are one to talk." He leaned conspiratorially toward me. "This chap has a new girl every time I see him."

"And you don't have an eye for a good-looking woman, Buster?" Beamish held Varian's gaze until he looked away, smiling. If Varian had affairs, he was certainly discreet. I never saw him with anyone.

"How are you getting on with the receptionist from the consulate?" he said to Beamish.

"Camille?" He cocked his head. "It is a sacrifice I must make to help our cause." I remembered the tough-looking blonde at the desk the day I met Bingham. If he was seeing her, he was a stronger man than me.

"Does she help you with the visas?" I said, leaning toward him. Sure, I knew that the ARC was the legitimate front for more clandestine work, but they were still careful with the amount of information they let me in on. Beamish looked uncomfortable.

"The ARC needs all the help it can get," Varian said carefully, "and Camille helps."

"A little," Beamish added. "She has an expensive cocaine habit, and I suspect she is selling information to both sides to fund her habit."

"It must be dangerous, though, the work you do?"

Beamish stared me down. "Not at all. We simply help refugees with visas, give them money for food and hotels. What could be dangerous about that?" I realized I had overstepped the line.

"Of course, I understand." I drained my cup and stood. "Good to see you both."

"Are you leaving? Breton and the others will be here soon. I thought you'd come for the meeting," Varian said.

"I am sorry, I have an appointment," I lied. The truth was, I was still so in awe of Breton, the thought of being in this small café with him intimidated me. He was the magus around which an ever-changing cast of writers and artists fluttered, moths to a flame. He knew—that's what his eyes said, every time he looked at me. He knew. I felt, somehow, that if my gaze met his, I'd turn to stone.

"Will you be up at the château on Sunday?" Varian asked.

"I wouldn't miss it." I glanced at Beamish. "How come I never see you up there?"

"Beamish prefers to stay in town," Varian said.

"One of us needs to." As Beamish looked at me, I felt my cheeks burn. "There are too many people playing games around here."

I walked on through the narrow streets, deep in thought. I had no idea, then, how remarkable Varian, Beamish, and all of them were, of the risks they were taking. On the surface, Varian seemed like the archetypal preppy—oh sure, if you saw him up at Air-Bel letting his hair down, there was a different side to him, but you'd still say he was straight as a die. Beamish, I couldn't figure out. He was smart, real smart, no hiding that, but it wasn't obvious in the way it was with Varian. He was, as the French say, *un peu dans la lune*. But there was another side to him—when I was up at the château one day, I heard Danny saying that Beamish had fought with the Republicans down in Spain. I admired him, I guess. I wish I'd known him better.

I found myself at the jewelry store before I knew where I was. The old woman was just closing up, turning over the sign on the door, but she let me in. The old brass bell on a hooped spring over the door tinkled. It was warm inside, a little stove behind the counter glowing in the dim light.

"There, that bracelet, please." I pointed to a silver charm bracelet, with stars and shells, in the window. The woman wrapped it in tissue paper and put it in a small red box for me. I walked out of the shop on air, buoyed up at the thought of giving it to Annie the next day. I rounded the corner of the street with a spring in my step, and then someone grabbed my arm.

"I thought I'd seen a ghost," he said.

"Quimby?" My bowels went slack. I would have run, but he had me by the arm, and I didn't want to make a scene with so many people around. Quimby was the one man who could destroy me, and I didn't want him spouting off to the police if we started a fight. He pushed me into a dark alleyway. I could see in the half-light the expressions rolling across his face as he put two and two together.

"Well, well. I was right." He tightened his grip. "What on earth do you think you are doing? I went back to the house to get you and the paintings and found it all burnt to hell. I had the buyer all lined up."

"It's not what you think," I said quickly. My heart was jumping around in my rib cage like a cricket. "I didn't—"

"Kill them?"

"How can you say that?" I pulled my arm free. "You owe—"

"I owe you nothing, you shit," Quimby said, spittle flecking my face. "The thing is, the paintings I have left are selling like hotcakes...."

"My paintings," I said, squaring up to him.

"I'm going to sell the lot before I get the hell out of this dump." He pushed me back against the alley wall, the heel of his hand pressing into my sternum. "Speaking of which, how much have you got on you?"

"I'm not giving you any money."

"You will give me exactly what I want, if you know what's good for you."

"I need time."

"That is one thing we have plenty of," Quimby said. "We're all trapped like rats here. Just remember, one word to the authorities—"

I searched in my pocket, felt the red jewelry box under my fingertips. I pulled out the notes I had left and handed them to him. Luckily I had hidden most of the money I'd rescued from the Château d'Oc under a loose board in my hotel room, and I had already put down the money for my ticket to America once boats became available. "That's all I have."

"All you have, or all you have on you?" He sneered. "Don't try and play games with me. I know how much you took from the château. There was always plenty of cash in the desk. I want another five hundred francs next Friday. I'll meet you outside the Notre-Dame de la Garde."

"I don't have it."

"Then find it." Quimby tucked the money into his breast pocket. "I want you to keep a low profile. Not that you would be hanging out in the kind of hotels my clients are staying in." He pulled on a pair of black kid leather gloves and turned up his collar. "I wouldn't want them to bump into you, that's all. And in case you get any ideas about not showing up, you should know I've been following you for a couple of days. I know all about the ARC, and that pretty little blonde." My mouth went dry. "You should also know that I have certain photographs of you in Vita's studio. . . ."

"Rubbish, you're bluffing."

Quimby calmly pulled out his wallet and slipped out a black-and-white photograph folded in four. I fought the urge to retch. The night returned to me. The flash of Quimby's camera reflected in the mirror near Vita's easel, the pop and hiss of the bulb.

"Don't you dare threaten me," I said quietly. The blood rushed and sang in my ears. Could I thump him, steal his wallet? But Quimby had said "photographs"—he had more, somewhere? I racked my brain, trying to remember that night.

"I'll do what I damn well like." He tucked the photo away. "And don't think about disappearing in this cesspool of a city, or I'll be straight round to nice Mr. Fry with the rest of the charming photos I took at the Château d'Oc."

"You wouldn't dare. I'll . . . I'll . . ." I was right. Panic washed through me, chill and sickening.

"What are you going to do? Bump me off?" He laughed, a quick exhalation through his nose. "Or *did* you do it?" I saw his teeth gleam in the blue streetlight as he turned away, smiling. "Who cares? For what I'll get for the paintings I'll risk dealing with a murderer."

Quimby was clever, that's for sure. He wormed his way straight to the heart of the thing that kept me awake at night. Did I kill them? Sometimes, in the sleepless hours, I still wonder if I pulled that door to and sealed their fate. I stood in the alleyway for a few minutes after Quimby left, shaking with shock and cold.

TWENTY-SEVEN

Flying Point, Long Island

2000

Sophie

The light is dazzling, flaring on the water, on the white sand. Sophie tastes salt on her lips as she bites the bottom one, searching in her bag for her phone. She is some way from the Lamberts' house, alone. She has ignored the insistent ring of the old-phone tone twice already, and she goes to switch it off but then sees it is Jess.

"Where are you?" he says the moment she answers.

"Flying Point." Sophie sinks down on her haunches and looks out to sea. "I can't talk now." She rakes her hand through her hair. "It feels like I've walked miles. I'm going round and round in circles. . . ."

"Listen, be careful, okay?"

"What do you mean, be careful?"

"I've been doing some snooping around for you." She hears the slight slur to his words, the background noise of a bar somewhere.

"I can look after myself."

"I know, I know." The phone muffles as he tucks it beneath his jaw. "But I've something that might make a difference."

"To the story?"

"To how much you care about the story. To us."

Sophie exhales and glances over her shoulder. She settles down on the sand. "Go on, then."

"Tell me what you know about your dad's family."

"What? Where's this going, Jess?" Sophie frowns with frustration. "My great-grandfather was from London. He married an American girl, Sophie, who I'm named for. They had two children, my great-aunt Vita and my grandfather Sam. There was some kind of argument, and Vita went off to France before World War Two. When my great-grandfather was killed, Sophie moved back to the U.S. with Sam—I think she met a GI, or something, in London?"

"Right so far." Sophie's eyes narrow at his cocky tone. "Go on."

"Vita, as we know, died in France." Sophie squeezes the bridge of her nose. "I'm going to get to the bottom of that."

"And what about your grandfather Sam?"

"I . . . I don't know much about his past." Sophie hears Jess exhale a short, soft laugh.

"Go on," he says.

"Sam met a girl in New York sometime in the early fifties, and they had a kid—my father, Jack Cass."

"Nope, not necessarily."

"What do you mean, 'nope'?"

"I mean, what if Sam Cass isn't your grandfather?" Jess sounds triumphant. "I can't believe you didn't check this out—"

Sophie leaps up and paces along the shore. "What are you talking about?"

"It's basic Journalism 101. Take everything you believe to be true that you are basing your story on, and make damn sure it is before you start work. I knew you would have taken this for granted. You trust people too much, Soph." She hears him take a hit of his drink. "Old Sam must have been a stand-up guy, because he married a girl with a small baby." Sophie hears the rattle of ice cubes. "Who knows, maybe it was a lavender marriage and he had something to hide himself; they didn't have any more kids—"

"You're drunk." Sophie closes her eyes, and the bright corona of the sun flares red and orange behind her eyelids.

"I may be drunk, but I'm right. There's a blank on your daddy's birth certificate under 'Father.'"

"Why are you doing this?"

"So that you'll give up on this dumb story, and come to Paris with me. The great Jack Cass was a bastard. There's no family connection now, no magical free-spirited Great-aunt Vita that you clearly wish you were more like—"

"That's low." Sophie shakes her head. "Dumb story?"

"Hey, don't shoot the messenger," Jess says. "It's not your story, Cass. Let the past go."

"Do you really think I care any less about it because of this? You're right about one thing, Sam was a stand-up guy. Whatever the deal was with their relationship, he and my grandmother loved one another, Jess—really loved one another, and they loved Dad."

"I didn't mean—"

"I grew up listening to Sam's stories about Vita, and if you don't get how inspiring hearing about a woman who was creative, and smart, and not afraid of anything was to a kid, then that's your loss." It feels like something has broken free inside her. "If you thought shattering my dreams would make me settle for you, then you were wrong."

"Hey, Cass, hold on—"

"Do you think I care for one moment if Vita's not a blood relation? She's family, Jess. We loved her, and she died. She was younger than me, and I just want to find out the truth, for me and for Dad."

"Yeah, it's all about Daddy. . . ."

"What was I, Jess? Your idea of the perfect girlfriend for the great American writer?"

"Soph, you were—you are, perfect for me—"

"Perfect pedigree? You loved the idea of that, at first, didn't you? Jack Cass's daughter. My dad may have been a bastard as you so charmingly put it, but he was still a better writer than you'll ever be."

"What happened to you?"

"I grew up." Sophie raises her chin. "I owe it to him to write this story, and then I'm done."

"Paris?"

"No, Jess. You've always been so hung up on proving that you are better than my dad, and you've just shown me you are nowhere near the man he was. He was human, and fallible, and wonderful, and he loved me and my mom. You've never loved anyone but yourself, Jess. I deserve more than that."

"You've met someone, haven't you," he says. Sophie thinks of their conversation in the bar the night before. "Is it serious?"

She glances over her shoulder, feels her stomach tighten at the thought of Harry. She's angry, but there's a fierce inevitability to it. "Nothing's happened." She realizes it's not true as she says it. *Nothing's happened—yet.* "It's over, Jess. It was over with us when you left me, and now I'm over you."

"Good luck to him, whoever the hell he is." Jess's words roll together, angry and hurt. "He's going to have to be one hell of a man to shape up to your daddy. I mean, what was it about him, eh? What did Jack Cass ever do for you that I couldn't? I know you. I know there's something you haven't told me."

"Thanks, Jess," she says calmly. "Thank you for making one decision a whole lot easier." Sophie turns and gazes out at the endless blue sea. "Take care of yourself. Good-bye."

Sophie cups the phone in both hands, fights the urge to throw it out to sea. She wants Jess, and his jealousy, gone, gone for good. *What did Jack Cass ever do for you?* Her chest rises and falls, her heart a staccato beat. *You'll never know now, Jess.*

"How was ballet?"

Sophie can remember her father's voice, still. She remembers the feel of her mittened hand in his, how she leaned in to the warmth of his overcoat, her head resting against his hip, the soft leather of his jacket—the smell of tobacco and motorbike oil. Steam rose from the pavement vent at their side as they waited to cross West Seventy-ninth Street. She remembers it all.

"Ballet was good. I'm ready for the exam next week."

"Good girl. Always give one hundred and ten percent, remember that." She feels him tighten his grip on her hand as they walk on up Broadway.

"I'm starving. Can we get a milkshake?"

Jack glances at his watch. "Your mom needs some groceries from Zabar's, and I've got to get back to work, honey. We'll be at the apartment in a few minutes, can't you wait?"

"I'll be quick, I promise." Sophie points at an old drugstore on the side street, its neon sign and chrome silver front blurred by the first snow falling. "Come on...." Her hand slips from his, and she backs away, daring him. "We can share a chocolate one."

"You're on," Jack says. He scoops her up into his arms and runs toward the drugstore.

Sophie remembers pushing open the door of the drugstore, the old bell ringing high above her, the warm draft of air. They sit at the lunch counter, her feet swinging above the chrome bar of the stool. The windows are steamed up, the streetlights and headlights beyond a pastel blur. It is busy. They have to wait for their order. She remembers the anticipation, swinging impatiently on the stool, round and round as Jack flicks through *The New York Times*. Finally, the waitress hands over the metal mixing cup and two glasses, two red-and-white-striped waxed paper straws.

Sophie has thought of this moment so often, it has a hyperreal quality. The red of the Formica counter is vivid. She sees her small hand on the counter, reaching for her glass, the smooth flow of the milkshake, hears the hiss of the coffee machine. Just as Jack begins to pour, the shop bell rings again.

Sophie's stomach lurches now with fear.

TWENTY-EIGHT

VILLA AIR-BEL, MARSEILLE

1940

VARIAN

"T*imeo Danaos et dona ferentes,*" Varian murmured, gazing up at the murals in the library. "Beware of Greeks bearing gifts." From the hall below, voices drifted up and among them the clear sound of a young American woman, saying, "And this is for the children."

"You shouldn't have," he heard Danny saying. "Thank you, Miss Guggenheim."

"Peggy," Varian said, jogging downstairs. He was struck as usual by her warm and anxious gaze. It always seemed out of place, somehow, in such an angular, confident woman. Her hesitation, her nervousness, made him want to protect her. Even her slightly bulbous nose added to the charm of her face.

"What a darling place you've found!" Peggy Guggenheim stepped across the black-and-white tiles of the hall and turned in a slow circle, taking the house in. "How clever of you, Varian."

"It was nothing to do with me." Varian glanced at Mary Jayne. She leaned against the doorway to the living room, smoking a cigarette, one arm crossed over her rib cage. "Miriam and Mary Jayne masterminded the whole thing." He registered her slow approval. "We're very happy here," Varian said. "May I take your coat?"

"Oh, no, my dear. It's frightfully cold." She pulled the collar of her dark sable coat tighter, burying her head farther down. "Aren't you freezing?"

"You get used to it." Varian ushered her into the living room.

"I'm so pleased to be here, at last. The artists talk of little else except Breton's Sunday salons." She cupped the curl of her hair in her palm and buoyed it up. "Air-Bel and Countess Lily Pastré's estate at Montredon are like sanctuaries in a dark night, the calm eyes of the storm. . . ."

Varian raised his eyebrows at Mary Jayne as Peggy walked on.

"Lily's a remarkable woman," Peggy said. "I believe Masson is in hiding with her, is he not? And Pablo Casals, Josephine Baker. Under any other circumstances it would be a marvelous party, wouldn't it?"

"Come and warm up, Peggy," Mary Jayne drawled. "Can I get you a drink?"

"A cognac, perhaps? Just to warm up." Peggy curled up on the rug before the fire, her thin legs tucked beneath her body. "Well, who are you?" she said to Clovis, who rolled over on his back, paws cycling the air. "I've met old Dagobert, but you are a handsome young fellow, aren't you?"

"Thank you," Varian said.

"Not you, my dear, I meant the dog."

Varian laughed. "I know you did, Peggy. He's mine, for my sins, aren't you? He's a scoundrel. Can't get him to do a damn thing I want him to."

"Poodles are clever dogs," she said, smoothing Clovis's belly. "You have to make him think it's his idea." She glanced up at Mary Jayne and took a balloon glass of cognac from her. "Thank you, darling."

"Your earrings are adorable, Peggy."

She touched the tiny paintings set in gold dangling from her ears. "Tanguy painted them for me. Do you like them? Now, you must tell me everything. How are you? Will you be going back to the States soon?"

Mary Jayne shrugged. "Perhaps."

"You must, it really is time for us to hightail it out of here, don't you think?" She sipped her drink. "Why, I've spent the last couple of months packing up my art collection single-handedly." She inspected her broken, torn nails. "At least the paintings are safely on their way to Grenoble now."

"The museum agreed to store them for you?"

Peggy nodded. "Now, I just need to get myself to safety." She looked up at Mary Jayne. "If you are leaving for New York soon, may I take your room here?"

She frowned. "I'm not leaving." She glanced at Varian. "Yet."

"I've been wanting to ask you about something," Varian said to Peggy.

He watched as Mary Jayne settled on a sofa on the other side of the room. The sound of a woman's laughter drifted through from the open door.

Peggy scowled. "I suppose all those ghastly fake surrealist wives have taken roost here, too? I—" She broke off and flung her arms up in greeting. "Jacqueline!" Peggy put her glass on the hearth and jumped up.

Jacqueline strode into the room, her full coat swinging. She brought the fresh scent of cold air and the woods with her. "Peggy." She opened her arms in an embrace. Varian noticed that both women kept their eyes open, their faces strained as they kissed once, twice. "What a marvelous surprise. Are you staying?" The edge to her voice made him think of paper cuts.

"A couple of days. I have some business to finish up, and then I'll be back again. I adore it here, it's just like Paris, don't you think, with all the surrealists wandering around in a vague way?"

"How delightful. We must . . ." Jacqueline followed the direction of Peggy's gaze, and her voice trailed off as she realized Peggy wasn't paying the slightest attention. Peggy's face lit up as André walked into the hall, nudging the main door closed with his shoulder. His arms were laden with branches and kindling. She rushed forward, beckoning to Danny and Gabriel.

"Boys!" she cried. "Come and help me. Monsieur Breton should not be carrying logs. It's like seeing Leonardo da Vinci take out the trash."

André carried the wood through. "Nonsense, Peggy," he said. "We are all doing our bit to help run the château, and this is a delightful chore." He tossed the wood into the fire basket and turned to his wife, taking Jacqueline's coat from her shoulders. Aube ran into the room and flung her arms around her father's leg. She glared at Peggy. "You remember our daughter?"

"Of course! Charming," Peggy said, taking up her spot in front of the fire by Varian again. As the Bretons busied themselves with unwrapping scarves and gloves, Peggy leaned in to Varian. "The child's a pest in cafés. I mean, he's clearly besotted with her, terribly indulgent. Don't you think that's what happens if you have children after forty?" She took a cigarette from Varian's silver case and waited for him to light it. "Thank you." Peggy rested her head back against the marble pillar of the fireplace and exhaled. "He must have mellowed. I remember a story about an outburst in Paris when a woman with a baby carriage bumped into him on the street. He rounded on the poor woman and said, 'If you must shit out a child, keep it away from me.' But look at him now, with the girl, he adores her, don't you think?" She stretched and sighed. "Do you have children, Varian?"

"My wife is keen. In fact, she's hoping I'll bring home a war orphan."

"Instead you're bringing her a poodle?" Peggy roared with laughter. "Varian, you're incorrigible. Oh, it is good to sit still for a while, isn't it? I feel like I have been running for months."

"How did you get out of Paris in the end?"

"My dear, it was a close-run thing. Can you believe the idiotic life we were living there? Everyone was determined to party that summer. Do you remember the ridiculous craze for yo-yos? Why, Cartier even made a gold one. Such nonsense." Peggy shook her head. "Why, right up until the last minute we were sitting in cafés drinking champagne while trains were pouring in with machine-gunned refugees. The day Hitler stormed Norway, I walked into Léger's studio and bought a 1919 painting."

"I heard you have been buying a lot of work," Varian said carefully.

Peggy laughed throatily. "People accuse me of profiteering—well, let them. The artists need money. Picasso, if you can believe it, had the nerve to turn me away at the door of his studio, and said, 'Lingerie is on the next floor.' Hateful man. But then, I loathe myself sometimes." She sipped her drink. "I got out on June twelfth, two days before the Nazis marched in. I'd been stockpiling *bidons* of gasoline on my terrace."

"A good move."

"Well, I just bundled my maid and my two Persian cats into the Talbot and hightailed it out of there. I tell you, it is marvelous to be here, just marvelous."

"Do you know the Bretons well?"

Peggy pursed her lips. "I wouldn't say I was part of the surrealist circle in an orthodox sense, but I am a great admirer of Breton." Her eyes dilated as she looked at André. "Have you not noticed the effect he has on people? No one is immune to his charm."

Varian shifted his arm and spoke quietly to her. "Listen, Peggy, if you really want to do something to help these artists, I realize it must be tempting to head to the U.S. as quickly as possible, but I wondered if you had paid any thought to my suggestion that you take over the ARC from me. Those blithering idiots in New York have no idea what's really going on here, and we need someone good if the office is to carry on its work."

"Of course I have thought about it, in fact I talked to the American consul about it only this morning." Varian's heart sank. "It's preposterous. What do I know about refugee work?"

"About as much as I did when I took over this job," Varian said. "You've got to remember, Peggy. I was an editor at Headline Books. I am an editor . . . that is, if they'll keep my job open any longer. I was only meant to be here a couple of weeks. I need to get home, to work and to my wife."

"I simply can't help. The consul advised me to have nothing to do with you all." Peggy glanced at him. "Though of course I don't pay attention to everything he says."

"The thing is, Peggy, this work is taking its toll on my health." He hesitated, thinking of Eileen's latest letter. "And my marriage."

Peggy placed her hand on his. "You are doing marvelous, wonderful work here. But I'll be honest, the black market atmosphere in Marseille terrifies me. The very thought of arrest . . ." She shivered. "I daren't think what you are really up to, behind the scenes, to get all these people out safely. I'm not cut out for espionage. I'm sorry, Varian, I just can't. You do understand?" She picked up her glass. "I am happy to give you money, though, and I guarantee I'll pay for the passages of the Bretons and Max Ernst to America. . . ."

"André," she called. "Does the thought of America excite you? I was thinking when I establish my gallery, you could use it as the court for your surrealist gatherings."

"Thank you, Peggy." His face grew somber. "America is . . . necessary. I cannot say I like exiles a great deal."

"Oh, my dear, it will be splendid—"

"Have you met Max?" Varian interrupted Peggy, quickly changing the subject when he saw André's discomfort.

"Not yet. I find his work quite dazzling," she said.

"I believe he has a similar effect on women, too."

"Varian, you are naughty." She cocked her head. "Though I am quite seduced by the idea of him, and his work."

André paced at the center of the living room, reading from a letter from Marcel Duchamp. Varian looked around the room—people had squeezed onto sofas, shared chairs carried through from the dining room. Jacqueline sat near the fire, with Aube curled asleep in her arms. *His voice is mesmerizing, like a spell,* Varian thought. He smiled to himself at the expression of awe on Gabriel Lambert's face. *What is it with men like Breton? This power they carry? He's more like a shaman than a poet.*

As Breton held court, Varian thought of that morning. He had gone out early to walk in the grounds while it was silent. They had all stayed up late the night before, as usual, so no one was up yet, or so he thought. He walked quietly downstairs, his socks slipping on the wooden stairs. At the landing he paused and listened. Behind the closed doors he could sense breathing. Varian padded down to the hall and sat on the bottom step to pull his shoes on. He buttoned up his coat and slung his binoculars around his neck.

The crisp air was like a tonic to him, clearing the pain of his hangover. *I'm drinking too much,* he thought, marking off the dull ache of his kidneys, his head, his ulcer. He breathed deeply as he walked, one gloved hand balled in the palm of the other. His thoughts fell into the rhythm of his steps as he ran through the urgent cases they had coming that week. Of the clients most in danger, the German politicians Hilferding and Breitscheid were still in hiding, and they were no closer to getting the editor Bernhard or "Baby" Mehring, the poet, out.

The sound of an ax chopping wood caught his attention, and Varian raised his binoculars, looked ahead through the forest. A thin, worried-looking man with gray, sunken cheeks was swinging halfheartedly at the trunk of a birch in the woods. *"Bonjour, monsieur,"* Varian called. *Someone else can't sleep.* The man turned quickly in surprise.

"I am not stealing."

"It is none of my business. We don't own these woods."

"Thumin said it would be all right. I am paying him." His eyes darted. Varian thought of a thrush he had held in his hands once, the quick-fire beat of its heart, how fragile its bones felt. He saw the man staring at his binoculars.

"I was hoping to see some birds." Varian suddenly realized the man was frightened. "Do you live in the village?"

"I am Bouchard."

"Varian Fry. How do you do." He stepped forward, his hand extended. Bouchard made no move to shake his hand, so he awkwardly folded his arms. "You live over by old Thumin? I've seen your daughter, Marianne, around." He said no more, seeing the sudden flash of concern on the man's face.

"You are at Air-Bel?"

"I hope we don't disturb you?"

Bouchard chewed at the inside of his cheek. "We hear the music, at night. We see the people coming and going from the parties."

"Perhaps you and your family would like to come over one evening, to meet everyone?"

"No. I don't think so." He swung the ax. "We are quiet people, Monsieur Fry. Your friends would do well not to ruffle feathers here. We do not like 'artists' and . . ."

Go on, say it. Degenerates. Say it. "Is that a threat?"

"A threat? No. Just some neighborly advice." The ax hit the trunk of the tree, splintering the wood. The elm's bare branches shook and rattled above them.

Varian cursed under his breath as he stalked back to the house. *Ignorant bloody peasants. . . .* In his heart, though, he knew Bouchard was right. Air-Bel was attracting too much attention with the nonstop parade of flamboyant characters making their pilgrimage to the Sunday salons. *Perhaps it would be safer to keep a lower profile.* The glimmer of a candle in the greenhouse distracted him. Holding his breath, he stepped a little closer and peered through the misted glass. Among the dusty leaves, he saw André sitting at a small table, sheaves of paper with green script littering the books in front of him, scattering to the cracked terra-cotta floor. A candle flickered at his elbow. He wore a heavy green wool dressing gown, and he had his head in his hands, his fingers raking his thick chestnut hair. His eyes were squeezed closed in absolute despair. Varian felt the hot prickle of shame. He felt like a voyeur, a gawping tourist outside the cage of a lion.

Varian studied André's face now as he paced magisterially within the circle of artists and writers. André had said to him one night that he had no time for empty moments of depression, though he seemed plagued by them. *Not a trace of that anguish now,* Varian thought as he sipped his wine. A shriek from the hall stopped Breton's soliloquy. He pushed his way through the crowd, Varian on his heels.

"What is it?" Varian said. Breton was kneeling over the prone form of the maid, Rose. She had lost a scuffed shoe and had a hole in the bottom of one stocking. Gabriel appeared at Varian's shoulder and inhaled sharply.

"Is she all right?" he said. Varian heard the anxiety in his voice. Rose lay at the bottom of the stairs, vomit staining her white apron red.

André scooped her into his arms. "It's red wine, not blood," he said. "But I will examine her just to make sure."

"Monsieur Breton!" Madame Nouguet rushed forward. "You must not soil yourself. I'll fetch the gardener. . . ."

"Nonsense, madame," he said, carrying the girl upstairs.

"Such a marvelous man," she said, wringing her hands.

"She'll be fine," Varian said to Gabriel. "Come on, have another drink, old chap." He clapped him on the back.

"I'm sorry," Gabriel said. "When I saw her lying there, it just . . . it reminded me of something." *Of someone*, Varian thought.

"Why is André dealing with the wretched girl?" Peggy said. "A great man like him. The girl was covered in vomit." She looked as though she were chewing wasps.

"André is a doctor, did you not know that?" Jacqueline said smoothly. She squeezed past with Aube in her arms, the little girl's head curled peacefully in the curve of her mother's neck. "It's late. I must get the little one to bed." She glanced at Peggy. "Sleep well."

"A doctor?" Peggy said.

"I had no idea," Gabriel said to Varian as he handed him a full glass of wine. "I still find it remarkable to see him . . . I mean, he's a legend. To see him collecting wood, or tending to that girl . . ."

"She's an alcoholic, clearly." Peggy clicked her tongue. "I could smell it on her as she served the soup."

"I think she may have drunk a little too much today because she was feeling guilty," Varian said.

"Guilty, why?"

"She forgot to feed the cow this morning, and the beast's bellowing was heard by one of the villagers. The authorities came and took it away this afternoon."

"You have a cow?"

"Had, Peggy. We had a cow. We gave its milk to the children."

"Goodness, how bucolic."

"You know it is all Chagall talks of. Will there be cows in America."

Peggy roared with laughter. "No, my dear, you misunderstand him. Chagall adores cows, identifies with the stupid beasts himself, I believe. Why, didn't he plan to have a cow on his business card? What he means is will they allow silly creatures like him into America."

"Well, I never." Varian glanced up. "Peggy, have you met Gabriel Lambert?" He saw a look of alarm cross Gabriel's face. "Peggy Guggenheim, a great patron of the arts."

"I know." He shook her hand. "How do you do, Miss Guggenheim."

"Perhaps you know Gabriel's work?" Varian said to Peggy.

"Some agent—Quimby, dreadful man—tried selling me some paintings in the summer. They were quite charming, but not my thing." She waved her hand. "Of course they are very accomplished, my dear, but decorative, wouldn't you say?"

"Peggy makes me laugh," Varian said quietly to Gabriel as she bustled away. "Have you noticed how she always answers everything with a question?" He raised his glass, puzzled by the flushed look of relief on Gabriel's face. "Your good health."

"He hasn't been here, has he? The agent she was talking about?"

"An agent? No, I don't think so." Someone turned up the radio, and a few couples began to dance in front of the fire. Varian raised his voice above the hum of conversation and the beat of the jazz tune. "Why, are you looking for him?"

"No," Gabriel said. "He's looking for me."

TWENTY-NINE

Flying Point, Long Island

2000

Gabriel

The thought of Quimby has me on edge again. Still, after all this time. I screw my eyes closed against the memory of him, just for a moment.

"Gabriel?" The girl's voice is close by, insistent. "We're not done yet. Come on. What happened next?"

"It was that night I finally started to relax around the place." My heart is fluttering in the cage of my ribs, but I'm not going to let on to her, oh no.

"Even if Quimby had been sniffing after Peggy Guggenheim and her fat wallet?"

"Yeah, well, if he'd tried her in the summer, I just had to hope he wouldn't bother chasing her up again now she was in Marseille."

"Go on, then. Tell me what happened next." The girl sits beside me again.

⁂

Breton—I never felt comfortable enough to call him André, he was always Monsieur Breton to me—well, he came back downstairs after half an hour or so.

"Rose will be fine," he said, rolling down his sleeves and fastening the heavy links in his cuffs. "A sore head and a few bruises, but nothing more serious." Peggy rushed forward and took his arm.

"We had no idea you are a doctor, my dear! What other secrets do you keep?"

"Plenty," he said, bowing that great head of his slightly. "I was a medic in the Great War, and recently," he said. "Like my dear friend Dr. Mabille." I saw her bridle a bit at that. Everyone knew she'd refused to cough up for Mabille's ticket to America. Peggy argued that he was just the surrealists' doctor, not an artist of note. Breton was gracious enough not to push the point further. I guess he felt, they all felt, beholden to her.

I slept at Air-Bel that night, for the first time. All the rooms were full, so I curled up on one of the sofas beside the dying fire and had the first good night's sleep I'd had for months. I felt safe, I think it is as simple as that, and I knew that Annie slept in her house nearby. It is a terrible thing to be afraid all the time. Everyone was terrified, because of the Gestapo, just waiting for that knock in the night. And me, I was petrified at the thought that Quimby might expose me. It felt like I was living on borrowed time, that I could lose everything, and Annie, at any moment.

Around seven A.M., people began shuffling downstairs. Varian and his group set off to catch the tram into town to open the office, and as I sipped my coffee at the window I watched him walking abreast with Danny and the others, Clovis racing ahead of them. They reminded me of gunslingers in an American western.

"Morning," Mary Jayne said as she poured herself a steaming cup of coffee. "Are you coming into town?"

"Perhaps later. I was hoping to see someone."

"Marianne?" She flashed me a quick smile. Aube rushed into the room and ran to me. I picked her up and swung her onto the crook of my hip. "You have quite the way with little girls," Mary Jayne said. "How old is Annie? . . ."

"Sixteen."

"Cradle snatcher," she said, winking at me. "Then again, I'm not one to talk. Listen, if you're going to hang around for a while, why don't you make yourself useful? When Raymond and I were walking in the woods yesterday, we saw a few last mushrooms."

"Has the cold not killed them off?"

"Dear boy, you are asking the wrong person; all I know is the season runs late here. I'm amazed Thumin missed them, but you could ask your little girlfriend to help you see if there are any more. Watch out for Thumin, though, don't let him catch you thieving."

I dared not ask for Annie at her front door, so I crept into the back garden of the house and tossed a few pebbles at her bedroom window. I saw her face appear behind the glass, and I signaled to her to meet me in the woods. As I waited for her, I gathered the few mushrooms I could find, then sat beneath an oak tree and scraped at the earth with my fingers.

After half an hour, I heard her footsteps running toward me, twigs cracking beneath her boots. She waved when she saw me.

"What are you doing? You look like Little Red Riding Hood with that basket." She leaned down and kissed me. "Or maybe the Wolf."

"I thought there might be some truffles. Don't they grow under oaks?"

Annie laughed. "You need a dog, or a pig for that. Do you know nothing about the countryside?"

"Perhaps Varian could train Clovis."

"A poodle hunting truffles? You are funny," she said, laughing. "I'm sorry, I couldn't get away. *Maman* wanted me to go into the market. I don't know what's wrong with her, she just won't leave the house these days. I can't stay long. She thinks I'm on the way to the tram."

"Well, we shall go into town together." I scrambled to my feet, and we walked hand in hand into the woods.

"So what have you found?"

I lifted the red-and-white gingham cloth and showed her the mushrooms. "Mary Jayne asked me to find what I could for Madame Nouguet."

"The cook?"

"Do you know her?"

Annie shook her head. "I overheard a couple of women from the village trying to get information about the house out of her at the tram stop." She smiled up at me. "She wouldn't talk, by the way. Your friends are safe."

"I wish you'd come and meet them one night, you'd love them."

"I can't, you know that. My parents practically lock me in my bedroom at night." She leaned against me. "I think they are afraid some handsome artist is going to scale the wall and carry me off."

"That sounds like a fine idea." I bent down to pick another mushroom. As we walked on, Annie offered me a folded shopping bag.

"It's been raining, so you should look for snails, too," she said, and I wrinkled my nose.

"I've never liked them."

"Gabriel, it's not about what we like, it's making do with what we have." She kicked aside a tree stump near the tumbledown wall and lifted an old rock. "There," she said, pulling snails from the wall. "Put some herbs in the bag and leave them to digest them for a few days."

"I don't know how Madame Nouguet is feeding everyone," I said. "You know, she had taken to locking the half-pound bread rations in the pantry overnight, but someone figured out how to take the door off its hinges." I laughed. "We all chip in some rations, but everyone is starving on stewed carrots and rutabagas."

"Stop it, you're making my mouth water."

"You know, yesterday, Varian caught the goldfish from the pond to add to the stew?"

Annie laughed. "Is that the American?"

"Yes, have you met him?"

She shook her head. "My father was moaning about some man spying on him with eyeglasses." She brushed her blond fringe away from her eyes. "He should be careful. People are suspicious. If they start thinking spies are hiding out in Air-Bel . . ."

"Oh, don't be ridiculous.'

"Really, you must watch out. It's not like Paris, Gabriel. This is a small, provincial village—people talk. One stray bit of gossip—"

"Then let's give them something to talk about." I pulled her into my arms and kissed her. For once, she didn't resist. I could smell the cold earth on my fingertips resting against her neck. "I have something for you," I said, and reached into my pocket. "I was going to wait until Christmas, but—"

"But you can't wait?" Her eyes widened as I handed her the red box. "Oh, Gabriel, you shouldn't have!" She eased back the lid, and her lips parted, smiling. "It's beautiful!" She held up the bracelet, looped over her fingertip. "I've never had anything so lovely."

I took the chain from her and fastened it around her slender wrist. The silver stars glinted in the morning light. I held her hand and raised her wrist to my lips.

"I'll wear it always," she said.

"You know, one of these stars is Venus," I said, touching the bracelet. "It shines night and day, like my love for you...."

"Marianne!" a man shouted. I looked up to see her father striding through the forest toward us. He was pale with rage, a shotgun slung over his arm and a rabbit dangling by its feet from his fist. "Who the hell are you?"

"Papa," she said, running to him. She held him back as he pushed his way toward me.

"Who are you?" he yelled.

"Sir, my name is Gabriel Lambert."

"You stay away from my daughter, do you hear? I'm warning you, if you so much as look at her—"

"You'll what?" I stepped toward him, my fist clenched. The blood sang in my ears. Annie shook her head, pleading with me not to do anything.

"Don't you threaten me." He dragged her after him. "You are to have nothing to do with those people, do you hear?" I heard him telling her.

"Let me go!" She struggled, but he held on to her. She craned her head back around to me. "Gabriel!" she shouted.

"Leave him," old man Bouchard said. "This is too much. I warned you. They will bring nothing but trouble to us, do you hear? It's time they left us in peace."

THIRTY

VILLA AIR-BEL, MARSEILLE

1940

VARIAN

Varian cleared the steam from the mirror on the marble stand. He was exhausted, and his hand trembled as he ran it over his jaw. He glimpsed movement at the edge of the garden through the window and stepped closer, clearing a space in the condensation with his fingertips. *Just some birds.* Varian exhaled. He had been on edge for days. Steam rose from the bowl of water as he lathered up the shaving soap with the brush and rubbed it into his face in even circles.

"Okay, Lena, the next letter is to Alfred H. Barr, director of the Museum of Modern Art, New York," he said, forcing himself to concentrate. "Dear Alfred . . . ," he began. His secretary sat at the small table by the window, her shorthand notebook balanced on her lap. It was a crisp morning, and beyond her he could see the pines emerging from the mist. The gaunt face of a stranger looked back at him from the mirror. In the greenish light of the lamp, he looked sallow, and deep purple shadows ringed his eyes. The razor rasped against his skin as he dictated the letter, each methodical stroke revealing pink, vulnerable skin. "Best regards, etc., etc." He rinsed the razor, thinking of the letter he had received from Eileen that week. *Think of me,* she said. *I do,* he replied, *but your husband is a changed man. Don't think of trying to change me back.*

"Varian!" he heard Mary Jayne shout, hammering on the door.

"Just a minute," he said. He quickly finished the last couple of strokes, wincing as the razor clipped his jawbone. He splashed water on his face and wiped the last of the soap away on the towel. "What's the matter?" He flung open the door.

"I'm sorry," she said, her gaze darting over his dressing gown, unsure where to look. "It's the Sûreté." She walked him over to the window overlooking the driveway. Outside, two police cars and a *panier à salade* wagon were pulling up.

"Damn," he said, and dabbed at the cut on his jaw, thinking, *This can't be good.* He grabbed his address book and threw it into the fire. "Listen, Lena—go down with Mary Jayne."

"What will we say?" She fingered the brooch at the throat of her blouse.

"Nothing, say nothing at all. I'm going to get dressed. I'm sure it's just routine inquiries."

"These Sunday parties have drawn too much attention to us," Mary Jayne said. "We need them to keep a lower profile."

You're a fine one to talk, he thought, *hanging out with that punk.*

"Stall them," he said, striding across the room. "Is everyone else up?"

"They're having breakfast."

"Good," he said, grabbing his suit trousers. "Make sure everyone looks as relaxed and normal as possible."

"Normal?" Mary Jayne laughed. "In this joint?"

By the time Varian raced down to the hall, Mary Jayne had opened the door to the police, and the inhabitants of the Villa Air-Bel were drifting into the hall. A burly policeman barred the front door. Varian caught the look of curiosity on André's face turn to alarm and then carefully disguised calm.

"Good morning, Detective." Varian strode toward him, his chin high and shoulders thrust back. "How may we help you?"

"Monsieur Fry? I have a warrant to search the premises."

"What's the meaning of this? We protest and reserve all rights."

The detective calmly began to pick his nose.

"Formidable," André murmured from the corner of the hall.

"We can make this easy, or hard, Monsieur Fry," the policeman said, inspecting his index finger as he stepped closer. "We have a warrant." Potent, stale cognac breath emanated from him like sea fog. He reached into his pocket and waved the papers in front of Varian with the same fingers that had recently been up his nose. Varian saw a carbon copy of the chief of police's warrant to automatically search any premises suspected of Communist activity.

"As I said, we protest and reserve all rights," Varian said slowly and clearly. "We have nothing to hide. Do you work with Detective Dubois? He's well aware of our humanitarian work at the ARC. In fact—"

"Detective Dubois will not be serving on the Marseille force much longer."

"Since when?"

He shrugged. "He leaves soon. Dubois is being posted to Rabat."

Poor devil, Varian thought. *No doubt someone blew the whistle on him.*

"Now, is everyone here, including the servants?"

Varian glanced around and saw Rose, Madame Nouguet, and the young Spanish nanny, Maria, huddled by the kitchen door. The Bretons and Jacqueline's sister stood together in the corner. "Yes, we're all here." *All except Danny and the others from the ARC,* he thought. *Let's hope they stay out of the way.*

"We intend to search the house from top to bottom," the detective said.

"In that case, perhaps you would like some coffee? Madame Nouguet, would you mind?" He watched as the relieved servants raced to the kitchen. "May I ask why you are searching the house?"

"We have had reports of suspicious goings-on."

"Such as?"

He checked his papers. "I believe young Mademoiselle Breton has been telling her classmates about how sad her parents were at the death of their friend *vieux* Trotsky."

Jacqueline held tight to André's arm. "Inspector, she is just a child, she doesn't understand."

"Still, it is suspicious. We cannot be too careful. Why, only yesterday we received a call about a young woman carrying a heavy suitcase to the house."

"That was me." Jacqueline's sister stepped forward defiantly. "I am visiting. The suitcase contained clothes for Jacqueline and the child, that is all. I'll show you."

"We'll see." The detective signaled to one of the policemen. "Go with her. Make a thorough search of the room, and the suitcase." He looked at each person in turn. "Now, all firearms must be surrendered. . . ."

Varian joined Mary Jayne by the green-tiled stove as the detective droned on. "Do you have anything incriminating on you?" he said under his breath once the police weren't looking. "I have to get up to my room. I left a fake passport on the dresser."

"You should be more careful." She glanced at the young policeman nearby. "Fine. I'll distract him. See if you can persuade them to let you up."

"Excuse me . . ." Varian strode over to the detective. "I need the lavatory."

The man looked at him in irritation, then signaled to one of the policemen. "Go with him."

Varian thought quickly as they walked upstairs. "Have you been on the force long?" he said.

"A couple of years."

"How do you find it?" They walked on up to the next floor.

"Pas mal." The boy shrugged.

"Here we are." Varian closed the bathroom door and waited, his head leaning against the door as he caught his breath. He pulled the chain and ran the taps, wetting his hands before he opened the door. "Thank you," he said to the policeman. He brushed his nose with his index finger. "I could do with a fresh handkerchief, would you mind? I'll just pop into my room and fetch it," Varian said, hoping he wouldn't follow him in.

"Fine." The boy slumped against the wall and crossed his ankle over his leg.

Varian grabbed the passport and looked around him frantically, darting backward and forward. *Oh God, oh God,* he thought. There was no time to lever up a floorboard or loosen the mirror, his preferred hiding place in his old room at the Hotel Splendide. He threw the passport up on top of the wardrobe and caught his breath. Calmly, he pulled open the top drawer of the dresser and slipped out a neatly folded handkerchief. As he walked out of the bedroom, he blew his nose. "Thank you."

They arrived back downstairs just as André was placing his service revolver on the table in front of the policemen. A couple of typewriters and guns were there already. "Good," the detective said, checking the Breton family's papers. "Did you find anything else up there?"

"There are a lot of books, and papers," a young policeman said. "I don't know what most of them are, but we found this." A portrait of Marshal Pétain as a Gallic cock dangled from his hand.

"*Ce sacré crétin de Pétain?*" the detective roared. "You are calling Pétain an idiot? This is revolutionary propaganda!"

"*Non, monsieur,*" André said calmly. "You misread. *P-u-t-a-i-n,*" he spelled out. "Whore."

Varian hid a smile. He saw Mary Jayne signaling to him, and he wandered over, pretending to warm his hands on the stove. "Did you get it?" she said.

"Let's hope they don't look too close."

"Good. Listen, cover me, will you?" She opened the door of the stove, and as she tossed on a fresh log, Varian saw her slip in a ball of paper from her pocket.

"Will this take long?" he asked the policeman walking toward them. He blocked his view of Mary Jayne.

"That depends," the man said. Varian glanced at Mary Jayne and saw her face fall. He followed the track of her gaze and saw Raymond being marched at gunpoint across the terrace by another policeman.

"That's all we need. What's he doing here?" Varian hissed to her. "I thought he was in jail?"

"He was. I helped get him out," she whispered.

"*Chéri!*" Mary Jayne cried, throwing her arms around Raymond before the policeman could stop her. "*Mon amour, mon amour!*" He kissed her, and Varian saw him slip an envelope into her pocket.

"Come on," the policeman said, dragging him away toward the detective. "I found him hanging around outside."

Varian watched as Mary Jayne stuck her hands in her pockets and walked over to Jacqueline. He saw her speak quickly to her and nod her head toward the young blond policeman by the terrace window. Jacqueline raised her chin and sauntered over, swinging her hips seductively.

"Do you have a light?" she said, leaning against the window frame.

"Of course, madame." He fumbled in his pocket. Jacqueline inhaled and licked her lips.

"Thank you. What a gorgeous lighter. Did you buy it here?" She ran her red fingernail down the engraved metal.

Behind the man's back, Varian saw Mary Jayne lift the edge of a Chagall painting of a flying cow they had hung on the wall. She slipped the envelope behind it and walked away.

"*Bon,*" the detective said after several hours. "All the rooms have been checked. . . ." His voice trailed off as two more policemen walked in from the terrace, Danny between them. All three were panting.

"He tried to make a run for it," one of the policemen said. Danny's face was bright with anger.

"Ah, another joins the party. *Bien.* We go."

"Go where?" Varian said. "You assured us this would not take long. We are a busy, and legitimate, relief organization—"

"We have a few more questions, Monsieur Fry, and I would like you, out of the goodness in your heart, you understand, to accompany me to the station."

"We are not under arrest?"

"Bien sûr." The detective opened his palms. "We have nothing against you. You will be back in an hour, you have my word. The servants and the mothers with young children may remain here. We are not animals, Monsieur Fry."

Jacqueline turned to André, flung her arms around his neck. Aube nestled between their legs, glaring at the policemen. Varian caught Jacqueline's whispered words: *"Courage, mon cher, courage. . . ."* She turned her furious gaze on the policemen, the tiger's teeth around her neck jangling.

Varian squatted down and rubbed Clovis's ears. "Do we need to bring anything?" he said to the detective.

"No, no. It will not take long, I assure you."

As Varian followed André out of the house, he heard him laugh and say, "Not long?" as he slipped a book from the hall table into his pocket.

"Stay, Dago," Mary Jayne said, beckoning to Rose to hold the dogs back. "Keep them on their leashes until we've gone." She buried her face in the warm, springy fur on his head. "Now, you be good for Rose and Madame Nouguet, you hear?" She glanced up to see Raymond struggling as the police pushed him into the back of the wagon. "If anyone comes for the kids, you give them hell," she whispered, and kissed Dagobert's nose.

"Come on," Varian said, offering her his arm. "Let's show these damn fools how to do it."

"Varian, I'm afraid," she whispered. He looked down at her, saw the terror in her eyes. Compassion loosened the tight coil of anger in him, like sunlight unfurling new leaves.

"Don't worry, my dear. They can't touch us." He put a protective arm around her and glared at the detective as he swept out of Air-Bel with Mary Jayne at his side. "Come on, chin up," he whispered.

"I can't," she said, her voice shaking. "Varian, what if—"

"You can, and you will, Mary Jayne. We're Americans." He helped her into the back of the wagon. André, Danny, and Raymond already sat in the shadows on the narrow bench opposite, straight backed and pale faced. *We are safe as Americans, but what of the others?* The thought of his friends in Vernet, or some other camp ringed with barbed wire, sickened him. Varian felt his guts weaken with fear.

⁂

"How long have we been here?" Mary Jayne whispered, glancing around the packed police station.

"Hours. I don't know." Varian checked his watch. "Jeez, it's six o'clock. They can't keep us much longer, surely?" The room was crammed with people waiting to be interviewed. "Why are they taking so long with André?"

"Don't you know, my dear? He has a list of convictions as long as your arm."

Varian paled. "You're kidding me."

"Back in the day, he was quite the bad boy. Jacqueline tells me there are at least twenty-five counts on his charge sheet."

"Christ! Why did no one tell me?" They sat squeezed together on hard wooden benches, the fug of hot bodies and wet-dog smell of tweedy winter clothes hanging in the air. "Hey, kid!" he called, signaling to a boy selling newspapers on the street. He wriggled his wallet free from his pocket and peeled off a few notes. "Go to the restaurant next door and bring us a bottle of wine and some sandwiches, okay? You can keep the change." The boy ran off. "Are you okay? What do you think this is all about?" he asked André as he joined them.

He shrugged and pulled the book out of his pocket. "Who knows? They want to round everyone up in a raid, they can do, with no reason."

"I wish I'd had the presence of mind to bring a book," Varian said.

André turned the pages and sighed. "But of all the books in the château to pick from, I end up bringing one I wrote."

"Ah, good!" Varian said, spotting the boy weaving his way through the crowd with their food. Mary Jayne handed out paper cups and tore the sandwiches into pieces until there was enough for the group. Varian sighed with relief and chewed his cheese baguette with his eyes closed. "Damn, that's good. We haven't had a thing since breakfast."

At nine o'clock, a door opened and a file of policemen strode into the packed room. "Make ready," one of them shouted. The noise grew, a hubbub of cries.

"Where are you taking us? We are Americans!" Varian shouted, taking Mary Jayne's arm and protecting her from the crush of bodies.

"Fry, Bénédite, Breton, Gold . . ." One by one their names were called, and they followed in line through the back of the police station to where the trucks were waiting. *Is this how it goes?* Varian thought, his breath pluming in the cold night air as he stepped into the gaping darkness of the truck. He heard others breathing there, nervous, short gasps in the darkness. *Perhaps at the end people do as they are told, meekly like animals? Not all of us fight, resist.* He felt Mary Jayne's hand on his arm as the doors slammed shut.

"Where are they taking us, Varian?" Her voice shook. "I don't know what they have done with Raymond. . . ."

"Killer can look after himself." He put his arm around her, steadied her as the truck lurched away. In the darkness, he tried to follow the path the truck was taking. *We're heading toward the port,* he thought. *That makes no sense. If they were going to ship us off to one of the camps, we'd head to the station.* The truck bounced along the cobbles, and Varian caught the tang of the Quai des Belges. "We're stopping."

The truck doors flung open, and a policeman signaled to them: "Out."

One by one they jumped down, and Varian blinked in the blue streetlights. Hundreds of people were being herded out of trucks just like theirs. "What's going on?" he said.

"They are forcing everyone onto the ship," André said, pointing behind them. Varian turned to see the huge hull towering over them.

"My God, it's the *Sinaia*," Varian said. The masts soared above the deck, and two vast chimneys with white bands running around them rose into the night. He felt vertigo sweep over him as he gazed upward. "I traveled around Greece on this a few years ago."

"Now that is a marvelous coincidence, my friend."

"Make sure we stay together," Danny cried out as the crowd jostled them. Varian grabbed Mary Jayne's arm and kept her close as they were forced up the gangplanks. He felt the rock and sway of the boat beneath them, the creak of the boards. Far below, the black sea sloshed against the pier.

"If I'd known they were taking us on a cruise, I would have packed my bathing costume." Mary Jayne's smile faltered.

"Don't worry," Varian said. "They can't do a damn thing to us. . . ." His voice trailed off as they stepped into the hold of the boat. His eyes adjusted to the darkness. "Christ, how many people have they got on board?" The hot, animal smell reminded him of cattle pens, the tang of sweat and fear. Above the stinking pallets of straw, a perfect square of stars hung, the only air from a hatch in the deck. Deep in the bowels of the boat, someone played a Spanish flamenco tune, melancholy and plaintive.

"Over there," a policeman said, pointing to the far corner of the deck.

"What about bathrooms? Where will we sleep?"

The policeman indicated the floor. Squalid straw pallets had been hastily thrown down. *"Pipi?"* He pointed up to the top deck.

"And food? Water?" Varian demanded.

He shrugged and pointed at a tin bowl on the floor nearby. "Tonight it is too late. Perhaps tomorrow you will be lucky." He swung his gun over one shoulder. "Choose one person from the group to collect food for you all. There will be a loaf of black bread and a pail of coffee to share in the morning."

"Why, it's a regular five-star resort," Mary Jayne said. She shivered in spite of the press of bodies. Varian shrugged off his jacket and draped it around her shoulders. "Thank you." She looked up at Varian. "I'm afraid. Where do you think they are taking us?"

"I don't know." Varian looked at Danny.

"You two will be fine," he said. "We have to try and get word to the American consulate, somehow. As for us . . ." His voice trailed off as he gazed around the ship.

"They can't hold us here, can they?" Mary Jayne's voice shook. "What—what will they do to us? I'm worried about Killer."

"I imagine Monsieur Couraud can take care of himself," André said. He took off his coat and spread it out on the nearest straw pallet, gesturing for Mary Jayne to sit down. "Courage, my friends. This is going to be a long night."

THIRTY-ONE

Flying Point, Long Island

2000

Gabriel

It's something that kids like Sophie will never understand, or at least I hope they won't. This was a so-called civilized European country, and they were just rounding up people from their homes, from the streets, and slinging them in holes barely fit for animals. They held them in three boats, four forts, and some of the local cinemas without explanation. In all, about twenty thousand people were rounded up, just to tidy the streets for Pétain's visit.

"So where were you when all this was going on?" she says.

I sway on my feet as I stand, the breath rasping in my throat. The sun seems to flare and arc above the horizon, luminous as phosphorus. I can hardly see her, the light's a halo around her, and I cover my eyes.

"Gabriel, I said, where were you?" She walks at my side as I stagger along the beach.

"With Annie, of course. When you are young, and in love, you steal time together whenever and however you can."

I had arranged a rendezvous with Annie at the public library in the Palais des Arts on place Auguste-Carli. Her parents could hardly object to her studying, and it was somewhere warm and quiet to meet. It thrills me, even now, thinking of the anticipation of seeing her. The silence, the peace of the library, the quiet breathing of the people bent over the old desks, studying. One day I saw Breton there, his head in his hands as he studied a pile of leather-bound books. I didn't dare disturb him, of course.

It was one of our favorite places to meet—we changed the stacks each time, just in case Annie's mother followed her. This time I was waiting in ornithology. Varian was a big bird-watcher, and he had taken me out in the grounds of Air-Bel, let me try his binoculars. He was a member of some fancy American club—the Audubon Society—and he knew all the Latin names of the birds, their calls, everything. I went early to the library, spent hours flicking through heavy leather books with marble endpapers. The illustrations were dazzling—the clarity and colors. I remember a "meet the artist" lecture in the city thirty years back, when some chinless art historian was pontificating about why one of my most celebrated works was called "Bird." "Oh, it must be because of this and that," he said, "freedom, peace, it's a homage to Brâncuşi or Picasso's doves, clearly. . . ." I was bored by then, so I just let him prattle on. I wasn't about to tell him it was named for an afternoon of erotic anticipation spent flicking through bird books while my friends were being rounded up like cattle. The shame of that makes my cheeks burn even now. The streets were strangely quiet by the time I walked back to my hotel. Then, when I went out to Air-Bel on Sunday, I found out what had happened.

"Bit late by then," Sophie says, her voice floating on the breeze.

"I did everything I could." I ball my fist up on my chest. I can feel my heart jumping around beneath my ribs. "It took me three days to find out where they were holding everyone."

"Wasn't that a risk for you, to go down to the docks?"

"I didn't give a damn. I owed Varian, all of them, everything." The guilt is bitter as lemon juice, still. "Of course, when I was on my way to the *Sinaia*, who did I bump into but Quimby?" He appeared out of nowhere from a narrow side road like the sudden smell of gas.

"Well, what a fortunate surprise," he said. "I was just on my way to your hotel."

"No," I said. "We agreed you wouldn't come there."

"Would you rather I came out to the château?" He stepped so close, I could smell his sweat and cologne. He repulsed me, but I wouldn't back away. I pulled out a pack of cigarettes and lit one, the flame dancing in his spectacles. He moved back a pace, leaned against the damp stone wall. "I'm out of cash."

"I'm not giving you any more money, I can't."

"Oh, I know you haven't got any on you," he said, inspecting his nails. "Or in your room."

"You *have* been to my hotel!" I said. Thank God I had entrusted Annie with the money. If I couldn't get to her, there's no way Quimby could get past Monsieur and Madame Bouchard.

"You really are peculiar," he said, still admiring his buffed fingernails. "For one left with so little, you are remarkably picky about your things." He looked up at me then. "I don't care where you've hidden the cash, but go and get it. I want another five hundred francs by tomorrow."

"Or what?"

"Or I'll march right into the ARC and tell them everything." He dusted off the shoulder of his overcoat. "Oh, and in case you are thinking of bumping me off or anything silly like that, I've taken . . . precautions. And I've left a letter with my concierge to be passed to Monsieur Fry should anything happen to me."

"I'll get it," I lied. I just wanted to get to the docks. I pushed past him and kept running, doubling back on myself again and again through the winding streets to make sure he wasn't following me.

At last I reached the *Sinaia*. Maybe you've seen that photograph of Marcel Duchamp standing on the prow of the boat that eventually liberated him from Marseille in 1942? He was heading out to Casablanca, and he stood up there like a ship's figurehead, waving, full of joy. People think of boats as great symbols of liberty, but the *Sinaia* did not seem like that to me. I joined the crowds of women and children on the docks, shouting up to their imprisoned men. The huge anchors tethered the boat, chains plunging into the choppy ocean. All I could see were cranes and rigging, ropes straining, birds shrieking in silhouette. It terrified me. I shielded my eyes, looked along the row of faces. It took me a moment to make them out, but then I spotted Fry, head and shoulders above everyone else.

"Hey!" I yelled, waving my arms above my head. "Hey! Varian!" They were too high, too far away, for me to hear what he was shouting to me. I saw him talking to someone at his side—I couldn't work out who, but then I saw him swing his arm back and throw something.

I pushed through and shoved some kid aside who was reaching for whatever Varian had thrown. It was a note, wrapped around a ten-franc piece. I gave the coin to the boy and waved the note in the air to show Fry I had it.

I went straight to the U.S. consulate, just as Varian asked. I knew better than to trust the receptionist by now. I just asked to see Harry Bingham and waited quietly for him. It can only have been a few hours, but it seemed to take forever. Bingham finally appeared at the door of his office, his kind, gentle face breaking into a smile.

"Ah, Monsieur Lambert. We met before?"

"Briefly."

"I'm sorry to keep you waiting. It's been a hell of a day with the aftermath of all these raids." He ushered me into his office. "How can I help you?" I explained what was going on as quickly as possible and watched his face set hard with anger. We stood by the window, looking down on the queue of people snaking along the pavement two abreast to the consulate. The café tables and chairs were piled up for the day, stacked between the plane trees.

"From up here, everyone looks the same," he said quietly. "Look—hat after hat, faceless, anonymous." He paused. "The trick is to make people care, you know, to name them to the world. Men like Fry are making a real difference." He laughed dryly. "You know what the U.S. officials call all the paperwork, all the hundreds of letters Varian keeps them tied in knots with? 'Fryana.'" He paused. "I've seen too many people's grief and anger turn to disillusionment. Not with Fry. He and his little tribe of amateurs are outwitting the Vichy stooges with sheer intellect, and the drive that comes from knowing they are serving justice." Bingham sighed. "I envy them. My hands are tied here. The consul general, Hurley, wants nothing to do with the ARC, and Consul Fullerton isn't a bad man, but he's cautious. Often the best I can do is to give an affidavit in place of a passport." Of course, that wasn't true. I found out after the war that Bingham was immensely brave. He helped many, many people and rescued Lion Feuchtwanger, the prominent German Jewish literary figure, from a Vichy detention center. Feuchtwanger had been one of the first to denounce the brutality of the Nazis, so of course they came after him. Harry sheltered him and his wife, Marta, in his own house and helped them escape to the United States. Bingham was a good man, a righteous man, just like Varian.

Ever the diplomat, he kept his thoughts to himself as we stood at the window, and he simply picked up his coat and hat and told the girl on the reception desk that we were going out on official business. I had to laugh at the look on her hard, painted face as outraged people swarmed around her desk, gesticulating and shouting.

The first thing we did when we reached the center of town was stop at a bakery, and Bingham bought a tray of sandwiches. The car drove onto the dock and pulled up beside the armed guards at the foot of the gangplank.

Bingham stepped out of the car and took the plate of food. He was a tall man, like Fry, and imposing, and I saw the crowd part before him like Moses.

"Good day," he said to the guards. "My name is Hiram Bingham and I am the American vice-consul. You are holding American citizens on that boat, and I will be seeking their immediate release." He handed the plate to one of the guards and pulled out his business card. He wrote on the back, *To Fry, with compliments, HB*, and tucked it beneath the waxed paper. "Now, perhaps one of your colleagues would be good enough to deliver that to Mr. Varian Fry and his colleagues." The guard opened his mouth to protest, but Harry's look stopped him in his tracks. "Meantime, I'd like to have a word with your boss, if you'd be kind enough to point the way."

Less than an hour later, Fry and André walked down the gangplank, Mary Jayne between them. I watched from the shadows as Bingham clapped him on the shoulder. It shook me to see Varian in that state, filthy and unshaven.

"Thank you, Harry," he said. "What a relief. We'd managed to get up to see the captain, but if it wasn't for you, God knows how long we would be stuck on the boat."

"Is that all of you?"

Varian shook his head. "They've held Danny."

"Do you know why?"

"He's done nothing," Mary Jayne said, taking the blanket Harry passed her from the car and pulling it around her shoulders. "Those animals." André stood at her side, pale and dignified, his face dark with stubble. "You know we've had nothing but stale bread and water for days? We've been sleeping on lice-infested straw, and pissing in—"

"Mary Jayne," Varian said, "it's over now."

"Jesus!" she said. "It isn't over, it's just beginning, don't you get it? They're holding Danny to get at you, Varian. They're trying to scare you into quitting. They can't hold you because they don't want to anger Harry's lot."

"Is that right?" Varian said to Bingham.

Harry opened the car door, ushering Mary Jayne in. "They won't rest until the ARC is closed down, you know that, Fry." He took off his hat and ran his hand through his hair. "Don't worry about Danny, I'll have a word with Dubois."

"He's being sent to Rabat."

"Maybe he'll be able to pull some strings one last time." His face fell as he turned. "I don't rate Danny's chances without his help."

THIRTY-TWO

Villa Air-Bel, Marseille

1940

Varian

"I did warn you," Beamish said, handing Varian a large glass of Armagnac. "I make it a rule to clear out when a fascist head of state is coming to town."

Varian raised his glass. "I'll bear that in mind, next time."

Beamish squatted down and raked the fire in Varian's room. "They've put an effigy of Pétain on La Canebière that's eight meters high. The bloody fascists have been parading in front of it all week." When Fry didn't respond, he looked up. "Are you okay?"

"Me? I'm fine." Varian leaned his head against his hand. "I just . . . I thought . . ."

"What? That you were untouchable?" Beamish settled back in the chair opposite Varian. "You thought that as an American you were a superior being, beyond the local rules?"

"No," he protested. "Not—I don't know."

"No one is safe, not now." Beamish swirled his glass, watching the flames of the fire through the amber liquid. "This was just a general *râfle* to clear up undesirables for Pétain's visit to Marseille. Worse will come."

"But why did the police come all the way out here? I can understand clearing up the Vieux-Port and La Canebière, but—"

"I told you it was a bad idea to move out here, but again you wouldn't listen. La Pomme is provincial. Air-Bel's neighbors don't like the motley band of bohemians and artists coming and going—especially the girls. Other women envy people like Jacqueline at the best of times. Last time I was on a tram back into town I heard a couple of old women at the stop bitching about her. You're too conspicuous out here. You'd all be safer in town."

"I can't ask a man like Breton to hide out in a fleabag hotel or a brothel."

"I'm sure if you asked him nicely, he'd rather be in a *maison de passe* than a concentration camp."

"Don't be facetious. Someone's betrayed us to the authorities, and I'm going to find out who." Varian bit his lip.

"Do you think Couraud has something to do with this?"

Varian thought for a moment. "No. He's a crook, but he wouldn't put Mary Jayne through that." He pinched the bridge of his nose. "I wish she'd listen to sense. That damn punk is going to drag her down with him, mark my words. You know he made her hide an envelope stuffed with forty thousand francs during the raid?"

Beamish whistled softly. "Where the hell did he get that kind of cash?"

"Where do you think? Stolen, no doubt." Varian swirled the drink in his glass. "No, I reckon the person who betrayed us is a local. I'd bet my last dollar on it being that Bouchard fellow next door. He warned me as much."

"Maybe he doesn't want his precious daughter corrupted by 'degenerates'?" Beamish's head rolled back and he flexed his shoulders wearily.

"I'll talk to Lambert."

"Does it really matter? It could have been anyone. People are squealing on their innocent next-door neighbors because they looked at them the wrong way in 1929. It's the perfect excuse for old prejudices and slights to get an airing."

Varian checked his watch. "Come on. André said he had some kind of announcement."

Varian and Beamish strolled into the crowded living room, and Danny nodded at them from the far corner. His wife sat at his side, and their little son hung around his neck. *The poor kid is probably worried his dad will go away again*, Varian thought. He turned as Jacqueline's sister walked in, talking to Mary Jayne.

"Those fools thought I had a suitcase full of dynamite, can you believe it? Just because Air-Bel is near the railway bridge, they thought I was going to blow up Pétain's train!" She laughed. *It's not funny,* Varian thought. *Who saw you with your suitcase? Who told the police?* He walked across to the darkening windows and looked out over the deserted grounds. The branch of a tree scraped against the glass. It felt to him like a thousand pairs of eyes were watching the house.

"Varian," Gabriel said, joining him.

"Do you ever feel like you're being watched?"

"All the time. Do you think someone's following you?"

Varian shook his head. "I don't know. I think someone is spying on us, on the house. I don't know why, or who." He rubbed his eyes with his thumb and index finger beneath his glasses. "Ignore me, I'm just being paranoid."

"No, I don't think you are."

"Look, Lambert, it's none of my business who you see, or—"

"Are you talking about Annie?"

"We have to keep a low profile, old man. I've heard talk, that's all. We're ruffling feathers in the village, and now someone has betrayed us."

"I promise, I'll deal with it—" Gabriel started to say.

"Thank you, my friends, for joining us," André said. Varian clapped Gabriel on the back and turned to listen to André. "These are dark days," he went on, pacing in front of the fire. *Like a lion,* Varian thought, the flickering flames illuminating his mane of hair. Breton's voice washed over him as he talked of the war and of everything to come. "I propose," he said finally, "that this festive season we play a game, the greatest game we have ever played." He stopped pacing and looked slowly around the room from artist to artist. "I have studied the *Jeu de Marseille* in the library on place Carli. The original tarot deck was named for this city." He pulled a pack of cards from his breast pocket and fanned them out like a magician. He dealt a card on the table and four cards ranged around. "As you know, I often used to consult the cards myself." He placed his finger on the central card. "We are poised in a void, my friends. We will redo the symbols of fate and we will create a new deck that will answer our questions—what is certain, can harm, is hovering, and has been overcome." He shuffled the cards back into the pack. "I propose that we create our own *Jeu de Marseille,* a collaborative deck, a work of art that will burn away our days of anxiety and waiting...." The group burst into applause and excited chatter.

"I heard W. B. Yeats drew his own tarot trumps," someone shouted from the back.

Breton raised his voice. "We will reimagine the suits. No simple hearts, diamonds, clubs, and spades. I don't want to change the rules of the game, I want to change the game!" he cried, throwing the cards high into the air. The men and women gathered in the room erupted in cheers and clapping. Varian watched as the cards tumbled down in the firelight, and André cried: "To Love, Dream, Revolution, Knowledge! To the *Jeu de Marseille*!"

THIRTY-THREE

Villa Air-Bel, Marseille

❦

1940

Gabriel

I heard Breton say once that what he loved, whether he kept it or not, he would love forever. I've always been like that, passionate and true, but I've mellowed, just like everyone does with age. When I think back to the night I went storming across to the Bouchards' house, I hardly recognize myself. I was so angry, I had lights dancing in front of my eyes. It was them, the Bouchards, it had to be. Who else lived close enough to Air-Bel to spy on what was going on? And Annie's parents had made it very clear they wanted her to have nothing to do with me. Well, I wasn't about to give up so easily. I loved her—I would love her forever.

I flung the old gate back on its hinges and marched up the pathway. It was late, but I could still see a glimmer of light through the downstairs curtains. I hammered on that door so hard, my knuckles ached.

"Monsieur Bouchard," I shouted.

"*Attendez, attendez!*" I heard footsteps on the other side of the door. "Who is it?" He didn't open the door even a crack. I heard a window open above me, and I looked up. Annie looked like an angel, her blond hair falling around her shoulders, the white of her nightgown brilliant against the ink-blue star-filled sky.

"What on earth are you doing?" she whispered. "Are you drunk? Go away. This will only make things worse—"

"No." I saw her frown at the anger in my voice. "Someone has betrayed everyone at Air-Bel to the police. Varian, André, Mary Jayne, all of them have been locked up on some goddamned prison ship for days."

"Oh God," she said, reaching to pull the window closed. "Stay there. I'm coming down." I paced the frozen path, my footsteps scuffing the ice. I could hear her now, arguing with her father on the other side of the door. Then I heard her mother talking low and fast.

"Let him in," I heard Annie say clearly.

Her mother sounded desperate. "No good will come of this, I told you. If people see him hanging around here . . ." The little dog chimed in, yapping and scratching at the door, trying to get at me.

"So let him in before someone sees!" Annie was exasperated. "I know Gabriel, if you don't open the door, he'll stay out there until the whole village wakes up." At that I heard the bolts slide back, and the door opened. The damn dog shot out and growled at me, its white fangs bared. I started to walk to the door, and it went for me, biting my ankle.

"Coco!" Annie shouted as I hopped around swearing, trying to shake it off my leg. "Coco!" She grabbed the dog and pulled me into the house. I had never been inside the Bouchards' home, and I was surprised by how empty it was. From the outside it looked like a gracious old stone house, but inside the living room the furnishings were little more than a battered dark wood table and chairs and an uncomfortable-looking horsehair couch. Annie gestured that I should sit down, and sure enough, it was as lumpy as a sack of rocks. "I'll put her in the kitchen," she said, stroking the trembling dog in her arms. I don't know if it was jealousy or my throbbing ankle, but I hated that dog at that moment.

"What do you want?" Old Bouchard stood in front of the grate and took out his pipe. "I thought I made it clear, you are to have nothing to do with our daughter, or I'll—"

"Or you'll what?" I said, cutting him off just as he started packing tobacco into the bowl of the pipe. I sprang to my feet. "Betray us? How dare you? Because of me, you betrayed all of them?" I realized at that moment that I wasn't just angry—I was guilty, and afraid, too.

"Gabriel," Annie said. "Don't talk to my father like that."

"Don't you see?" I rounded on her. "He threatened me, said he'd get everyone kicked out of Air-Bel." I glared at Bouchard. "Thanks to you they were all locked up. Thank God the American consul got them released—"

"We did nothing." Annie's mother sat in one of the wooden chairs, her back straight. "It wasn't us."

"Gabriel, honestly, it could have been any one of the villagers. It doesn't take much for people to turn on strangers." Annie cupped my hand in hers. "I promise, it wasn't my parents who turned them in."

"You should hear the gossip," Madame Bouchard said. "They are having drunken orgies there. That blond American girl nearly slapped a woman in the café, I heard, and that other one, the one with the crazy outfits and the teeth strung around her neck like some voodoo priestess, well, everyone is talking about her." She rocked slightly as she talked. "Everyone is talking. No one is safe."

Monsieur Bouchard walked across and laid his hand gently on his wife's shoulder, and she stilled. I felt the anger in me ebbing away. "Go," he said. "If you care even a little for Annie, go away and never see her again."

"I can't do that." My fingers interlaced with hers. "I love your daughter. I intend to marry her." I felt her squeeze my hand. When I looked at her, her eyes shone with love.

"No good will come of it. We have lived quietly here, safely. . . ." Bouchard was afraid, I realized. What was he hiding?

"Papa," Annie said, "we can't hide like animals. They will find us soon enough anyway."

"What are you talking about? Who will find you?" I said.

Bouchard gazed at me, clearly thinking whether to talk or not. "I am only telling you this because I want you to go, do you understand? If you breathe a word of this to anyone, I swear . . ." His wife reached up to touch his hand.

"Marianne is of Jewish descent," she said. "I am Catholic, but my husband's family is Jewish." I felt the truth come together in me like a smooth stone falling in a well of cold water. I looked at them and tried to imagine them young and in love. What must it have taken for them to defy their parents, to marry outside their religion? I could see no trace of that passion. Their eyes were ashes.

"That is why I cannot work anymore," he said, his voice bitter and angry. "This so-called Statut des Juifs forces my people from our jobs, our livelihood. They take our money, our public voice. What will be next, I ask you? Our lives?"

"We have lived here for years, quietly," she said, her hand on her husband's arm. "We do not want to draw attention to ourselves—that is why we want Marianne to have nothing to do with you and that crowd at Air-Bel."

"If we keep our heads down, we will be safe."

"Do you think so, Papa?" Annie's voice broke with frustration. "No one knows what the Nazis are capable of."

"I vomited when I heard about the statute," Bouchard said. "It is the beginning, only the beginning."

That was the first time I saw him as a human being, as a man, rather than an obstacle to overcome. Who was it said "Something horrible happens when you claim certainty"? I will never, as long as I live, be able to understand how that self-appointed so-called master race believed they had the God-given right to destroy the Jews. I saw tears glint in old Bouchard's eyes as he looked down at his wife. He turned to me and blinked quickly. "Don't you see? No one pays any attention to us here."

"Not yet," Annie said.

"You've been seen," Madame Bouchard said quietly. She glared at me. "Oh, you think you've been so clever, the two of you, meeting up for your walks, and in town, but don't you know there are eyes everywhere? That nosy old bitch from the farm up the road cornered me in the market and said, 'I see your Marianne is courting, then?'" Annie looked at her feet. "Imagine, hearing it from her how you have been sneaking around in the woods and the fields."

"I am sorry, *Maman*." Annie tightened her grip on my hand and looked up at her parents. "I love Gabriel, and nothing you can do or say will change that. I want to marry him."

"No, I forbid it," Bouchard said. "What you must understand, Mr. Lambert, is that not only am I Jewish, if you marry her, Marianne will be Jewish in their eyes too."

"I don't understand?" I thought of the gold crucifix she always wore.

"You see, the Vichy government has made the law against the Jews even harsher here," Madame Bouchard said, going to her daughter. "The Nazis said that anyone with more than two Jewish grandparents is considered Jewish."

"In France," Monsieur Bouchard said, "you need only two Jewish grandparents and a Jewish spouse." His eyes brimmed with tears. "Your mother, I believe, was Jewish. Marianne told me, because she thought I would be pleased."

I thought quickly. I had made a grave mistake in telling Annie. "You misunderstood, darling," I said, skipping back a generation. "My grandmother was Jewish, but she married outside the faith. The Lamberts, my parents, were both Catholic." I saw old Bouchard exhale, but I dared not breathe easy myself, not yet. If we married and the truth came out, it would be a death sentence for Annie.

"My wife, I hope, will be safe," he said. "I don't care what they do to me, but my wife and daughter must be saved. A Jewish father is no great recommendation these days." He hung his head as Annie went to him.

"I love Gabriel," Annie said. "Please, give us your blessing."

He shook his head. "No. This man has Jewish blood, he is part of that . . . that degenerate crowd at Air-Bel. No good will come of it. If you love my daughter, Monsieur Lambert," he said, unable to look me in the eye, "you must never see her again."

THIRTY-FOUR

Villa Air-Bel, Marseille

1940

Gabriel

I stumbled my way back through the darkness to Air-Bel, looking down at my pale hands. It was like I could see it there, the blood—of Vita, of them both. The thought of adding Annie to the list made the bile rise in my throat. I turned my anger on Quimby, and my fists clenched. I punched the gate as it swung closed behind me. The pain was keen, but it calmed me down.

"Clovis!" I heard Varian's voice somewhere behind me. "Clovis! Where are you?" I could hear him marching through the undergrowth, twigs snapping beneath his feet. "Who's there?" He swung the beam of the flashlight toward me. "Is that you, Lambert?"

I squinted and covered my eyes. "Has he run off?"

"No." Varian strode toward me, the flashlight beam swinging across the dead grass and wintry ferns. "That bastard Raymond Couraud has kidnapped him. Can you believe it? I thought maybe he tied the dog up out here somewhere. When I get my hands on that little punk, I'll—" He broke off at the sound of a car racing up the driveway, a shower of gravel on the terrace. Varian broke into a run, and I raced after him. Just as we rounded the corner of the house, we saw Killer stumble drunkenly from an old black Citroën 11 cabriolet. Mary Jayne ran out and took hold of him. The Bretons and Danny's family trailed behind her, alarmed by the disturbance.

"You idiot," she said to Raymond. "What on earth do you think you are doing?"

"He had fun, didn't he, Mathieu?" he protested, pointing to where Clovis sat on the backseat between two of Killer's gang, panting contentedly.

"He sure did," said an olive-skinned man with slicked-back hair. "Hello, Mary Jayne. You look lovely this evening."

"You asshole," Varian said, grabbing Killer by the collar of his jacket. He pushed him back against the hood of the car. "I swear, if you ever touch him again, I'll—"

"You'll what, you American pansy?" Killer flicked away his hands, squared up to him. "You prig. I'd slit your throat in a heartbeat."

"You don't frighten me." Varian glared down at him. "You leave him alone. And you leave us alone. I heard all about the stash of money you hid here. Don't you get it?" he said, turning to Mary Jayne. "You stupid girl. If they had found that, it would have been enough to have us sent back to the U.S. It would have destroyed everything, just because of him." Varian put his hands on his hips. "You have to make a choice, Mary Jayne. It's him or us."

"What?" She turned slowly to him. "How dare you?"

"You are jeopardizing the entire operation."

"I choose Raymond," she said, taking Killer's arm.

"Then you are making the wrong decision."

"We'll see about that."

"I think you should leave."

Mary Jayne stepped closer and murmured, "You pompous ass."

"And you, my dear, have proven yet again that you are nothing but a spoiled little rich girl." He lowered his head and whispered in her ear, "Your charm, and ease, and beauty will no doubt get you through life, but you need to grow up and get some backbone. Life isn't like a story from F. Scott Fitzgerald for most of the world, Mary Jayne, not all of us tool around Europe in our private plane, following the snow and the sun when the whim takes us. I know you. I know what you are. You're not a kid anymore. All the planes, and jewels, and elegant dresses can't fill the hole in your heart. . . ."

Her eyes blazed, glistening with tears, but her voice was steady. "You're wrong. You are wrong about me. Ask them, ask any of them. I am brave, and kind to my friends, and generous—"

"Oh, sure, I can't argue with that one. But then it is easy to give away that which you've never had to work for."

"You know nothing about me, and you know nothing about Raymond."

"Killer?" Varian sneered. "He's a punk, Mary Jayne. The kid is sore with me because of what I represent, he's outclassed by Breton, so out of spite what does he do? Kidnap a puppy. Some great man you've got yourself there."

Mary Jayne raised her chin. "You have no idea—"

"If you want to be really kind to your friends, do the decent thing and leave."

"This is my house. I found it."

"If you continue to stay here, and see Raymond, you are putting the lives of your friends, of Danny and his family, in danger." That seemed to hit home. I saw her face crumple as she glanced over at her friends.

"All right! You don't have to go on." She sauntered over to Killer, swinging her hips. "You've got yourself a lodger for the night. Okay?"

"Okay, *chérie*." He put his fingers in his mouth and whistled for Dagobert. The dog bounded down the steps to the car and leapt into the front seat. "Looks like Dago is driving us back to town."

"At least he isn't drunk." Mary Jayne pushed the dog aside and settled behind the wheel. "I'll be back to collect my things in the morning," she said without looking at Varian.

Danny rushed forward and passed her a sweater. "Take this," he said, "you'll freeze." Mary Jayne reached up and squeezed his hand.

"Thank you, darling. Now, you keep this lot in order, eh?"

"Are you sure you know what you are doing, Naynee? You will be careful?"

"Naynee? You haven't called me that in ages." There was a slight tremble to her smile. "You were always cautious enough for the two of us." Mary Jayne started the engine. "Of course I don't know what I'm doing, but what can I do? I'm not going to let Varian boss me around like some stuck-up schoolteacher."

"I could knock your heads together sometimes." Danny looked uncertainly at Raymond. "You know I'm here, if you need me," he whispered. "Please be careful. We've all heard the rumors that he and his buddy Mathieu bumped off some hood in the Vieux-Port. Raymond has dangerous friends."

"I know." Mary Jayne slipped the car into gear. "But I believe in him," she said, looking at Varian, "and nothing you, or anyone else can say will change that."

Varian grabbed Clovis's lead and lifted him from the car. Killer vaulted over the door and slid down into the space. "So long," he said, flipping a salute at them as Mary Jayne turned the car and sped away, the taillights disappearing into the night.

THIRTY-FIVE

Villa Air-Bel, Marseille

※

1940

Varian

Varian tied a red ribbon to the fir cone and passed it to Aube. "Now, why don't you make it beautiful," he said. "What color shall you paint it?"

"Red! Like a magic tree!" Aube clapped her hands. She sat at Jacqueline's feet in the dining room. Aube propped the china doll her parents had given her that morning for her birthday against the fireplace and fanned out her printed cotton apron. The doll's slim white legs and tiny black shoes stuck straight out from the white underskirt as though they were emerging from a shell.

"There," she said to the doll, "you must stay warm, little one."

Jacqueline dragged across her sketchbook and sighed. She tucked a pencil behind her ear and flicked through her drawings.

"They are wonderful," André said. He was leaning against the door, watching them.

"Hello, my darling." She closed her eyes as he leaned down and kissed the top of her head.

"That is what I was saying to Jacqueline," Varian said. "She must paint."

"It's hopeless," she said. "I can't work at the moment. I mean, I love it here. With all our friends coming and going, it feels like old times, but . . ." She frowned and looked down at Aube's golden head, bent in concentration. André squatted down beside his daughter and helped her dab red paint on with his fingertips. Varian felt like he was intruding, so he stood and went over to the fire, raking the embers. He saw Breton look reflectively at his hands, smear the red between his thumb and forefinger.

"There, Papa!" Aube said, lifting the bright red pinecone.

"It's beautiful," he said.

"What do you think, Varian?" she said.

"Marvelous," he said.

"Come, let's hang it on the tree with the others." Breton lifted her into his arms, and they walked out into the hallway. Danny and Varian had dug up a fir tree from the forest and planted it in a terra-cotta pot as a surprise for the children. The artists had painted the branches white and everyone had joined in, painting stars and butterflies, abstract shapes, and ribbons of colored paper chains. Now, in the firelight, it looked magical. Aube reached up and placed the little red fir cone on one of the branches.

Varian looked up as the front door flung open, and the decorations danced in the cold wind. "Thank God, Beamish," he said as his friend strode into the hall. He took a deep breath, felt some of the tension in him ebb away.

Beamish pulled off his woolen hat and ran his hand through his hair, nodding a greeting to them all. He was out of breath and gestured to Varian to follow him.

"Where have you been?" Varian said quietly.

"Not here," Beamish said.

"Come on upstairs. We won't be disturbed there."

~☙~

Clovis lay sleeping in a pool of lamplight on Varian's bed beside a half-read copy of Virgil, his paws working as he chased rabbits in his dreams.

"Come on in," Varian said, holding the door open for Beamish. Clovis bounded from the bed, welcoming him with delight.

"Thank God, Beamish. The cops have been at the office looking for you. I thought they might have got you, too."

"Do they have an arrest warrant?"

Varian nodded. "They were looking for 'the one who calls himself

Hermant.'" Beamish squatted down and rubbed the dog's ears. "I told them you had resigned some weeks ago and I had no idea where you are."

"Thank you."

"How was Banyuls?"

"Good. Everything is running smoothly at the border."

Varian got to his feet. "We had a bit of a blow while you were away. Little Bill Freier has been picked up."

"Damn. Really?"

"Someone must have ratted on him. The cops walked in and found him surrounded by all the paraphernalia of his forging operation." Varian blinked quickly. "I daren't think what will happen to him." He noticed the look on Beamish's face suddenly. "What is it? Something's wrong."

"Not really, considering the cops are after me. I've, well, I've had some news. A post has come up for me at the University of California at Berkeley."

"I didn't know you'd applied."

"I hadn't. An old professor of mine arranged it through the Rockefeller Foundation." Beamish lowered his eyes. "He's a good fellow. I think he looks on me as something of a wayward child. He knew I'd made it through the fighting in Spain. I think he's worried my luck might run out."

"You? Never."

"He may have a point. I've had a good run."

"Congratulations." Varian shook his hand. "Of course, you must take the job."

"But what about our work here?"

"You think you're irreplaceable?" Varian couldn't hold on to his smile. "It's not safe for you anymore, my friend."

"Was it ever?"

"Damn, we had some times, didn't we?"

"The best of times."

"And you, my friend . . . you are the best of all of them." He cleared his throat. "It's probably just as well you are leaving now the cops have you in their sights. When will you go?"

"Tonight."

"So soon?" Varian felt like a mountain climber watching his rope snake free from its anchor.

"I won't risk going back to the hotel for my things, but I'll take whatever you need me to, from here, papers and so on." Both men felt the charged atmosphere. "I'll head straight back down and on through Spain and Portugal, then to New York."

Fry reached for his briefcase and sorted through the papers. From an envelope he pulled a torn slip of colored paper. "There, this matches up with the half our people have at the border. They know you, of course, but we may as well keep the sequence and take the next slip they are expecting."

"Of course."

"I can't imagine you'll have any difficulties. They've helped nearly a hundred people over the mountain routes in just six months. You can stay in their rooms for as long as you need, and work with them in the vineyards near the border until it is safe for you to cross over."

"Won't people be suspicious?"

Varian shook his head. "If anyone notices, they always say our clients are friends who have been unable to *rejoindre leurs foyers*. I do love that phrase, the idea of returning to your hearth, your home. . . ." He fell silent. "You have your visas and passport ready?"

"You know me, I'm always *en règle*."

"I've never seen a man with so many IDs." Varian poured them two drinks. The bottle was almost empty, and he finished it off between them. On the nightstand he saw Eileen's latest letter. The words *much love—if you're interested* leapt out at him. Beneath it, he glimpsed the dog-eared corner of the telegram from the committee in New York: *Replacement arriving. Return to US soonest.* He knew another fitful night's sleep lay ahead. Every night was the same—he awoke at four A.M., worrying about the refugees, his marriage, his health. Now, it no longer helped to go to bed half-cut. He always woke stone-cold sober at four, unable to rest and sleep, succumbing finally just before his alarm went off. *I was never qualified for this job,* he thought. *I only volunteered because there was no one else. It was only supposed to be a few weeks. I've been demanding New York send over someone with experience of a situation like this for months, but now* . . . Varian's heart stilled as he realized nobody had experienced anything like this before. There was no precedent, no one better qualified for the job than him. He had no option but to stay to the end, whatever that meant. These people needed him. He blinked quickly. "We're going to miss you around here." He turned and smiled, handed his dearest friend in Marseille a drink. "To Buster and Beamish," he said, chinking the glasses.

"May we always be one step ahead of them," Beamish said, and downed his Armagnac. "Right, what can I take out with me?"

Varian took his copy of Virgil from the bed and slipped out a couple of thin sheets of onionskin paper, filled with tiny writing. "I've been waiting for the next client to leave, but you may as well take these."

Beamish reached for the tube of toothpaste by the basin and squeezed some out until it was half-empty.

"I don't suppose you have a condom?" Varian said, rolling the papers tightly. Beamish flashed him a quick smile and reached into his pocket. He slipped the documents inside the condom and slid them into the opened end of the tube. He refilled the toothpaste and rolled down the end.

"What will you do now?" Beamish said, wiping his hands. "Will you leave for New York?"

"How can I? Someone has to hold this place together." He glanced at Beamish, a faltering smile on his lips. "I sent them a telegram. Do you know what their response was? The committee has stopped my salary."

"They're trying to force you out?"

"And Headline won't keep my editing job open any longer."

"What does your wife say?"

"Eileen wants me on the next boat out of here." Varian laughed. "But I never did like being told what to do. I think I might move back into town for a while. I'll take a room at the Hotel Beauvau. Like I say, with you gone, we need someone on hand in town." Varian shivered. "It is kind of cold here, too."

"I didn't want to say anything, but this place is like an icebox."

Varian's stomach gurgled. "Don't say that, you'll make me think of food. I dream of steak and ice cream."

"When I get to America, I shall eat a steak in your honor."

"Are you sure you won't wait and come by the office in the morning?"

"I don't think so," he said, unable to look Varian in the eye. "I'm not good at long good-byes."

"Me neither." Varian offered Beamish his hand. "Take care, old boy."

Beamish glanced up at him. "I'll see you soon, in New York?"

"Do I always say that? It seems to give them confidence."

"Like I said, maybe it is you who needs reassuring."

Varian's throat was tight. "You take care, you hear? And I will see you soon, in New York, or California, Dr. Hermant, or whatever your real name is."

"Hirschman," Beamish said, slipping his hat onto his head. "Albert O. Hirschman, but don't tell a soul." He gazed out the window toward the sea in silence for a moment, and Varian saw him smile one last time in his reflection in the dark window, before he turned and was gone.

THIRTY-SIX

FLYING POINT, LONG ISLAND

2000

GABRIEL

"Is it true," Sophie says to me, "that everyone was making love like crazy during the war?"

"What?" I stop and lean over, my hands resting on my thighs. "Jeez, woman. Is that all you kids think about? Everything was different then. Normal rules didn't apply. People changed their partners, their lives, their names. Wartime . . . peacetime . . . we're all making it up as we go along."

"I kind of admire people who have the guts to invent their own lives," she says. My head hangs down as I try to catch my breath, but I can see her legs up ahead.

"You're nuts if you think you're going swimming. You'll freeze your ass off."

"I just want to put my feet in the water, wash off the blood on my leg," she says. She peers back at me over her shoulder as she peels off her stockings, her hair blowing long and wild in the wind. I can't make out her face, just those blue, blue eyes looking at me defiantly. Blue? I could swear they were green earlier. Must be the light. "Come on, Gabriel, live a little."

"Not so much of your cheek, missy. I told you 'Mr. Lambert' will do just fine."

"Stop avoiding the question, *Mr.* Lambert," she says, tossing her stockings down on the sand like a shed skin.

"You young people think you invented sex," I say. "The thing is, when death's all around you it gives living an edge, makes you take risks you wouldn't otherwise."

"Is that how it was with Annie?"

"None of your damn business." God, I hate journalists. All these years poking and prying like the fame of my public work gives them rights to my private life. I haven't spoken to any of them since 1970-something, and this was a mistake, today. I'd never have agreed if the girl's mother, Paige, hadn't called my son. My head snaps up and I've a good mind to tell her to get lost, but she's run off down ahead into the shimmering water, and there's such a grace and lightness to her that I'm lost for words. "Annie was a good girl," I yell after her, my words snatched away by the wind.

~⚘~

Annie, Annie, Annie . . . As I close my eyes, I think of that first time. I'd spent the day helping Varian and the boys move the ARC into bigger offices at 18, boulevard Garibaldi. The place they were taking over had been a hairdresser's salon. I guess they had split in a hurry because they had left all their equipment—mirrors and brushes, bottles of potions, all kinds of junk.

"Is that the last of the boxes?" Varian asked, looking up from his desk. "Thanks for your help, Gabriel."

"What do you want us to do with all this?" Gussie said, pointing at the pile of hairdresser's equipment.

"Chuck it out, would you? We need all the space we can get in here." He gazed over to where the team were unpacking files from brown boxes. Roses bloomed across the wallpaper behind Lena's desk, framing a small white marble fireplace. He seemed miles away, in some kind of detached reverie. Varian had seemed distant for the last week or so, ever since Beamish had left.

"Here," I said to Gussie, "let me help you." I grabbed one end of a big mirror and helped him out the back door to the alleyway and the bins.

"It's good of you to help," Gussie said.

"The least I can do," I said. "I wish I could do more." The truth is, I felt like a fraud. The guilt's as fresh now as then. Oh sure, some people are pathological liars—untruths are as natural to them as breathing—but not me. I just wanted to do any little thing that was good, and true, to help them. We carried box after box of junk out into the alleyway, making a great pile. "What do you think will happen to this stuff?"

"It won't last long out here," Gussie said. "We're probably being watched as it is. You wait and see, as soon as it's dark someone will be down here and away with the best of it to sell it on."

I thought of Annie. "Say, do you think it would be okay to take a couple of things for my girl?"

"Sure," Gussie said, pulling the door closed behind him. "Take whatever you want."

I headed out to La Pomme that afternoon with my pockets stuffed with hairbrushes, clips, shampoo. On my lap I balanced a little gilt-framed mirror. It made me think of Snow White: Who is the fairest of them all?

Annie and I had grown bolder—the confrontation with her parents had brought everything to a head, and now I had figured out how to sneak up the back stairs of the Bouchards' house through the old hay barn and along the roofline to her bedroom window. If we weren't allowed to see each other in public, then we would do it under their noses.

Annie opened the French windows of her room. They swung back from the wrought-iron balcony, and she stood aside, waiting for me to jump in. She had been working on the loom by the window, and she held a hank of blue silk in her hand.

"Wait," I said, "let me pass this to you."

"What on earth have you got there?" She put down the thread and took the mirror from me.

"It's a present," I said, vaulting over the balcony. I closed the window after me, drawing the drapes.

"I swear you were a cat in a past life," she said, kissing me on the cheek. She was like the heroines of courtly love to me, worthy and chaste. Devastatingly chaste. "You never make a sound."

"Are they here?"

Annie nodded. "*Maman* is in the kitchen, and Papa is asleep in front of the fire downstairs. I said I had a headache, so I've gone to bed."

"Poor darling," I said, pulling her to me. "Let's see if we can do something to help." She let the mirror fall back on the bed and wrapped her arms around my neck.

"I missed you," she said, taking first my lower lip and then the top one between hers. I felt her tongue glide against mine, quick as a fish among the reeds. Oh, those afternoons were an exquisite torture, the silence, the fear of being discovered. They were the most erotic hours of my life, without doubt.

Her hands slid beneath my coat. "What have you got in here?" she said, reaching into my pockets. "Have you held up a beauty salon?"

"Not exactly." I emptied my coat of brushes and bottles, setting them down on the kidney-shaped glass-top dressing table. Annie's bedroom was the only properly furnished room in the house, it seemed. The chintz drapes on the dressing table were faded but good quality, and her bed had a wonderful, deep down quilt that I longed to curl up under every time I saw it. Now, with children of my own, I can see that Annie was the Bouchards' world. They wanted her to have everything they did not. Then it seemed only right that someone so beautiful should have the best of everything.

"Are these really for me?" Her eyes sparkled. "You promise you didn't steal them?"

"I promise." I set the mirror up against the dressing table and guided her to the stool.

"What will I say to Mother? She'll notice."

"Hide them in your wardrobe, or under your bed," I said, letting down her hair. I ran my fingers through it, felt the heavy weight of it. "It can be a secret." I pushed aside her hair and brushed my lips over the nape of her neck, felt the fine strands against my cheek. "Let's play hairdressers."

"Oh Gabriel, you're ridiculous! We're not children."

"Okay, you do your hair, and I'll just watch." I lay back on her bed, the springs creaking and sighing.

"Shall I put it up?" Annie turned this way and that in front of the mirror. She reminded me of Velázquez's Venus. I could almost picture Cupid hovering over the dressing table as she looked at herself.

"Why not?" I pulled my sketchbook from my rucksack. That was the first drawing I did of her, the first of thousands, as it turned out. It was quick and full of longing for her. I caught her, pinning her hair up into a chaste chignon. No, that's not quite right. There's nothing chaste about that drawing. I was weak with desire for her, my head swimming with exhaustion, the sketchbook barely concealing how much I wanted her. "Annie," I said without looking up from the drawing.

"Mm?" she said, hairpins in her mouth.

"Darling, would you take your blouse off?" I could see the shock in her eyes. "Just so I can see the line of your body better." I wondered if I had blown it, if she would throw me out. Night was closing in, the gray light falling outside, and a storm wind rattled the window. Annie's bedroom was small and cozy, up in the eaves of the house with its sloping ceiling. She took the pins out of her mouth one by one, holding my gaze. It was agony. Then, her fingers drifted to the little mother-of-pearl buttons on her white cotton shirt. One by one she undid them, and then, finally, she eased off the blouse. It slipped silently to the floor. She looked at herself in the mirror, her fingertips running across her collarbone, between her breasts. The thin silk camisole she wore outlined the curve of her rib cage. I was afraid to move, but I had to touch her. I was breathing hard as I marked in the final strokes of the drawing, and then I crept forward, padded silently across the room to her. I knelt behind her, slid my hand across the flat of her stomach as I kissed her neck. "Annie," I said, my voice little more than a whisper. She turned on the stool and allowed me to nudge open her thighs. She told me later she had decided that morning that she was ready, that I was the one, but I expected her to stop me. Instead, I felt her hand on my belt, the soft white skin of her thigh above the edge of her wool stocking. And then, and then . . . I thought I might faint at any moment. She led me to the bed, and we slipped beneath the quilt. We dared not undress in case her parents discovered us. The thought that we might get caught . . . well, that only added to the illicit joy of being with her. Everything fell away—there was no war, no house, nothing beyond our mouths and our hands on each other. We were the world, and the world was in us.

THIRTY-SEVEN

BOULEVARD GARIBALDI, MARSEILLE

1941

VARIAN

"Happy New Year," Danny said, closing the door to Varian's office. "How was it in Cannes?"

"Not good." Varian sat back in his chair. "And now the Thyssens have been arrested. Not that I care much for Nazi financiers. The net's tightening and it's bad news for our operation. If they've taken the Thyssens, what hope is there for clients of ours like Breitscheid and Hilferding? They were prominent German statesmen, but Hitler is gunning for them now."

"It's the first arrest of many, I am sure of it," Danny said. "Now we know the Nazis intend to use Article Nineteen."

Surrender on demand. "Is there any news of what has become of the Thyssens?"

Danny shook his head. "There's nothing in the press."

"When I was up in Vichy, the first place I went was the U.S. Press Bureau. They were beside themselves—if this story broke, there would be a worldwide scandal, but the censors have stamped right down on it. I don't hold out any great hopes for them, I have to say. . . ."

The main door of the boulevard Garibaldi office flew open, and a young man stepped inside before Gussie could stop him. He put his hands on his hips and surveyed the ARC like a conquering hero. A stooped, gray-haired woman clasping a hard alligator handbag in both hands slipped through the door behind him and stood, waiting.

"Here we are, Miss Palmer," the man said. He marched across to Lena's desk and, ignoring the young refugee family talking with her, thrust out his hand. "Jay Allen of the *Chicago Tribune*, and now the ERC."

Lena pursed her lips. "How may we help you, Monsieur Allen?"

"Why, New York has sent me to take over this place," he said. "Haven't they cabled?"

"They said something about sending a replacement," Varian said coolly. He strode across the office. "How do you do?" His handshake was firmer than strictly necessary. "Why don't you come through where it's quieter?"

"Excellent idea, old boy." Allen turned, searching for the woman who was still cowering by the doorway. "Miss Palmer," he bellowed, beckoning to her.

"Everything okay?" Danny said as he slipped by.

"It will be," Varian said quietly, ushering Allen and Miss Palmer through.

He closed the door behind them and gestured to the chairs in front of his desk. He opened his mouth to speak, but Allen interrupted.

"I was expecting more of a welcoming committee."

"There's a war on. Banners and balloons are hard to come by." The men glared at each other. "Let me introduce you to everyone—"

"That won't be necessary." Allen leaned back in his chair and laced his hands behind his head. "This is how it's going to work. I will not be coming into the office myself. I will be continuing my work for the North American Newspaper Alliance, and Miss Palmer will be taking orders directly from me, running the day-to-day goings-on in the office."

Varian glared at him in silence, unable to believe what he was hearing.

"If I may, Mr. Fry," Miss Palmer said, her voice little more than a whisper. "New York has asked that we tail you for a few days, see how the office operates. . . ."

"A few days? It will take more than a few days."

"Well, that's no good," Allen said. "I've got to get back up the country. I have a story to—"

"Hold on a minute." Varian leaned toward him. "You think you can just waltz in here—"

"Listen, I'm the foreign correspondent for the *Chicago Tribune*, and—"

"I know perfectly well who you are, but you surely don't mean you intend to continue working for them and running the ARC?"

"Why not? I'm not afraid of hard work or tough situations."

Jumped-up, would-be Hemingway, Varian thought, and chewed his lip.

"Besides," Allen went on, "as I said, Miss Palmer is going to be my eyes and ears here when I'm not around."

"You fool. You have no idea about the work we are doing here." He leaned closer and spoke clearly, quietly. "We are working eighteen-hour days, often seven days a week—you think you can do that part-time?... Well, do you?"

"Yeah, well, we'll see about that." Allen stood, his wooden chair scraping back on the boards.

"This is ridiculous. I'm not leaving."

A slow smile formed on Allen's lips. "Varian the contrarian. You've been asking for someone to take over this joint for months."

"That was early on."

"Changed your mind, have you?"

"The situation has changed, not me."

"Mr. Fry," Miss Palmer cut in, "you asked for someone to relieve you."

"Someone capable."

"You stuck-up son of a bitch." Allen thumped his fist on the table. "I'll show you. Whether you like it or not, Fry, I'm here to stay and you are heading out on the next boat or plane home."

"Who was that?" Danny said to Varian once Allen and Miss Palmer had gone.

Varian reached for the bottle of cognac on his desk. "My replacement."

"I thought you wanted to go back to America? Haven't you been saying for weeks how worried you are about your job, and Eileen?"

At the mention of his wife's name, Varian paused pouring his drink, then doubled the measure. "It's not that simple anymore. With Beamish gone . . ." He hesitated. He'd always hidden much of the clandestine work from Danny and the others. "I'm damned if I'm going to leave the office in the hands of that fool and see all we've worked for go to hell."

Danny stared at him, held his gaze. "Boss, if you ever need help, you just have to ask. We all know how much Beamish did."

Varian sensed that he knew what was going on. "Allen has no idea of the gravity of the situation. He thinks he can just handle all this work on the side as he continues to send reports home." He knocked back his drink. "Well, let's just see how much he can handle, eh?" He flipped through his diary. "I'm going to Nice tomorrow to see Gide, Malraux, and Matisse. Those idiots in New York think it's just a question of saying: 'Well, hello, Mr. Matisse, would you like a one-way ticket to New York? Oh, you would, splendid. I'll just chat with the nice visa people, and we'll put you on the next boat out of here.'" Varian swirled the drink in the bottom of his glass. *They have no idea,* he thought. *No idea about the fake passports, and visas, of the constant fear everyone is living in.* "They think everyone will just jump at the chance of going to the promised land. Half the artists of Picasso and Matisse's stature think they are untouchable, and the other half would rather die on French soil than leave."

"Boss, you seem awfully tired. Are you sure it's not time for you to go home?"

"Hell, no." Varian raised his dark-ringed eyes and looked through to the main office at the queue of refugees snaking out the door and onto the pavement. "The ERC wants Matisse and his like to leave France immediately? Let's just show Mr. Allen how difficult this job is."

Miss Palmer flinched as a parakeet swept across the palms. Water dripped somewhere in the conservatory, the sound muffled by the green leaves blocking the light from the vast glass windows. Up ahead, Matisse shuffled along the tiled path, leaning on a cane. At his side walked Varian and a doctor. He wore a red velvet dressing gown and a purple paisley turban. His orange leather slippers flapped gently as he walked.

"Are you sure we can't convince you?" Varian pleaded. "I am most concerned about your health."

"Thank you, young man," Matisse said. "Monsieur Fry, it was most thoughtful of you to bring a medic with you."

Varian took Matisse's arm and helped him back into the wicker bath chair set up beside his easel. Specially adapted brushes on long bamboo sticks sat in a jar at his side, and an unfinished nude in india ink was pinned to the board on the easel. Around the legs of Matisse's chair, Varian saw multicolored offcuts of paper strewn across the floor like confetti. A large pair of silver scissors sat on the table beside him, resting on a stack of cerise and orange paper.

Matisse caught his breath. "I am not a well man, as you say. I have no interest in leaving my home, my birds." He pointed up at a pair of yellow cockatiels. "Who would feed my birds?"

"You may not be able to feed your birds yourself, soon," Varian said.

Matisse laughed, a light gasp of air. "The Nazis cannot scare me. Why would they be interested in an old man who paints dreams?" His head rolled to the side, and he looked at the empty champagne bottles on his desk filled with wildflowers. "They call me a degenerate, but all I have ever done is paint the beauty in the world. Is that a crime?"

"No, far from it. It's why you have so many friends in America who wish to see you safe."

Matisse reached up and patted his hand. "Tell my friends I thank them from the bottom of my heart, but I will not leave my home."

"Stubborn old coot," Varian said, pulling his hat down over his eyes as they stepped onto the bustling Nice street.

"For intellectuals they are either brave or naïve. Gide, Malraux, Matisse—we couldn't make any of them see sense." Miss Palmer shook her head. "I don't know what to report back to Mr. Allen."

Told you so, Varian thought to himself. "It's a tough job, Miss Palmer, but I'm sure you're up to it." He glanced over his shoulder at her as he tipped his hat. "I'm sure you're both up to it."

"Of course we are." Miss Palmer's eye twitched as she buttoned her coat against the biting January wind. She pulled up her collar. "Have you booked your ticket yet?"

"Lena's taking care of it."

"Good." Miss Palmer's face betrayed her suspicion. "I'll see you in the office on Monday, Mr. Fry."

Varian strode away through the town. He headed toward the Promenade des Anglais in silence, his thoughts rolling round and round in time with his footsteps. Varian jogged down the steps to the beach and sat down to take off his shoes and socks. He rolled up his trouser legs and walked on across the cool beach. He stood at the shoreline and gazed out to sea, curling his toes against the sand. *So,* he thought, *the Foreign Policy Association won't keep my job open editing at Headline in New York any longer, the Emergency Rescue Committee has stopped my salary here because of Allen, and my wife is threatening to leave me.* He took a deep breath and sighed. *But I have this. I have all this, and there is much to do.* The winter sun broke through the clouds, glittering on the horizon. He realized, in spite of everything, he had never felt more alive.

THIRTY-EIGHT

Marseille

1941

Gabriel

There's something about the threat of imminent demise that can send the most godless man hurrying on his knees to church. Annie's always had her faith, and I've envied her, truth be told. All the years she's worn that same little gold cross she had when I met her—I guess her mother must have given it to her at her confirmation. We raised our kids to respect all faiths—Annie still lights a candle for her father and my mother on a Friday night and so on. If there's one damn thing I can't bear, it's intolerance and the stifling insistence that someone's right and the other guy isn't. The moment you're certain about something, the game is up.

Quimby and I had argued about religion one night at the Château d'Oc, and I'd said I was agnostic or words to that effect. I imagine Quimby found it amusing to make me meet him up at Notre-Dame de la Garde to hand over his hush money. Not that I minded. I'd rather have met him far away from where we might bump into anyone from Air-Bel, or Annie. Once I'd caught my breath, I liked it up there. The view across Marseille, and out to sea, you wouldn't believe. Everything looks better from a distance—lives, lovers, cities. You miss the grit and boredom of everyday living, just get to see the good bits.

It was cold up there, with the wind blowing around the hill, and I felt the chill of the stone through the seat of my pants as I sat on a wall looking out toward the Fort Saint-Jean and the big old lighthouse. It was peaceful, though, and somehow I forgot about my wet shoes and chilled feet, and I felt myself still. Maybe that's happened to you? It's like a glimpse behind the curtain, when the chatter and the nonsense falls away, and you hear yourself clear and true? Well, I held on to that moment, and I took my chance. I made myself a pact with that little gold Virgin up on top of the church.

I said to her: *I know I've done bad things, the worst. I know I've not been to church, or prayed for years, but if you save my Annie, I swear to you I will be a good man. I will put all of this behind me, and I will live a good life. I will do good work, and raise fine children, and I will leave this world a better place than I found it.*

It wasn't much as prayers go, but I meant every word. I put my hand into my pocket and felt the smooth paper of the envelope holding my exit visas. Varian had told me that morning as he'd handed them to me that there was a flood of refugees leaving France now that they were authorizing visas again. He reckoned that the Gestapo had most of the refugees they wanted trapped and at their mercy.

I saw my own tormentor sashaying toward me along the path. "Gabriel," Quimby said, tugging off his leather gloves. "Do you have it?" I slid a wad of notes toward him on the wall. "You're very quiet today."

"What is there to say? You're blackmailing me."

"No need to sulk." He flipped through the notes. "You don't mind if I count it?" I caught a couple of rough-looking sailor types looking at him as they walked out of the church and hoped he might get mugged on the way back down the hill.

"Good, all there," he said, slipping the money into his breast pocket. "Same time, same place next week?" He cocked his head. "Or perhaps you'll be gone then?" I said nothing. "I saw you going into the ARC this morning. I imagine you have your exit visas, as they seem to be handing them out like gobstoppers at the moment."

"If it wasn't so tiresome, it would be flattering the way you follow me around."

Quimby put his fists on the wall and leaned toward me. "I'm just protecting my investment, dear boy." He licked his lips. "I don't know how you do it, day after day."

"Do what?"

He moved closer, I could feel his stinking breath on my cheek, but I was determined not to recoil. "Aren't you consumed by guilt, when you see all those hopeful, desperate faces lined up outside the ARC?"

"Go to hell, Quimby."

"I'll see you there first, Gabriel." He pulled his gloves on. "Tell me something, did you do it? Did you kill them?"

I closed my eyes and breathed deeply. Bright flashes of color and light swirled behind the lids as I thought of the fire, of the hand reaching through the grille on the door. I jumped down from the wall and squared up to him, my face close to his. "Why, are you afraid I might come after you next?"

"Not that it matters, either way. I don't care. You've done me a favor as long as I get my money." He pursed his lips. "Do give my regards to that luscious little cutie you're dating. When are you going to tell her you're leaving? Time's running out."

The thought of admitting the horrible truth to Annie made me feel sick. That morning, I had confirmed my passage on a boat heading via Martinique to New York. I just hoped, somehow, I could persuade Annie's parents to let her come with me. I hadn't enough cash to pay for another ticket, not with everything I had been giving Quimby. I hoped they would have the money. Papers were another thing entirely. There had to be a way to get her out of France safely. My own visas crinkled in my pocket like a guilty secret as I stood.

"Oh, and just in case you are thinking of skipping the country without saying good-bye, remember, I'll find you." The sunlight flared on Quimby's spectacles as he turned away. "I think there might be a very good market in the U.S. for artworks by the illustrious Gabriel Lambert."

"No, you wouldn't!"

"You can run to America if you wish, but you can't hide from me, Gabriel. Remember the photographs. I can destroy you any time I feel like it. I own you. I created you." A smile curled across his pale lips. "And we have a great future ahead of us."

THIRTY-NINE

Villa Air-Bel, Marseille

1941

Mary Jayne

Mary Jayne shouldered open the heavy main door at Air-Bel, the wind rustling the heavy velvet drapes in the hall.

"Hello," she called, "anyone home?" She looked up as the maid, Rose, crossed the hall from the dining room, carrying the remains of breakfast on a tray. "Where is everyone?"

"Good morning, mademoiselle." She shifted the weight of the tray. "The Bretons have traveled to town together to try and secure their tickets."

"And Monsieur Fry?" Rose nodded toward the drawing room, and Mary Jayne tossed her coat on the chair. Her heels clicked across the tiles as she followed the sound of men talking. "Hello, Danny," she said. "What are you boys up to?"

Varian and a couple of the men looked up from the papers they were talking about but said nothing and turned their backs on her. *Typical of Varian to sulk,* she thought.

"It's . . ." Danny hesitated. "Things are rather difficult at the office. Miss Palmer has just upped and left for the States."

"I'm not surprised. I ran into her and that chap Allen at the consulate. The woman looked like she'd keel over from a heart attack the first time someone said 'boo.'"

Danny shouldered on his overcoat, and Varian picked up his homburg from the table. Danny scooped the papers into a file and tucked them into a canvas knapsack.

Well, I'm not going to talk to him if he's going to be that rude, Mary Jayne thought, glaring at Varian as he swept by without acknowledging her.

Danny saw the expression on her face. "I'm sorry, it's a bad time. Allen is giving Varian hell, and Breitscheid and Hilferding are being as difficult as usual."

"Those old sons ah bitches," Mary Jayne said, imitating Charlie's elegant southern drawl. "What have they done now?"

"We sent a car to Arles to pick them up, at great expense, which would drive them safely to Lisbon. Can you believe it, they turned it down flat?"

"I can believe anything of them. They think they are untouchable."

"Well, they are under house arrest now."

"Danny!" Varian yelled from the hall.

"Are you okay?" Danny asked Mary Jayne.

"Me? I'm fine and dandy," she lied. *As fine as a girl who has just found out her lover has stolen all her jewelry can be.* Mary Jayne chewed at her lip as she remembered returning to her hotel room to find the place had been turned upside down. When she challenged the concierge, he had described in perfect detail the man who had gone to her room. *How could he? How could Raymond betray me, after all I have done for him?* She had wept as she'd folded away her clothes and retrieved the empty jewelry boxes scattered around the room. *I'm not having it,* she had decided. *I'm going to find him, and I'm going to get every last jewel back.* She thought of her father, her grandmother, overcome with regret. *Varian was right, damn it, he was right all along. How could I be so stupid? Well, this is my own dumb fault for trusting him. Love? Killer doesn't know the meaning of the word.*

FORTY

Boulevard Garibaldi, Marseille

1941

Varian

Varian paced the office, waiting for Danny to return. "Were we followed?" he said as Danny appeared from the alleyway and locked the back door.

"No, I couldn't see anyone."

"There have been people on our tail for weeks, ever since the *Sinaia*." Varian ushered him into his office and locked the door. "Listen, I need to talk to you before the others arrive." He picked up his telephone and listened, before replacing the handset and pulling the wire from the wall.

Danny leaned against the fireplace. "Now Beamish has gone, perhaps we will all have to do more. You can't do this by yourself, however much you love playing at espionage."

"It's not a game, you're right," Varian said. "But the truth is there's a hell of a lot of fun to be had in rescue work and you have to find it whenever you can, or we would all break down. Regular depression, ennui, has no place here, and I for one am glad of that." He cleared his throat. "Even if our less official work is too much for some to handle."

"You're talking about Miss Palmer, aren't you?" Danny said. "You get a kick out of riling people, don't you? Is that what happened? You scared her away?"

He held Danny's gaze. "What we are doing is a kind of miracle day after day."

"One gets used to miracles. However they are being performed."

Varian leaned on the desk. "This is what I need to talk to you about. As you may know, or suspect, we have been helping people with fake visas and passports." Danny came and sat quietly by the desk as he talked. "There is more to the covert work that the ARC has been doing, and you're right, I need your help more than ever now that Beamish has gone." He folded his arms. "For the time being we are just going to carry on regardless, and pretend Jay Allen doesn't exist. We receive income from many people, not just the committee in New York, and I can't in good conscience simply hand everything over."

"Mary Jayne alone has given thousands," Danny said, "and this office does work far beyond the remit from New York." He paused. "Just tell me what we can do, boss."

"It's dangerous work. Are you sure you want to be involved?" Varian sat back in his chair and placed his fingertips together. "Very well. I think the best, the safest, option is to divide the work that Beamish and I have been doing between a few of you."

"That way if one of us is picked up, they won't be able to get all the information out of us?" The Adam's apple in Danny's throat jumped as he swallowed.

"Let's hope none of us will be picked up. If they do get one of us, then at least the others can carry on." He paused. "We have three problems. How to get people out, how to get false papers, and how to get dollars from our patrons into France from the U.S." He looked directly at Danny. "From now on, I want one of you to be in charge of land routes. He'll liaise directly with the guides at the border to get our clients out over the mountain and sea routes." Varian leaned forward. "I'd like another of you to take care of the fake passports and documents. Bill Freier has been picked up, but we have found a new supplier, and Gussie will continue to courier them across the city for us." He smiled, thinking of young Justus Rosenberg. "The boy has the face of an angel. No one would suspect him of running forged papers."

"And what about me?"

"I'd like you to take over some of the most challenging work Beamish was doing. As you know, he had good contacts with some of the . . ."

"Shadier elements?"

"Precisely," Varian said. "I want you to be in charge of laundering money."

"Hold on a minute—"

"Listen, how else do you think we have been bankrolling all this? With the donations from the committee?" Varian laughed. "We've been moving money in and out of the country for the refugees via Corsican gangsters. It would be far too suspicious if the authorities knew of the huge sums we are clearing through the office. Camille, the receptionist at the consulate, introduced Beamish to some gangsters, who in turn introduced us to Charles Vinciléoni, who owns the restaurant Dorade. Beamish came up with a way to launder funds. When one of our clients headed for America needs to get out, they give us their francs. Instead of running it through the books, Beamish clears the funds through Vinciléoni. A fellow called Kourillo is in on the deal. He realized that this would be a good way for some of his associates to get their money out of the country, too. The middlemen take a commission, of course—"

"Even Beamish?"

"Naturally. The gangsters would be suspicious otherwise. It's a three-way split between Kourillo, Vinciléoni, and Beamish. What they didn't know was that Beamish gave his commission straight back to the ARC. Once we have the funds here, we tell the office in New York how much to deposit in the client's dollar account. The client then picks up the cash once they are home free in the States." Varian paused. "It also means that any funds donated in New York can be picked up as francs here without going through the official channels. The police have no idea what is going on."

"And you trust these guys?"

"Trust is the wrong word. These guys have a finger in every pie—white slaves, the black market, dope." He thought of them all sitting around the stone-topped table in Vinciléoni's restaurant. Everyone was drinking cognac except Vinciléoni, who drank a glass of bicarbonate of soda. "There's little choice but to deal with gangsters in Marseille. I know this must go against the grain for you, but we need help however we can get it." He held Danny's gaze. "Will you do it, and take care of the accounts?"

"Will I cook the books, you mean? Is that what he was doing all this time?" Danny tilted his head back and nodded. "Sure. After all, who would suspect an ex–police official?"

"Good," Varian said. "I'll take you with me to the next meeting. Kourillo has offered to sell us some gold worth fifteen thousand dollars for eight thousand."

"That sounds too good to be true."

"I know. We're screwed if they catch us with gold, but we have to look at every opportunity, every crazy scheme to get our clients out of here." Varian looked at Danny. "It's up to us, my friend, and we are running out of time."

FORTY-ONE

Flying Point, Long Island

2000

Gabriel

Where is she? The damn fool girl has dived into the sea. She must be crazy. I can see her, just, doing a lazy crawl out toward the horizon. "She's mad," I say, and slump back onto the sand. There's no fat on me these days, and my bony haunches ache as they hit the beach. I reach into my pocket and pull out my battered old brown leather wallet. It's worn and smooth as a stone, and over the years it's shaped itself to my hip. I open it up and flip through the photographs of all the kids, back through the years like watching the leaves of a calendar fall away. There it is: March 1941. The photographer Ylla turned up at Air-Bel, and she took photographs of the artists and the Bretons—maybe you've seen them in books about the surrealists. There's a gorgeous one of André and Jacqueline sitting with their little girl, Aube, beneath that huge old palm tree on the terrace. They look so happy and contented. It's heartbreaking when you think what was to come. Maybe the photo of them play fighting had more in it. They're standing beside a tall range of windows, opaque and dusty like the corroded silver of an antique mirror. They've both taken the stance of a boxer, fists raised, weight balanced back on their legs. Jacqueline is wearing a pair of wide-legged pants and a plaid shirt. If you glance at the photo quickly, it looks like they are dancing.

Air-Bel was a refuge for us all, and that's the feeling you get when you look at Ylla's photographs, how happy we were there. It was a place apart from time. Ylla took this photograph I have in my hand of a kid called Gabriel and his girl, Annie. There's so much love in our eyes, the photograph is radiant, even after all these years. I flip it over, and there's Annie's writing: *I love you, this much, always.*

It wasn't like real life didn't touch us there. I remember one Sunday in March, the little nanny Maria was hysterical. The Vichy government had suddenly rounded up all Spanish men and deported them to the Sahara to build the railroad. Just like that, no warning. They had taken her father, and I never did manage to find out whether she ever heard from him again. Imagine that, when the people you love most in the world could be taken from you in a heartbeat, not because they are good or bad, but just because of the chance of their blood.

I sometimes wonder why it didn't make me more bitter, all of this. The thing is if it changes you for the worse, then they've won, the fascist bastards have dehumanized you, and they've won. I never gave up, not once, not even when it looked like everything was lost.

I rub my thumb across the photograph. I remember we went into town the night that Maria's father was taken. Annie was pretty shaken up by it, and we wanted to do something defiant, however small. We heard that a bunch of the artists were meeting at the café Au Brûleur de Loups. They were planning something, and we wanted to be part of it. I remember her walking through the packed café to our table, to me, and the head of every man in there turned to watch her walk by, but she saw only me. She sat on my lap and put her arm around my neck.

"So? What are we going to do tonight?"

"Wait and see," I said. I was playing with the silk rose the café owner had put in a vase on our table, and I offered it to her.

"We can't take that," she said, laughing.

"When we get married, I will fill a church with roses for you."

"Gabriel . . ."

"I mean it. I don't care what your parents say. I love you, Annie, and I want to spend the rest of my life with you."

FORTY-TWO

BOULEVARD GARIBALDI, MARSEILLE

1941

VARIAN

"Is it done?" Varian said, looking up from the papers on his desk as Danny walked in.

"Yes, I buried the cases under the pine trees at the back of Air-Bel." He slumped down on the chair in front of the table. "That artist, what's his name? Gabriel Lambert? He almost caught me. Scared the life out of me, I thought it was the cops."

Varian smiled. "Was he out walking with a pretty blonde as usual?"

"That's right." Danny took the glass of cognac Varian offered him. "What's been happening here?"

"Well, the good news is we have our friend Mehring safely away."

"Baby? Thank God for that. How did you manage it?"

"As you know, our friends Breitscheid and Hilferding felt bunking down in the bowels of a ship was beneath them."

"The fools. Even if the cabins were all sold out, they should have jumped at the chance of getting out, particularly Hilferding—he's Jewish, isn't he?" He crossed his arms. "Well, they're in trouble now. Their exit visas have been withdrawn. It's a bad sign." He glanced at Varian. "Have you had any luck with your passport, boss?"

Varian shook his head. "I'm in exactly the same boat as many of our clients, now. Instead of renewing it, the idiots at the consulate have confiscated it until I leave."

"It's ridiculous! They are putting you in grave danger."

"Since Miss Palmer's hightailed it home, I have no choice but to stay, whether the U.S. government likes it or not."

The men turned as one at the sound of fists hammering on the front door. Varian felt his heart leap to his throat. He checked his watch. "It'll just be the others," he said.

Danny pushed back his chair and unlocked the front door. Gussie ran into the room, gasping for breath. "They got them," he said. "They got them—"

"Slow down, Gussie," Danny said.

"They've arrested Breitscheid and Hilferding—the Gestapo have them."

"Oh God, I was afraid of this," Varian said. "When?"

"I overheard two Vichy cops in the Vieux-Port crowing about it in a bar: 'Two of Hitler's greatest opponents have been rounded up. . . .'"

"Damn, we were too late." Varian took his glasses off and threw them down on his desk. *Charlie had it right about them: "Those couple ah sons ah bitches are asking for trouble."*

"It's not good." Gussie looked down at the floor. "Hilferding is dead."

"Oh God, no." Varian slumped back in his chair.

"The Nazis found the poison he always carried on him, but he managed to hang himself in his cell."

"And Breitscheid?"

"They are sending him to Buchenwald."

Varian took off his glasses and rubbed his face with his hands. "Thank you, Gussie," he said. "Keep your ear to the ground. We have to get as many of our people as we can out immediately. If great statesmen like them are being arrested, what hope does the ordinary man or woman have?"

FORTY-THREE

Marseille

1941

Gabriel

I remember that night like yesterday. The artists who met in the café Au Brûleur de Loups decided to take part in the "battle of the walls," painting graffiti on the streets of Marseille. The BBC were putting out broadcasts, telling people to paint *VH—Vive l'honneur* ("Long live honor") on the walls. Or sometimes it was *VV—Victoire et Vengeance.* Either way, everywhere you looked there were red and black Vs. It was a small defiance, but it annoyed the hell out of the fascists. Of course, they were clever and eventually pretended like it was their idea to paint *V* everywhere, *V* for *Viktoria,* some old Teutonic word they dug up. They started printing posters with big white Vs on a red background, even stuck a big one on the Eiffel Tower for a while. But in the early days, it was ours. Everyone was fired up. We agreed to meet the next night, at eleven o'clock in the Vieux-Port.

Annie wasn't allowed out, of course, so we had to wait until her parents were asleep. I'd half dozed off myself, waiting by the garden gate for her. "Wake up," she said, sliding down onto my lap. She showered my face with kisses, and my hands slipped down to her hips. "Oh no, you don't," she said, springing up. She grabbed the pot of paint at my side and hid it in her basket, then ran off across Air-Bel's lawn. "We have work to do!"

You had to be careful, of course. There were Kundt Commission and Vichy cops everywhere, but we managed to do about ten walls that night, before we ran out of paint. Just as I was doing the last *V*, I heard Annie gasp: "The flics!" She was keeping watch at the end of the road, and she ran toward me, her feet splashing in the gutter.

I slung the empty paint tin into a bin and grabbed Annie. By the time they walked past, we were in each other's arms, kissing. I heard them whistle appreciatively and flicked open an eye, watching them until they turned the corner. "That was close," I said, giving Annie my full attention now. We hadn't managed to be together for a week or more, and my whole body hummed with desire. Every kiss, every touch, every look, lit up the night.

"Come with me, to my hotel."

She shook her head. "What if someone sees me? My mother would ship me off to a convent if she thought we had been to a hotel together."

"Perhaps that would be the safest place for you."

Annie shook her head and laughed. "You're crazy."

"Crazy with wanting you."

"Let's go home," she said. "We have a couple of hours before Papa wakes up." She slipped her arm through mine and leaned into me. "I wish we didn't have to hide, Gabriel. Wouldn't it be wonderful, to be together, always?"

My stomach twisted with guilt. How could I tell her I was leaving? I looked down at her face, at the love and trust there. I'd realized something else sitting up on the hill saying my little prayer. I was going to marry her, and I had to find some way for us to be together. We rounded the street onto La Canebière to catch our tram back to La Pomme, and I summoned up all my courage. "Listen, Annie, we need to talk. . . ."

Her face fell, and she pulled away. "I don't believe it. Mother warned me it would be like this, that if you gave a man what he wanted, then he'd use you up and throw you away. How could I have been so stupid?" She began to run toward the tram stop.

"Wait!" I shouted, running after her. People were turning to look at us. I grabbed her arm and stopped her. "I love you," I said, holding her tight. I kissed her then, and her spine arced back. "I love you, but I need to tell you something. . . ."

"Well, well, my favorite lovebirds." Quimby strolled toward us out of the darkness. "I was just having a late supper in the café over there, when I saw you run past. Not a lover's tiff, is it?"

Annie looked at him askance. "Gabriel, who is this?"

"Has Gabriel not told you about me? I'm a dear friend of the family."

I pleaded with him, with my gaze. She couldn't find out like this, not like this. "Quimby is an old business associate," I said. "We'll be concluding our work together tomorrow."

"Tomorrow?" He tossed his scarf over his shoulder. "Excellent. Shall we meet at the usual place?"

I couldn't get away from him quick enough. Quimby was one of those people who taint everything around him just by his presence, and I wanted Annie away from him as quickly as possible. I spotted a tram coming and bustled her onto the car.

"Who is that man?" she said.

"No one, it doesn't matter."

"You're shaking." She put her hand on my arm. "He's not no one. Why are you afraid of him? . . . Gabriel?" She refused to budge. It's something I've always loved about Annie. She's straight as a die. My whole life has been built on so many lies, I don't know what's truth anymore, but Annie always cut straight to the heart of something. "Are you in some kind of trouble?" I felt her lips against my ear. "I don't care," she whispered, aware of all the people around us. "You can tell me."

"I will," I said. "But not here." I put my arm around her, and my head sank to hers. I closed my eyes. I felt scared, suddenly, for the first time, after staggering blindly through the horrors of the last months. More than anything, I couldn't bear the thought that what I was about to tell Annie might drive her away forever.

We jumped down off the tram and began to walk toward Air-Bel. Annie stopped me beneath the railway bridge, just as a train thundered overhead. "Gabriel," she said. "I'm not walking another step until you tell me what's going on." She settled her back against the tunnel wall, and I put my hands either side of her. The train passed by, and the vibration through the brickwork stilled.

"I'm sorry," I said hoarsely.

"Sorry? For what?" She reached up and touched my face. "Gabriel, are you crying? What's wrong?"

"No, I'm not crying," I said, embarrassed, wiping at my eyes with the back of my hand. I was, of course; I've always been a weeper. Never make it through an old movie without a tissue or two, not like Annie, she's the tough one.

"Stop it this instant. You're scaring me. Whatever it is can't be anywhere near as bad as you think."

"It is. I've done something terrible."

FORTY-FOUR

Flying Point, Long Island

2000

Gabriel

"What did you do, Gabriel?" The girl is there, suddenly, her face close to mine. I feel her breath, the breeze on my cheek. "What did you tell Annie?"

"The truth, missy, what you've been waiting for." I close my eyes as she exhales. "Annie said to me: 'Gabriel Lambert, nothing you can say will stop me loving you.' I said: 'That's just it. I'm not Gabriel Lambert.'"

I sense the girl sitting just in front of me, the fading sun a halo of light behind her head. "At last," she says. "Tell me the truth, just like you told Annie."

The truth? It's all so long ago now, I can hardly remember where one life ends and the other begins. I was in Paris on June 14, 1940, when the Nazi tanks shook the pavements and their vile black boots goose-stepped down the streets I loved. That day, a boy arrived home from art school to find his mother had killed herself. I was eighteen, but still more boy than man. You could smell the gas as you walked upstairs to our studio. Or could you? Maybe we didn't even have gas, I don't remember. She'd barred the door and by the time the concierge helped me take it off its hinges, it was too late. Our neighbors rushed in and screamed. I remember their bent figures crowding around her, my mother's foot as small as a child's extended beyond their swirling skirts, a hole in the bottom of her shoe patched with newspaper. That's what spooked me the night the maid fell downstairs at Air-Bel—I think I'd blocked the image of my mother's body until that moment, seeing her sad little foot with its hole in the stocking and everyone crowding around.

The funny thing about life is it's not consistent. You can go through years, even decades, without aging, then bam!—something happens, and you wake up older. Loss, war, disease . . . these are the things that ravage you and burn the lines on your palms and your face. I reckon this is why time moves slowly when you're a kid, why summers are never as endless and sunlit again. When the knocks are coming thick and fast, as they did the summer of 1940, you grow up quickly. It's not the length of years, it's the weight of them—that's what makes people old.

There was no note, no good-bye. I have no photographs of my mother, and my memories of her are confused. All but the image of her small foot, the battered shoe. Helene was fifteen when she fell pregnant with me, to a boy a couple of years older. She never stopped loving him, even though he had abandoned her the moment he found out she was having his child. She named me after him, encouraged me to be an artist, like him. She raised me, groomed me, even, to be just like my father. Sometimes I wonder if she's looking down and regrets quite how well her pupil learned his lessons.

My mother was an artists' model, and more, I don't doubt. That's how she met my father. We lived in the eaves of an old house in the Marais, in a single room with a roof that leaked. She slept in an old còt, I on the cushions from our single chair. The room I remember more clearly than my mother—the slant of the light on a winter's afternoon, the smell of cabbage, the almost edible fug of must, and dust that settled on the place like a shroud.

It wasn't the chichi district it is now. When I went to a show at the Picasso Museum a few years back, I walked past our old building. I've tried to find her, of course, but they just took my mother's body and dumped her in some unmarked pauper's grave. It's like she never existed. But she was a good woman, and she did her best with the little she had. I guess she lives on, in my work. It's because of her I am who I am.

One of her clients must have taken pity on us when I was thirteen or fourteen, and when I showed some talent he paid for my art lessons out of charity. Or guilt, who knows. I remember wondering at the time if he was my father. My mother was nearly thirty-four when she died, but she looked decades older. When I look at thirty-year-olds now, they are soft like children. Not my mother. When the Nazis invaded Paris, she snapped like a brittle twig. As I cradled her body in my arms, she weighed little more. In my memory, a copy of Stravinsky's *Firebird* is looping on a record player near the window, the needle sliding, bumping across the smooth end of the record, a soft hiss filling the air. But maybe I invented that. I don't see how we could have afforded a gramophone, and she would have pawned it by then if we had. My mother had given up on happiness years before the Nazis marched down the Champs-Élysées, but her dream, her fantasy of art and freedom and Paris, kept her going. When that died, her spirit went with it, but she gave me a parting gift. I learned early on how easy it is for people to disappear.

The girl, Sophie, can't be much older than I was when my mother died and I joined the great exodus of people fleeing Paris, heading south through France away from the gray Nazi tide sweeping across the country like slops from a mop bucket. Everyone was terrified. All many of us had left was our name. Some of us didn't even have a piece of paper to remind us who we were. Stateless, *apatride*, we were trapped, fleeing who knows where, with no hope of escape without paperwork or visas. The roads from Paris sparked with fear in the night. If the troops caught up with us, what would happen? People talked in choked voices of concentration camps. I could tell you about the nights I spent sleeping in ditches, or barns if I was lucky. Whenever I see a herd of deer now, and one senses something, a predator, and raises its head, and all the others follow suit before they flee, I think of the nights I spent huddled in dark spaces with men and women, and children. I see their faces.

I could tell you about sheltering under cars as enemy planes strafed the columns of refugees snaking south. I could tell you how it feels to squeeze yourself between the earth and the hot metal chassis of a car, whose faint blue-painted sidelights illuminate the long grass near your hand. Can you imagine how it feels when a bomb explodes nearby, and every cell in your body reverberates, and you don't know for a moment if you are alive or dead? Your ears are shrill with blood, but you can just hear the moaning of those hit at point-blank range, behind you. Never look back. Like I said, the ones who look back are the ones who turn to stone, or salt. You have to keep moving forward to survive. I could tell you how it feels to walk hundreds of miles and find yourself cowering, your face in the dirt, and see bullets ricocheting like hailstones inches from your head. I could tell you how sick you feel when the four-year-old child hiding up ahead isn't so lucky.

That moment has stayed with me my whole life. What was left of the good, of the boy in me, broke then. Now, when I picture myself lying in the ocher dirt, trying not to cry, it makes me think of that line of Mehring's: "Hope cracks and crumbles." Even now when I cradle my sleeping great-granddaughter in my arms, I think of that little girl. I was surrounded by people, but completely and utterly alone. I left everything that was pure, and soft and true, on the side of the road, and the shell of a man staggered up and walked on past the grieving mother.

But do you want to know about that? The world has compassion fatigue. You've heard stories like my sorry loss of innocence before, haven't you? I was a refugee, just one more face among the nameless thousands lucky to make it out alive. I can see from the look on Sophie's face that all she sees is the sorry old husk of the great man of art. She wants Vita, to conjure her back like a spirit at a séance.

"Okay, okay," I say to her. Flick back in time. Imagine you are this boy who has lost his mother and the only home he has ever known. Your heart is broken—you just want to look your father in the eye and tell him she's gone. Of course, part of you hopes for a reconciliation, that he will accept you, love you, even. Night after night you wonder what it will be like to meet this man. You have been on the road for weeks, scavenging food from hedgerows, drinking water from streams and puddles. You are tall and broad and strong, so you can look after yourself, but you look like a bum, your unshaven face is dark with dirt, your hair is thick and long. The look in your eyes has the weariness and knowledge of a man. All you know for sure is that you have to get away. All you have is an address written in your mother's hand, an unknown village in the Languedoc, a pin in the map gleaming like a beacon. On the road south, the companions you found peel off group by group, to Toulouse, to Spain, to safety and escape, they hope. The refugee telegraph crackles, word of mouth, sightings of friends and family in distant towns. By the time you stumble into the nearest town to this village you have pinned your last hopes on, just as the light is falling, the beauty of the sunset makes no impression on your broken senses. Birds settle on the terra-cotta tiles of the church like five o'clock shadow, but you don't see them. You are shattered, heartsore, all you want to do is sleep. In the nearest bar's cloakroom you wash yourself as well as you can, and you order a beer, a *pression*, with your last centimes, and it is the best, the coldest, beer you have ever tasted in your life before or since. After this, you think, who cares what happens. Then someone slaps you on the back.

"Lambert!" he says. You turn your head slowly, his voice and face swimming in and out of your senses like you are a prizefighter on his last legs, cornered. "Where the hell have you been, you old dog? I haven't seen you for years. Are you still with Vita? No one's heard from her in an age."

"Vita?" You have no idea who this man is, you realize, but he knows you, it seems. It takes a moment for you to click that he has mistaken you for your father.

"He's squiffy," he says to his companions. "Thank God some things don't change. Lambert's been on one of his benders." You look at the group and wonder if you are hallucinating. There is Pierrot and Pierrette, a jester, a Roman legionnaire, a bear. "Are you coming to the party, at least? You must! One last fling before we all get the hell out of here." They drag you away from your drink and bundle you into an open-top car. *Why not*, you think. *Why not play along?* Perhaps there will be food at this party. What harm is there in pretending to be your father, just for a while?

"He doesn't have a costume," Pierrette says. A mask is handed to you, a Venetian carnival mask, gold, with a long nose, and a black cape is draped over your shoulders. Your head sways as the car swings around hairpin bends, up, up into the green mountains. Your eyes are heavy, lead weighted. When you awake, they are climbing out of the car and walking along a gravel path lit by torches, through the great wooden gates of a château. You follow them.

You wonder if you are dreaming. "What a darling idea to hold one last party," someone says as you knock back a drink at the bar. You pour another. "A last cry of freedom," someone dressed as Nero declares, holding a slopping glass of red wine aloft. "Damn them all to hell." Then the band quiets, and all you can hear is a girl, laughing in the shadows of the plane trees. The drummer pounds a beat, one-two, one-two, thumping faster and faster, your heart can't help but keep pace. The trombonists stand, swinging out a tune, and all faces turn to the gate like sunflowers following the course of the sun. And then, she is there.

Vita rode into my life—literally. She galloped through that gate on a horse—I'd like to say a white horse, but really it was a crazy-eyed bay.

Did I say she was naked? The torches in the night scorched the earth between me and her. It was as if the noise of the party, the people, fell away around us. There was only her and the flames dancing in the night. Then there was a flash of light, a pop. Some guy dressed up as a faun with green body paint and shaggy thighs was taking a photograph of her. His yellow horns poked out of his hair just above the camera.

Then the party erupted into cheers, and the horn section of the band rolled into "Sing, Sing, Sing." Vita pulled the horse up short, gravel scattering under its hooves. It reared up on its back legs, turned a circle on its heels. Everyone thought it was part of the show, but she told me later she was scared to death. She jumped down soon enough, and the host cut through the crowd of wild dancers and draped a sheet over her like a toga.

"Your best yet, Vita," he said.

"Happy birthday," she said, kissing him on the cheek. "I never could resist a bet." Then she pushed her way through the crowd toward the bar and picked up my drink.

"What are you staring at, big nose?" she said to me, glancing over the rim of the glass of wine.

It took a moment for me to realize what she was talking about, and then I remembered the mask. "That's my drink."

"It's a free country." She paused. "Or was."

"I like your crown," I said.

She touched her hair, the delicate circlet of gold leaves. "It's a coronet of myrtle leaves. I made it myself, modeled on the Macedonians." She swayed in perfect rhythm to the music, her hips undulating with the liquid grace of a cat. "Dance with me."

"I don't know how. . . ."

Vita dragged me into the heart of the crowd. "Just feel the music," she yelled in my ear, and swung away.

I remember now the drums, the thump of the drums reverberating in my chest, how the swirling masked faces swam before my eyes, and at the heart of it all was her, jiving and swinging, so terribly alive. That is what I remember most about her, how much her name suited her. I had never met anyone like her. "Who are you?"

She stepped closer to me, ran the nail of her index finger over my lips. "I am the poisoned chalice. I am Helen astride the Trojan horse."

"You're certainly melodramatic."

"No, this is the bit where you are supposed to say: 'Of course you are, Vita, quite as lovely as Helen,'" she said, waving her fingers in the air. "You're not terribly good at this, are you?" She tilted her head. "Have I seen you before?"

"I don't think so. I'm just passing through."

"Oh goody," she said, and took my hand, pulling me toward the garden. We were breathless by the time we found a quiet dark spot beneath the trees.

"No, really, who are you?" I said again, catching her by her waist.

She pulled off the cascading blond wig and ran her fingers through her dark bobbed hair. "Does it matter?" she said. She backed away from me and slipped the toga from her shoulder. She was naked and lovely, moonlight dancing through the leaves, across her skin. When you look at all the art deco paintings and sculptures of her now, they are alive with that grace.

I'd like to say I seduced her then, but the truth is I was clueless. Vita took charge. She placed my hand on her breast and kissed me. "We could die tomorrow," she whispered, her lips tracing my jaw beneath the mask, my neck. "I don't want to die without having made love tonight." I pulled the mask from my face, and in the darkness, my blood coursed with the distant beat of the jazz band, the hypnotic buzz and hum of the cicadas in the grass around us. I felt my whole being contract to my lips as she kissed me, like running the film of a firework exploding in reverse, and then, predictably, in sudden, wonderful release I came the moment she touched me.

"Oh God, I'm sorry, I—"

"Don't apologize." She laughed softly. "We have all night." She curled herself around me, skin on skin. "Forget everything. The future doesn't exist tonight, nor the past. . . ."

"Only memories?"

"They change." She slid her hand down my stomach. "All that matters now is you, here with me, tonight."

War is like that for some, you see. It heightens everything, makes you more of what you are, makes you want to do something life affirming, the most natural thing in the world. We were young, and crazy with fear, I think. She was the first woman I had ever been with, and dazzling is the only word for her. When I woke at dawn, I was alone, sleeping on the dew-wet grass with a canopy of leaves above me and a fragile gold coronet placed over my heart.

FORTY-FIVE

Flying Point, Long Island

2000

Gabriel

"Gabriel," Sophie says, "we're running out of time. Tell me about the house where you lived with Vita. Tell me about what happened at the Château d'Oc."

"It was a magical place, but of course I sold it after the war," I say to her, and begin to rattle out the same old lies I've told over the years to anyone who was curious enough to delve back that far.

"Stop it. Tell me the truth, Gabriel."

"I . . ." Oh God, the truth. The blood is singing hot in my ears, a volcano surging.

The truth is I hated the Château d'Oc. I was terrified the first time I walked up the dirt track to my father's house. There was no paved road in those days, just an earth track cut through the trees, climbing up the mountainside. Someone at the party gave me directions, and at dawn I stumbled off along the driveway lined with burned-out torches. I heard them laugh and say, "My God, Lambert must be pissed."

It didn't take long to walk there, an hour or so, in spite of my lungs. You have to remember I was an eighteen-year-old boy and all sinew and muscle then. It would take a month of Sundays for me to do that walk now. Each step brought me closer to the village, to the address my mother had written so many times on letters begging for help that I knew it by heart.

All I knew about the house, about my father, was hearsay and gossip. He had run away the moment my mother became pregnant. They were little more than children themselves, so perhaps it's no surprise he ran like a scalded cat. He became a fashionable artist, grew wealthy in the early 1930s, and married some young heiress, Rachel West. She died in a car crash, and he took up with one of his models. His society clients couldn't get enough of his paintings of languid nudes and his flattering portraits of society women with their strings of pearls and greyhounds. Then, he disappeared.

My mother was relentless, though, and finally tracked him down to the Château d'Oc. We never visited, of course. Ignoring her letters was one thing, but I think she couldn't have borne it if he had rejected her face-to-face. I could see its turrets and pink-tiled roofs above the tree line now as I walked, snaking round and round its fortified base, the road coiling in like the track of a labyrinth. I passed rough cottages built into its base, where scrappy, boss-eyed dogs stared at me with their yellow eyes, yawned, and stretched. Beyond a small chapel, I caught my breath. I stood for a while, looking out across the open hills just beginning to tremble with the dawn chorus of birds and crickets, a red sun flaring over distant mountains. I'd imagined this for years, his home, his land. Finally, I was going to meet my father. Sometimes I pictured myself embracing him, sometimes thumping him on my mother's behalf. I'd never expected to feel so uncertain. My footsteps crunched across the stones littering the road. I remember thinking clearly that I had come to the end of my journey. More fool me. It was only just beginning.

A peeling piece of paper was tacked to the gate with a rusted thumbtack. I could just make out the name "Lambert." I thought the blue gate looked rotten, its paint flaking at my touch. The château wall seemed to grow organically from the hillside, and the gate was flanked by ferns and ivy that brushed my arm. The swollen gate swung open, dragging on the earth beyond, and I hesitated.

That was my moment. The split second that time seemed suspended and gut instinct or my guardian angel told me to walk away. To keep going. To head to Spain, or Marseille, or some other way out. But, what did I do? I shouldered it open, walked straight in, and the trap sprang shut.

Across a courtyard littered with broken chairs and a dried-up fountain, the first person I saw was Vita. She was sitting on the kitchen doorstep, eating a baguette with strawberry jam smeared on her lips. Wasps muzzed around the open jar at her side, and a bowl of black coffee steamed patiently by her ankle. I remember the shock on her face, how her silk flowered robe gaped open and she knocked the coffee over as she ran toward me. The empty white bowl spun on its side.

"What the hell are you doing here?" she whispered, glancing back over her shoulder. She pulled the robe tight and belted it with a scarlet sash. "I couldn't believe it when I woke up and saw your face. Christ, what a mess. What a ghastly, hideous mess. He'll kill you if—"

"Can I help you?" A man leaned in the kitchen doorway, a burgundy paisley robe doing little to conceal his nakedness. His hair was wet from the bath, and he looked at me with pale, myopic eyes. I recognized him from the party—the faun with the camera. A smear of green still edged his jawline. Was this him? The man I had hated and loved my whole life?

"I'm looking for Lambert," I said. There was a strange expression on Vita's face, something I couldn't place.

"Are you indeed?" The man sauntered over. "Well, I'm Alistair Quimby, his dealer. Any business you have with Monsieur Lambert, you can discuss with me." He pulled a lorgnette from his pocket and grimaced as he settled it on his nose. He stopped short. "Good God," he said, and stepped closer to me. I recoiled as he paced around me, felt his gaze snaking from my ankles up to my face. He pursed his lips in amusement. "Let me guess."

"I believe he is my father."

"Do you? Well, you wouldn't be the first one, lovey, but we've never seen one quite as good as you before, have we, Vita? This divine creature is Lambert's muse," he said, waving a pale hand in her direction. He looked me over one more time as if he were inspecting a prize bull, then beckoned me to follow him into the house and walked away.

"Go. Go now," Vita said under her breath, and pushed me away. "I never would have spent the night with you if I'd known who you are."

"I don't care," I said, my heart already full of desperate longing for her. "I don't care if you're married to this Quimby fellow."

Vita gasped out a short laugh, little more than a breath. "I'm not married to *him*. I'm with Lambert, you fool." She looked up at me in the dawn light as the sun rose over the dark bulk of the château's walls and struck me. She raised her hand, shielded her eyes. "It's incredible."

"What's your name?" Quimby called.

"Gabriel Lambert," I said.

"Ha. Of course it is." He turned to me. "And your mother is . . . ?"

I told him, and that she had died recently.

"Condolences," he said without much conviction, and clapped his hands. "Well, Gabriel Lambert, prepare to meet your father."

The first thing I noticed about the house was the smell. Even now, when the calibration of mothballs, dust, cigars, and garlic is just so, I go time traveling back to that old château on the hill. The second thing was how dark the house was. The windows were little more than glazed arrow slits, cut into the walls of the château, so deep a man's arm could barely reach the glass. Clearly there was no housekeeper. The frames of the engravings hung in the entrance lobby were thick with dust, untouched for years.

The kitchen was clean enough—whitewashed stone walls, a long scrubbed pine table with benches either side, and a high-backed settle hard up against the open fire, which was lit and dancing even at this hour. Above the table, a Bec Auer gaslight shed its greenish glow. "I'll make some more coffee," Vita said, and stalked off toward the scullery, swinging a metal kettle in her hand to pump some water.

"Follow me, young man," Quimby said, his pale finger dancing over his burgundy shoulder like a maggot on a steak. Out in the hallway was where it started to get a little crazy. Kilims littered the large flagstones, slipping beneath my feet as I walked after him. Every wall was hung with African masks: beady, glassy eyes and gaping mouths with ivory teeth everywhere I looked. Every tabletop was piled with yellowed journals and papers. "Lambert is quite the collector, as you can see," he said airily. "Primitive art has been a great inspiration to him." I glanced down a curving flight of stone steps.

"What's down there? The dungeons?" I thought of the old woman who babysat me at night when my mother was working. She told me once that in the old stories, the monster is always driven out. Our Minotaurs and Calibans live alone in their labyrinths on the edge of town.

"Once upon a time. Now Vita has her studio down there. She says it's 'womblike.'" He turned to me. "Frankly it gives me the willies." He brushed some dust from the shoulder of my jacket and flattened down my collar. Close to, he smelled sour. His breath was stale with cigarettes, and his lips were chapped and stained from too much red wine the night before. His eyes were cold as a pike's as he smiled, and his yellow pointed teeth reminded me of the horns he had worn to the party. "Smarten yourself up a bit, old boy. Lambert still cares about appearances in spite of everything."

In spite of everything? I wondered what he meant, but as we passed an old gilded mirror glimmering darkly above the open fire in the hallway, I paused and smoothed down my hair. I hadn't shaved for weeks, and the dark beard made me a stranger to myself. The silvering on the old mirror had worn away at the back, and I had to weave my head around to find a patch that did not show only a partial reflection.

"Come on, you'll do."

I followed him upstairs and craned my neck to look up at the wide spiral of mahogany banisters disappearing into the darkness of the house like a nautilus shell.

"Most of the château is closed up," Quimby said, padding noiselessly up the stone steps ahead of me in his purple Moroccan slippers. "It's hard to keep these old places going without staff." We reached the first landing. "Right. Wait here. I'll go and wake him." He knocked softly on the double doors at the heart of the landing and opened the door. A draft of warm air breathed across the landing like a sigh, sickly and sweet.

I remember pacing the landing for some time. I could hear Vita knocking around in the kitchen downstairs, the crackling of the fire in the hallway below, and, from within the room, the rise and fall of male voices. I remember thinking it strange that you couldn't hear any clocks ticking. Houses like that always have a few longcase clocks knocking around, marking off the hours. It was like time stopped. I don't know what I was expecting—sure, part of me hoped my father would walk out of his bedroom, bleary with sleep but delighted to discover he had a son. For a moment, I let myself imagine some guy embracing me, holding me at arm's length, exclaiming, "Well, I never!" The bedroom door opened again, and I heard Quimby say:

"Just wait. He's perfect, I promise you." He beckoned to me. "Come on, Lambert will see you now."

I stepped into my father's room sick with dread. The heavy red velvet drapes were still closed, and the only light came from the smoldering fire in the grate. I blinked, my eyes adjusting to the darkness. My hearing seemed more acute, and I could make out the wheezing breath of a man. With the dust and the smoke, I could feel my own lungs tightening up, I can tell you. I turned to the heavy four-poster, and against the white sheets I began to make out the dark shape of someone. Of my father. The coal of a fat cigar glowed as he inhaled.

"Gabriel Lambert," Quimby said with a flourish, "meet Gabriel Lambert." I felt like he was laughing at me, at us, and my cheeks burned with humiliation.

"Of course your mother named you for me." My father's voice was breathless and harsh. "The woman never got over me. All those letters, Christ." He leaned forward in the bed and stubbed out his cigar in a Chinese ashtray on the bedside table. The firelight flickered over the purple silk drapes of the bed. Still, I could not see his face. "I'm not at all surprised she stole my name for you, too." He laughed bitterly. "All those years, calling herself 'Madame Lambert.'" I blinked. Perhaps it was the smoke from the fire or the dust, but my eyes pricked with tears. "Well, step closer. I can't see you." I felt as wary as Red Riding Hood.

Vita barged open the door and dumped the tray into Quimby's hands, coffee cups rattling. "Good grief, no wonder. You can't see a thing in here with the drapes closed all day." She flung open the curtains, and my father recoiled in the bed, his hand shielding his eyes.

"Not all the way, Vita." She closed them slightly, so that a thin shaft of sunlight cut through the room, illuminating the tangled roses of the faded rug. "Step forward, boy." I moved to the line and raised my chin. I heard him gasp. "Well, well." He threw back the bedclothes, and again, that sweet, heavy scent caught at the back of my throat. Vita chattered on as she set out the coffee on the table beside the fire, but I watched him in silence as he struggled out of the bed. He walked toward me in darkness, a white nightshirt falling to his knees. We were the same height, I realized, the same build, shadows of past and future meeting. "It's remarkable," he murmured. "It's like looking in a mirror."

"It's like you've been reborn," Quimby added.

My father circled me. Unnerved, I kept my gaze ahead, waiting for him to stop in front of me. This he did, and as he stepped into the light, I tried not to cry out in shock.

By that evening, I had grown a little more accustomed to my father. In the dim gaslight of the drawing room, he sat in a red velvet wingback chair, talking to Quimby beside the fire. The heat was stifling, and sweat stuck my shirt to my back as I laid white plates on the mahogany dining table next door. They gleamed in the shadows like four full moons.

"Syphilis," Vita whispered to me as I helped her set the table. "In case you were wondering."

"Oh God," I said under my breath.

"You're fine," Vita said tetchily.

"I didn't mean that."

"We're both fine." Vita threw down the last of the napkins and stalked toward a large Chinese gong. She plucked up the carved beater and thumped the gong—the note vibrated through the house, through my chest like a heartbeat. I was so nervous, eating was the last thing I felt like doing, and the smell of the mushroom soup turned my stomach. "Dinner is served," she called.

Lambert and Quimby joined us, still deep in conversation. My father leaned heavily on an ebony cane as he walked and barely glanced at me as he sat at the head of the table. Only when he raised his glass in a toast did he look directly at me.

"As Plautus said: 'I wined, I dined, I concubined—'" He broke off into a hacking cough.

"Perhaps good food, good friends, good health, would be more appropriate, my darling," Vita said, handing him a napkin.

The children of depressives are alert to the subtlest shifts in mood—they are very good at reading people. Living with my mother all those years had trained me well, and I learned a lot about my father during that first meal. He hid his bitterness well, but I saw something flicker over his face as he looked at me. Jealousy. I came to the conclusion that the corruption of his skin was the final manifestation of whatever poison twisted in his heart. He must have been quite something when he was my age, all that vanity and greed cloaked in beauty. No wonder my mother with her desperate unhappiness fell for him—she must have realized no one could make her more exquisitely miserable than him. Now, he lolled at the head of the table, his bow tie loose around his neck, like some young buck at a party. I wondered if he forgot sometimes, if he thought he was still as he had always been, forever young. Perhaps that was why all the mirrors in the house reflected darkly or had been hidden away.

My father drained his glass. "To hell with this, we should be having champagne, celebrate the return of my prodigal son." He clicked his fingers at Quimby. "Fetch a bottle, will you?"

Quimby hid his flash of annoyance rather well. I guessed he must be used to it. He dabbed his lips with the heavy linen napkin and scraped back his chair. I heard the sound of his footsteps going down to the cellar echo through the silent house, and the fire crackling in the grate beside the table. My cheeks were burning under the intensity of my father's gaze, but I was determined not to let him intimidate me. Quimby returned with a dusty bottle of Dom Pérignon in his hand. "Shall I?" He began to peel away the foil and loosen the wire cage.

"Do it like a man." Lambert lurched from the table and grabbed the bottle. "Watch, boy," he said to me, lifting a tarnished saber from the mantelpiece. "Always slide the blade along the seam," he said, warming up with a couple of short slides, the metal scraping on glass. "There!" he cried, slicing the neck of the bottle neatly. The champagne gushed, and Vita casually leaned forward with a glass to catch the flow.

"Gabriel?" she said, passing me a glass.

"In one!" Lambert cried. It was the first time I had tried champagne, and the bubbles caught in my throat, making me cough. "Come on, boy, drink!" Red faced, ashamed, I knocked back the wine. "That's more like it." He filled my glass again. "Drink!"

"Darling, stop it," Vita said, reaching out her arm.

"Go to hell." He pushed her away and concentrated on me. "Drink." So I did. I drank the whole damn bottle and I've hated the stuff ever since, but I proved something to him that night.

Vita cleared the plates in silence, her gold shift glimmering in the candlelight.

My humiliation over, Lambert turned his attention to her. "Why are you so tarted up? I can't believe you still have that ghastly dress," he said.

"It's a special occasion."

"I told you when I met you, you don't have the tits for it."

"Why do you always have to be such a shit, Lambert? Why can't you be nice for once?"

"Whoever said artists had to be *nice*," he yelled after her as she carried the plates to the kitchen. "We're all heartless, selfish bastards," he said to me, "don't think you are any different, dear boy," and drained his glass, catching a dribble of red wine with the back of his hand. He gestured at Quimby to fill his glass and turned to me. "Oh dear. Have I embarrassed you?"

My cheeks were burning, the champagne lurching in my stomach, but I held his gaze. "Not at all."

"It's quite remarkable, isn't it, Quimby?" He staggered to his feet and walked around to my chair, lowered his ravaged face beside mine. "He's identical." I tried to keep my head steady and not to recoil. He was, what—only seventeen years older than me, but close to, I could see clearly the corruption of his face.

"Identical? In your dreams." Vita thumped down a board of sweating cheeses on the table. "How old are you now, Lambert? Thirty-four, thirty-five?"

"I'm thirty, if I'm a day."

"As I said, in your dreams. The boy's mature looking for eighteen, but you . . . ," she said, her voice low. "Do you know, Gabriel, your father is so vain that his new passport and papers still carry a picture from over ten years ago?" She raised her chin defiantly. "And a false birth date by the sounds of it—"

"Go to hell," Lambert yelled. He heaved himself up from his chair and limped outside to the terrace.

I don't like conflict, never have, but they thrived on it. Half an hour later, they were dancing in each other's arms on the terrace like Beauty and the Beast, moonlight gilding the beads of her gown. Their argument upset me, though, and that night I couldn't sleep. I was jealous, too, I admit it. The memory of his hands on her ate away at me, and I tossed and turned, fitfully, in my bed, the sheets tangled around me. No breeze came through the open window, and the heat and weight of the empty rooms soaring above mine weighed on me like a tombstone. The house seemed alive at night, full of sighs and creaks. The scream of a fox jolted me awake, and I sat bolt upright in the bed, my heart racing. It was hopeless trying to sleep, so I padded downstairs, feeling my way through the dark house. The cool stone wall was rough to the touch. I remembered someone had told me if you were lost in a maze, all you had to do was hold your left hand to the hedge and follow it around. Is that true? In the hallway I paused. A faint, reddish light glimmered from the stairs to Vita's studio. I began to feel more confident at the thought of catching her alone. Perhaps there was still a chance she might want me as I wanted her. Yes, I know, did I have no scruples? She was my father's girlfriend and all that, but I was eighteen, for goodness' sake. I may have looked mature, but I can tell you I wasn't exactly thinking with my brain in those days.

My footsteps on the stone stairs were silent, and I followed the spiral down. I frowned as I made out Lambert's and then Quimby's voice.

"Do you think he'll go for it?" Quimby was saying.

"Of course he will!" Lambert's words were thick and slurred.

"I think you should just do the decent thing and let the boy go on his way," Vita said. That annoyed me—"the boy." Vita wasn't much older than me. It's funny, that throwaway line stuck with me. It always makes me think of that Noël Coward song "Mad About the Boy." You could picture Vita saying it somehow: "My dear, I'm simply mad about the boy." Well, blame it on her or him—maybe that's why I've spent my whole life thinking I'm Peter Pan. In my head I never aged past 1940. A lot of moons, a lot of years, have come and gone since then, but part of me burned as bright as phosphorus that year.

Vita turned at that moment and must have spotted my foot on the stairs. "Gabriel, is that you?"

"I'm sorry, I didn't mean to intrude." I pushed the heavy, iron-braced door fully open.

"Well, don't just stand there, come in," she said. "Whatever you do, don't slam that door, though. The handle's broken."

I wedged the iron bar propping the door open and rattled the handle. "I can fix this for you, if you like. I'm good with things like that."

"See, Vita, the boy's good with his hands." Lambert raised his chin. "Takes after his old man."

"Could you, Gabriel? The whole damn place is falling apart." She cast a surly look at Lambert.

"What do you expect me to do? We're out of cash, dear heart."

"Which is what we were just talking about, Gabriel," Quimby said. There was a sibilance to his French pronunciation that made my skin crawl. When Annie and I took our first grandchild to see *The Jungle Book* at the cinema, Kaa, the snake, reminded me of Quimby. "Your father has a business proposal for you."

"We have a proposal for you," Lambert corrected. "You'll make enough cash to get out of France, too, Quimby, if Gabriel will help us."

"Help you? With what?" I said.

"Here's the deal." Quimby settled back on the high wooden stool beside Vita's easel and made a bridge with his hands, pointing at me with his index fingers. The way his thumbs were cocked, it looked like a gun. "Lambert will house you, teach you all he knows about art . . ."

"Which is no more than a father should do for his son," Vita muttered.

"And in return?" I held Quimby's gaze steadily.

"You must agree to impersonate your father."

"That's ridiculous!" I cried. "He's seventeen years older than me."

"Hear us out," Quimby said. "Before the unfortunate effects of Lambert's condition, he was a handsome man—youthful, tall, olive-skinned like you. He wore a black beard, like you, had longish dark hair . . ."

"Like you," Lambert said. He had the glazed expression of a bored cat toying with a mouse. I noticed when he looked up at me as he leaned in to the candle flame to light his cigarette, his eyes remained black, the pupils fully dilated.

"All we need you to do is meet some rich American clients of mine who are thinking of buying up everything your father has ready. They collect art deco, and already have several of Lambert's best pieces, but they realize this is a buyer's market."

"Fuckers. People like Peggy Guggenheim are just profiteering," Lambert said.

Quimby coughed delicately. "Like I said. It is a buyer's market. Artists are selling at rock-bottom prices, and they want to clean up before they get out of France."

"The thing is, Gabriel," Lambert said, "they want to 'meet the artist.'" He glanced at Quimby. "Clearly they think they will get a better price if they deal with me rather than with Quimby alone. Of course I can't meet them like this." He waved vaguely at his face. "No one would buy a beautiful dream from a monster."

"Hush." Vita reached out and touched his arm, but Lambert pushed her away. I realized then from the look on her face that she loved him, in spite of everything.

"They'll never fall for it," I said.

"I've looked at your sketchbook." Lambert tapped at the dog-eared book on the table beside him.

I grabbed it, held it to my chest. "How dare you go through my things?"

"Your things?" He roared with laughter. "A few pairs of darned socks and a sketchbook?"

"You have no right . . ."

He sneered, waved me away with a hand that I recognized as my own. "I don't know what you're bothered about. It's not as if you have much."

"But you will." Quimby stood and walked over to me.

"And if you're worrying about being busted by the clients," Vita said, "I used to be an actress—"

"That's one word for it," Lambert said under his breath, lurching back into an old armchair in the corner of the studio. A cloud of dust rose up as he sat, legs spread straight ahead of him. I noticed there weren't any holes in the bottom of his hand-tooled, supple shoes, not like my mother's.

Vita ignored him. She put her hands on my shoulders and led me to the huge mirror she had placed by her easel. "I can help you age your features a little, put some gray in your hair to match Lambert's." My hackles rose as she ran her fingers through my hair, brushed the skin at my temple. It was less the thought of art lessons from my father than the idea of being alone with Vita, her face close to mine like this, that made me agree to their plan.

As I left, I loitered on the stairs and listened to their conversation.

"Do you think he can pull it off?" Lambert said.

"Of course he will." Vita's voice came and went as she paced the studio.

"We have to get to the States," Lambert said. "I've heard of an American 'angel' in Marseille who is spiriting artists to the U.S. We just go and find this guy, and we're out of here."

"Everyone knows you've always been an outspoken critic of Nazism," Quimby said. "Naturally they will help an artist of your stature."

I heard Lambert cough. "Frankly I'm scared for my life."

"Don't worry. The sale of these paintings will pay for your passage to New York," Quimby said.

"And mine," Vita added.

"What about the boy?" Quimby said.

"What of him?" Lambert laughed, a cold little laugh that made my stomach curl up and harden. "It's a little late in the day to be paternal. After we pull this off, he can stay here if he wants, or he can just disappear again. He's nothing, a nobody. The Nazis will leave him alone."

When someone tells a boy he's worthless, that he doesn't count, it can go one of two ways. Either you believe them, resign yourself to second best, to being a nobody, or you decide to prove them wrong. Perhaps that is what I have been doing my whole damn life, trying to prove my father wrong. I wanted to show Gabriel Lambert that I was as good as him—hell, I wanted to prove I was better than him, who am I kidding. Vanity, greed, talent—they were just some of the gifts my father gave me. I have no illusions about my personality. I never did a thing I didn't want to, I was just as driven and selfish as my father. Maybe that's why I did so good a job, how I fooled so many people. There's the same uncompromising clarity in our work—even after all the people who had known him personally died, his work lived on, and not once did anyone question Gabriel Lambert's progression from decadent art deco nudes to big old angry abstracts, not once . . . well, not till today, this girl. The critics all put it down to the influence of Breton, of Duchamp, to the torch that these European greats passed on to the new generation of American artists that I became part of. They never doubted for a moment, because there is a perfect, true note in our work, like the way a soprano hitting a high C makes your hackles rise and glasses shatter. I became so adept at imitating my father's art and life, now even I don't know where he ends and I begin.

Like him, I have devoted my life to art, have done what I wanted to, needed to, without compromise. This work has, if you like, left the world a better place. Does that make mine a good life? Has everything I have done in the last sixty-odd years redeemed one unforgivable act? Looking back at that boy on the stairs now, I think it's kind of ironic. For once in my life, I did exactly what someone asked me to do. I disappeared.

FORTY-SIX

Flying Point, Long Island

※

2000

Gabriel

Sophie stretches out on the sand beside me. "So how did it work, Gabriel? How did this transformation come about?"

"I was a quick learner, it's as simple as that. And I was motivated—boy, was I motivated. I wanted to show that bastard just what I was made of."

※

Is it fanciful to say that my father enjoyed my company? I wonder. He had many faults, but he was true to his word, and when I wasn't out fooling people with more money than sense into buying Quimby's stash of my father's—or should I say "our"—paintings, we worked in the studio from dawn till dusk. Lambert's studio was out across the courtyard in an old barn, where they had opened up the north-facing roof for skylights. Week after week, he had me practicing my drawing, turning out little oil sketches in the manner of his work. He spent the days sitting on the sofa, smoking, teaching me everything he knew about art. Around the house he was listless and apathetic most of the time, but when we were working I saw the fire in his eyes flare up, briefly. I saw what he once was and could imagine him as the toast of Paris.

There wasn't any question of asking me what I wanted to paint—when

I showed him some of my modern pieces, he tossed the canvases into the corner of the studio. He said: "You are the son of a great figurative artist, and that is what I will teach you to paint." Anyway, I must have done all right because one day toward the end of October I found him pacing in front of the piles of drawings and paintings I had done. He had them spread out on the big oak table he had by the barn door. I watched him for a while, saw him pause beside a painting I was particularly proud of, a copy of one of his early works, so good that even Quimby couldn't tell I'd done it.

"Not bad," he said without turning to me.

"What do you mean, not bad?" I said, laughing. "Quimby said it was perfect."

"Quimby's a fool," he muttered, and pointed upward. "There's only one source of perfection in the world, don't you forget it." He turned to me, but he was looking past me toward the courtyard. "Sometimes he gets it just right." I followed his gaze and saw Vita doing her calisthenics, turning cartwheels across the yard. "Right, you're ready," he said to me as he limped to the door. "Vita!" he yelled. "Vita." Moments later she ran into the studio.

"What is it? Are you all right?"

He tossed aside his cane and gathered his purple dressing gown around him as he fell back onto the sofa. I saw him wince with pain. "It's time to teach this boy how to paint properly from life. I don't know what kind of nonsense they've been filling his head with in Paris, but we shall sort him out." Vita glanced at me apologetically. "You will model for him."

"Oh." I saw her cheeks flush. "I couldn't, I mean, I—"

"My dear girl," he said, "you're surely not going to play the blushing ingenue at this late stage." He seized his cane and lifted the edge of her blouse with it. "Come along, off with it." Vita looked horrified.

"That is no way to speak to your muse, dear heart," she said, trying to make light of it.

"I'm sure we could find another model, p-perhaps a girl from the village . . . ," I stuttered.

"N-n-nonsense!" Lambert said, imitating me. "A girl from the village? That's like asking a donkey to run the Grand National." He glared at me with those black eyes of his. "If we are to complete one or two of my unfinished paintings, you need to work with the woman who inspired my finest creations."

"It's fine, really." Vita glanced at me and shook her head as if to say, *Stop complaining*. I realized if we made too much of a fuss, my father would know there was something between us.

Was there? I've often wondered that over the years, whether Vita felt anything for me, anything at all. I know she loved Lambert, but there was something in her face, when I caught her looking at me sometimes. I don't know if she wanted me or just wished Lambert were still whole and healthy like me. Perhaps I was just a reminder of what might have been. All I know is my heart was in my mouth as she disrobed behind the screen in Lambert's studio.

"Put some music on, boy," he said, dragging at a cigarette.

"What did you mean, about the unfinished paintings?" I asked him as I flipped through the stack of albums beside the gramophone. I selected Debussy's orchestration of Satie's *Gymnopédies*. I'd heard Vita listening to it one night as she sat alone at sunset, looking out over the hills. It suited her somehow—gentle and beautiful. It suited the melancholy sadness in her that she tried to hide.

"You didn't think I was teaching you everything I know out of the kindness of my heart, did you?" My father's eyes glimmered. "Quimby's nearly sold all my finished work, and all the last editions of the prints. I haven't had the energy to work for some time, and he reckons he can sell anything I can give him at the moment. We'll start with that." He gestured toward a large canvas leaning face-to against the wall.

"No."

"What do you mean, no?"

"Passing myself off as you is one thing," I said, struggling, "but to forge your work as well?"

"What on earth do you think I've been teaching you for? Stop blathering and listen. You have to talk convincingly to the buyers about the work. It's not enough that you look like me, you have to *be* me." He leaned forward and whispered, "You will do exactly what Quimby and I tell you to. What if we were to tell the police that some young con artist has been impersonating me, selling off stolen work . . ."

"You wouldn't."

"Try me." I carried the painting he pointed at to the easel and pulled off the dust sheet. My lips parted as I stood back to inspect it. "I've done the hands and face, as you can see. The rest should be easy enough for you." Vita's face gazed out of the painting. Her life-size body, arms raised sinuously above her head, her legs at full stretch, on tiptoe, had been sketched in.

"It shouldn't take too long for you to finish, a week, perhaps." A week? A week of looking at Vita, in this pose? I didn't know whether to laugh or cry. It was exquisite torture. "Any fool could finish the background," he said. There was the suggestion of a familiar Lambert motif in the background, an art deco design like a metallic mosaic. His work had all the glamour of Tamara de Lempicka, but there was something else to it, a raw sexuality. "It's the line of her that you must be careful with." He reached out and slapped Vita on the backside like a racehorse as she walked past. "That is the true signature of a Lambert painting."

"Oh God, not this one," Vita said. She paused in front of the canvas and wrapped a faded floral kimono around herself. "I'm sure he's a sadist," she said. "I had the most awful cramps in this position, but would he stop? Would he hell." She stalked away and unwound a rope tied to the beam at the side of the podium in the studio. "And it's bloody freezing in here. If you're going to have me pose all morning, at least light the sodding stove." I rushed forward and clumsily stuffed balls of newspaper and kindling into the wood burner. I struck a match, and as the flame caught, I looked through the dancing light to where Vita stood, winching down a small noose.

"A little higher," Lambert said. His voice was low, and I felt my cheeks burning. I tried to busy myself stoking the fire, but I glanced at him. His gaze followed Vita as she climbed onto the podium. She slipped the kimono from her shoulder, her gaze locked on his. It was as if she were stripping for him alone, and I felt like a voyeur. I could hear him breathing as I walked around to the easel and sorted through the brushes. When I looked up, she was quite naked, her hands looped into the noose for support as she took on the pose in the painting. The heat of the crackling fire, the buzzing of the cicadas in the grass, and the bees muzzing the lavender outside made my senses vibrate. The smell of turpentine and oil paint inflamed me. I turned to her, my brush in my hand, and tried to forget it was Vita. Tried to forget that I had kissed that rib cage slick with sweat, felt her move beneath me. "Perfect," Lambert said softly. "Perfect."

And she was. The truth is that painting had all of us in it—my father, Vita, and me. That's its complexity and beauty. Lambert finished it—two tiny dots of white on her pupils breathed life into the whole thing, like the touch of a god. That painting turned up at Sotheby's in New York not so long ago. It had stayed in the family of the old guy who bought it in 1940 all these years. I don't know how anyone could have let it go. I went into town to see it one last time. The director is a friend, so he let me in after hours to see my painting—our painting. They had it spotlighted at the center of the gallery, up against a black velvet wall, the heart of the collection. I recognized the work of the framer—he'd done a good job, a deco key design picked out in silver against the gilding, echoing Lambert's motif. The painting had "it," that something that makes a work of art unforgettable. I brought my old Sony Walkman with me and listened to the cassette of the *Gymnopédies*, rewinding it over and over again as I sat in the dark gallery alone with her. The music, the plaintive oboe and soft strings, worked its magic. It was like having Vita in the room with me. The line, the pigments, shimmered with Lambert's genius, my teenage lust, but more than anything with her, with Vita. Looking at her in the peace of that gallery, I wasn't an old wreck of a man, I was a young boy again, and I wanted it, I wanted the magic. I could have bought the painting anonymously, of course. I won't pretend I wasn't tempted, but I couldn't have it in the house I share with Annie. It would have felt unfaithful.

The last time I'd seen it was when Quimby returned to the Château d'Oc at the end of October to collect the paintings. I don't think I've ever hated anyone more than Alistair Quimby, I tell you. I stayed out of his way, as much as I could. That is, when he hadn't got me dressing up as Gabriel Lambert to sweet-talk some old fool of an art collector into handing over more than they should have for one of the paintings.

"Shouldn't these be signed 'studio of'?" I said to him as we loaded the last of the canvases into the back of his old gray Citroën van. I tucked a blanket around the end of Vita's painting as if I were swaddling a child.

"Nonsense, dear boy," he said, tightening the straps around the blankets so the paintings stayed upright as he drove. Quimby slammed the door shut. "Think of Gainsborough, Rubens, do you really think any of the great prolific artists really painted all their own work?"

"It's forgery."

"No, it's not."

"Well, I bet Gainsborough never had his son impersonate him."

"Hush, dear boy," Quimby said, patting my hand. He stepped a little closer. "Don't pout. You know, you should have some fun. All work and no play—"

"Quimby." Lambert's voice was harsh. Quimby stepped away and slid a pair of round rose-colored sunglasses down from his hair.

"I was just thanking young Gabriel for all his work."

"Hadn't you better get a move on? It will be dark before you reach Marseille."

"Yes, yes." He shook Lambert's hand. "I'll send for Gabriel once I've secured buyers."

"This will be the last time, won't it?" I said.

"I said so, didn't I? I heard Peggy Guggenheim is buying anything she can get her hands on for a good price."

"She's never bought any of my work," Lambert said.

"There's always a first time." Quimby turned to me. "You've done a good job. No doubt now you want to get back to your own work?" I caught the smirk on his face and thought uncomfortably of how Quimby had surprised me in Vita's studio the night before, how the flash of his camera had cut through the darkness of the cellar. Vita was sitting on the stool beside her easel, watching me paint one of the abstracts I was working on. They were never Vita's paintings. They were mine. Lambert pushed past Quimby as he took the photograph, lurched toward my work. His ghastly face, twisted with laughter, reflected in the mirror side by side with my own. Click, the camera went. I remember the pop of the flash, the smell of it. Even to this day, the memory of their laughter, their ridicule, makes the bile rise in my throat. That's what I saw in the photograph Sophie showed me—not Vita, not the paintings, but the truth about us, about Gabriel Lambert. The two of us, side by side. Past and future. Both of us. And the girl knows, I'm sure of it.

~∞~

I found Vita curled up asleep in the armchair in her studio that evening. I didn't want to wake her and began to step away.

"Lambert?" she mumbled sleepily. "Is that you?"

"No, it's me."

"Oh." She rubbed her eyes and yawned. "It's getting harder to tell you two apart. Even your footsteps sound the same now. Or at least, they sound how his used to. If you know what I mean."

"Have you been working?"

Vita laughed. "Trying to. It's hopeless. I've come to the conclusion my destiny is to be a muse rather than an artist in my own right." She gestured languidly at a pile of torn sketches littering the floor. "Lambert says I have failed to progress, and he's right, damn him. Perhaps I shall return to the stage. . . ."

"I thought you might like to go down to the village, for a drink?" I said quickly, before I lost my nerve. She looked so beautiful, curled up on the chair. I longed to kiss her again. It was like some kind of divine joke that I had spent my days, weeks, forced to look but not touch, to study every inch of her in detail under the watchful eye of my father. I could draw her still, if I wanted, in absolute perfection.

"No, I don't think so," she said. She stretched as she stood and looked into my eyes, blinking once, twice, like a cat. "That's not a good idea."

"It's just a drink."

"We both know you are asking me for more than a drink."

"Vita," I said, desperately reaching for her. Before I knew what was happening, my arm was around her waist, my mouth searching for hers.

"Gabriel, stop it. Stop it!"

I backed away, my heart thumping. "I'm sorry. Please forgive me, I . . . I've never felt like this about anyone before." Frustration balled in my chest, I could hardly breathe. "It's just being near you, all the time—I can't, I can't bear it."

She pulled her embroidered shawl around her shoulders and crossed her arms. "You dear, sweet boy."

"I'm not a boy—" I said, my voice breaking.

"Shh! Lambert will hear you." She stepped closer and kissed me on the cheek. "Gabriel, I'm very flattered, and it's understandable that you feel confused, after what happened at the party, but the thing is, I love Lambert. He's a grade-one shit in many ways, but I love him, and I can't leave him, not when he is so ill." She took my arm. "I don't know how long he has left, but I want to be there."

"I understand." I didn't, of course. I was eighteen and randy as hell.

I couldn't for the life of me see how a woman like Vita could choose Lambert over me.

"I'm not feeling so great myself," she said. I noticed for the first time the dark circles under her eyes.

"You don't think . . . ?"

"No, of course not. It's just some bug or rotten food, or something." She shook her head and sighed. "Of course it's not syphilis. Lambert and I have always been careful. We've never been lovers, you do know that?"

"No?"

"He was already ill, when we met." She glanced at me as we started to climb the cellar steps. "His wife, Rachel, infected him." She pursed her lips. "She must have been a piece of work, spoiled bitch. Imagine being unfaithful to a man like Lambert? No wonder she killed herself when she found out what she had done."

"She did?"

Vita nodded. "Lambert was in pieces when I met him. She'd just died, and he couldn't work. He knew what was coming, too, how ill he was going to become."

"And then you came along."

"Then I came along." She smiled sadly. "I asked him to marry me, you know, but he won't. He says he doesn't want me to be tied to a monster."

"I'm sorry," I said, and meant it. Now I knew why she was so unhappy. "Your father was . . . is a remarkable man. Never forget that."

"But isn't it difficult, for a woman like you, I mean?" My chest was tight with jealousy. "What do you get out of this? Don't you ever—"

"Need someone? It was part of our agreement, that every so often I could have a little 'adventure' if I felt I needed it."

"He knew?"

"Of course he does. I'd never go behind his back." She squeezed my hand as she turned to go upstairs to bed. "He knew where I was that night, but not who I was with." She looked into my eyes. "You turned out to be more of an adventure than most, Gabriel. Lambert must never know about us. It would break his heart."

I've never been a good sleeper. Overactive imagination, that's what Annie always says, but I've never slept worse than I did in my father's house. I remember lying in bed one night in October, thrashing around like a sprat in the bottom of a bait bucket trying to get comfortable.

I couldn't stand it anymore, thought perhaps I'd be better after some fresh air, so I pulled back the blankets and struggled into my clothes. I leaned against the wall of the staircase as I stumbled downstairs. The fire in the hall cast long shadows, steps zigzagging up the curving wall like teeth. I was heading for the kitchen, but then I heard Vita and Lambert arguing down in the cellar.

I know, I know. I should have gone on, ignored them, but I could hear her crying, and I was worried he was drunk and might hurt her. None of it would have happened if I had just gone on walking out into the night and caught my breath under the cold sky of a thousand stars. But I padded downstairs.

"Whose is it?" he was yelling.

"I don't know." Vita was sobbing now.

"Tell me." I heard Lambert throw something across the room, the mirror above her desk shattering. "This was never part of the deal, Vita. I don't want to be a father. Children suck the bloody life out of you, and leave you a husk. I can't paint around a screaming infant. . . ."

"You can't paint anyway!"

"Go to hell, Vita."

"You don't have to do anything," she said. "You'll never see it."

"You have no idea! The noise, the squalor. You'll get fat and . . ."

"And what, Lambert? Hideous to look at?"

"That's not fair."

"Do you think I love you less, for what you are?"

"I just want one part of my life to remain perfect. One part. Is that too much to ask?"

"I'm not a sculpture, or a painting. I'm real, and I'm alive, and I just want a child so that when . . ."

"When I die? Is that it?"

"I don't want to be alone, Lambert. It would be like having a part of . . ."

"What?"

"Nothing."

The silence pushed me back against the wall of the cellar stairs.

"Oh, Christ, no . . . Him?" Lambert said. "Not him."

"Lambert . . ."

"In my own house, with my son, how could you?"

"It's not what you think!"

"I'll kill him!"

"Lambert, no, please—" I heard the sound of his hand hitting her, the thud of Vita hitting the floor.

"Leave her alone!" I yelled, my hand clutching at the wall.

Lambert knelt at her side. "Vita . . . Vita . . ." He cradled her head. Blood was already trickling from her ear.

"What have you done?" I cried.

"She fell, hit her head on the table." I glanced across. As she had fallen, a candle had knocked over. Flames were beginning to lick the red velvet drapes behind her easel. As usual, the place was littered with cloths smeared with oil paint and meths. An arsonist couldn't have done a better job. I winced, the smell of smoke filling my nose.

"Lambert, you have to get—"

"You, you little bastard," he said, struggling to his feet. "After all I've done for you."

"It wasn't like that—I didn't know," I said. "Vita didn't—"

"You thankless, heartless piece of shit." He shoved me hard, back against the door frame. I felt the metal rod Vita had propped the door open with fall away as I stumbled. I looked beyond my father, to where the flames were leaping up the drapes. Vita lay on the floor, her pale arm extended toward me. I felt like I was about to pass out.

"Lambert, you must—" He thumped me then, and I fell back onto the stairs. I saw him reaching for the door.

"Go to hell."

"Lambert!" I shook my head, the blood shrill in my ears from the blow. I jumped up as he went to slam the door, grabbing the handle on this side. The handle that I had said I'd fix but hadn't. I pushed against the door with all my strength, keeping it open.

"Get out of here," he said. "I swear to God, I'll kill you if I see you again."

I felt my feet slipping, skidding on the stone floor as he pushed against me. My arms were shaking as I clung on. "The fire," I gasped.

"Get out!" With a final shove, the door slammed shut, and I fell backward.

For a moment there was silence. I imagine he must have turned and seen the fire rising, licking the ceiling. I heard him cry out, then the handle rattled.

"Fire!" He thumped on the door. "Fire! For God's sake, the fire! Get us out . . . get us out of here!" I tried the door. The lock was jammed fast.

"I can't . . . I can't open . . ." Bright lights danced before my eyes.

"Oh God, oh God," I heard him cry out. Smoke snuck beneath the door. I threw myself against the heavy wood again and again, but the door wouldn't budge. "Help us!" he cried, coughing and choking on the smoke. I pulled open the tiny metal grille in the dungeon door and looked in, terrified by what I might see. His eye appeared there, briefly, blocking the light of the wall of flame, and then his fingers snaked through the grille. I reached up and touched him, repelled and afraid.

"I'll go and get help," I said, but we both knew it was hopeless. There was no fire brigade here, no way to pump water down, no locksmith who could cut them free in time.

That image has stayed with me my whole life, his fingers touching mine—again, I think it was the only time we touched. Like God giving life to Adam in the Sistine Chapel. The deaths of Vita, of our child, of my father, marked the end and the beginning of my life. I've asked myself if I could have saved them somehow, whether Vita knew or if she was already dead. For sixty years I have blamed myself. If only I had fixed the damn door. It's the smallest things blindside us and change our lives forever.

"Go," my father said. He took away his hand and stepped back to meet his fate. I peered through the grille, saw him take Vita in his arms, cradling her. "Go!"

FORTY-SEVEN

Flying Point, Long Island

2000

Gabriel

I lie back on the sand beside the girl. "If only..."

"What happened next, Gabriel?" Her voice seems far away.

"I don't... I don't know. I must have collapsed, outside the château somewhere. The next thing I knew, I woke up in bed."

"Monsieur Lambert?" I could hear the woman's voice, but it seemed to be floating toward me out of a thick fog. "Monsieur Lambert?" I sat bolt upright in the bed, gasping for breath.

"Hush," she said. Dry old hands pushed me back against the soft pillows. My shoulder was throbbing, and it was agony every time I breathed in. "The doctor thinks you have cracked a couple of ribs," she said. "Try and lie still."

"Vita...," I said, my voice a thin rasp.

"Oh dear," she said. I tried to follow her dark figure in the shadows of the lamplit room. I was in a single bed, the old brass frame gleaming in the firelight. The room smelled of violets—the stale, sweet air laced with the tang of cat pee.

"Where is Vita?"

"Oh dear, oh dear..." She tucked in the lace-trimmed sheet. I recognized her as the old widow who lived in the gatehouse near the entrance to the Château d'Oc. She had been a sculptor, I believe, and several figure studies were ranged along the mantelpiece, their shadows flickering up the wall like a Greek chorus in the firelight. A ginger tabby slipped unnoticed into the room and curled up on the pink chintz chair by the hearth.

"Please, I must know." I took her hand and saw that mine was bandaged. Dark blood had dried on the ridge of my knuckles, and my nails were torn and dark. Her hand was gnarled with arthritis, twisted and bulbous as an old tree root. I remembered then that Vita told me this was how the woman had ended up in the Languedoc, unable to work any longer. She said that my father let the widow live there rent free because she had been married to one of his old teachers.

"Monsieur Lambert. I am so sorry, your wife . . ."

She had mistaken me for my father. "You don't understand, I am not—"

"I do wish there was someone I could call, to be with you?" I shook my head. "There are friends, perhaps? I don't feel you should be hearing this from a stranger . . . well, a neighbor, though we've never met." She looked away again, blinking. "I recognize you, of course, from the newspapers. You haven't changed at all, you are just as my dear Philippe described. He always said you were a remarkable boy, such talent—his star pupil. . . ." I stared at the ceiling as she chattered on, trying to collect myself. "I am so grateful for your kindness," she said finally. "After Philippe died, I didn't know what to do."

"This house is your home for as long as you need."

"Thank you. I am so glad to meet you at last, to say that face-to-face. Of course, I understand that artists need solitude, and I never wanted to intrude. Your wife was always quite insistent about that. I assume Vita was your wife? And your son . . ." She looked away. "I don't mean to pry. Vita told me your son had come to visit. I hoped to have the chance to meet him, but I know you value your privacy at the château, and I didn't want to pry. Oh dear, oh dear . . ."

I flinched. "Are they dead?"

"Oh dear," she said again and again, fussing over the blanket. "My condolences, Monsieur Lambert. They took away two bodies this morning. They were too . . . They asked me who they were. I knew you, immediately, of course, and told the police the only other people at the château were your son and your wife. I saw Monsieur Quimby leave some time ago, that's what I told them. I knew it was just the three of you at the château. Not that I pry." I turned my head away, tears pooling in my eyes. "By the time the fire brigade arrived from the town, the fire had swept through the lower floors of the château. They found you on the steps to the courtyard, half-dead from the smoke. Of course, I offered to take you in. The doctor said you must have complete rest—"

I pushed back the blankets and staggered to my feet. My right arm was in a sling, and my ribs were bandaged. I caught my reflection in the oval mirror over the dressing table and saw my right side was a livid purple, bruises seeping beneath the white bandages. "I have to go back," I said.

"Are you sure that it's safe, Monsieur Lambert? The authorities will have to have reported the fire." She lowered her voice. "If the Nazis were to hear that you have been hiding here . . ."

"I haven't been hiding," I said, shrugging on my father's identity like my old jacket. "This is my home."

"Of course, of course." I could see she was thinking as I dressed. "Monsieur Lambert, I have heard rumors." My breath caught in my throat. What was she talking about? Had she glimpsed my father? She knew the truth, she had just been humoring me.

"Rumors?"

"Your satirical cartoons are well known in certain circles. Why, Philippe had several framed in his study in Paris," she said. "France is no longer safe for people who have spoken out against fascism. Of course, they were not published in your name, but people gossip. Philippe worried that you had lost your way, artistically. Success can do that, sometimes."

"I never stopped working, he needn't have been concerned," I said, struggling into my shirt. The woman untied the sling, and I winced as I slid my arm into the sleeve.

"You are a prominent artist, Monsieur Lambert," she said, doing up the buttons. "It may be wise for you to leave now, if you feel you can travel."

I was intrigued. This was a side to my father I hadn't seen. All the time he had been hidden away in his castle, he had been penning anti-Nazi cartoons. No wonder he was worried.

"I've heard many of the artists are flocking to Marseille," she whispered, tying the bandage at the nape of my neck. "They say there is a man there, an angel from America, who is spiriting people out of the country. There is a man in Arles you can pay fifty francs to find out his name and address." She found a scrap of paper and wrote down the name of a café. "He is there each day at twelve P.M., apparently."

"Then you must come, too, madame." I thought of the *bidons* of gasoline Quimby and Lambert had been stockpiling in the barn and Vita's pretty little red Peugeot 202 cabriolet. "I shall drive us to Marseille," I said with more confidence than I felt. The most I had done was drive the car around the courtyard with Vita yelling instructions.

"No, no. They will not bother me and Artus." She beckoned to the old cat. "We have done nothing of importance."

"Thank you, madame," I said, and walked toward the door as weak and gangly as a newborn foal.

"Be careful!" she called. "Promise me you will rest once you are in Marseille!"

The house was silent in the twilight. I realized I must have slept through a whole day. The smell of burning hit me the moment I walked through the gate in the wall. Furniture had been dragged out into the courtyard, where it lay dark and sodden. Lambert's papers and journals caught at my feet, blowing limply in the wind like wet autumn leaves. I bent down, wincing, to pick up one yellowed journal, and peeled back the pages, stopping at a cartoon of Hitler as the Grim Reaper, presiding over a marching army of skeletons. The fluid line of the drawing was unmistakably my father's, but it was signed only with a cartoon of a feather—an Egyptian glyph. Years later, when I remembered this and looked it up, I discovered it was the symbol of Maat—of truth, justice, and balance.

I hadn't the maturity then to look beyond the surface of what my father had become. I saw a ruined man rather than a loyal husband, a good friend, an artist of conscience. Once in a while his drawings come up at auction, and I add them to my collection. If I had stopped then to look at the piles of journals and magazines littering my father's house, I might have seen a different side to him, but my chance had gone.

I staggered as I climbed the kitchen steps. Weak light leaked through the narrow windows of the house. I paused at the steps to the basement and listened to the silence, the slow drip of water from the ceiling. There was nothing for me here, now, I realized. In the hall mirror, I looked at myself, at my dark beard trimmed to match my father's, at the gray hair Vita had bleached at my temples.

"I am Gabriel Lambert," I said aloud, my voice echoing through the house. It was as if by naming it, by naming the monster that stood before me, it would come alive. I padded up the staircase, wheezing. My lungs were never the same after that fire. Aside from the stench of smoke, the fire had barely touched the first floor. I went first to my own room and lit a fire in the grate. Into it I threw every last scrap of my old life—my clothes, papers, my sketchbooks, even. Gabriel Lambert Jr. was dead. The only reminder of his life was the name on a death register somewhere, together with Vita's, forever. Next, I searched my father's bedroom, found the key to his desk. I pulled down a soft leather Gladstone bag from the top of the wardrobe and tossed it onto the bed. It was filthy—my fingers were coated with dust. I remember turning them over in front of my face, the bandages black with ashes. Whose hands were they? From the desk I took everything I could find of value—cash, the deeds to the château, bankbooks, his papers and passport. Sure enough, just as Vita had said, the photograph was at least ten years old. The face that looked back at me was my own.

FORTY-EIGHT

Marseille

1941

Gabriel

"Who are you?" Annie said.
"I'm sorry," I said, over and over. I'd imagined, sometimes, it would be a relief to be unmasked, for the whole story to come out, but God, the guilt was unbearable; it still is. What if it was my fault? I've asked myself that time and time again over the years since Quimby put the seed in my mind. It's funny how a single comment from someone can burrow down inside your mind like a parasite and blight your whole life.

All I cared about now was Annie. "You see?" I said to her. "I can't marry you, not while we are in France. If I did, and Quimby told the authorities who I really am, then you would be classed as Jewish, and I'm terrified what they would do to you. My father's parents were Catholic, but my mother was Jewish—if we marry, then the statute will apply to you, too."

Annie rocked on her heels, biting her lip. "Who are you?" she said. "Who are you?"

"Please, don't leave me," I said, hanging my head in shame. That's when she slapped me, hard.

"You lied to me."

"I know."

"Look at me, Gabriel." I could see the fire in her eyes. "Give me one good reason why I should forgive you."

"I love you, and I'll never lie to you about anything again as long as I live." I've been true to my word, that I can tell you.

Annie pulled herself up to her full five feet two inches. She smoothed down the collar of my jacket. "Let me get this straight. I thought I had been seduced by a thirty-something-year-old successful artist, but I've really been made love to by his penniless eighteen-year-old son?"

"It sounds terrible when you say it like that."

"At least Papa will be relieved about one thing. He said you were too old for me."

"You mustn't tell him."

"Why on earth not?"

"Varian and everyone at Air-Bel will know."

"But why should they care? They are your friends. It's wartime, Gabriel, thousands of people are living under assumed identities." She thought for a moment, and I saw her face cloud as she realized. "Oh God, you're leaving, aren't you?" She began to back away from me. "That man Fry's helping you get your papers . . . your father's papers. You've been planning to leave, all this time?" Her voice rose in despair. "How could you?"

I grabbed at her wrist. "You don't understand, I want you to come with me. They mustn't know who I am. They can help me get papers for you, and we can marry in America, I'm sure of it. Quimby has taken all my money, but I'm going to ask your parents to pay for your passage—"

"To America? Are you mad? As if they'd let me go, let alone marry you. And anyway, they have no money. Haven't you seen our house? Papa hasn't worked for months. They had to sell everything. If it wasn't for the pittance we make from sewing, we'd have starved."

"I didn't know," I said, and my head dropped. "I'm sorry."

Annie covered her ears as another train thundered overhead. Once it had passed, she took my face in her hands. "I love you," she said. "I will always love you, but the odds are I will be rounded up with all the other Jewish families, and who knows how long I have."

"No," I said, my throat thick with tears.

"It is what it is, Gabriel. I'll do everything I can to fight back, but you . . ." She paused and kissed my eyes, my cheeks. "You have a chance," she said, her voice little more than a whisper. "I want you to go, and live a wonderful life, Gabriel, for both of us. I want you to go to America."

"I won't leave you."

"Yes, you will," she said firmly. She stared at me in the way she's looked at all our children since when she's going to make damn sure they do what she wants. "You are Gabriel Lambert. You are going to America."

We walked up to Air-Bel hand in hand, in silence. I felt like that fellow Varian told me about—Sisyphus, struggling under the weight of all my guilt and sorrow. The lights were on in the house, in spite of the early hour.

"Looks like they've been having a party as usual," Annie said, and we stepped through the door. A man in a dazzling white sheepskin coat stood next to a pile of canvases strapped together. He reminded me of a bird of prey with his flash of white hair and those sparkling blue eyes of his.

"How do you do?" he said, stepping forward to shake my hand. I saw him eye Annie appreciatively as he kissed her hand. "Max Ernst."

"Ernst?" I said. "How marvelous to meet you. I am a huge admirer of your paintings. I'm Gabriel Lambert, and this is Marianne Bouchard."

"Ah, you are Marianne," he said. "Yes, I can see why your father might be worried."

"There she is!" Monsieur Bouchard marched through from the kitchen. "Where have you been hiding her? I searched the grounds, the house." He grabbed her arm, but Annie struggled free. "Did you think I wouldn't notice you were gone? You left your window on the latch and it was banging in the wind. Your mother and I have been worried sick."

"I'm sorry, Papa."

"I suppose you have been with him," he said, pointing at me. "We forbade you to have anything to do with him."

"I assure you, Monsieur Bouchard, Marianne has been perfectly safe," I said.

"Papa, I'm here now," she said, and glanced at me. "Besides, Gabriel is leaving for America soon. You will have nothing to worry about then." She ran toward the door. "Good-bye, Gabriel. Good luck."

"Annie, wait—" I ran after her and caught up with her on the drive. I took her in my arms, but she wouldn't look at me. Moonlight gilded her hair, her skin silver. "I love you," I said. "This isn't the end." I heard footsteps behind us.

"Gabriel." Varian reached out and took hold of my arm firmly. "Let her go." He glanced back at old Bouchard. "This will go badly for us all if you make a scene."

I stepped away. "Please, Annie—" Bouchard shot me an angry look as he dragged her away, but it was tinged with relief.

No, no, no, I thought. It would never be good-bye, not with Annie and me.

"Courage, mon frère." Max clapped me on the shoulder and steered me back toward the house. "One must sacrifice everything for love."

"That's just what I was thinking," I said, looking back over my shoulder, watching Annie and her father disappear into the dark night.

FORTY-NINE

Villa Air-Bel, Marseille

1941

Varian

Spring came early that year at Air-Bel. Varian sat high in one of the plane trees on the terrace, his back against the trunk. The plum trees were in blossom, and irises poked through the sodden leaves beneath them. From the pond, where he had caught the last of the fish a few months ago, toads croaked, spawning. He could see a female lying belly-up, dead, after releasing her strings of eggs.

Varian glanced up into the tree as he heard a lark sing. It was as though the house were awakening from the winter. Lizards basked on the warm stone walls again, and a magpie rooted through the leaves of a yellow fuchsia on the terrace. He laid his head back against the bark and imagined the sap rising through the tree like a pulse.

He stretched out his hand and spun the small framed ink drawing by Wifredo Lam that he had just suspended from the branch, ready for the auction. The colors glinted in the morning sun like jewels. Through half-closed eyes, he gazed out to the Mediterranean. *This is the kind of place you could live forever,* he had written to his father the night before.

He glanced up as he heard the kitchen door open. Madame Nouguet was pushing the gardener out of the door, looking nervously around her. He was tucking his shirttails into his trousers and pulling up his braces. Madame Nouguet's cheeks were flushed, her hair worked loose. Varian smiled as the man leaned in for one more kiss, and, swept away, she threw her arms around him. They broke apart, and the gardener stalked off toward the greenhouse, his shoulders hunched. The passionate affair between the cook and the gardener was the talk of the château. Mary Jayne was scandalized—she could not understand what the normally prim cook saw in the man. "He smells of compost," Varian overheard her say one night. He thought of Cupid, bow taut, arrow swinging blindly. *Who else will he hit?* he wondered as he scrambled down from the tree. *It's like spring sickness.* Even the two rabbits they had brought back from the country for breeding for the pot had just had their first litter.

Varian watched the gardener amble off toward the vegetable patches, where they had planted string beans, radishes, tomatoes, and lettuces. The thought of the vegetables made his mouth water. *I must have lost twenty pounds*, he thought, feeling his waistband sag as he put his hands in his pockets.

A group of figures made their way up the driveway, ready for the Sunday salon. The doors and windows of the château were flung open to the balmy air that morning, and the celebrations moved outdoors. Already, it was impossible to imagine the biting cold of the winter. The breeze on his face, on the skin at the open neck of his shirt, was like a caress. He was glad to be back, *to be home*, he thought. It felt like these gatherings were running on borrowed time. The artists would be leaving soon, Gabriel Lambert and the Bretons among them, he hoped. His face clouded as he thought of Breitscheid and Hilferding. After the news of their arrests was confirmed, he had grown more determined to get everyone else out safely.

At least Monsieur and Madame Bernhard are safely on their way now. Varian rubbed the bridge of his nose as he thought of all the plans they had tried to get them out of the country. Now, at last, another contact had come good and the Bernhards were being taken via underground routes and hiding places through Spain to Portugal.

Varian raised his hand as he saw Gussie walking across the terrace. He jumped down from the tree. "Morning, what a fine day."

"I think I have some news that may make it an even finer day for you," Gussie said. They stepped to one side to let a crowd of artists past, and Varian leaned against the ivy-clad wall.

"So?"

"You know our friend Mr. Allen was heading up-country to get an interview with Pétain?"

"In his dreams. No one can get close to Pétain."

"Well, according to some of the journalists I just bumped into in town, our friend crossed over into the Nazi-occupied zone without permission."

Varian raised his eyebrows. "Did he now? Not a terribly good example for a man who is supposed to be heading up a relief center. What have they done with him?"

"He's been arrested. The best he can hope for is that they'll trade him for one of the Nazi journalists later on." Gussie winked at Varian and walked on. "He's out of your hair, at least."

Varian clenched his fist and pumped his arm in the air. The sun seemed brighter suddenly, the colors of the garden more vivid. Men whose names he had known only from books on art, literature, politics, greeted him as an old friend on their way to pay homage to Breton. Varian felt like the ringmaster of a circus, keeping the house in check. *I wish Miriam could have got back here to see all this,* he thought. *She'd have got such a kick out of it. If only their visas had panned out. I hope they get down to Lisbon some other way.* He thought guiltily of Mary Jayne, how she was missing this, too. *But she'd made her choice. If ever Cupid was blind—* His thoughts cut off as Aube wove around his legs and ran toward the lawn, chasing Clovis. Rose and Maria raised their arms high, the glasses and bottles tinkling on the trays they were carrying. They set them down on the trestle tables set up on the terrace.

"Thank you, girls," Varian said, reaching for the corkscrew.

"Will that be all, sir?"

"Thanks, we'll be fine." It was the servants' day off, and Varian always had the impression they couldn't get away fast enough from the Sunday parties. *Maybe they're afraid.* He'd never been able to get over the sense of being watched, not since the *Sinaia* arrests. The sun gleamed on the glasses, the bottles glowing ruby in the morning light. *Let them watch,* he thought as the cork slid out of the bottle with a mellow pop, and he raised the bottle of red wine to his lips.

"*Santé,*" Jacqueline said. She walked with her arm around André's waist, his hand upon her shoulder. She took two glasses from the tray and poured a glass for them.

"Do you think the auction will be a success today?" André asked Varian.

"There are some remarkable pieces. I'd love to buy them all myself, if the ERC hadn't stopped my salary." *At least that should change now Allen is out of the picture.* Varian gazed up at the canvases strung from the trees. "There should be a good turnout for the Ernst exhibition alone."

"Is Peggy coming?"

"I'm not sure. She said she'd be back soon."

"I have a feeling her interest in Max is not entirely professional," Jacqueline said. "Once she sets her sights on a prize she won't give up until she's won it, or bought it. She'll be back, if I know Peggy."

There was no food that day, but there was wine and an infectious sense of joy and optimism. Varian orchestrated the auction, waving a wooden hammer in the air like the conductor of the philharmonic.

"What will you give me for this Masson drawing?" He pointed to the last gilded frame in the trees, and Danny scrambled up to turn the picture toward the crowd. Varian took the bids, calling them out with the rolling tone he'd heard an auctioneer use at a house sale in Connecticut when he was a child. The bids rose steadily. "Sold!" he cried.

As the auction wound down and the crowd dispersed, following André inside to see the sketches for the *Jeu de Marseille,* Fry settled back in a wicker chair. The midday sun beat down on him. A group of Spaniards was clearing the pond for swimming. He felt lazy, fug-headed with contentment. Clovis lolled over, his tongue hanging from the corner of his mouth. The dog flopped down at his side, and Varian distractedly ran his fingers through the springy fur on his head, felt the hard, narrow skull beneath.

"Varian!" Danny called, running along the terrace. He was gasping for breath and clutched his side as he ran toward him. His pale face was flushed, alarmed.

"What is it?" His moment of peace evaporated. The wineglass slopped as he put it on the table, and red seeped into the white cloth. There were people milling around them still, so Danny nodded his head toward the garden. They walked on in silence until they were out of earshot, Clovis weaving among the box hedges ahead of them. "Well?"

"It's the Bernhards."

Varian stopped walking. "No, not them, too?"

"I just heard. They were picked up in Madrid."

Varian slumped onto a stone bench beside the pool. "How did they find them?"

"It was their papers. The new transit visas are obvious fakes, if you know what you are looking for."

"This is terrible. Which other clients have we got going out?"

"I don't know, but I'm going straight to the office so we can recall them all."

"Good. Is there anything we can do for the Bernhards?"

"I'm sorry, boss." He was shaking. "We can't seem to do a damn thing right at the moment."

"Christ, it's not your fault. We're all up against it. You mustn't blame yourselves, you hear?" Varian rubbed his thumb against his lip, thinking quickly. "Our days of grace are over."

"And you?" he said. "It's not safe here for you now."

"I don't give a damn. The U.S. government won't help us, the French want us out, so to hell with all of them. I'm going to stay and fight it out just as long as I can." Varian thought for a moment. "Listen, we're going to need more funds. Kourillo reckons he can sell half the gold for us at a favorable exchange rate. I was going to meet him in town tomorrow, but I've got to go up to Gordes to see Chagall with Bingham. Will you meet him at midday?"

"Sure, boss. I'll dig the gold up tonight." Danny squeezed his shoulder. "I'll need to take it in two cases, it's too heavy for me to carry in one lot."

"Good man."

"Boss, are you sure we can trust him? It was mighty suspicious that the cops turned up at Air-Bel with a warrant to search for gold and foreign currency a couple of days after Kourillo sold it to us."

"Trust him?" He raised his head and focused on the distant sea. "I wouldn't trust him not to sell his own grandmother if he could get a good enough price, but what choice do we have?"

FIFTY

Marseille

~~~~~~

1941

Mary Jayne

"Mary Jayne!" Raymond grabbed at her arm as she walked out of her hotel.

"Go away, I have nothing left to say to you." She struggled free and hurried on quickly toward the tram stop. The morning crowds of people on their way to work milled around the pavement, and people stared at them as they pushed by.

"Wait, hear me out," he called after Mary Jayne.

"I can't. I'm late for work."

"For that stuck-up ass Fry?"

"Don't you dare," she said, swinging around. Mary Jayne slapped him, hard, the force of the blow stinging her palm.

"I deserved that," Raymond said, cupping his cheek. "I've been trying to see you, but the doorman wouldn't let me into the hotel."

"Good." Mary Jayne strode on, keeping her gaze straight ahead. "I told him if you came anywhere near me to call the cops."

"Please, I beg you."

"The great gangster, begging now?" She rounded on him. "How could you?" She glanced around, self-conscious, aware of the people staring, a crowd forming around them. She was standing by the door to a church and motioned at Raymond to follow her inside, away from prying eyes.

The church was empty, only the scent of incense from the morning mass lingering, rows of votive candles glowing on a tiered stand near the altar.

"I'm sorry," he said quietly. "I love—"

"Love?" she murmured, her voice low and husky. She gazed up at the stained-glass window nearby, a cloak of shifting color moving over them as the sun emerged from behind a cloud. "You don't know the meaning of the word. I feel like such a fool for telling everyone they were wrong about you."

"Mathieu threatened me. He said the gang would kill me if I didn't take your jewels."

"Killer was afraid of being killed?" She laughed. "I don't believe you. I think you were in it together. I think all you ever wanted from me was money."

"No," he said quietly, shaking his head.

"I never want to see you again. Do you understand?" He reached for her. "I mean it," she said, turning away. She wrapped her arms around herself. "I don't know what to believe anymore. That hoodlum Mathieu offered to bump you off, you know that? He said he wanted me for himself, can you believe it?"

"He always wanted you." Raymond's face crumpled. "That's the only reason he gave your jewels back. He'll kill me now, for sure."

"Well, that's your problem, not mine. I've done all I can."

"It can't end like this, *bébé*."

"Don't call me that. You have no right."

Raymond took hold of her arms. "Come with me. We can run away from this place, start again. . . ."

"And what? Keep on running? Always looking over our shoulder in case Mathieu and his gang have found us? God only knows what you have done to cross them, but they want you dead."

"I love you."

Mary Jayne turned her head away. He pressed his lips to her hairline. "It's over," she said.

"No, never. Not with us."

"It's over," she said again, her voice hoarse, breaking.

"I'll always love you."

Mary Jayne unclipped her handbag, pulling out her wallet. "Write to me once in a while. Tell me about all the battles you have won, and all the women you've destroyed with that black heart of yours." She handed him a roll of banknotes.

"I don't want your money."

"Take it," she said, forcing it into his hands. "Take it, and get yourself to England somehow, like you always said you would. Take it, and make something good of your life, Raymond. Prove them wrong." Mary Jayne embraced him, her throat tight with emotion. She screwed her eyes closed, trying to stem the tears she was too proud to let him see. "Prove me right."

FIFTY-ONE

Gordes

1941

Gabriel

"I assure you, Monsieur Chagall, we love 'cows' in New York," Varian said for what must have been the hundredth time. I couldn't figure it out. Here we were with one of the world's greatest living artists, and they were talking about cows? I'd managed to hitch a ride with Varian and Harry Bingham out to old Chagall's place in Gordes. When I miss France, I think of that day. Chagall lived in an old girls' school, a huge, beautiful old place. That day was perfection—the almond blossom was out, and the air was drenched with perfume. I'll never forget those hills—the gray green and sage, the dark flames of cypress. I think it is what heaven will look like, and I could understand why Chagall was reluctant to leave. I'd always been a big fan of his work, but the man himself was leaving me cold.

"Meh," he said, and shuffled toward an easel in the corner of the studio, draped with a white cloth. "I do not think I can work in America."

"My God," I heard Varian whisper to Harry, "it's like dealing with a recalcitrant child."

"Stick with it, Fry." Harry walked over to Chagall. "The thing is, monsieur, our sources tell us that soon people of Jewish descent will be rounded up."

"The anti-Jewish laws disgust me, but I am safe. I am an artist, a celebrated artist, and a French citizen. They would not dare to touch me." I could see from the expression on Varian's face that he thought they wouldn't think twice.

"Monsieur Chagall," Bingham said in his measured, pleasant tones, "you must listen to Mr. Fry."

"We're running out of time," Varian said. "I implore you, let us help you. We can arrange everything—papers, visas, tickets."

Chagall ignored him. He threw back the dust sheet from a painting of a young girl, flying free in space. "This is *Three Candles*."

"Let me take a photograph," I said, ushering Fry, Bingham, and Chagall toward the canvas. The painting was sublime. The girl reminded me of Annie.

"Please, at least come and see us at the ARC office, so we can talk through exactly how we can help you," Varian said to Chagall. I was half listening, caught up in the beauty of the girl, flying free.

Of course, by the time Chagall came to town in April, they had started rounding up the Jews in earnest. Varian had to go storming into police headquarters and say to them, "You do realize you have just arrested Monsieur Marc Chagall, one of the greatest artists in all of France, in the world? If I make one call to *The New York Times*, you will feel the full force of the U.S. government." Varian fought for Chagall and look how he repaid him. I can't figure out human nature sometimes. But then again, like I said to Sophie, why do people assume artists are going to behave like nice, normal people?

Anyway, I owe Chagall. That painting changed my life. I knew now what I must do. On the drive back down to Marseille, all of Provence unfurled beneath us, rolling green hills spreading down to the sea. Through the open window, I could hear cicadas humming. The sunlight through the window of the car was warm, and the leather seat was comfortable. I stretched out on the backseat, dozing as Varian and Harry talked in the front. Maybe their goodness was catching. On that drive I decided to do the first selfless act of my life, and there was a peace in that. I reconciled myself to my fate, and perhaps that made me appreciate the beauty of the countryside, the company of two good men, even more, because I knew it was all about to end. I'll never forget that drive—I felt a rare contentment the like of which I was not to feel again for years.

Varian dropped Harry at the American consulate, and we drove on in companionable silence to Air-Bel.

"Is everything okay, Gabriel?" he said, parking up on the drive. "You haven't said a word on the way back."

"I was just thinking about Chagall's painting."

"Beautiful, wasn't it?" He turned the engine off and stretched out his arms. "You know, some people said to me in New York, 'Why on earth are you risking your life to save artists? Why are they more important than ordinary men and women?' When you look at a painting like that, you just know it's the manifestation of everything good in a civilized society. If we don't keep the flame of culture burning bright, then what will we have left when the fighting is done?" He took off his glasses and rubbed at the bridge of his nose. "My friend Alfred Barr says that art exemplifies freedom. A painting like that is a symbol of freedom."

That was exactly how I felt when I looked at Chagall's painting—free.

FIFTY-TWO

Boulevard Garibaldi, Marseille

1941

Varian

The outer door of the boulevard Garibaldi offices was splintered and dented. "Thank God we changed the locks recently," Varian said to Gabriel as they let themselves in to the ARC. "If they'd have got through this door, they could have torched all the files."

"Who do you think did it?" Gabriel said.

"Probably those Vichy fascist kids Gussie noticed hanging around the last few days."

"They're just trying to scare you."

Yeah, or their bosses are, Varian thought, *and it's working.* The frequent searches, the suggestions that they would not be at all surprised to find Monsieur Varian Fry floating in the harbor with his throat slit, were all beginning to take their toll. "To hell with them, we've got work to do." Varian flicked on the lights as they walked through. "Morning, Gussie," he called.

"Morning, boss." Gussie swung his legs around from the cot in the kitchen and stretched, yawning.

"Quiet night?" Varian glanced at him and noticed the iron bar beneath the camp bed.

"Not exactly." He slid on his shoes. "I didn't think it was worth waking you all unless they made it through the street door. I don't think they'll bother trying again."

"Good chap." Varian peeled off a couple of notes from his money clip and gave it to him. "Listen, go get yourself some breakfast and head up to Air-Bel for a rest. We can hold down everything here."

Varian flicked on the gas stove and ran a kettle of water. "Right, we've got a busy day ahead," he said as the staff began to file into the office. He spoke to one or two of them and handed over the most urgent files. Finally, he turned to Gabriel. "Okay. Why don't you tell me what the hell is going on? I thought everything is in order? You're sailing on the *Paul Lemerle* with the Bretons."

"No. There's been a change of plan."

Bloody artists, Varian thought. *It's terrible to say it, but when some of the most troublesome ones get picked up, it's almost a relief not to have to deal with them.* The kettle whistled on the stove, and Varian frowned as he poured the steaming water over coffee grounds in the jug.

"Look. We have little time left, and much to do." He poured them each a cup of coffee. *At least there's some good news. Who knows why, but the Bernhards have been released and they are on their way to Lisbon. Thank God,* Varian thought, offering up a silent prayer of thanks. *Out of Hilferding, Breitscheid, and Bernhard, at least we managed to get one of the three out.* Varian slumped down in the chair at his desk and sipped at the scalding coffee. His mouth tasted metallic and his head was thumping. The thought of the day ahead exhausted him. They had stayed up until the early hours celebrating the news that the Bretons' French exit visas had come through, and Varian had drowned his guilt about Danny's arrest in drink after drink.

Just as it seems there's a glimmer of hope, Varian thought. *My poor, poor Danny. Kourillo's to blame.* He paled at the thought of the lost gold. *The crook's an agent for the police and the Gestapo, I'm sure of it.*

"Danny's lawyer came in yesterday," Gussie said, shrugging on his coat.

Varian beckoned to Gussie to follow him to a quiet corner, away from Gabriel. "Is he formally under arrest?"

"They've booked him for trading in gold, and transferred him to the Prison Chave."

"Oh God, no," Varian said, raking his hand through his hair. "Did anyone from here manage to speak to Danny?"

Gussie shook his head. "His lawyer saw him for ten minutes. He told me that Danny took the first case of gold, and Kourillo was waiting for him at his hotel on rue Thubaneau for the pickup, just like you arranged. Kourillo took the two thousand dollars in gold, and handed over the francs. When he came with the second case, Danny thought he was being followed, so he tried to walk on by, but Kourillo rushed down the steps and shook his hand. That's when the flics picked Danny up. Three guys jumped him."

Judas, Varian thought. "You're sure he has been charged?"

Gussie nodded. "They've thrown the book at him."

"Damn, damn, damn," Varian said under his breath. "Right. This is what we are going to do. I will go down to the station and take responsibility for it myself."

"You can't do that, boss," Gussie said quietly. "The office depends on you. Danny knew the risks."

"Damn it, we have to do something."

"Danny cooked up a story," Gussie said. "He's told the cops that some of our grateful, wealthy clients have paid us in gold."

"Did they believe him?"

"I doubt it."

"Damn them to hell," Varian said, and balled his hand into a fist, pressing it against his forehead. "I pass that prison twice a day walking to and from this place. I hate to think of Danny in there." He fell silent, his shoulders hunched. "Right. I'm going to see Vinciléoni. I'm going to make it known that we want a hit put on Kourillo."

"Are you sure, boss? Do you really want his blood on your hands?"

"They won't kill him. I just want to scare him out of town. Kourillo is one of their own. Vinciléoni will just tell him to get lost. I simply want to send a message that they are not going to mess around with us again." Varian strode past Gabriel to his desk and reached for his hat. "People disappear in Marseille all the time—only last night some English guy, Quimby, turned up in an alley with his head bashed in. It was in the papers this morning."

"An English guy?" Gabriel interrupted.

"Yeah," Gussie said. "I doubt they would have bothered to cover the story if it was just the usual Marseille ruffian, but they are speculating he was some kind of spy."

"Look, Gabriel, we'll have to do this later. Can you book a time with

Lena? . . . Say, are you okay?" Varian looked properly at Gabriel for the first time. "What happened to your face?"

Gabriel touched the gauze taped to his cheek. "Nothing. I looked at a guy the wrong way in Snappy's bar."

Varian shook his head. "I tell you, you'll be glad to get out of this place. Nobody's safe anymore."

FIFTY-THREE

Villa Air-Bel, Marseille

1941

Gabriel

"Did you kill him?" Annie whispered to me, closing the Bouchards' back door behind her. I could hear her parents talking in the house—it wasn't safe for me to stay long.

"Of course not." I hoped my face didn't show a thing. "Quimby had it coming. I bet I wasn't the only person he was swindling. They're saying he might even have been some kind of agent, or spy."

"At least you won't have to spend your whole life looking over your shoulder, now." When she looked up at me, her expression reminded me of an old stray dog who lived on our street in the Marais. He must have been thirteen or fourteen, a grizzled, charming old thing. We'd give him scraps if we could, which he accepted with all the grace of a down-on-his-luck nobleman. I came back from school one day to find him locked up in the back of the warden's van. We all knew what that meant. The man wouldn't budge, wouldn't let him go. I railed against it, banged the bars, but the old dog just stuck his nose through and nudged my hand. He looked at me with exactly the same brave expression Annie had.

"Annie, I'm sorry—"

"Don't, Gabriel, please." She pressed her fingers to my lips. "Don't make this any harder than it is."

"You will come, tomorrow, to see the boat off?"

"Of course. Even my parents are coming. I think they want to make sure you've left the country." She turned my hand over in hers, traced the long, firm arc of the lifeline with her index finger. "There, you've years and years ahead of you. . . ."

"I don't want to spend them without you."

She shook her head, unable to look me in the eye. "You have to go, now. It's too dangerous here." She touched the bandage on my cheek. "My poor darling," she said. "You have a chance to get away from here. You can start a new life. No one knows you there. You'll just be Gabriel Lambert, not the father or the son. You can just be yourself, the very best self you can be." She raised her gaze, her eyes glistening. "Promise me, Gabriel. Promise you'll never forget me." I held her close, her head against my chest, my lips in her hair. "Live a good life, for both of us, Gabriel. Make it count."

FIFTY-FOUR

MARSEILLE

Tuesday, March 25, 1941

GABRIEL

Dawn's silver light washed the horizon, crept wave by wave across the shore. The Quai de la Joliette was crammed with people by the time I arrived, carrying only my rucksack. I was leaving as I had arrived, with nothing more than the clothes I stood up in. I had even sold my easel. Once again, I had no money, no home. I had skipped out of the hotel owing the last of my bill.

I could see armed guards keeping the crowd separate from the passengers. People were so desperate to get out of the country, they would try anything. I saw an old man on his hands and knees, trying to creep past the guards, but they caught him and cracked his ribs with the butts of their rifles for his trouble.

"Where are they?" I said under my breath. I saw Varian then, shepherding his clients toward the gangplanks. I saw Breton, his hair gilded by the morning sun, carrying Aube in his arms. He was hand in hand with Jacqueline, and they pushed their way through. I've always hated crowds, and the noise, the shouts, the hot jostling figures, terrified me. My palms were sweating, my skin prickling with anxiety. All the Bouchards had to do was bring Annie to the docks, that was all. What if I never saw her again? I checked my watch. They were ten minutes late. The *Capitaine Paul Lemerle* was making ready to sail, sounding its great horns, steam pluming up into the air from the huge chimneys. *Where is she?* I looked frantically around and saw a lamppost to one side. I clambered up and looked around the bobbing sea of heads and hats.

"Annie!" I yelled above the noise of the crowd and the ship's horns. "Annie!"

"Gabriel!" I could hear her, followed the sound of her voice. There! I saw her pale hand waving like a drowning woman's, reaching out of the dark sea of hats. I jumped down and pushed my way through toward her, my heart thundering, my breath coming in short, tight gasps. I knocked over a man, tripping on the legs of someone who had fallen. Then she was there, in front of me.

"Annie," I whispered, burying my face in her hair and holding her tight to me, tears in my eyes. Her parents shoved their way through. I saw my anxiety painted on their pale, drawn faces. I held Monsieur Bouchard's gaze, and he nodded. "Come," I said. "It's time." I held on to Annie's hand and shielded the Bouchards with my arm. We fought our way through to the front of the crowd, until I found a rifle pointed at my chest.

"No further," the guard barked, "passengers only."

"He is a passenger," Annie said. She turned to me. "I may never see you again. It's just hit me, that you are really leaving."

"No," I said. "I'm not leaving. You are."

I saw the confusion on her face, and it felt like the noise, the crowd, fell away. It was just me and her. "Annie, it's all arranged. The ARC has helped me get your papers in order, and I'm giving you my ticket." I put the strap of my bag over her head, tucked it under her arm safely. "I knew you'd refuse if I told you before. It's all in here. Tickets, papers—"

"No," she whispered, tears brimming in her eyes. "I can't let you sacrifice your crossing . . . yourself, for me."

I took her in my arms, held her tight, my lips against her cheek. "Annie, after everything I have done, please, let me do one good thing."

I felt her shake her head, she pushed me away. "No, I won't let you. I won't go. I can't leave you . . . ," she said, turning to her parents.

"Marianne," Monsieur Bouchard said, taking her face in his hands, tears pouring down his wrinkled cheeks. "You are getting on that boat."

"No, Papa," she said, a sob catching in her throat. She looked at her mother. Madame Bouchard reached into the carpetbag she was carrying and forced a bundle of money and clothes into her hands.

"My child, my child . . ." Her face crumpled as she held her daughter one last time, rocking her in her arms, her eyes screwed closed as she whispered to her. "Go," she said finally, breaking away.

"Mama, no!" Annie screamed, reaching out to her, but her mother pushed her toward the boat, weeping.

"Go now. God bless you, my darling girl. Go!"

The ship's horn blew, and I dragged Annie, crying for her parents, to the bottom of the gangplank. I handed over the ticket and papers for inspection. The official stamped them and unclipped the chain to let her climb aboard.

"Listen to me . . ." I soothed her like a child, like I have all my own children and grandchildren down the years. "I love you," I said, embracing her. I breathed in her clear scent of sunlight and lavender one last time. "I love you. Wait for me. When I get to America, we'll be married, I promise. . . ."

"Gabriel," she cried out as the guards pushed me back with their guns. "I love you!" The official took her arm, hurried her up the gangplank. "I'll wait for you. However long it takes, I'll wait."

I reached toward her, fought to stay at the front of the crowd for one last glimpse of her. "I'll see you," I cried, "I'll see you in New York!"

FIFTY-FIVE

Marseille

1941

Varian

The great ropes loosed from their mooring posts, snaked free into the water. The *Capitaine Paul Lemerle* heaved, like a black cliff breaking free above the crowd. Varian waved, craned his neck to see the Bretons up on deck.

"Bon voyage," he cried, echoing the shouts around him. *It worked*, he thought, his heart soaring with elation. *It worked. Thank God, they are away.* Next to them, he saw Marianne. The poor girl looked terrified. He followed the direction of her gaze and saw Gabriel Lambert, fighting his way to the front of the crowd, tears pouring down his face. He thought of the letter he had received that morning, delivered by the concierge of Alistair Quimby's hotel. It made no sense to him. *Clearly that guy Quimby had some kind of grudge against him.* Varian had simply screwed up the note and tossed it in the bin. Gabriel Lambert's file was closed. *It's too late now, and there are hundreds of other people needing our help. Whatever the truth is, Lambert gave up his passage, and that's a selfless act. Good luck to them. I hope they find one another again.* Varian smiled sadly at the love written clear on Gabriel's face as he waved, as he blew kisses to Marianne with both hands.

They had only just managed to get her papers in time. Varian remembered Gabriel pacing up and down in the office the day before.

"Please, you must help her."

"Listen, old chap—"

"You must!" Gabriel slammed his hands down on the desk.

"Look. I can see how much you care about this girl, but she's not . . ."

"Not what? Not a great artist? Not important enough?" Gabriel was shaking. He held out a golden cloth, an embroidery that spilled onto the table. "She made this."

"Lambert, it's hardly on a par with your work."

"She is young, and bright, and good. What price is a life, Varian? What makes one life more important than another?" He rubbed the heel of his hand between his eyes. "How can you say that my life is worth more because of a few paintings?"

Varian sat back in his chair and sighed. "You are willing to sign over your passage to America to her?"

"Yes, without hesitation."

"Listen. We've always had a rule here that we will only help people to escape that are known by people we trust. Can I trust you?"

"Yes."

"The ARC cannot officially help her to obtain papers."

"I'll do anything," Gabriel said. "I will pay whatever it takes to get her papers in order, for forgeries—I'll do them myself if necessary. . . ." His voice trailed off as Varian looked at him sharply. "I don't . . . I don't know quite how you have managed to do what you have done here, but I am begging you, please help Annie."

Varian sighed. "All right. You're in luck. It would have been different a few months ago, but now that they are letting boats sail for Martinique, all she will need is a French exit visa."

"Thank you, thank you . . ." Gabriel clasped his hand. "I'll never forget this, Varian, never."

"There will be time for sentiment later. I'll get one of the men to bring Annie's visa to you tonight. Let's make damn sure she is on that boat, too."

"You'll never know how much this means." Gabriel hesitated. "Why do you do it? Why do you do all of this, put yourself at risk for us all?"

"Why?" Varian said, as though it had never occurred to him to ask the question. "You know, I keep a phrase of Emerson's with me always." He gazed out of the window, reciting from memory: "'There are men to whom a crisis, which intimidates and paralyzes the majority, comes as graceful and beloved as a bride.'" He turned and smiled at Gabriel. "I do this simply because it is the right thing to do. Charlie always said it's the duty of the strong to protect the weak. All I can tell you is I've met the most remarkable men and women of my life in the last few months. I've met people whose work I've loved my whole life. You know," he said, laughing, "all I knew about people outsmarting the Gestapo was what I'd seen in movies, but when the committee in New York said 'You're it' and sent me out here, I had to learn fast." He stood and guided Gabriel out of the office. "The thing is, I believe in freedom. I feel a deep love for these people and gratitude for the happiness their work has given me. I had to come and help them when they needed it." He took off his glasses and rubbed the bridge of his nose. "You remember Miriam? She always said it made her think of that verse in Ruth: 'Your people are my people.' That's what it comes down to."

"You are remarkable. If I ever have a son, I'll name him for you."

"I always hated my name," Varian said, laughing softly. "I wanted to be called Tommy." They shook hands. "Good luck, Gabriel. What will you do now?"

"I thought I'd head into the countryside. I hope I can be useful to the Resistance."

"Talk to my men. They can help you."

"What about you?"

"Me? I'm going to get Danny out of jail, and then I'll hold out here as long as I can. Besides, it is easy to become attached to a place, especially when it is a country as beautiful as France." He opened the door for me. "You know, we are all at war as surely as our brave boys on the front lines. One must bring them all back home, or at least one must try. That is all I can do, bring as many of you home as I can."

Varian stumbled as the crowd surged, fought to stay on his feet. A guard nearby brandished his pistol, cocked it up into the air.

"*Arretez!*" he warned.

If only we could round them all up, every single name on that list, and spirit them away on a boat like this, Varian thought. He waved as Jacqueline lifted Aube to see the boat leave the Vieux-Port. The sea lurched and swelled, slapping against the quay as the engines roared. A woman on the deck dropped red rose petals, spiraling, drifting down to the sea.

"Varian!" Mary Jayne yelled, pushing her way through the crowd. He reached out to her and put his arm around her, shielding her from the crowd. They gazed silently at each other for a moment, like equally matched creatures deciding whether to fight or make peace. "Well done," she said, and dug him in the ribs. "You did it."

"We did it," he corrected, "but only just." He shielded his eyes and looked up to the deck. "Are you okay? Where's Killer?"

"He's gone." She looked up at Varian. "Thank you."

"For what?"

"For not saying 'I told you so,' like everyone else has." She shielded her eyes. "Where are they?" He pointed up to the deck. "I'm so glad," she said, her voice catching. "Good-bye!" she called. "Good-bye!"

Varian cupped his ear, craning to hear what André was shouting as the ship pulled away, guided out of the harbor by the pilot boats. He shook his head, mimed that he couldn't hear. "I'll see you soon!" he cried, waving as the boat pulled away. "I'll see you in New York!"

"So," Mary Jayne said, glancing up at him. "What now? Friends?"

"Friends." Varian offered her his arm, and they walked in silence along the quay. "I think it's time we got you safely home, too, don't you?"

"Home? I don't even know where that is anymore." She looked toward the cathedral, the sun glinting on the Virgin high above the city. "Nothing will ever be as extraordinary as this year in Marseille, will it? We shared our finest hours, my friend, our finest hours."

FIFTY-SIX

Flying Point, Long Island

2000

Sophie

An old red truck pulls up in front of the beach house, and Marv clambers out. "Hey, Tommy," he says.

"Hey, Marv, how are you doing?" Tom lifts the last of the boxes into the back of the station wagon. "Who's this?" He squints his eyes in the sunlight.

"Pleased to meet you." Sophie steps forward and offers her his hand. "I think you're expecting me? Sophie Cass."

"This is Tom Lambert, Gabe's eldest," Marv says. "This here's the girl Gabe's been talking to himself about for the last few weeks."

"I know who you are," Tom says. "We tried to cancel a hundred times, but you wouldn't listen. When your mother rang, the only reason I agreed to see you was to tell you face-to-face. Gabe doesn't need this. Dad is . . . well, he's not been well for some time, but the last few days he's grown more confused. It's like he's lost in his own world. He really doesn't need you dragging up all this stuff about the war, and Vita, not now. It's all so long ago—what does any of it matter anymore?"

"I promise, I won't take up much—"

"Anyway," Tom says, stepping toward her, "it's too late. You've missed your appointment, and we have to get going."

"Look, I've walked for miles." Sophie folds her arms. Her skin is tanned, her hair windblown. "I wouldn't have been late if Harry hadn't dumped me on the wrong beach."

"I found her thumbing a lift on the road to town." Marv leans in to Tom. "Did I do the right thing bringing her here?" he whispers too loudly. "Gabe was talking to himself again, earlier on in the café—well, it was like he was talking to her." He points at Sophie. "I thought it might be important."

Tom throws a tarpaulin over the boxes. "Sure you did right," he says clearly, angling his head toward Marv's good ear. "What does it matter anymore?"

"Talk of the devil," Sophie says as Harry's pickup bounces along the dirt road and pulls to a stop beside Marv's.

"I'm sorry," Harry says, holding up his hands as he walks toward Sophie. "I felt bad and I went back to find you, but you'd gone already." He glances at his father. "We'd decided this morning we were going to send you on a wild-goose chase, and hoped you'd just give up if Gabe had gone by the time you found the house." His eyes are clear and blue as he looks at Sophie. "I was just trying to protect Gabe. He's not been that strong lately, especially since Grandma died."

"Annie died?" Sophie's eyes widen. "Oh God, when?"

"We lost her a few days ago—" Tom kicks at the ground, his voice breaks. "We haven't made it public knowledge yet. She was only diagnosed a few months ago, and she went downhill fast. Gabe . . . he's taken it pretty hard."

"I just can't imagine Gabe without her," Harry says. Sophie looks across at him, holds his gaze, tears pricking her eyes. "He's not well himself, but he was with her every moment she was awake, right up to the end."

"I'm so sorry." Sophie's throat is tight. "Why didn't someone tell me? I would never have—" She looks up at a sound from the house, her eyes glistening. Some of the great-grandchildren are playing in the garden, the flames of a last bonfire sparking into the sky. "Excuse me." Sophie walks toward the fire. Her hand shakes as she reaches for her phone.

"Honey?" Paige picks up on the first ring. "Are you okay? I saw you'd tried to call."

"I'm here, finally."

"Have you seen Gabe?"

"Not yet." Sophie closes her eyes. "She died, Mom, Annie died."

"Oh God, when?"

"A few days ago. I feel terrible for pushing and pushing to see Gabriel over the last few months. No wonder they were trying to keep me away. I don't know what to do—" She sensed something and glanced back at Harry, who was leaning against his truck, watching her. "I can't put him through this when he's just lost the love of his life."

"Do the right thing, Sophie."

"Mom, I'm so confused. And Jess told me . . ."

"What's he done now?" Sophie hears the edge in her mother's voice.

"He's just told me that Dad was illegitimate."

"Oh, that?"

"Mom, what do you mean, 'Oh, that?'" Sophie's voice rises. "Why didn't any of you tell me?"

"Darling, what does it matter? Of course, it was still a big deal in the fifties. You know what your grandmother was like, she always was independent, said she didn't want Sam to think she was trapping him into marriage. But Sam made her see sense in the end. They married after your dad was born. My guess is your grandmother was so stuck on the idea of doing it all herself that she wouldn't give Sam's name when she registered the birth. Simple as that. Maybe they never bothered changing the certificate later. You know what they were like, always so focused on the day. My bet is they just didn't look back. I promise you, your grandparents had one of the best relationships I've ever come across."

"Thank God. Vita, the story . . ." *My story*, Sophie suddenly realizes. She feels like she is watching a carefully constructed puzzle slot into place. "I thought . . . I thought it meant we weren't related. Dad always loved telling me the stories about her."

"Honey, you only have to look at you. You're the spitting image of her—Jack always said you reminded him of the paintings he'd seen of her."

"I know."

Paige clicks her tongue. "Typical, Jess couldn't even let you have that, could he? Just like that control freak to think he can destroy that link to your dad. Forgive me, darling, but I always said Jess is a narcissist. Love isn't about what you take from someone, it's about what you give."

"I was just . . . I was thinking about Dad." Sophie sits down by the bonfire, hugs her knees. "I wish—"

"Sophie, it was just his time."

"He died because of me." Her fingertips tremble, running across her right collarbone, searching for the indentation, the daily reminder of where the bullet nicked her shoulder. She had told Jess it was from a broken collarbone—described the pony, the fall, in vivid detail.

"He died protecting you," Paige says gently. "I know you never talk to me about your work lately, because you think it will upset me, but you don't have anything to prove. You don't have to pick up where he left off."

"If I hadn't insisted we go to the drugstore, he would still be alive. Think of everything he would have written."

"Sophie, you can't think like that. It was your dad's choice. He tried to talk the gunman out of holding up the drugstore, and he protected you when the guy started shooting."

Sophie closes her eyes. She hears the crackle of the bonfire, and her nostrils flare at the acrid smoke. She remembers it all. The sound of her father's voice, calm and sure, telling the guy to hand over the gun. She remembers his silhouette blocking the light. Then the screams as the shots rang out, the weight of her father's body, shielding her. How the bullet nicked her shoulder as he slumped down. "He died in my arms."

"I know, honey, I know." Paige falls silent. "You have to let go of this and move on, live your own life." She laughs softly. "Your dad was no angel, trust me, and he'd be the last person who would have wanted you to think that. He died as he lived, doing what was right, standing up to the bad guys. It's as simple as that. He was doing the right thing, the brave thing." She pauses. "I was just thinking about you out there today, about Gabe and Annie."

"What about them?"

"It's nuts—I've never admitted this to anyone before, but your dad had a huge crush on Annie. Every man who met her did—she was like the Long Island Bardot. You know that photo I gave you, of Annie and Gabe?"

Sophie searches in her bag. "It looks like she's in her thirties?"

"I hadn't even met your dad yet, when he took that. I found his journals after he died, and that was tucked in there."

"Did he and Annie—"

"God, no!" Paige laughs. "Not for want of trying on his part. It may have been the swinging sixties, but there was only one guy for Annie.

Gabe didn't like it one little bit, though. Well, just look at his expression in the photograph."

Sophie smiles. "It looks like Annie's holding him back."

"Gave your dad his first black eye, just after that photo was taken." Sophie hears her mother sigh. "First of many."

"Did you know Gabriel well?"

"No, I never could understand why he wasn't friendlier—I mean, with the connection to Vita and all." Paige thinks for a moment. "Maybe like your grandparents, he just didn't want to look back. A lot of that generation just wanted to put the war and all the losses behind them. But I'm convinced that's why they ended up out here—Vita's mother was from East Hampton originally. Maybe after he lost Vita and his son during the war, it was a way of being close to them."

"His son?" Sophie hesitates. It is on the tip of her tongue to tell her mother about her doubts. "What about Annie?"

"She was older than me, obviously, but she was lovely, very down-to-earth. We'd see them both at parties and gallery openings occasionally. I lost touch with her when your dad convinced me to move to the city." Paige hesitates. "I don't know why I never looked them up again, when I moved back to Montauk. Maybe . . . maybe I was a little jealous of her, if I'm honest. It all seemed so natural and easy with them. The success, the troop of beautiful kids, that gorgeous house." Paige laughs sadly. "She was so kind to me, but I couldn't help envying her. After I lost your dad, I just couldn't face seeing all . . . well, all that happiness when I was trying to cope raising you by myself. Even you've been won over by Gabe and Annie's love story, haven't you?"

"I guess I have." The knowledge settles in her, strong and true. "I want that, you know?"

"I know," Paige says. "If I've learned anything, you have to fight for it. Sure, they made it look easy, but marriage is as much about sacrifice and compromise and forgiveness as moons in June." She laughs softly. "Maybe if each of you is willing to give more than you get, you stand a chance."

"Was it like that with Dad?"

"When I first met Jack, I thought we'd set the night on fire, we loved one another so much." She pauses. "Oh, God, it goes by too fast. What a fool I've been. I wish I'd seen Annie again."

"I'll tell Gabriel you say hi."

"You will be careful, won't you? I know he's what—ninety-something, now? He had a hell of a temper on him in the old days, though."

"I'll be careful, I promise."

"See you soon?"

"Sooner than you think. I've decided to take you up on the offer of the barn."

"Seriously? That's wonderful."

"I've even found a contractor." She glances back at Harry, who is watching her. "I don't need much—just water and electric."

"All mod cons? We can do better than that." Paige laughs. "It's the right decision, take your time and find your feet. You're always happy when you're out here, and Mutt will love it."

"I've got to go."

"Sure. And Sophie . . ."

"Yes?"

"It's just beginning, you know. Forget about all the what-ifs and what-might-have-beens." Sophie hears the love in her mother's voice. "Your story's just begun."

FIFTY-SEVEN

Flying Point, Long Island

2000

Gabriel

I lie back on the sand and close my eyes, listening to the surf. I try to push that anxiety from me, the bittersweet relief of seeing Annie leave Marseille. I'm there, on the docks again, seeing the only sure light in my world sailing away.

"Don't go." I'm floundering, caught in nets I wove myself.

"Go? I'm not going anywhere."

I blink, shield my eyes from the overhead sun. The girl is above me now, her blond hair ablaze in the light.

"You?"

She comes closer so I can see her face.

"What is it, Gabriel? It's like you've seen a ghost."

Someone is crying out, a strangled whimper. It's me, I'm frozen like a dreamer caught in a nightmare, stifled and mute.

"Hush," she says, brushing the hair back from my brow. "Don't fight it now."

"You?" The breath is tight in me now, no respite. "Vita?"

"Sophie? Vita? What's the difference? Names are irrelevant." Her face hovers over mine, and I see, I see. Those lips, the pillow crease, her golden hair tumbling around me like flames.

"No, not you," I say, blinking away tears. "I don't want you here."

"Tell me the end of the story, Gabriel."

"I can't. I'm tired . . . It's too long ago."

"It's important," she insists. "You need to remember it all." She shakes me so my head rolls from side to side. "Did you do it, Gabriel? Did you kill Quimby?"

"I lied to Annie, one last time. I did it. I did it for her." My voice is a whisper. I never meant to kill him. I followed him down from our last meeting at the cathedral on the hill to the city, to the Vieux-Port. I just wanted to find out where he was staying, so I could get back as much of the money as I could for Annie and destroy the photos. I saw him go into some seedy hotel, and I waited until nightfall. As I waited, I got angry, thinking of everything he had done to me. I didn't trust him to leave me and Annie alone. Then I remembered he had a photo in his wallet, too. I decided I'd follow him and rough him up a bit, scare him away. If Varian and his guys could get tough with the gangsters and bullies, then so could I. He came out just after six. He must have realized he was being followed. I saw him go into the alley behind the café Au Brûleur de Loups. He was hiding in a doorway. For years, the memory of his face looming at me out of the darkness has haunted my nightmares. Quimby had a blade, and he jumped me, slashed at my face. I saw the surprise on his face when he saw it was me, and then he went for me. He had me backed into a dead end, waving that knife around. He wanted me dead, he said. I had no choice but to fight him. I knew he'd never let me go.

It's not like in the movies. The fight didn't last long. I was younger than him, and stronger, and I managed to get hold of his arm and knock the knife from his hand. Quimby backed away and put his glasses in his top pocket, then raised his fists. I told him to give up, but he said nothing would give him greater pleasure than to smash my face in. He was bluffing. I could see him peering at the floor, trying to see where the knife had gone, but he couldn't see a damn thing, and the alley was full of potholes and puddles of oily water. I hated him at that moment. I had no choice, I fought for my life, for Annie, and I thumped him with all my strength. He reeled away toward the wall, and I pushed past. I could hear him coming after me, the sound of his feet on the cobblestones, and then . . . then it just stopped. He fell, you see. Fell or tripped on something and hit his head on one of the sharp stone doorways jutting out into the alleyway. I went back to check, but he wasn't breathing.

"It wasn't your fault," the girl says.

"He wouldn't have been there if I hadn't followed him from the hotel."

"But you didn't kill him."

"I just wanted to scare him, that's all. He'd threatened to tell Varian. They wouldn't have helped Annie."

"Fry's team never knew who you are? Only Quimby and Annie knew the truth?"

"How could I tell them, even later? I was so ashamed." That is the greatest punishment of all, perhaps. All this, this beautiful life with its fragile happiness, has been built on a lie. Is it your own life, if you can't claim it as your own?

"Tell me about Varian."

"He . . . I lost track of him, toward the end."

"Did you contact him again?"

I shake my head. "I gave to the International Rescue Committee, as Fry's organization became, as much . . . as I could."

"Anonymously," the girl says.

"Of course."

"But you couldn't bring yourself to see him. Were you guilty because of what you had done?"

"Yes."

"Good. So you should be, lying to good people like that."

"Please don't . . ."

"Poor Varian. Everything that came after lived in the shadow of Air-Bel." She sighs. "And Mary Jayne, what of her? She wrote to Fry just before he died, and do you know what she said?"

I know. She said: *We shared our finest hours, my friend.* "But there have been other fine hours since then, simple hours full of work, and love, and family."

"Mary Jayne spent the last of her days in a villa in the south of France she christened 'Air-Bel.'" The girl reaches out her hand and points at the house, at my home. "Just like you, Gabriel." I think of Annie, sitting on her chair out on the deck looking out to sea, wrapped in blankets, and behind her, the old flaking sign we painted together: *Air-Bel.*

"Annie," I gasp.

"Tell me about Annie, Gabriel. Did she make it safely to America?"

"Annie . . . waited. Years. Years and years."

"You were trapped in France, weren't you?" Her voice soaks into me like sunlight. It comes from far away. "You went into hiding, fighting with the Resistance, didn't you, Gabriel, do you remember now?" I try to nod. "Just like Danny and the others." I feel her shaking me. "Stay with me, Gabriel. Do you think you made amends, for all you did and didn't do? For Vita, and your father, and Quimby?" I whimper. "Shhh," she murmurs, strokes my cheek. "Do you think all the years of working, all the years of loving your family and living quietly, atoned for that? How do you live a good life with such guilt?" The girl pauses. "What about the man who killed Annie's parents? Do you think he felt guilty?" I close my eyes as her voice, Vita's voice, whispers close to my ear. "All those nights Annie stood on the shore wondering what happened to her mother and father. Do you want to know what happened? They were captured, Gabriel, just like Annie always feared. Her father was shipped out to a concentration camp." I feel her breath on my cheek. "When you were all playing games in Marseille, no one had even dreamed of the horror to come, of the Holocaust, but it swept them away. Her mother was shot on the platform as they took old Bouchard away. She tried to run past the guards, to go with him."

"How do you . . . How do you know all this?"

"I'm everywhere and nowhere, Gabriel. That's what you will find."

"Please," I whisper. "Get Annie . . ."

"I'm almost done, Gabriel," she says. "After the war, you finally reached New York, didn't you? Do you remember arriving at Ellis Island, and Annie was waiting for you?"

"Annie." My breaths are shallow, useless.

"You were young, and penniless, but with Gabriel Lambert's name and your contacts at Air-Bel behind you, your work began to sell." I close my eyes as she strokes the lids with her fingertips. The images come thick and fast then. Annie sitting up in bed holding our first son, the love and amazement on her face as she looked at him. The old van we parked on the spot overlooking the beach, our first night talking by a bonfire here on the shore, our dreams for the future unfurling to the stars. We lay there watching the midnight-blue velvet sky lighten and the morning star shine for us. Then I see the timbers marking out the space that we called home. Annie in dungarees, painting the walls, her stomach swollen with our second child. One after another, the images come, fragments of a simple life. Our life. And I feel such happiness, such joy.

FIFTY-EIGHT

Flying Point, Long Island

❦

2000

Gabriel

Inside our sanctuary, our Air-Bel, my other son and daughter and their children are closing up the house for the season. Dust sheets billow like sails, falling silently across the furniture in the shadows for the last time.

"Marv? You okay?" Tom says, touching my old friend's arm.

"Oh, me, sure. Listen, like I said, Gabe was in the café just now."

Tom slams the tailgate closed. "Damn, is that where he's got to? He said he was going for a walk. Albie was supposed to be keeping an eye on him, but Dad gave him the slip."

"He seemed . . ." Marv chooses his words carefully. "Well, he seemed a little lost."

"Just so long as he wasn't upset. He has good days and bad days. We only just convinced him to throw out the Christmas tree."

"That was a good thing you did for your mother. I know how much he wanted her to have one last Christmas here, even if it was August." He looks up as my second son strides over, arms laden with bags. "Hey, Albie," he says. "How are you kids holding up?"

"Day by day." Albie leans on the car, dumps the bags into the back. "Dad was amazing, you know, he cared for her right up to the end, would hardly let anyone near her."

"It's good that she came home," Marv said. "They loved it here."

Tom looks back at the house, watching Sophie. She is talking to the kids now. She squats beside them, helps the littlest toast her marshmallows over the fire. The men wander over. "You know, we used to say we hoped they'd go together. It was impossible to imagine the one without the other." He shakes his head. "Dad's been pushing himself too hard. The last few weeks, all he's wanted to do is work when he wasn't with Mom. He spends hours in the studio, just talking to himself."

"Can I see him, now?" Sophie asks.

"Shame you weren't really in the café with him," Marv says. "It was like he was pouring out his whole life story to you." He shakes his head. "Even ordered you a stack of pancakes."

"That's Dad for you, always did have a good heart." Tom thinks for a moment. "He knew you were coming. His lawyers had told him about some old photographs, or something? It seemed to upset him."

"Oh God, I'm sorry—" Sophie says.

Tom sticks his hands in his old blue jeans. "Dad's still fine if he's working, but everyday things . . ." He shrugs. "We normally get to the mail before he does. As long as everything is routine, he's okay." He sorts through his bunch of keys.

"At least he's still working," Sophie says.

"Yeah, but no one can figure out what on. The whole studio is jammed with blue canvases. He spends days just painting a single canvas blue, then moves on to the next one, just the same as the last."

"That's it? Nothing but blue?"

Tom shrugs. "There's a tiny white dot, like an opal, on each one, but that's it."

Venus, Sophie thinks. *The morning star, guiding him home.*

"I hate seeing Gabe like this," Marv says. "He's always been amazing for his age." He shrugs. "Maybe it'll be good for him to be with you kids in the city for a few months. The winters are hard."

"I know." Sophie glances at Harry. "My mom lives in Montauk. I grew up out here, and I'm moving back." He holds her gaze and smiles. Impulsively, she pulls her files of research from her satchel. "In fact, my dad took this photo of Gabe and Annie, years ago, at some party."

"They were friends?" Harry looks at the picture Sophie hands him and passes it on to his father and Marv.

"At least, Mom and Annie were," Sophie says.

"Really?" Harry turns to her. "Your mom just mentioned that you were related to Gabe's old girlfriend during the war, Vita?"

"Yeah, Vita," Marv says. "Gabe's been yacking away to her too, the last few days. Vita this, Vita that . . ."

"Aren't you full of surprises?" Harry says to Sophie. His look quickens her heart, she feels her stomach free-fall.

"Unexpected?" she says.

"Look at that." Marv's face softens, gazing at the photo. "The image of Gabe, that's what you are, Harry. Can't be much older than you are now."

"Keep it," she says to Harry.

"You sure?"

Sophie nods. "I'm sorry," she says quietly to him. *Do the right thing.* Her mother's voice comes to her. She throws the file of notes and photographs onto the fire, watches the paper buckle and hiss in the flames, the faces of Gabriel, his father, and Vita disappear. Harry stands close beside her.

"Is that your story?"

"It was."

"I don't get it? Why . . . ?"

"I can't do this to Gabe now. I never would have hounded him if I'd known about Annie." She pauses. "Besides, something my mom said really hit home. I've got to let the past go and live my own life. What good would it do now, pulling apart Gabriel's life for the sake of a story? Sometimes we need to believe in fairy tales."

"Thank you." Harry squeezes her hand.

"I'd better be on my way, Lil's waiting on me." Marv pulls down his cap. "See you kids in June at the start of the season?"

Tom hesitates a moment too long. "Sure."

"You are going to bring Gabe out here again next year?"

"Marv, the doctors . . . they just don't know how long he's got left."

"Damn." Marv blinks rapidly, his yellow-tinged eyes pooling with tears. "I . . . Oh, damn it. This place just ain't going to be the same without Gabe and Annie."

"Maybe you'll come and see him in town?" Tom checks his watch. "Listen, we've got to get going. Harry, why don't you and Miss Cass—"

"Dr. Cass." He glances at her.

"Sophie," she says. "I'm so sorry. You've lost Annie, and now Gabriel?"

"The doctors said he has a little time," Tom says. "We just don't know how much. Harry, why don't you drive over to the diner to fetch Gabe while I get the kids in the car and the shutters bolted down before the light fades? Thanks, Marv."

"Sure, Dad," Harry says, and gestures to Sophie to join him. They begin to walk to his truck, his hand resting on the small of her back.

"No, that's just it," Marv interrupts. "I tried to call you, but your phone's been cut off. He walked out of there about ten minutes ago, still talking away to . . . well, her." He points at Sophie. "Damn it, you know what I mean."

"Which way did he go?" Albie starts to run toward the coast path.

"He was heading toward the beach. . . ."

"Mary Jayne!" Tom calls out to his sister. "Dad's missing."

They come running then, my children, Sophie among them. I honored Varian just like I said I would—the names of the good people who changed the course of my life live on in my children and in theirs. Their heels kick up the sand as they run to the crest of sea grass. My grandchildren run with them, down the steps, across the empty white sands.

"Dad!" Tom yells.

Then they see me, lying on the shore, a streak of palest blue.

FIFTY-NINE

Flying Point, Long Island

2000

Gabriel

I am here, and there, Vita is right—everywhere and nowhere. With them, and not.

"Not bad," Vita says, looking around the walls of my studio. "A Chagall, Matisse . . ." She peers closer. "Duchamp? These should be in a museum."

"They will be, soon," I say, "when the house is cleared." Oh, I know the kids haven't been able to tell me what I've known for weeks. My heart is giving out. Today they were going to take me away, away from my home of over fifty years. They are good kids, but I don't want to go. I take a last look at my collection, at the art that has filled my soul for years. "None of us would be here without Varian, without all of them. Sometimes I think we left our hearts at Air-Bel. . . ." And I think of him, walking down the drive that last time when the police came and arrested him and forced him out of France. The last time I shook his hand, he was holding the copy of *Terre des Hommes* that Danny had given him. That's what great art does—that's why these men and women counted. It shows us what makes life worth living.

"Is this great art?" she says, gesturing at the stacks of blue canvases. "What is all this?"

"You have to imagine it, when it is installed." I picture the canvases laid out as I have numbered them, in a circular white-walled space. The blues merge to infinity, from darkest indigo through Prussian, ultramarine, cobalt, to heavenly cerulean and back, and there she is, a tiny white dot of life, Venus, the morning star, always there night and day. It is our endless sky, mine and my love's, the sky we saw when we lay on the beach and looked to heaven and talked of the future. "It's for Annie, always," I say.

"Tell me, do you ever think of me, of Vita?"

I beckon her on and go to a locked wooden chest in the corner of the room beneath the window. I take the key down from its hook, and the smell of cedar fills the air as I lift the lid. I lift out a fold of linen and unwrap the gold embroidered cloth.

"I carried you with me," I said as I put the gold wreath of myrtle leaves on her head. "I'm sorry I couldn't save you, and our child. I'm sorry I couldn't save my father. Forgive me."

"There," she says after a time, and touches my forehead. I feel myself lift, like a ship weighing anchor. "We got there in the end. It's time to let go," she says gently, and I am on the beach again, and my children are running toward me. "I'll wait with you, while they come," she says. "You carried us all. You weren't the only young boy who took on the burden and fortune of his family." She strokes my forehead. The light is flickering, flashing behind my eyes. I see my father's face next to mine, in the photograph. The light flares. Our faces merge, become one. My eyes blink open, see endless blue. "When I look into your eyes, I see the ghosts of your father and mother, of all of us, staring back." I know she tells the truth.

"I can't . . . what if, what if Sophie tells everyone? What will it do to my children if they find out I've lived a lie?"

"It will be okay, Gabriel, you're almost there, now." She soothes my brow. "I know some nights the weight of carrying us, of all that guilt, has been too much, but a new day always begins." She looks out across the beach. The children are running toward us. "You know, sometimes it's been like a spectral army standing shoulder to shoulder with you, fists in the air, showing them that they didn't win, that we live on and we didn't give in." She leans down and kisses my brow, and the light fills my eyes, all fades to white. "You'll live on in them, too. Nothing matters more than the love we leave behind." The sea, the light, it is so beautiful. "Relax. She's coming for you. Not long now."

"Dad?" I hear Tom's voice calling me back. I hear Harry's voice above him, frantic, calling for an ambulance.

"I know CPR." Sophie kneels beside me on the sand as they gather around. I feel her lips against mine, breathing life into me, her hands against my heart. I am like an old engine, winding down. Just for a moment, it catches. "Gabriel," she says, turning my face to hers. "Gabriel, stay with me."

I try to raise my hand to touch her face. "Vita?"

"Sophie, my name is Sophie Cass. Jack and Paige's daughter." She smiles down at me. There are tears in her eyes. "Vita was my great-aunt."

"You look . . . like her." My voice is a whisper. Sophie leans closer, unable to hear. "Please, don't destroy"—I gasp for air—"my family."

"I won't. Vita loved you. Both of you. That's what matters, not some story."

Relief floods through me, and I close my eyes.

"She's proud . . . of you."

It's true, you know, what they say, that your life flashes before you. I feel Sophie's hands on me again, her urgent lips forcing air into my lungs as I slip back, but I am far away, free at last to run down the years as the people I love most in this world gather around me, and the sea rolls on regardless. I see my arm fall to my side, the shepherd tumble one last time from my hand.

Then, she is there. Annie, my Annie, is walking along the shoreline, and she is young, and beautiful, and she has the sun in her. She's come back, this woman I have loved my whole life, and she has come for me.

And it has been a good life, because of one good man. And I have lived a simple life and done good work. And I have loved, oh, I have loved. My heart is light with thankfulness.

I see her now, Annie, my Marianne, dancing and turning in the snow at Air-Bel, dancing to the music of life itself, and I see her, and I feel her touch. I see her holding our children, and I see them, and I feel them, I am back, I am back. I never knew, I never knew I was alive until I held them.

I see her now.

Annie walks to me with the fluid grace of the girl. She tilts her head as if to say, *What are you doing there, Gabe?* and she kneels beside me in the sand, takes me safe in her arms. Annie lies down beside me, and I'm not scared anymore. I've missed her, so much, but now she is here with me, and we'll never be apart again. She lies with me, and I am home. I am filled with so much joy I could fly right up there above the beach, the sea, our world, with her. I can't bear it, it is so beautiful.

It all falls away.

I loved, I am love, I am free.

Author's Note

This novel weaves fiction with factual events at the American Relief Center (Centre Américain de Secours) in 1940–41. My admiration for Varian Fry and his team grew immeasurably the more I learned about them and the artists they saved. The "real" characters are fictional versions of just a few of the remarkable people involved:

Varian Fry (born 1907) was arrested and forced out of France on August 29, 1941. The ARC was raided and closed down on June 2, 1942, but the members of his team continued his work underground.

Fry received little thanks for his remarkable work during his lifetime. Now, the Consulate General of the United States in Marseille sits on place Varian Fry. After the war he divorced Eileen, but he married again and raised a family. In 1971, when Fry published the *Flight* portfolio of prints in aid of the International Rescue Committee (the organization that the ERC became), he struggled to convince artists to take part—though he was responsible for saving many of their lives.

He was honored with the International Rescue Committee's medal in 1963 and the Croix de Chevalier de la Légion d'Honneur by the French government in 1967. He died alone in his sleep later that year at only fifty-nine. A manuscript lay at his side. Varian Fry died surrounded by his incomplete notes for a new memoir, by his memories of Marseille.

In 1991, the U.S. Holocaust Memorial Council awarded him the Eisenhower Liberation Medal. In 1994, he was named "Righteous Among the Nations" by Yad Vashem—an honor bestowed on non-Jews who helped Jews during the Holocaust. It was an honor shared with Oskar Schindler and Raoul Wallenberg. He was the first American to be honored in this way. Warren Christopher (U.S. secretary of state at the time) said: "Even today, Varian Fry's tale of courage and compassion is too little known in the United States. . . . We owe Varian Fry our deepest gratitude, but we also owe him a promise—a promise never to forget the horrors that he struggled against so heroically, a promise to do whatever is necessary to ensure that such horrors never happen again."

Some of Fry's Colleagues

Danny Bénédite was released from prison and took over running the ARC after Varian was forced out of France. The onetime police official went on to become a leader of the underground Resistance. He died in 1990.

Hiram "Harry" Bingham IV (born 1903), Varian's "partner in crime," was abruptly removed from his diplomatic post as vice-consul in Marseille in 1941. He went on to serve in Portugal and Argentina, where he traced Nazi war criminals. When he was overlooked for promotion, he left the U.S. Foreign Service in 1945. Like Fry, Bingham has been honored with several awards for his remarkable humanitarian work. He died in 1988.

Dr. Miriam Davenport (born 1915, Boston) married her fiancé, Rudolf, and escaped with him to America. They divorced, and she remarried twice. She worked for Albert Einstein and became a prize-winning artist. She gained a Ph.D. in 1973 and died in 1999.

Charles Fernley Fawcett (born 1915) followed up his daring work at the ARC with spells in the RAF and the French Foreign Legion. After the war, he performed in more than a hundred films and was a veteran of several conflicts. He continued to help humanity as a freedom fighter and was involved in Afghanistan in the 1970s and the cause of refugees. This modest hero received many decorations, including the French Croix de Guerre and the Eisenhower medal, and died in London in 2008.

Bill Freier (Wilhelm Spira) survived Auschwitz and a series of concentration camps including Buchenwald and Theresienstadt. Mina gave birth to their son during his imprisonment but suffered a nervous breakdown after the war and died in 1953. Spira died in 2000.

Mary Jayne Gold (born 1909, Chicago) escaped to the United States in 1941. After the war, she divided her time between New York and the south of France and named her Saint-Tropez villa "Air-Bel." She never married or had children, but she maintained her contact with Killer. She died in France in 1997.

Raymond Couraud escaped France in April 1941. Killer rewarded Mary Jayne's faith in him and became a hero of the British Special Operations Executive and the Special Air Service.

Albert O. Hirschman (born 1915, Berlin; aka Albert Hermant, aka "Beamish") had a long and distinguished academic career and became one of the world's leading experts on economics. He taught at Columbia, Yale, and Harvard Universities and was Professor Emeritus at Princeton University. He died in 2012.

Justus "Gussie" Rosenberg (born 1923) attempted to escape via the Pyrenees but was caught and arrested. He escaped, joined the Resistance, and managed to get to the United States after the war, where he completed his studies. He is Professor Emeritus of Languages and Literature at Bard College and co-director of the Varian Fry Foundation.

Some of the Clients

André (1896–1966) and Jacqueline (1910–1993) Breton arrived safely in New York after being detained in Martinique. They later divorced, and both remarried. Their daughter, Aube Breton-Elléouët (born 1935), is a distinguished visual artist.

Marc Chagall (born 1887) was finally convinced to leave France after he was arrested by the police in Marseille. Fry secured his release. He died in 1985.

Peggy Guggenheim (born 1898) and Max Ernst (born 1891) finally met in Marseille. Max said, "When, where, and why shall I meet you?" Peggy said, "Tomorrow, four, Café de la Paix, and you know why." They escaped to the United States together and married. They later divorced, and Guggenheim established a museum of modern art in Venice, founded on the paintings she rescued from war-torn France. She died in 1979 and Ernst in 1976.

As Fry himself complained writing his memoir, *Surrender on Demand*, trying to write this story with its "hundreds of characters is worse than

War and Peace." In the confines of fiction, it is necessary to simplify the true story—it was not possible to include all the people involved in the remarkable rescue operation in Marseille, but this in no way diminishes the contribution of Fry's unnamed colleagues. The Varian Fry Institute and Varian Fry Foundation both have excellent Web sites with information about all the people who helped Fry in Marseille and the full events of this time.

Many more of the world's greatest artists and intellectuals were saved than the original two hundred names on Fry's list. Some fifteen thousand people came to the ARC seeking help, many of them "ordinary" relief cases. The organization gave aid to more than 560 families and took food parcels to those detained in concentration camps. More than two thousand people were rescued.

There is a dedication at Harvard University that expresses Varian Fry's tenacious humanitarian spirit well: "To one who dared to defy authority and attempts at restraining the human impulse for good." The Emergency Rescue Committee of New York, for which he did such remarkable work, became the International Rescue Committee—it continues to operate in more than thirty countries, aiding refugees and victims of oppression whenever and wherever it is needed. Fry's legacy lives on.

Acknowledgments

I would like to thank Professor Justus "Gussie" Rosenberg for his generous help writing this novel and Aube Breton-Elléouët for her kind permission to conjure a version of her five-year-old self. Thank you to Dr. Sarah Wilson, Jean-Jacques Lebel, Pierre Sauvage, Richard Kaplan, Paul B. Franklin, and Marisa Bourgoin of the Archives of American Art; Michelle Harvey of the Museum of Modern Art, New York; Constance Krebs of the Association Atelier André Breton; and Laurene Leon Boym for their help with my research.

Thank you to Professor Jon Stallworthy and Lorna Beckett of the Rupert Brooke Society, for their kind permission to quote from Rupert Brooke's "The Great Lover."

My thanks to the incomparable Sheila Crowley, Rebecca Ritchie, and the team at Curtis Brown and to my wonderful editor, Anne Brewer, and all at Thomas Dunne for their help with this story.

As ever, love and thanks to my husband and family for their support and encouragement. This much. Always.